THE BEAR AND THE LAMB

FATED OUTLAWS

BOOK ONE

HALLE OAK

ISBN: 979-8-9905358-8-6 (Paperback)

PRAISE FOR HALLE OAK

"The Bear & Lamb had me by the throat from the very first chapter. Look up BDE in the dictionary and you'll find a picture of Kodiak's ... face. If you also love a 'She makes him better, he makes her worse [complimentary]' dynamic, you'll be swept away by Alice and Kodiak's outlaw love story."

— ALLIE OLEANDER, AUTHOR OF 'WILLING PREY'

"The Bear and the Lamb is a fresh take on dark western romance. Kodiak is every morally gray outlaw that ever made you question your morals for the sake of some good d*ck. The way his darkness attempts to corrupt Alice while her love for him brings him back into the light is a story for the ages. The Bear and the Lamb is perfect for anyone who loves gritty, historical romance with vivid imagery but with more modern progressive values."

— POPPY FITZGERALD, AUTHOR OF "ASTRAY" AND "EXILE"

Kodiak will take you on the ride of your life. Are you ready?

— LAYNA JAMES, AUTHOR OF THE FORT BENDER SERIES

Brilliant! Halle Oak has crafted a gripping outlaw romance, complete with blazing guns, scorching on-page chemistry, and a dangerously tempting anti-hero.

— J.B. LAREE, AUTHOR OF THE RUNAWAY HEARTS SERIES.

To Arthur Morgan

CHAPTER 1

ALICE

By dark, the once riotous inn has settled into a quiet hum, marked by the incessant ticking of the mantle clock. Most of the guests have retired to their rooms, save for a few lingering over their evening meals in the dining room.

The stairs groan beneath my steps as I ascend to the observatory, where a brass telescope waits under the glass dome. I haven't much time. Joseph's just returned from a long stay at his family's head office in Cincinnati, but maybe I can steal a few minutes with the stars before he notices I'm gone. I adjust the telescope, aligning it with Ursa Major—the constellation I've tracked for days. Its familiar pattern twinkles from the deep black, an old friend amid countless celestial bodies.

"Callisto," I greet her. "So lovely to see you again."

Since I was a girl, the sight of her has soothed me with a familiar calm. I reach for my clothbound notebook where it rests on the desk beside the flickering light of an oil lamp. Flipping to a fresh page, I sketch the constellation.

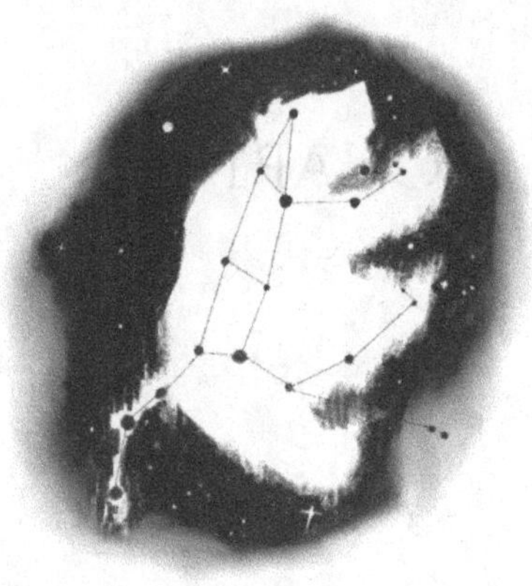

July 17th

    I traced an imaginary line through Merak and arrived straight at Polaris, the ever-faithful North Star. This was the shoulder and flank of Ursa Major—the Great Bear—standing guard in the northern sky.

    Heavenly Father, I pray for my own Great Bear: a protector who, like the bear's bright stars, can guide me out of the darkness.

The scratch of my pen is the only sound in the otherwise silent room, the rhythm of ink on paper like a secret between me and the cosmos.

The evening's observation concluded, I hurry downstairs and slip out of the inn through the back door. The short cobblestone path to our private residence crunches beneath my feet. Crickets chirp in the hedges, their shrill songs twisting my stomach tight. Joseph will be cross I've come home so late.

I rush up the porch to the front door, the beveled-glass pane revealing the gaslight from within. As soon as I enter, I'm struck with Joseph's cigar smoke. It overpowers the pleasant lemon oil I'd used to clean and polish earlier.

"Late," he barks from the parlor. Face buried in a ledger, he doesn't so much as lift his head. I don't answer, just step inside. The floorboards—wide-planked walnut, edges softened by braided rugs—gleam faintly under the chandelier.

Light flickers across the ivory wainscoting of the parlor walls, gold dancing over the rosewood settee with its worn cranberry velvet, faded along the back where guests lean too long. Joseph sits in his armchair beside the hearth, lamp light darkening the angles of his face.

"The guests required tending to, sir."

"The guests always require tending to," Joseph retorts, engrossed in his ledger. "It is hardly proper that a man of my stature should sit cooling his heels like a footman while his wife stargazes at her leisure. It's this kind of disrespect that would see my brother succeed the family business, while I piddle away at a roadside country inn. Had I a proper wife, I'd be the one working in the city office, managing the luxury hotels."

It was my father who handed me over to the Sherman family for the price of keeping his farm afloat. Signed me away like livestock to a man twice my age, then kissed my cheek and thanked me for my sacrifice. I doubt he imagined Joseph would spend the years since wishing for a refund.

"My sincerest apologies, sir."

"Off to bed," he orders with a flick of his wrist.

I exhale. "Yes, sir."

I rush upstairs while he appears to be in a forgiving mood. Inside our bedroom, a carved mahogany four-poster bed sits against the far wall. I pull down the shades and shut the lace curtains.

Standing in front of the vanity, I study the reflection staring back at me. Tired—worn thin at the edges, like fabric pulled too tight for too long. My eyes search the face for something—resolve, perhaps, or recognition—but find only weariness.

Water splashes at the wash stand as I rinse away dust and sweat. With stiff fingers, I slip into my nightgown, folding the day's clothes into a neat pile. I drag the brush through my hair —tug and release– smoothing the chestnut strands into order.

The bedroom door creaks open.

My hand freezes mid-stroke. In the mirror, I watch Joseph enter. He undresses without ceremony, letting his clothes drop where they please. His belly, his sloping shoulders—all briefly exposed before he pulls on his long, linen nightshirt. The bed creaks beneath his weight as he settles into it.

I pick up his clothes. Place them in the basket. My pulse begins to race, the way it always does when I prepare to lie beside him. He's been away with his brother, Virgil. Something for the family business. Maybe travel has worn him out and tonight I will be spared.

His breath, hot and thick with cigar smoke, brushes my shoulder. The bristle of his mustache grazes the back of my neck.

"On your belly," he commands. Not cruel, but expectant. The way a finishing school matron might correct a young woman's posture.

I obey. A lump swells in my throat, and I swallow it down. It will not last long.

My mind slips away. I leave this room, this body, and drift toward the stars.

I think of Callisto.

A nymph, taken against her will by a god who called it love. Changed into a bear for the crime of being desired. Alone, she bore her son in the woods. And when he grew, he raised his bow, not knowing the beast before him was his mother. Just before the arrow flew, Zeus transformed her into starlight. Into Ursa Major.

Her stars point the way to the North Star. For generations, the lost have followed that fixed light in the sky toward salvation.

Hold fast, I tell myself. You, too, will be transformed. Your suffering will not go unrewarded.

I repeat the words silently, like a prayer, over and over, until Joseph's body collapses against mine. His sweat clings to my skin, his breath ragged. He tugs the nightgown down over my legs, then rolls onto his back.

Silence returns at last.

And finally, I let myself breathe.

CHAPTER 2

ALICE

Cold, slick fabric clings to my fingers as suds slip in rivulets down my wrists. The rhythm of scrubbing and rinsing merges with the cicadas' song, rising and falling with the breeze. Footsteps shuffle behind me. Gideon, the porter's son, approaches, hands clasped behind his back. "Miss Alice," he says, his too-short trousers revealing his skinny ankles.

He lifts his hands. Nestled there is a smooth stone threaded with crystalline veins. "I found this by the creek," he says. "It's for you."

I take the stone, feeling its cool weight in my palm with a smile. His chest swells.

"This is lovely, Gideon. Thank you."

"You're welcome, Miss Alice."

I pat the spot next to me, and he sits eagerly.

"Mr. Sherman said the astrometers are coming back. Did you hear?"

"Astronomers," I correct gently. "And yes."

"It's a big group of 'em, I heard."

"Mmm." I wring water from the linens, scrubbing them against the board. "They're visiting to study the night sky from the tower. There's talk of a comet passing soon."

His mouth parts, eyebrows springing up. "Ain't never seen no comet before."

I hold up the stone. "They're made of rocks just like this, traveling through space around the sun."

"No kiddin'." He pauses. "You got anything inside that needs mendin'?"

"Not today. Don't the horses need tending to?"

He tugs the hem of his trousers, as if he could coax them longer. "I ain't been near the stables much."

"Why not? You love the horses."

"The new hand. Lucas. He's been...teasin' me, 'bout m'trousers and other stuff. Pa says if I don't stand up to him, I'll be picked on my whole life. I want to, Miss Alice. It's just... he's so much bigger'n me."

"Well, if he lays a finger on you, tell me, and I'll straighten him out."

He grins at that, then leans in. "Lucas don't know nothing about your supplies. I hid 'em good."

My heart tightens with gratitude, and unease.

"Where?"

"In the hayloft. Behind a loose plank in the wall."

Relief softens my shoulders. I brush my thumb across his cheek. "Thank you, Gideon."

That night, once the guests settle, I slip into the stables by the glow of my oil lamp. The ladder creaks as I climb to the loft. At the wall, I find the loose plank.

Behind it sit two burlap bags.

I pull them out and check the contents: a canteen of water, jerky, biscuits, canned beans, corn, stew, and salmon; a leather pouch holding twenty dollars in one-dollar bills and a scatter of quarters, dimes, and nickels; one change of clothes; and a pair of sturdy work boots.

My fingers skim each item like a familiar ritual. My escape kit. But even with all this, there's something missing. Something I'll need if I'm to make it beyond the roads, the woods, the highwaymen, and the wild animals.

A pistol.

Women vanish on the trail. A gun would offer protection.

I just have to find one without drawing suspicion.

After breakfast service, Fred appears with weekly provisions, the wagon wheels kicking up dirt, horses huffing under the heat. Not a hint of a breeze moves the air. My blouse clings to my back. Fred brings the horses to a halt, hops down, wipes his brow, and stretches. I smile, imagining Gideon copying the same motion, as if his young bones were just as weary as his father's.

Lucas meets Fred at the wagon, and the two of them start unloading provisions and linens. I watch from the porch as they make several trips.

I lift the top bundle and spot a bolt of cotton duck fabric—stiff, weighty.

Perfect.

I pull it free.

"Miss Alice," Lucas says, tipping his hat. The sun has browned his arms, the tops tinged pink.

"Lucas," I answer coolly.

"Mr. Sherman around? Fence by the south pasture's down. Need his say-so before I fix it."

"Mr. Sherman and his brother are in the city for the auction. Go ahead and fix it."

He hesitates. "Reckon I oughta wait for Mr. Sherman's word."

My grip tightens on the fabric, but I keep my tone even. "If a horse gets out, you'll be in more trouble for doing nothing. I trust you know how to fix a fence."

He draws in a slow breath. "Yes, ma'am," he says, turning to leave.

I watch him go, biting my tongue. Heaven forbid one of them take an order from a woman. I should've let him face Joseph's wrath, but a bad day for Joseph is always a worse day for me.

Fred approaches again, empty crate in hand. "Got your change, Miss Alice."

I lower the fabric bolt and wipe my palms before taking the small cloth bag. Inside: two dimes, a quarter, five pennies.

"Actually, Fred, wait here a moment."

He nods. I head inside the office, unlock the tin change box and retrieve a small bag of nickels, dimes, and quarters. Back on the porch, I hand the bag to him.

"Could you exchange these for bills next time you're in town? Too much loose change to manage, and the guests would appreciate it too."

"Sure thing, Miss Alice." He tucks the pouch away.

Once he's gone, I log the transaction in the ledger—minus the five cents per dollar that won't return to the inn. That portion has another home: hidden between beams in the hayloft.

When night falls, I retreat to my sewing room. The Singer gleams beneath the lamp as I unroll the cotton duck.

Earlier, I'd found a worn pair of trousers in the laundry pile. I lay them out, trace their shape, ready the panels. The crank hums, the needle darts, and thread binds cloth. By the time I finish, the trousers are plain and sturdy. I hold them to the lamplight, inspecting the seams.

At first light, I walk to the stables with the new trousers under my arm. "Gideon," I call.

He raises his head from the horse he's grooming. "Miss Alice?" He wipes his hands and hurries over.

"I've got something for you," I say, offering the folded pants.

He takes them with both hands, awed. "These are for me?"

"Of course. I think they'll fit better now that you've grown."

Before he can respond, boots thunder across the yard. Lucas barrels in, breathless.

"Gideon! Mr. Sherman needs shackles and a chain. Quick!"

The trousers fall onto a hay bale as Gideon bolts into a stall. He returns with heavy iron and hurries out. I follow.

Inside the inn, the scent of copper thickens the air. Joseph and Virgil drag a man from their wagon—injured, limp, skin gone pale. Blood blooms across his shirt. His boots scrape the steps as they haul him to an empty guest room.

"Chain him to the bed," Joseph orders.

Gideon obeys, fastening a shackle around the man's wrist and looping the chain through the bedframe, leaving roughly five feet of slack.

"What are you doing?" I move toward Gideon.

Joseph grabs my arm and yanks me back. "He could be dangerous," he snaps. "We can't take chances."

"That's no excuse for cruelty!" The words erupt from me. "He needs a doctor, not chains."

A flash of movement—Joseph's hand strikes my cheek.

"Calm yourself, woman." He jerks his chin at Gideon. "Keep her out of the way."

Gideon approaches. "Are you all right?"

I force a smile. "Just startled."

"Maybe some fresh air'll help," he says.

We sit on the porch. My cheek still burns. The fields waver in the afternoon gold.

Joseph appears. "Back to work, son."

"Yes, sir." Gideon hesitates.

"We found him under suspicious circumstances," Joseph says. "Fits the description of a known criminal. Until we know more, we're being cautious."

I say nothing.

"He needs care," he adds. "That's where your strengths lie. Can you put aside your hurt feelings and help, or are your sensibilities too delicate?"

"If my sensibilities are so delicate, why would you have me alone, tending to a dangerous man?"

He scoffs. "He's quite helpless, Alice. I'd be surprised if he lives through the night. There's nothing he can do to you in that state, and I've no time to play nursemaid. "

No matter the man's crimes, the thought of such an awful death aches in my ribs. I lift my chin. "I will see to his care."

"Good. And keep it quiet."

ALCOHOL, linen strips, needles and thread, scissors, ointment, iodine. I gather everything I can from the medicine chest in the inn's office, my hands trembling as I place the supplies into a woven basket. I carry a kettle of boiled water wrapped in a dish towel.

Suspicious circumstances. Not a real explanation. And now here I am, tiptoeing up the stairs to tend to a strange man—one who will eventually wake to find himself chained like a prisoner.

I ease the guest room door open. A faint groan escapes his cracked lips, his blue work shirt clinging to his chest with blood and sweat. Boots hang off the bed, trousers still tucked in.

A shallow cut bleeds above his right brow. I check for more head wounds but find none. Unbuttoning his shirt, I work fast but gently. Maybe he's a ranch hand. A farmer. His body is built for labor.

My fingertips rest briefly on his chest as I watch the steady rise and fall of his breath. Sweat glistens across his neck. He's sun-darkened but pale in the cheeks. He's lost too much blood.

Then I see it. A small, clean puncture wound just under his ribs. A knife? Maybe. I lean in, ear to his chest. No gurgling. No wheeze. His lungs sound clear. It mustn't be too deep. Thank God. All I can do now is close it up.

Surely this will wake him. Shackles lock his wrists, chained to the rails of the iron bedframe. I didn't want them there, but right now I'm grateful. If he lashes out, at least I'll have a chance to flee.

I steady myself, open the iodine.

The moment it touches the wound, he stirs. Mumbles something.

"Shhh," I whisper. "You're safe. I'm closing the wound. I'm sorry—it'll hurt. Please try to be still."

He groans. A gasp tears from his throat as he jolts upright, chains clattering.

"Shhh, please. You're all right. You're doing just fine," I say, stitching fast. Sweat beads on his brow. His lip trembles as he bites down, suppressing a scream.

I wish to God we had something stronger whiskey.

When I finish, I wipe away what blood I can and bandage the wound.

"All done," I whisper, gathering the stained cloth and excess supplies into a small sack.

Then he shifts again, rolling slowly onto his side, exposing his back.

My breath stalls.

"Oh, good God."

The white linen beneath him is drenched in blood. No wonder his skin's gone ghostly.

I slice the back of his shirt open with the scissors. Beneath it, more blood, more wounds. One near the shoulder, another low by the kidney.

I move faster now, scrubbing the area clean, then pouring iodine over the wounds. He flinches but doesn't speak. Iodine pools in the gashes like a seasoned hog roast. I thread the needle and begin again.

When I finish, I tap his side. He rolls onto his back with a grunt.

"It's going to be all right," I murmur, dabbing a cloth along his lips. They're dry, cracked, nearly bloodless.

He barely moves, but his hazel eyes open for a moment. Stormy, unfocused. When they lock with mine, something flickers in me.

Who is this man?

"Miss Alice!"

A voice rings out down the hall. I jolt, heart hammering. I shut the door quietly behind me.

"Miss Alice?"

It's a maid. Mabel. She seems flustered, hands wringing against her white apron. I try to smooth my expression and tuck the panic away.

"Yes?"

"It's the sleeping quarters for the Astral Society meeting," she says. "We've had more confirmations than expected. We're two beds short."

I take a breath, steadying myself. "We can shuffle some of the regular guests."

"And the kitchen," Mabel adds. "Mrs. Baxter says we haven't enough ingredients she needs to feed them all."

"I'll send Fred into town. Make a list."

"Right away, Miss Alice."

She hurries off, leaving me lingering at the stranger's door, lost in the fog of the last hour.

No time to think. No time to feel.

There's far too much to do.

CHAPTER 3

KODIAK

I'm so goddamn thirsty. Tongue dry as a brick.

Sons of bitches stuck me good. My ribs scream every time I so much as breathe. Back's no better. Shoulder blades feel like they've been used for target practice. Ain't spilling blood no more, least not fresh, but my body won't quit reminding me I damn near died.

I'd count myself lucky to be breathing, if not for this iron shackle clamped on my wrist.

Can't rightly say how I ended up here.

Last thing I recall clear is riding out in the open country heading north from La Grange, Kentucky, where I'd squirreled away saddlebags full of what might've been the slickest job I ever pulled. Broad daylight. L&N train hauling near ten thousand in payroll cash.

Took it clean off the rails with two horses and a winch, timed just right on a bend. Only had to kill two—both guards, both armed. No civilians. Clean work. Smart work. The kind you grin about for years.

But I ain't grinning now.

Thought I'd picked a quiet place to camp. Deep in the scrub, tucked between two ridges. Fire low, horse fed, saddle off. My heart wrenches at the thought of losing that fine animal.

No shout, no warning. Just two shapes outta the dark. Badges, maybe. Maybe just hired guns chasing a payday. Said I was under arrest.

I laughed, I think.

Reached for my iron, but they swarmed me. Lost the gun. Fought barehanded. Might've had a chance if they hadn't brought knives.

Sharp steel. Cold, then hot.

They stabbed me till I stopped fighting. Till the light narrowed down to a pinpoint, and I figured that was it.

But it ain't.

There's more story, seems, just ain't sure what it is yet.

From the racket outside and the creak of boots passing the door, I reckon I'm in a hotel. Question is, who the hell locked me here?

Only clue I got is Alice.

Miss Alice. Miss Alice.

Christ almighty. The staff don't tire of calling that poor woman's name, asking her permission to sneeze or spit. Seems she's the one running the place, and that's the part I can't square. She's been tending me. Stitched me up clean. Keeping the fever down.

Pretty thing. Gentle touch. Tried to keep me easy. If a woman like that's gone and locked me up, maybe it's for her own protection, not knowing me from Adam. Maybe her people ran off the bastards who ambushed me and brought me here for mending. If that's the case, I'll heal up quick and walk out a free man soon as I can prove I don't mean her no harm.

Room's nice enough. I'm the filthiest thing in it. Smells like rosemary soap and lavender. Clean linen. White walls. Lace curtains. Washbasin and pitcher. One of those lithographs on the wall—farmhouse with a cow in the front yard.

A right respectable establishment.

But why am I here?

My only notion is I'm worth more alive than dead, and my keeper's just fattening me like a hog for slaughter.

CHAPTER 4

ALICE

Once the clamor of the day finally ebbs, I carry a tray with a bowl of broth down the dim hallway, my pulse thudding hard enough to feel in my throat. At his door, I knock once before easing my way in.

He lies exactly as I left him—flat on his back, chain secured to the bedframe, sunk deep in the kind of sleep that borders on unconsciousness. He hasn't stirred in days. I set the tray on the table and step to his side.

The bandages are clean. Scabs have begun to form. Bruises are shifting from purple to yellow along his ribs. His breathing is even beneath the blankets, and when my fingers brush his forehead—warm with fever, but not dangerously so—he doesn't react.

"Time for some broth," I murmur.

His eyes snap open—a quick, fluttering blink of hazel fractured with brown and green. His right hand jerks to his hip on instinct, reaching for a gun that isn't there. He scans the room like a man waking in hostile country. Then I sit on the edge of his bed, and some of that tight-held caution eases.

"Easy," I whisper, resting a steadying hand on his shoulder. "Try to sit up. You need food."

He pushes himself upright by degrees, breath catching as the chain drags across the iron frame. His gaze cuts from the restraint to me, dark with accusation.

Guilt crawls under my skin. "I'm sorry, sir. My husband insisted on the irons—for our safety, he said. I hope you'll understand."

I lift the spoon, and after a moment's hesitation, he leans forward enough to accept it. He swallows, exhales, and some of the hard edges in his face soften. By the fourth spoonful, he speaks, his voice rough, low, and controlled. "Where am I?"

"The Sherman Inn. Larkspur, Ohio. You're safe."

He doesn't blink. He simply lifts his arm and pulls, testing the restraint with a hard, deliberate jerk. The metal rattles. He lowers his arm again.

"I know," I say quietly. "And I'm sorry. How do you feel?"

Another spoonful. He swallows. "Alive."

"I'm glad. Can I bring you anything?"

He lifts the shackle. "A key would be nice."

Something in me curls tight. "Mister, if I had the key, I swear I'd use it. This wasn't my doing. I'm only here to care for you."

He studies me a moment. "Whiskey wouldn't hurt."

A surprised breath escapes me. "That I can manage. I'll return shortly."

"I won't go anywhere."

I hurry downstairs, snatch a bottle of rye and a glass from behind the bar, and climb back up. When I push the door open, he's on his feet, braced unsteadily, shirt open, shoulder twisting as he studies the sutures in the mirror.

"I'll fetch a fresh dressing," I say, guilt tightening in my throat. I wish I could give him clean clothes as well, but the irons make that impossible.

I set the whiskey down on the end table and turn to leave.

"Alice."

I freeze. Turn slowly. "How—how do you know my name?"

He perks up an eyebrow, mimicking a chorus of voices: "*Miss Alice, Miss Alice...*"

I stifle a reluctant smile. The walls must be thinner than I realized.

I wait. If he knows mine, it seems fair he gives his. After a silence that stretches a breath too long, I ask, "And you are?"

"William Archer. Arch, if you like."

He says it without hesitation, but something about it rings hollow. I smile anyway. "Pleased to meet you, Mr. Archer."

"Thank you. For the drink. And for stitchin' me up."

"You're most welcome."

He pours a measure, winces as he tips it back, then lets the rye sit a moment on his tongue. I clasp my hands behind me.

"Where are you from, Mr. Archer?"

He laughs—not unkindly, but as if the question itself were a jest. The sound is low, rusty. "I move around. Wherever there's work."

"Do you have people who will worry for you?"

"People?" He rolls the word around like a pebble. "Oh, I suppose folks don't count on me bein' in a place long enough to miss me."

"That is a lonely answer."

He glances at me over the rim of the glass. "Lonely ain't the worst thing. Easier on others."

I busy my hands with the tray, though there's nothing left to straighten. "Do you prefer cities, or the open country?"

"Country," he says, easy as breath. "So you run this inn?"

He seems eager to turn the talk, so I let him. "I suppose you could say that. I manage the staff. Keep the books, the linens, the kitchen when needed."

"Busy hands," he says, as if approving the notion. "You make a fair broth."

"You've Mrs. Baxter to thank for that."

"I'll be sure to thank her next I see her."

He's wry. It startles a laugh out of me. Awkward, this—making small talk with a man my husband has chained in irons. I ought to ask what happened on the road, but before I can, he nods at the shackles.

"You said this weren't your notion. Whose was it?"

"My husband's," I say, smoothing a napkin that needs no smoothing. "For the safety of the house."

"Safety of the house," he repeats, turning it over once. He sets the glass down. "How long you reckon I'm to wear 'em?"

"Until you're mended I suppose," I say. "Or until he decides." I hate the sound of it.

He studies me a beat, nodding pensively.

"I'll be right back with that dressing, Mr. Archer," I say, and step out.

That night, after tending to him again, I steal away to the observatory. I pray he'll be free before the Astral Society arrives. Their visit is the one bright ember in this gray life I lead. I need that peaceful reunion with the stars. Not a sickroom.

I adjust the telescope and lean in. Aquarius glitters across the darkness.

Then, a streak.

A flash so bright it seems to strike my chest. A star tearing across the lens, brilliant and immediate before it vanishes. I blink, breath caught halfway. In all my nights at this telescope, I've never seen anything so close.

It feels aimed at me.

July 30th

> *Lo! A beautiful sight unlike one I've ever seen. While peering through the telescope at Aquarius, a bright star fell from the sky and crossed my path. Is it a sign? A warning? In mythology, shooting stars were thought to be men thrown from heaven for their sins. Satan, too, fell like a star.*

Arch's eyes flash in my mind.

My pen stills.

Who is he, really? Why was he bleeding out in the back of Joseph's wagon? Who would want him dead? Why would Joseph bring him here?

This cannot be a coincidence. Something bigger is at work.

I feel it in my bones.

The next morning, Joseph sits behind the front desk, hovering over the ledgers. His presence alone sets dread stirring in my stomach. Hoofbeats *clip-clop* outside, wheels grinding over the dirt. I glance out the window—Fred has arrived.

I hurry to open the door as he and Lucas unload the supplies. Fred hands me a cloth bag.

"Bills you asked for, Miss Alice."

"Thank you."

Joseph watches the exchange. When Fred departs, he steps toward me.

"What's this?"

"Last week's takings, sir," I answer, calm as I can manage. I loosen the drawstring and show the stack of bills inside. "I had Fred exchange the coins. Easier to manage."

Joseph studies me—too long—before saying, "As long as it's accounted for."

"Of course, sir." I smile, though dread blows cold through my spirit.

He snaps the ledger shut. "Our patient must be relocated. Lucas will escort him to the residence after dark."

"In our home?" The falling star flashes through my mind— bright, sudden—and Arch's haunted eyes with it.

He scoffs. "Those rooms are for paying guests. That conference is far too important to risk any shortages. It's shameful enough we've been left with this country post while Virgil runs the city hotels."

"We're the only location with an observatory," I say calmly. "That counts for something."

"It counts for little—this piddly post with a farmer's daughter for a wife." His voice drips scorn.

The insult stings, but I swallow it. "I've done all that has been asked."

"A chair does what it's asked, Alice. Doesn't make it remarkable." He waves toward the ledger. "Now—enough.

That wounded man goes to the residence. The room is needed."

I press a steadying palm to the desk. "Couldn't you simply let him go?"

"I'm not asking permission," he snaps. "And he stays restrained."

Questions burn in my throat, but I swallow them all. There's a wall around Joseph no one breaches.

"I should check on him," I say softly.

I plate his lunch and climb the stairs, schooling my expression at his door.

"Mr. Archer," I say as I enter the room.

He sits upright now, boots on the floor, color returned to his cheeks.

"I've brought stew and bread. Something heartier than broth."

His focus moves from the food to me, gratitude softening his expression.

"You look well," I say, touching his forehead. Warm, but no fever.

"All thanks to you." He clears his throat. "I mean no disrespect, but I reckon I've mended long enough. I'd like out of these irons."

"Yes, of course, Mr.—"

"Arch."

"Arch," I correct. The word feels unfamiliar, weighty. "I don't rightly know why my husband insists on keeping you here," I admit.

Something shifts in him—dark, deep.

"What happened out there?" I ask. "Do you remember?"

He drops his attention to his hands. "Nothin' worth burdenin' you with."

"Maybe not. But it might explain why he won't let you go. You could be in danger."

"Your husband," he says slowly. "Who is he?"

I hesitate. "We are the Sherman family. This is the Sherman Inn."

"Sherman," he echoes. "Didn't realize I was patched up by their heir."

"You've heard of them." The moment it slips out, I regret it. *Them*, not us.

Recognition flickers behind those hazel eyes.

"Hard not to," he says. "Shermans own half the hotels from here to...a long ways."

"Yes. It's the family business."

"Business," he repeats, bitter. "If that's what you call it."

I press a hand to my corset. "What else would I call it?"

"Your husband always send you to do his dirty work?"

"I beg your pardon?"

His tone sharpens, slicing the air. "You his diplomat, or is he just too much a coward to face me?" He leans back with a hardened look. The breadth of his shoulders, the strong-cut jaw—dangerous things for a lonely woman to notice.

I breathe slowly. "I'm not here for him," I say. "You need to eat."

"Men like your husband don't chain up strangers for their health," he says. "Why hasn't he shown his face?"

"I don't know." I steal a quick glance toward the door. "I shouldn't be discussing this."

"Alice," he says quietly, "you're already in it. You've been tendin' to the man he's got chained. Question now is, are you goin' to let me go?"

My hands twist in my skirt. "I would if I could. But I don't have the key."

"Then get it," he says. Not threatening, simply tired of waiting.

"I'm sorry. I must speak to my husband first."

Before I can turn to leave, he grabs my wrist, grip hot, strong. After a moment, he eases—just enough to show me the choice in it.

"Alice."

My body stiffens.

"Free me, and I promise I won't let harm come to you. You have my word."

"I'm sorry," I whisper. I pull free and flee the room.

CHAPTER 5

KODIAK

I can hear Pa now, sobbing at the kitchen table. Servants long gone. Cupboards bare.

"You are a blight," he said, voice steady as a minister even with the whiskey. "This—our ruin—is your doing."

I was a small boy then. Now I understand a man might turn sour left alone, his one love in the ground, saddled with the reason she's there. But that boy didn't know better.

"I should say you are ill-suited to bear the name Randolph," he went on, setting the bottle down just so. "Yet the name is of such little account, you may keep it."

Ladies who once took his arm on a Sunday—Miss Carter from St. Mark's, Mrs. Hale's widowed sister—had found better suitors once the town learned he'd gambled off what was left. He wouldn't have fallen so low if I hadn't been born.

"Hope," he said, folding his handkerchief into a neat square beside his pistol on the table, "is a rope to hang yourself. All my best days are behind."

I've spent half my life trying to prove that bastard wrong. But sure as hell, life always sides with him in the end. Seems like I was wrong about where I'd landed. Thought maybe some Good Samaritan hauled me out of the dirt, trussed me up here for my own keeping till I could prove myself no threat. But the more I turn it over, the more it stinks. It was the Sherman brothers who stuck me, no doubt in my mind now. If that's the case, then this room ain't no sanctuary. It's a cage.

And the only key is Alice.

I regret scaring her. Truth is, she's jumpy enough without me baring my teeth. What I can't make sense of is what a woman like her's doing tangled up with the Shermans. When she spoke of them, I got the feeling she don't see herself as one of them, and I don't blame her. Sweet thing like that never could belong in a nest of snakes.

Maybe she could use saving too.

I been riding alone too long, doing business my way with no soul beside me to question it. Saving her ain't part of the plan—it's a burden, truth told—but in my gut, I feel like it was meant to be.

It started with that star.

Saw it drop clean out the heavens a day, maybe two, before the Shermans come tearing into my camp. Last time I seen a falling star, I was a boy. Same night I stood over my old man's body, blood warm at my feet. Learned my lesson then: world don't hand you nothing. You take, or you die.

And yet, here I am, thinking on signs like some stargazing dandy with his tarot cards and tea leaves. Maybe I've gone soft. Maybe I'm losing my damn mind. But something in this chain of events, something in Alice herself, keeps whispering there's a piece of work laid out for me.

I just don't yet know what it is.

CHAPTER 6

ALICE

The quiet plea behind Arch's eyes looms.

The supper I prepared—cold ham and succotash—lies untouched on my plate while Joseph's silver knife and fork go busily to work. We sit at the long, gleaming table in our private dining room. The air is thick with summer heat, and yet, my skin crawls.

Joseph didn't bring Arch here to protect him. He never does anything without expecting his due in return. This is madness, and to sit idle makes me no better. No less guilty. But what can I do?

"I expect you to coordinate with the cleaning staff," Joseph says, as if reading my mind. "Every room spotless. Every guest well-supplied." A wet speck of corn clings to his mustache, bobbing with every word.

"Of course, sir."

"And you'll keep clear of the parlor. Once the men settle, they'll take their smoke and drink there."

My mind catches on the words. I've dreamt of the wonder that settles over a gathering when the sky feels rich with discovery. Months of planning—menus, wine orders, letters. All of it to support an event I'm now forbidden to witness.

"Why must I keep clear?"

Joseph tears into his ham, loud and graceless. "You'd best keep watch over our patient. I won't have any irregularities."

I force a polite smile, tightening my hold on my fork. More than once, I've imagined driving it into his throat. But the cost would be too great.

"They're not here for cards and whiskey. They'll be speaking of the stars and—"

"I said no."

"One evening, Joseph. I've earned at least that much. What harm—"

The crack of his hand silences me. My head jerks sideways, a burst of white flooding my vision, the sting sharp as a struck match. My fork clatters to the floor.

"Enough," he says, and returns to his meal.

I sit, frozen. My fingers go numb around the edge of the table, every nerve strung tight as a harp. The scrape of his knife against the china fills the silence.

"Now," he continues, "I've arranged for your patient to be moved after the guests have retired. You'll accompany Lucas and ensure it's done."

I want to demand answers—who Arch is, why Joseph chains him like an animal.

But the metallic tang of blood in my mouth reminds me what questions cost.

FOOTSTEPS on the porch announce Lucas and Gideon.

"Gideon, what are you doing here?"

"Mr. Sherman said he wanted an extra pair of hands to make sure there weren't no mistakes." He wears the pants I made him, gun strapped to his hip.

"Oh," I say softly. "He's upstairs. I'll bring you to him."

The lamp inside Arch's room casts a pulsing golden glow. He sits at the edge of the bed where he's been waiting, a low chuckle rising as we enter.

"They sent the whole cavalry, did they?"

Lucas squares his shoulders. "Mr. Sherman asked us to escort you to your new quarters. We don't want any trouble."

Arch quirks a brow. "Course not."

Gideon steps forward with the key, hesitant. I glance at Arch, silently praying he'll come quietly. Once freed, he rubs his wrist. Gideon shackles his ankles, the chain long enough to walk but too short to run.

"Come on then," Lucas says.

We start down the path, Lucas and I on either side of him.

The night is cool, the cobblestones silvered by starlight. I glance up just as a brilliant streak tears across the darkness— another shooting star.

I stop without thinking, and the others follow my pause.

"You all right, Miss Alice?" Gideon asks.

"That's the second one this week," I say.

A hush falls over the men, no doubt finding my startlement peculiar. Blinking hard, I clear the fog and fall back into step.

When we reach the house, Joseph's cigar smoke still clings to the doorway, though he's long gone. Arch takes in the space as I lead them upstairs to the unused guest room. I'd made it ready earlier—window open to air it out, fresh linens turned down, a basin of water set for washing. I even let out the seams on a few of Joseph's spare garments. He's not as tall as Arch, but he's thick through the middle; trousers for a man built like that often carry extra fabric in the seat. Arch will have to wear them low on his hips, and they're not the prettiest pair I've ever stitched together, but they'll do.

Gideon crouches; metal scrapes and squeals as he opens the cuffs, then clinks together as he drags them away. I interject while I can.

"Might it be all right to clean him up? Let him change clothes? Before you shackle him again."

Lucas presses his lips together. "That ain't what Mr. Sherman asked us to do."

Arch laughs. "That's because your boss ain't got the balls to come up here and smell me himself."

I open my mouth, half a heartbeat from chiding Arch for his foul language like I would a drunk traveler, but I swallow it. Though a flush creeps up my neck, I square my shoulders. "Cleanliness is important for healing," I say. "Surely you want him mended."

Lucas and Gideon exchange a look. Finally, Lucas sighs. "Fine. We'll wait outside."

The door clicks shut, and the task before me sets my insides trembling, as though the ground itself has shifted under me. Arch is already tugging at his shirt. When I help him, the fabric rips away from his skin, sticky with sweat and blood. He hisses, but he doesn't complain.

"May I clean your wounds?" I ask.

He's shirtless, his bare torso stained with old blood, grime, and trail dust. He inches closer, rolling his shoulders back and lengthening his body as if to give me permission. "Do your worst."

I dip the cloth into the basin. Suds of homemade soap

bubble with hints of lye and rosemary. My hands are steady, but they don't feel as though they are. Not when I stand in his shadow brushing a cool rag against his broad chest. Not when his breath brushes the top of my head.

His shoulders are sturdy, chest all hard lines and scars. He looks dangerous. Dangerous and alive, and I despise the way that makes my stomach flip. He doesn't turn away. Doesn't even blink. The silence between us is deafening.

"You're frightened," he says, half a question.

I don't answer. Whatever it is, the power of this spell has teeth and honey both. My mouth dries as I chase a spot of rust-brown blood against the planes of his taut stomach. My goodness—he's solid as stone. Muscles clench under my touch, then ease, the shadows shifting with them. A pale scar tucks under one ridge, a freckle under another.

He tilts his head, watching me. "I ain't gonna hurt you."

The words land like a warning, not a comfort. He could break me in two if he wanted—*oh*, how he could break me— we both know it. The thought leaves me hollow, as though my ribs have been scooped clean, making room for sin to flood in. Shame rises fast, curling around me like ivy. Beneath it, a slick ache warms at the apex of my thighs.

I shove the cloth into his hand. "Do it yourself." I turn my back, my insides churning from how abrupt I've just been. *Foolish woman.*

Fabric rustles; water splashes into the basin—it sounds lewd. My palms sweat against my apron, neck burning with heat I can't shake.

He's quiet as he works, but every sound paints an obscene picture. I grip the dresser, staring at a framed pastoral scene, pretending not to hear the wet drag of cloth over skin. I keep my back turned while he strips off what's left of his trousers.

The shuffle of fabric, the grunt of effort, the creak of the bedframe—it all sounds louder than it should.

There's a pause, then the soft rasp of cloth being pulled up over his legs. He exhales hard, as if even that small task has taxed him.

"All right," he says at last.

I force myself to turn back, only to realize he hasn't put on trousers at all. He stands there in nothing but his drawers, thin cotton clinging tighter than it ought, cut too narrow for a man built like him. They ride low on his hips, fabric strained tight across the heavy swell of him. *Oh dear.* I wrench my curiosity away, barely stifling a gasp.

He notices. Of course he does. His smile unfurls slowly, edged with a darkness that unsettles me. "Don't reckon these were stitched for a man my size," he drawls.

My throat tightens, fingers fumbling with the trousers still folded on the bed. "I let out the ankle. They're cut a bit looser."

He stoops, stepping one long leg then the other into the trousers, drawing them slowly up his muscular thighs; he knows I'm watching. The waistband settles into place across his hips, the fabric fitting better than I feared, though not loose enough to spare me the sight of him. The length falls straight now, thanks to my alterations.

"Sit," I say, sharper than I intend. "Let me tend your wounds."

I kneel beside him, fingers brushing his side as I wind the cloth around his ribs. His skin is hot beneath my touch, muscles taut even at rest. He doesn't flinch. Doesn't speak. He only watches me.

My hands tremble, traitorous things, and I curse them silently. I pull the bandage snug and knot it. "There." I reach for the shirt laid neatly across the chair and shake it out. "Arms."

He lifts them slowly, and I guide the sleeves over his shoulders, fabric dragging across scarred skin. The nearness of him overwhelms me—the scent of rosemary soap and heat, the brush of my knuckles against the soft hair of his chest as I button him. At the last button, my fingers falter. His breath is there, warm against my hair.

"Feels better already," he whispers.

I busy myself with smoothing the fabric, as though the work itself can shield me from the weight of my unwanted attraction.

He's watching me, his attention prickling my skin. God help me. One look and the air in this room will combust.

Before the devil can tempt me any further, I jerk my hand back and blurt, too fast, too loud, "You can come back now!" My voice cracks in the quiet.

The door hinges squeal. Lucas and Gideon step in, their boots heavy on the floorboards.

"All finished?" Lucas asks, his attention cutting from the basin to the damp rags, then to me. He lingers a touch too long, suspicion tightening his features.

Arch leans back against the headboard, the faintest smirk tugging at his mouth, as if he's daring me to blush under their stare.

"He's clean and bandaged," I say quickly, forcing my voice steady. "You can see he's no danger tonight."

"Mr. Sherman said he's to be secured," Lucas replies.

Gideon moves forward with the iron, and it clanks against the brass bedframe.

Arch doesn't resist. "Don't worry," he drawls, tipping his

head toward me, hazel eyes gleaming with something unreadable. "I'll manage."

When the men leave, I cross to Arch and press my palm to his cheek. He's warm but not fevered.

"Touch a man's face that soft, Alice, and he'll start wonderin' how the rest of you feels."

Heat rises from my collar to my ears, and his words land low in my belly. He'd spoken them as if he knew exactly where they would land. My palm lingers half a beat too long before I snatch it away with a gasp, as if burned.

His grin deepens into something wolfish.

I smooth my apron, stepping back under the pretense of giving him space. "I'll see you've water for the night."

"That star business—superstition of yours?"

"Pardon?"

"You said you'd seen two this week. You reckon it means something?"

"Maybe. I've read they can be warnings or signs of hope. I'd rather think the latter."

"What do you believe?"

"I...don't rightly know."

He turns to the window, the sky beyond wide and star-strewn. "The night before—however I ended up here—I seen one myself."

My hand lingers on the door, though I ought to go.

"Tell me something, darlin'—how's a woman in a place like this know about fallin' stars?" He leans forward, elbows to his knees, chain drawn taut. His genuine curiosity holds me still.

"I read," I say. "And I listen. My father had an old almanac. When I was a girl, I'd sneak out with it, match the drawings to the sky."

"That so?" His mouth tugs upward. "So you fancy yourself a stargazer?"

I almost smile. "Falling stars aren't stars at all. They're stones from the heavens, burning up as they pass through the air. Some folks think they're omens."

"Sounds prettier the way you tell it. Me, I don't care what they're made of. I just watch 'em fall."

I move toward the door again, but he goes on.

"I ain't much for book learnin'. But I know men. Always have. When I was a boy, I'd ride the train into town just to study folks. Get 'em talkin', coax their secrets out on account of pride or the itch to brag. Funny thing—animals, like a rabbit or a snake, they'll match the brush or dirt, melt right into it. But city folks?" He gives a humorless smile. "They march to the slaughter, drunk on their own pomp."

"You study human nature, then?"

He scratches his chin as he seems to turn it over. "Suppose you could call it that. I can tell when a man's lyin' by the set of his shoulders, when he's scared by the drop of his eyes. I know when he's thinkin' of runnin' and when he's thinkin' of killin'. That's how I keep alive."

My pulse quickens, and not from fear alone. "And what do you see when you look at me?"

His reply comes with a bitter certainty, like an irrefutable truth he cannot abide. "I see a little lamb standin' in a den of snakes."

"You don't know me."

"No. But I know snakes. And I know the look in a lamb's eyes when she's wondering how long she's got. You're a lamb, Alice. Soft-hearted and sweet. But I reckon you could learn to bite."

A tightness coils in my chest.

"That mark," he says softly, nodding toward the fading bruise on my cheek, "don't belong on you. Your husband, that whole damn clan of Shermans, they ain't known for their kindness. Help me, and I'll see to it no one ever lays a hand on you again."

"Suppose I freed you. What then? You ride off, and what happens to me among snakes?"

"I won't leave you behind."

I almost laugh. Why should I believe him? Any man in his position would make the same promises—sweet enough to loosen a lock—then vanish once his boots touched open trail.

And what would he see me as, once free? Not the woman who could cook and sew, tend a fever, manage a house and its accounts. Not the one who could ride a horse hard across open country and read the stars to find her way. No, he'd see a liability. Just as my parents had. Just like Joseph.

"You've only known me these few days, Mr. Archer. Long enough to see me carry a tray and change a bandage, nothing more."

"That's plenty. Some folks won't fetch a sip of water for a man laid up, much less see to him proper." He huffs a short, quiet breath. "You kept me fed. Kept my mouth from goin' dry. Saw to it I was clean and comfortable. That's more than keepin' a man alive, that's kindness. And I don't take kindly to seein' a good soul bruised up."

The words settle over me like a blanket fresh off the line. No one had named my care so plainly before. It stirs something I've never known—something lovely and fragile, yet mysterious, like a rose blooming in the dark.

"Who are you? Really."

He studies me a long moment, then says, "I'm someone most folks wouldn't trouble themselves to treat so well."

CHAPTER 7

ALICE

His words linger, follow me back to my room and into bed, where I lie staring at the ceiling. He hadn't said more, but he hadn't needed to.

He's a criminal. A desperado, like one of those dreadful novels come to life. A man who robs and fights and boasts of it. He expects me to be revolted, and perhaps I should be. Yet the danger of him only makes him more magnetic.

What's the matter with me?

I squeeze my thighs together under the quilt, hating myself for the ache that builds there. That man is temptation made flesh. The work of the devil, surely. And yet, he has never said an unkind word to me. Never raised a hand, though he's had cause and opportunity. Wounded, shackled, cornered—yet he hasn't struck out.

So what if he's robbed and brawled? Men on the right side

of the law have given me more grief than any outlaw ever could.

Once the day of the Astral Society's conference arrives, Fred guides coaches onto the lawn and unloads trunks. Gideon and Lucas lead horses to the livery, where extra hay bales, oats, and buckets of water have been laid out. The inn hums with order and noise—rooms scrubbed, glasses polished, cellars stocked with the Society's favored brandy. But I feel removed from it, my thoughts caught elsewhere.

Joseph is too busy shaking hands, clasping shoulders, and making introductions to every man of consequence within reach to dwell on his prisoner. We haven't exchanged more than a few words since morning. Still, curiosity gnaws at me, burrows deep as a worm in an apple.

"Have you seen the humidor key?" Joseph asks suddenly, patting his waistcoat with irritation. From one pocket, he pulls a heavy iron key, a square-cut bit meant for a sturdier lock. I nearly gasp. I know that shape—the lock that chains Arch to his bed.

Joseph frowns at it, slips it back, then checks another pocket. "Ah. Here it is." He holds up a smaller brass key with a satisfied grin. "Fetch the cigars for me, will you? The gentlemen are expecting them."

I dip my head and hurry toward the case.

The first key. He must keep it on him. Always. If I slipped it from his pocket, what might it mean? A chance to end this insanity once and for all? Freedom for Arch, or ruin for me? Yet the image of that key lingers.

The racket of the Astral Society carries faintly through the walls, but the house itself is hushed. I slip into the room with a pitcher of water in my hands.

Arch stands beside the bed, fingertips touching the glass as he peers through the curtains. "You're hosting quite a shindig." He turns toward me, the sunlight catching along the lines of his features—broad shoulders, strong jaw. All of him shaped like he was built to step out of the light.

"Largest of the year," I say. "And how are you feeling?"

"Strong," he says, seemingly mesmerized by the activity outside.

I clear my throat and square my shoulders. "I'm glad to hear it. May I see how your wounds are healing, Mr. Archer?"

He nods slightly with a curious smirk, calloused hand rising to the top button of his shirt.

"You're awful formal this morning."

The comment makes me acutely aware of my own stiffness —the way I hold myself, rigid and upright, as if a single slip might betray my thoughts. Maybe it is the realization that any daydream I have entertained about Arch is just that: a fantasy. A futile mirage conjured by Satan.

Still, my hands struggle to remain steady as I help him. I loosen the bandage wrapped around his side, peel it away slowly, watching his face for any flicker of pain. He doesn't flinch, just offers the same tenderness that makes me lose my train of thought.

I dip a clean cloth in the basin and press it gently to the wound. He breathes in sharply through his nose, but says nothing.

There's salve in my apron pocket—phenol and lanolin. I set the cloth aside and fish it out as I examine him. The swelling has eased. The angry, raw edges have softened. Dipping two fingers into the ointment, I spread it over the gash in careful, circular strokes. It bites the back of my throat with its tang of burnt wood and medicine.

Surveying the expanse of him—broad chest, narrow hips, muscles carved like stone—I pause at the line of hair below his navel, that subtle trail disappearing beneath the low waistband of his trousers. A path no decent woman ought to follow. And yet my thoughts slip there all the same, warmth rising in my cheeks before I force my attention elsewhere.

"I'd tip you for your fine nursing skills, but I think that husband of yours took all my money."

A soft, surprised sound escapes my lips—too quick to stop. It catches me off guard, light and sincere in a way I hadn't meant to reveal.

He smiles. Not his usual smirk or flash of teeth. This one comes slower, unguarded, unsettling in its softness. A hint of warmth ghosts across his features, and he holds me there with it. For a heartbeat, it feels like we've spoken without a word.

"You know my name ain't William Archer," he says softly.

"I didn't think it was."

He angles his face away, almost bashful, a quiet huff of a laugh escaping him. When he faces me again, his features are disarmingly earnest.

"It's Archibald Randolph. But my friends call me Kodiak."

"Kodiak?" I echo, glancing back up. An exhilarating shiver chases down my spine.

"Like the bear," he says. "Big, mean bastard from up north. Biggest there is, far as I know."

The bear.

Ursa Major.

The constellation I traced, whispering to it beneath the stars. The protector in the sky. The guardian. A wish I almost forgot I made.

And now, here he is.

Could it be real?

Could the stars truly send someone?

"Kodiak," I say again. The name feels different now. Sacred.

"I'll admit, I like hearing you say it better than Mr. Archer."

I open my mouth, but the words catch. The air feels changed somehow. Dense, expectant. Like a great star straining at the edge of its life, ready to burst and scatter fire into the heavens. The way his presence narrows toward me dims the rest of the world until only this room exists.

He reaches down slowly. His fingers brush an errant lock of hair from my forehead, careful, tentative. "I don't know what your husband's got planned," he says, brushing knuckles down my cheek.

I let him. I do not for a moment intend to protest, even as he lifts my chin, holding my jaw with two rough fingers and the pad of his thumb.

"But I figure the reason he's kept me breathing this long is 'cause I'm worth more alive than dead."

"What do you mean?"

He pauses, then his hand slides lower, settling at my waist; his palm, firm and broad, anchors me. I should shove him away. Slap his hand. But his touch is so gentle my wits are useless.

"I mean there's a price on me. Big one. Thousand, last I heard."

He doesn't say it with pride, just fact. And with the ease of a man explaining something plain—practical and somehow sweet, with a touch of warmth beneath the grit—like a farmer chatting about planting season and not crimes worth hanging for.

"Ain't just for robbin' trains, though that's part of it. Some folks got real upset when I stopped their freight from making it where it was supposed to go. Truth is, I've caused trouble for men who don't like bein' embarrassed. Real high-up men. Railroad men."

His palm rests against my hip, the smallest motion of his thumb stroking lazy circles there.

"I ain't innocent, Alice. I've done bad things. But this ain't about right or wrong. It's about makin' a show. Somebody's payin' good money to see me hang."

"Why?"

"'Cause they can. Joseph and that other son of a bitch who ambushed me, they knew that. You said this is the biggest event of the year, which means once this big shindig of yours is done and the stargazers ride home, I'll be headed to a rope."

My chest aches with all I cannot give. All I have are words that taste like defeat. "I don't have the key."

His other palm moves to my nape, warm and steady, a quiet claim. The weight of his focus roots me to the spot. "Don't you fret, darlin'. I've got an idea."

He leans close, voice a hush meant for me and no one else. "Your husband thinks he took everything. He didn't. There's more than what he lifted off me." A pause, the faintest smile. "Men like him climb stairs for gold. Put that thought in his ear and he'll come to me—alone."

The sheer audacity makes me go still. To bait Joseph with treasure. To make him walk willingly into a trap. It's madness —and delightfully clever. I can already see the gleam that would kindle in Joseph's eyes. I press my lips together, heat rushing through me—not fear, but the thrill of strategy.

"And if he comes?"

His eyes fix on me, steady as stone, yet soft. "Then I'll make sure he sees sense. He gets his gold, I get my freedom." His thumb strokes my jaw, coaxing. "That's all, little lamb."

The name sweeps through me, tender and possessive at once. He draws me in with a single, confident motion. My front collides with his bare chest, his heat seeping through my corset. The rosemary soap lingers, mixed with his faint masculine musk. It's intoxicating, and I find myself swaying closer to breathe him in.

He leans forward—slow enough I could move away, but I don't. I cannot. His lips brush mine, a ghost of a kiss, faint as smoke, and it rushes through me like the first light of spring spilling across frozen ground. He lets out a long, slow exhale; the low growl of an animal warning others away.

When he draws back, his hand lingers at my cheek, thumb rough against my skin. I feel branded. Marked. My body betrays me, pulsing with a desperate, slick ache that makes my most secret flesh quiver.

The steady beat under his skin thrums against my hand when I touch his chest and wander upward, curling in the dark hair at his nape. It's soft as it tangles around my fingers.

"When I get out of these chains," he rasps, "I'm takin' you with me."

The words nearly buckle my knees. My mouth opens, but no protest comes. Only the silence, thick and charged, pressing in around us like the hush before the stars themselves break apart.

I RAISE my fingers to my lips; the surge of heat remains there. A longing. Then shame, heavy and unwelcome, threatens to flatten me.

Lord forgive me.

I want to believe God knows my heart, that a merciful God

understands a marriage born of debt and fear and obligation is not a sacred thing.

I was only a child during the famine, the winter that took nearly everything. Our farm withered beneath the frost, and the Shermans stepped in with a loan that kept my brothers and sisters fed. When my father couldn't repay, there were only two choices: give me up or watch our land burn.

A union made under threat is not holy.

So why does Kodiak's mouth feel like sin?

A delicious sin.

Oh, Father.

I hurry to the parlor, my mind a blur. The room is thick with cigar smoke and laughter. When Joseph spots me, his expression tightens just slightly.

"Well?" he asks. "Our guest has been attended to?"

"Yes, sir," I say, dipping my head. "But Joseph, he said something you should hear."

He waves a dismissive hand, attention fixed on the men debating across the room. "Later."

"No," I press, lowering my voice. "It was about money."

That earns his full attention. Of course it does. I knew it would. He excuses himself from the circle of men and leans close, his genial mask slipping. "Money?"

I clasp my hands to keep them from trembling. "It seemed like a riddle of some kind. He said there was a trove. Somewhere hidden, but not a secret. Worth more than any prize, he said."

Joseph gives a sharp, humorless laugh. "So the patient spins tales now? Tells riddles like Rumpelstiltskin?"

My pulse kicks hard, but I hold fast to the ruse. "He wouldn't say more to me. Only that he'd speak the rest to you."

Joseph's mouth twists, though not in amusement. He

studies me a moment longer, his hand resting on the back of a chair as if weighing whether to bother. Then he gives a curt shake of his head. "Not now. The guests require attending. If he's still telling tales once our guests depart, I'll hear his ramblings then."

I bite my lip, lowering my lashes. "He made it sound urgent."

Joseph raises an eyebrow. "Urgent how?"

"I—I don't rightly know." I wring my hands, feigning confusion. "He only said it was worth more than any prize. He swore the rest was only for you. What do you think it means?"

His jaw flexes as he dismisses my question with a wave of his hand. Gripping the chair, he appears to wrestle with the offer, then at last he gives a short nod. "Very well. I'll see him. But mark my words, if he's trifling with me, I'll know it."

My stomach turns liquid, but I'm careful to keep my face composed.

He brushes past me, his smile snapping back into place for the benefit of the gentlemen in the parlor. "Pardon me, gentlemen," he says easily. "A private matter requires my attention."

With sharp strides he's off, and I follow a pace behind, my hands clasped before me to hide their shaking. What have I done? What will Kodiak do?

The noise of the parlor fades as we move down the corridor toward the exit, into the sunshine, and along the cobblestone path. Each step closer makes my stomach twist tighter.

Once inside Kodiak's door, he glances back at me. "You stay here," he says.

"Yes, sir."

Joseph pushes the door open.

Inside, Kodiak stands by the window, one arm braced

against the sill, chains rattling softly as he turns. Sunlight slips over the planes of his face, and for a breath, I think I see the faintest curl of a smile.

Joseph steps in, closing the door behind him.

I press my back against the wallpaper, the hush of the corridor wrapping around me. Muffled voices bleed through the door—faint, indistinct. I can't make out the words, only their rhythm. The slow build and break of cadence. Their voices rise, and I hold my breath. I think of the distance to the inn across the yard, through thick wood walls and shuttered windows. The guests won't hear a thing. No one will.

I inch closer to the door, every inch of me strained with listening.

Something shifts in their voices. An edge now. A warning. A chain yanked, hard. It snaps loud against the bedframe. A grunt. Furniture scrapes. A sudden thud.

I flinch, drawing in a sharp breath. Holding it there, I listen hard.

Another sound. Lower. Rougher. Like someone choking. Then boots dragging, scuffling, stumbling across the floor. A second thud rattles the door.

Then stillness.

Nothing but the tick of the hall clock, the rasp of my own breath.

I raise my hand to the knob, then pull it back, heart galloping. I stand frozen in that silence, perspiration gathering on my nape, my mouth dry as cotton.

I wait—longer than I should—before my hand finds the knob again.

CHAPTER 8

KODIAK

Footsteps creak up the stairs and my heart kicks in my chest—not fear, but hunger. Same way a Kodiak watches an elk lower its head to drink. I sit, waiting, listening for the latch. Half hard already, thinking on looking that bastard in the eye as he takes his last breath.

The lace curtain breathes at the window, throwing patterns of light across the plaster. Plain brass bed under my wrist, five feet of chain hangs slack from the shackle to the footboard. The door eases open and in strolls that Sherman boy, puffed up like a show pony. Alice lingers behind him, trembling like a newborn fawn. Can't help but crack a smile knowing she did her part just fine, nerves and all.

The bastard squares himself between me and the door, shutting it behind him.

"Mr. Randolph," he says. "You look well."

"No thanks to you."

His mustache twitches, humorless. "Ordinarily, I would

delegate such work to lesser men, but I've heard of your cunning. I could not risk you bribing some unfortunate soul with promises of fortune. And now it seems you've fooled my wife into believing you have some hidden treasure. I knew it for nonsense the instant she spoke it, but I will not have you trifling with her, nor making sport of my household."

Yet here he stands.

"Mr. Sherman," I say, giving the yellow-bellied dog respect he don't deserve, "whoever sent you, I reckon they paid top dollar. Whatever it is, I can do better."

He studies a fingernail, exhales hard, weary-like. "Money is a poor motivator in my position. My family has no shortage. You have meddled in our affairs, and those of our esteemed associates in Kentucky. Train robbers such as yourself cannot be tolerated. It is a matter of honor, Mr. Randolph. Your death will not merely be an end, it will stand as a lesson."

Bleeding out in the brush ain't near as attention-grabbing as a noose.

"Honor, huh? Was it honor when your company men shot down every Shawnee over by Oleander spring? Spilled blood on holy ground just to throw up a fancy hotel? Or is it honor when you lay hands on that sweet-as-sugar wife of yours?"

That sparks a fire. He lifts his chin.

"I suppose my wife has sought your pity? As her husband, I may correct her as I see fit. I've no more time to waste, Mr. Randolph. My guests require me, and the law will see you disposed of soon enough."

He offers a nod and goes to leave. Been waiting on this cocky bastard to turn his back. He only drops his guard for half a moment, but that's all I need. I whip the chain up and over, iron whispering over brass, and set it clean under his jaw, right across the windpipe.

I yank him back till he's flush against me. Bedframe screeches across the floorboards. "Here's my fuckin' correction."

The terror in his soul kicks his heart up so fast I can feel it humming through him. He thrashes wild, swinging elbows, kicking back on his hinds like a spooked stallion. One catches me in the ribs sharp enough to sting. Pleases me some, knowing he's spending his last breath on nothing. Every scrap of fight wasted against what's already done.

We slam sideways into the washstand. Porcelain sings. The pitcher tips—water arcs and smacks the boards, running fast beneath his boots. He skids.

Dragging him down, I wrestle him to the floor easy. His fingers claw at his throat, desperate for so much as a hair of space between the bite of my chain and the skin turning red beneath. Mouth gapes wide to beg, to cry, but not a sound can break through.

Just as the strength drains out of him, I lean in close to his ear. "Don't you fret 'bout Alice. Your wife is mine now, and I'll keep her proper. While you're rottin' in the dirt, worms in your eyes, I'll be fuckin' her full, keepin' her moanin' my name, seein' her belly swell with my young."

My taunt gives him his last burst of fight. He jerks, froths from his lips, then goes limp. The rush of his life spilling out, of revenge under my hands, rips through me like release.

Silence takes the room.

Bed skewed off-square. Smell of cigar, wet wood, and iron thick in the air.

The door creaks open.

CHAPTER 9

ALICE

Joseph lies crumpled on the floor between Kodiak's legs. His face purple, lips parted in a frozen gasp. Kodiak lies behind him, sweat pouring down his face, his chest rising and falling with ragged breaths. The chain in his hand is taut, looped once around Joseph's neck like a collar.

I stagger back, frozen in the frame of the doorway. My whole body goes weightless, as if gravity itself has released me into space.

Kodiak unwraps the chain and lets it drop. It hits the floor with a final, metallic clatter.

I can't breathe.

Joseph—gone.

This is my doing. I tricked him.

What had I thought would happen?

God forgive me.

"Alice."

The voice snaps my focus to him.

"You hear me?"

I manage a faint nod.

"Good." He jerks his chin toward Joseph's body. "Where's the key?"

My stomach lurches. "I—"

"No time for panic," he says, voice calm but firm. "They'll be missin' him soon enough. You want me out of these chains; where's the key?"

The key. Joseph had the key. The man who ruled my life, reduced now to nothing but weight and flesh.

My fingers curl in my skirts.

How could I?

I lied. Led my husband to his death.

Surely there was another way. A path to freedom that would have spared my mortal soul.

"Alice," Kodiak says again, softer this time, but no less urgent. "Where is the key?"

My breath comes shallow, ragged. Joseph had the key. Now he's murdered, his waistcoat twisted askew.

My husband.

My stomach heaves. I press a hand to my mouth, swaying where I stand. I hadn't been ready for this, hadn't imagined it would be like this. Not tonight. Not so soon.

"I-I can't," I stammer. My pulse thunders in my ears.

Kodiak's voice cuts through the rising whirl of my panic. "Yes, you can." Easy. Solid. Grounded as a fencepost.

"You don't understand."

"I understand plenty," he says. "I know you're scared. But you ain't scared of me."

My throat tightens, my wits on the edge of failure. "H-how can I be sure?"

He doesn't flinch at the question. "If I meant you harm,

you'd already know it. You patched me up, stood close enough to touch, and I never laid a hand you didn't want. That's the truth, ain't it?"

My breath comes faster, my palms damp where they press against my skirts.

"Now listen," he says. "You've got one chance. One. Either fetch that key and we walk out of here together, or we both hang when the law comes lookin'."

The reality of it all closes in, bitter and final, yet it all seems like some ghastly play. A sickness settles deep in my gut. I want to run, to hide, to wake up from this nightmare.

But the way his eyes fix on me anchors me fast.

"Alice," he says, almost pleading. "Trust me."

UNCHAINED, Kodiak moves with a strength and certainty that chills me. Not the bedridden man of days ago but something else entirely. He shoves Joseph's limp body from his lap with a groan, and Joseph's head strikes the floor with a dull thud. My stomach lurches at the sound.

He crouches low with a wince, patting Joseph down, then slips a hand into the waistcoat pocket. Bills. Folded, neat, clipped with gold.

"Where's the inn keep its coffers?" he asks, slipping the bills into his pocket without sparing me a glance.

"Pardon?"

"Payroll. Expenses. Where's the cash kept?"

I scoff. "You will not steal from this inn."

His eyes snap to mine, sharp as flint. "How do you suppose we pay our way out in the world? Your dearly departed took everything I had, and I intend to get it back. Now, you can tell me and save us both a whole lotta time."

"What will happen to the staff?" My throat tightens. "They won't be paid."

He drags a hand down his face, sighing, muttering, then louder, "To hell with the staff, Alice."

"No!" I shout, surprising myself. The sound cracks through the sparsely furnished guest room. "These people are my family, and I won't steal from them."

He shakes his head, a low curse tumbling from his lips as he pushes past me. I stumble, my skirts brushing Joseph's outstretched hand. A dead man's hand. My God.

Kodiak's boots hammer like thunder down the stairs. I follow, heart slamming, whispering prayers between breaths. Fool. Criminal. Devil. And yet, I can't let him do this alone.

In the corridor below, I find him at Joseph's office, hand already on the knob. He rattles it, then shoulder slams the door once. The lock holds. He draws back and kicks with a pained grunt. The crack of splintering wood jolts through me as the door is sent flying wide.

"What are you doing?" I cry, panicked.

He doesn't turn. "Quit pesterin' me with questions, woman." Papers scatter off the desk as he tears inside and rifles through drawers. A fine wool Stetson rests atop a stack of leather-bound books. He lifts it, studies it a beat, then sets it square on his head. "I already told you, I ain't goin' to the gallows on account of the Sherman family. And I'll be damned if I leave this place empty-handed."

Kodiak lets his hand stray over Joseph's desk, hooks a tobacco pouch with two fingers, and shoves it in his pocket. At last, he faces me, expression dark. "Now, are you with me or not?"

For years I'd prayed for freedom, and briefly, I believed Kodiak had been brought to my doorstep to answer that prayer. It felt destined—stars and planets aligned—right up until the moment Joseph's cold, dead expression stared back at me.

God wouldn't answer a prayer with such a sin. I should have known better.

"You're a murderer," I say, almost a whisper, but sharp enough to stop his search.

"That ain't news to you," he says, then flings a heap of papers aside. "Shit," he mutters, gripping his side. He strides toward me until his shadow swallows me whole. "Those Sherman boys stuck me like a hog and chained me up, kept me breathing only so I might hang. I know you ain't one of 'em," he says, his hands closing at my waist.

Since we've met, he's taken liberties I'd never grant a man other than my husband, yet his ungentlemanly gesture makes me soften under his touch.

"I knew it first time I laid eyes on you. Too kind, too soft to bind yourself willingly to a Sherman. I know that clan. Rotten to the core, every last one of 'em. How'd he make you his, Alice? Tell me."

My throat tightens, heat climbing into my cheeks, my legs near failing me. He's twisting me with his words. I know it, but I cannot stop the pull. Surely he's done the same to a dozen women, at least. Convinced them they were goddesses just to have his way before leaving them like fools. Yet the truth spills from me.

"M-my father. Owed a debt to Sherman senior." I've never spoken the words aloud, not even to myself.

"Your father sold you to the Shermans?"

I flinch, heat prickling my skin, searing from neck to cheeks. "He didn't have a choice." My protest is weak even as I speak it. "The land was all we had. My brothers and sisters... without the Shermans' loan, they'd have starved."

"Bullshit," he says. His jaw sets hard, voice a growl. "Sherman would've found his head on a pike before I'd let him lay a hand on you."

My knees nearly give; my chest seizes with a shudder I can't suppress. It should horrify me. It does. But God help me, it stirs something deeper. No man has ever spoken of me this way. Not Father, who bartered me like livestock. Not Joseph, who took me like property. But this outlaw, this killer, says he'd spill blood to keep me safe, and the vow tears through me like a firestone ripping through the sky.

Shame prickles my skin, hot and unholy, because part of me leans toward him, drawn into the violence of his promise as though it were a kiss.

Kodiak's gaze narrows, darkened under the brim of his stolen hat. He sees it—sees me unraveling beneath his words. A slow smile, dangerous and knowing, curves his lips. "That got to you, didn't it?" He hushes, like his words are a secret meant only for me. "Little lamb, you tremble like I've already laid you down."

The shame sears hotter. My lips part, but no sound comes. I want to deny it, to call him ungodly, indecent. But the truth is there in my pulse, in the fire brewing in my belly. He knows it.

"You ain't afraid of me," he says softly. "You're afraid of how I make you feel." Pulling me closer, his breath is hot against the shell of my ear. "You're slick as rain, ain't you? Soaking through your pretty slip."

I gasp, the strain in my chest growing unbearable. How dare he speak to me this way? Yet I can't push him away, don't want to. And he doesn't let me go.

"Thought so. I can feel the heat rollin' off you. Never been near a real man, have you? A man who don't flinch, don't bow, don't hide behind ledgers and laws. Joseph was a coward. Your daddy too. But a man worth his salt? He risks his life for what matters. Kills for it if he has to. That's the natural order." His hands tighten around me, making me shiver. "And now you're near one, your body knows it."

"Enough." My voice breaks, limbs weak as I shove at him. "You will not speak to me that way."

He tips his head with a chuckle, loosening his grip but not stepping back. His fingers linger at my waist. "There's the teeth I was waitin' on. Only makes me want you more."

Gathering myself, I wrench free. "Mr. Archer—or Randolph, or whatever you choose to call yourself—you shall not steal from this house. I have funds set aside for just such a time, and if you'll cease playing the brute for a moment, I will fetch them."

He watches me long enough that my breath stutters, before he says, "Lead on."

The barn swelters in the midday sun, the odor of hay and manure thick as the dusty air. I pry loose the plank, burlap sacks waiting where I left them. Kodiak crouches beside me, broad shoulders blocking the light.

"Would you look at that," he says, surveying the gear, rations of canned food, and stack of bills. For a breath, I worry he'll snatch everything and run.

Boots scrape the packed earth below. I start, heart thudding. It's Gideon, his face pale.

"Miss Alice?" His voice cracks, then his focus shifts past me to the outlaw at my shoulder. Recognition sharpens his features. His hand fumbles to his hip, pulling a revolver he has no business carrying. He raises it, though it wavers in his grip. "You all right, ma'am?"

My breath knots tight. "Gideon, no!" I say quickly, pushing the words out steady as I can. "It's all right. He won't harm me."

Gideon doesn't lower the gun. "That's the outlaw, Miss Alice."

Kodiak shifts slowly, hands out and open as though calming a skittish colt. "Easy, boy. Ain't here to hurt her." His voice is a low rumble.

"Please, don't hurt him," I warn Kodiak. "Gideon, I'm safe. I promise."

Gideon lowers his weapon, face drawn with apprehension. As he studies the scene, I see the truth become clear to him, the realization settle. "You're leavin' with him?"

I nod.

His shoulders sag. A breath escapes him, weary as an old man's. "Reckoned the day'd come you'd be gone."

It tightens my chest, but before I can speak, Kodiak cuts in. "If you give a damn about Miss Alice, then listen good, boy. When they come askin', you tell 'em I killed Joseph and dragged her off. You do that, no harm comes down on your head. You understand?"

I glance at him, startled. Is this meant to shield me? To spare me the law's noose when he casts me off somewhere on the trail?

Gideon's voice breaks my thoughts. "Mr. Sherman's dead?"

"Yes," I whisper.

He swallows hard, a long silence stretching between us before he nods toward the yard. "I'll have a carriage ready at the gate."

"Smart boy," Kodiak says, then hefts the burlap sacks to his shoulder, his other hand pressing lightly at my back, steering me on.

At the carriage, Gideon steadies me as I climb aboard. His face seems older than his years—drawn, sorrowful. Before he steps back, he slips his revolver into my hands. "Just in case," he murmurs, cutting a wary flick toward Kodiak.

The iron chills my palm. My throat tightens. "Thank you, Gideon."

His lip trembles, his attention fixed on me as if trying to memorize every detail, then he forces himself to step away.

Kodiak gathers the reins. "Best you head inside, boy."

The whip cracks, and the horses surge forward. Wheels clatter over the stones, sunlight flaring as the inn drops away behind us.

CHAPTER 10

KODIAK

Once we hit open country, the truth settles in—ain't no turning back.

We're in it together now.

Alice sits beside me, staring off, looking low. Can't blame her. She blew her life apart, and I supplied the dynamite. Ain't a word I could say to ease her, though I've turned it over for miles. Just wish there was something I could do.

That's why I've always gone alone. No one needing, no one feeling, no one taking more than they give. Don't have to wonder if they're true or fixing to sell me out the first chance they get.

But Alice... Since the first time she turned them wide, unguarded eyes on me, I ain't been right. Locked up in that room, I thought on her skin till it near drove me mad. Soft hands. Sweet mouth. Tits heavy enough to fill both my palms. Thought of her baring one to feed my young near broke me. And the work it takes to make young—her body clutching me tight, trembling. Just the thought made me hard as iron. I'd spill blood from here to kingdom come to make her mine.

But sweating and patched up from a blade wound ain't the time. And sitting up here with the reins, catching how she's gone all downcast, I know taking what I want would only make it worse. Already spooked her enough. I've seen fear before—men facing the barrel, women when I step in their path. I love that fear. Tells me I've done my job.

But on her? Don't sit right. She's too pure for this crooked world. That's why I call her little lamb. Feels like fate. Like the future I never reckoned I deserved.

But I got to take care. Move too fast, I'll break what little trust she's given.

CHAPTER 11

ALICE

We ride. The carriage, a Mylord commandeered from one of the Astral Society guests, is led by two Clydesdales—one bay, and one roan with white blaze and legs. They slow their pace once we've left the town behind. I take shelter from the sun under the open carriage's black leather hood as a passenger, while Kodiak drives up front. Wheels clatter over stone, hooves pounding a steady rhythm that carries us away from everything I've ever known. Kodiak doesn't speak much, only says we're headed south.

But when dusk fades and the sky clears, the stars tell me otherwise. I know them like old friends—the Dipper, the North Star, the tilted line of Cassiopeia. They show me what he does not say, what perhaps he doesn't even know.

Not south. Southwest.

I am not sure why we've traveled in this direction, but I had no reason to ask. We've already gone further than I'd ever dreamed. We ride through the night until dawn bleeds across the horizon. And the further we go, the stranger it feels to be untethered. Back at the inn, my tasks had been marked out like minutes on a clock. Routine so ingrained, I scarcely had to think to carry it out.

But here, inside this rattling carriage, nothing holds me. Only the sky above, wide as eternity. The rush of wind, the groan of a leather harness, the smell of horseflesh and sweat. A world of earth and animals and stars. I don't know who I am without the chains of my old life.

At last, we stop beside a creek fringed with cottonwoods. "Trees'll give us cover," he says, his voice rough from hours of silence. Kodiak bends to inspect the horses' hooves, then leads them to water.

It's been a day since our last proper meal. I rummage through the rations, preparing a pot over a fire. It's less than ideal. Nothing fresh. But it will fill our bellies, and for a time, the work helps me forget my listlessness.

When he returns, he gives the small camp I've made a quick once-over. He squats by the fire, peering into the pot. The summer sun sets behind him, painting the sky in pink and gold. "I'da chewed jerky and called it a meal. You make it feel damn near civilized."

"It's the least I can do," I say. "I only wish I had more to give."

He watches the pot a second, steam curling up into his face as he tips his chin with approval. "You've given plenty. I'd be dangling from a rope by now if not for your kindness." His mouth crooks. "Hell, I'd be dinin' with the devil hisself."

The ease with which he speaks of damnation chills me. I

stir the beans, though they don't need it. "You've resigned yourself to such a fate?"

"I ain't resigned to nothin'." He flicks a twig into the fire, sparks jump. "I only know what I done, and what's waitin' for me past the grave. None of it pretty. But if that's the price for livin' honest, then that's the price."

I huff a breath I didn't mean to. "I've never heard a man call robbing and brawling an honest life before."

He gives a short laugh. "What's more honest than takin' what you need? Lookin' a man square in the eye and givin' him the choice—his life or his coin? I never lied about who I was."

Silence gathers with the dusk. Crickets start up along the creek.

"William Archer?" I ask at last.

"Ah," he says, with a slow nod. "You do have me there. Though what's a man's name worth, anyhow? Call me Arch, call me Kodiak—don't change the color of my blood." He rests back in the grass, tilting his hat forward to shade his face. "Man ought to be known by his deeds, not the word somebody pinned on him." He stirs the fire with a stick, sparks leaping.

The pot bubbles, and I dish the beans and salt pork into tin bowls.

He takes his portion with both hands, studying it a moment. "Same goes for a woman. Your deeds never cease to amaze."

Heat rises to my cheeks. "It's only beans and pork."

His hand shoots out sudden, quick as a pistol draw, catching a firm grip on my wrist. His voice lowers, serious. "It's kindness. And you ain't owed it to the likes of me. So you won't make it small, you understand?"

I swallow hard.

Loosening his grip, his thumb brushes softly against my skin before drawing back. "Not long as I'm here to say different." Sitting back in the grass again, he takes an eager spoonful into his mouth, bowl an inch beneath his chin. "Mmm," he says, touching two fingers to the wide, flat brim of his hat. "You doctored this up, ain't you? Seasonin' and such?"

I laugh, picturing the bare-bones fare he must live on alone. A fearsome outlaw who can scarcely boil an egg. "I had no spices to spare, but I brought a small jar of molasses."

"Mercy, woman," he says, with a grin.

A passing compliment, but I'm buoyant. Flying too high. I mustn't forget he's a criminal. An outlaw. A man not to be fully trusted.

We eat in silence, save for the hiss of insects, the rustle of wind in the trees. It grows dark. Tilting his bowl back against his mouth, he takes a final sip, then wipes his forearm across his mouth. I take the empty bowl from him, his hazel eyes fixed on me. The air feels thicker, charged. I busy myself with the bowls, stacking tin and scraping them clean. But my mind stays busy, the silence between us growing too much to bear.

"Do you usually travel with others?" I ask. "A band of outlaws?"

That earns a bark of laughter. He turns his head, teeth flashing in the dim. "Gangs? Hell no. Packs of squabblin' fools, cuttin' shares, takin' orders. Curlin' up around a fire together whisperin' stories like a buncha sissies. I've always gone alone." He pauses, chest lifting on a quiet breath, as if replaying the last week that changed everything. "Till now."

The kettle's warm with water, and I pour some into the pot to keep the sauce from sticking. "Why me?"

He shrugs. "Don't know. Somethin' in you. Felt like fate, I reckon."

The word fate strikes deep. I've wondered too, though I dare not name it. If destiny is designed by God, then how could salvation find me through a man like Kodiak? "I don't even know right from wrong anymore," I confess. I scour the pot with a rag. "Everything I prayed for is falling into place. Freedom. Escape. But you..." My throat tightens. "You're a sinner. You admit it freely."

"Ain't we all?"

I set the cleaned pot upside down beside the fire, brushing water from my hands. "Yes. But you commit mortal sins. Murder."

He doesn't flinch. Reaching into his pocket, he retrieves Joseph's tobacco pouch and sets a book of cigarette papers on his thigh. "I've killed. I don't make light of it. But most times it was them or me, and I aim to keep breath in my lungs. Don't mean I sleep easy after...least not at first."

As he rolls his cigarette, I rest on the soft earth beside him, blanket in hand. It's cool out, and I drape the wool cover over my shoulders. "So you've no code? No rules to guide you?"

He huffs, shaking his head as he licks the cigarette shut. "A code? No, sugarplum. I go with what feels right. And sometimes what feels right is ugly. Done cruel things. Been a real evil son of a bitch. Kindest thing I do for most folks is keep my shadow off 'em. But you—" His voice softens and he lets out a weary sigh. "I'd never have walked out of that place empty-handed. I'd have emptied the safe, robbed every last one of your lodgers blind. But you defended 'em like they were your own. And you tended me when I was half dead. Somethin' pure about you. And, well, you seemed to want out of there, and I'm a man of my word so..."

He trails off, letting the last few days speak for themselves. Could it be he believes I make him better? I turn to face him, my fingers twisting in the blanket. "I thought you might abandon me on the trail."

He's hooked his knife into the fire, and he fishes out a glowing ember, then kisses it to the cigarette, lit red. His expression shifts, shadowed and veiled in tendrils of smoke. "Alice," he says, as if it troubles him, "I gave you my word I'd take you. Truth is, that word ain't safe to keep. Men like me draw lead, and lead don't mind who it passes through."

"I am certainly safer traveling with you than I would be alone."

He holds up his hand in warning. "Best not say *safe* out loud 'round me." The fire cracks and he brings the cigarette to his lips, drawing hard. "Attracts bad weather," he says, words mixed with smoke as he exhales.

The stars are in their familiar places. All the preparation, the setting aside of coin and tinned rations—would I have had the nerve to venture out alone? All I needed was a pistol. Yet, Gideon easily provided one. They were not hard to come by if I'd ever truly put my mind to it. Perhaps it is time to fortify myself. If he leaves me, I cannot languish.

"I suppose I would find a way to manage if I must continue alone."

"I ain't gettin' rid of ya. I just can't make no promises. Ain't my nature. But for now?" He leans closer, elbows on his knees, the stars and fire alive in his eyes. "For now, I ain't goin' nowhere without you."

For now doesn't offer me much confidence. The stars twinkle above us, and perhaps I ought to pray for guidance. But no prayer comes, only the thrum of his words in my chest and the ghosts of what I've done.

As night stretches on, the subject of sleeping arrangements can no longer be ignored. There's but one tent. One bedroll.

The carriage is an option, I suppose, though it doesn't offer much shelter unless one sleeps beneath it. The prospect is rather unpleasant.

I clear my throat. "I've readied a tent."

"See that."

We drift off into weary silence. Nocturnal creatures sing their songs in darkness, the firelight dancing on Kodiak's rugged face.

"Perhaps we can take turns. I will sleep on the bedroll one night, and you—"

He chuckles. "Ah, I see what you're gettin' at. You're a proper lady and all that. Suppose stealin' a kiss don't give me license to lay beside you."

The reminder of our brief intimacy sends a shiver rippling through me.

"I done without plenty'a times. Go ahead and take the tent; I'll be fine by the fire."

"That's very kind of you."

We speak of little things after—the road, the weather, how long the rations might last. His voice is low, almost gentle now, and I find myself wishing the night could stretch on forever. But weariness presses on me, heavy as the blanket wrapped around my shoulders. "Here," I say, offering it to him. "The bedroll will be enough."

"Thank you, lamb."

The name he's chosen for me makes me smile. "You're quite welcome."

I slip into the tent, lying back on the bedroll. Through the flap, I watch him stretch by the fire, the glow outlining the breadth of his shoulders, the long lines of his body as he settles down in the grass.

The fire pops and cracks. The wind stirs the leaves. And

there he is, just a few paces away—so close I can almost feel his warmth. My breath quickens against my will. Foolish, improper thoughts churn in me, and I wonder if I was too hasty in insisting he stay outside. What harm would it be, really, to let him lie beside me? Yet I press my lips tight, willing myself still. Better to guard my virtue, even as my body aches for the opposite.

In the gray wash of dawn, I wake before him. Kodiak lies on his back, hat tipped low, one arm flung across his chest. The blanket has slid aside, leaving him half uncovered. My breath catches. Even at rest, the sight of him is indecent. The fabric stretched over a shape so large it makes my thoughts scatter. Heat rises to my cheeks, and I spin away, as if God himself had caught me sinning from the heavens.

To notice him is sin enough. To wonder is worse. And still, a treacherous thought rises in me, whispering how it might feel to have him pressed to me, inside me. My body answers with a quickening I cannot will away.

Horrified, I whisper a prayer.

Perhaps it was only the trousers. A poor fit, that was all. Yet the seams strained as though ready to give way. Had I packed needle and thread?

I busy myself with the kettle, pouring water over the last of the coffee grounds just to keep my hands from trembling. When I glance back, Kodiak stirs, dragging in a long breath. He stretches slowly before pushing himself up on an elbow. His hazel eyes catch me quick, sharp even in half sleep.

"You're up early." His voice is rough with sleep.

I keep my back turned, fussing over the tin cups. "Couldn't rest."

He hums, the sound deep in his chest, and I hear the shift

of fabric as he sits straighter. The sound alone brings back the indecent image. How could a man so sinful be made so perfectly?

He takes the cup I hand him, his fingers brushing mine. Warmth flashes, traitorous, through me.

"Well," he says, blowing steam from the rim, "ain't every day a man wakes under open sky with coffee waitin'—and a pretty face makin' it for him."

Curse the way his compliment tingles on my skin. I duck my head, pretending to mind the fire.

He takes a long swallow, sigh content, then tilts the cup toward me. "Next place we come to, I'll see about gettin' us more beans. Maybe somethin' sweet too."

"Where is that?" I ask.

"Little town down in Kentucky—Salt Lick. Place don't look like much, just a mill, a store, and a saloon where the whiskey's cheap. We'll stock up, fill our bellies proper. Maybe even see what kind of mischief we can stir."

I grin without thinking, an unexpected giggle bubbling to my lips. I've never imagined playing cards in some dusty town saloon. I scarcely let myself imagine being outside the confines of the inn. If I was in anyone else's company, perhaps I would feel frightened by the unknown, but there's something about Kodiak that makes me feel safe.

"Sweet mercy. Never reckoned I'd sit across from a smile so pretty. Careful, you smile at me like that in Salt Lick, you'll give folks the idea I'm the luckiest bastard alive."

My chest swells, and I shake my head, a flush consuming my cheeks. "You exaggerate." I busy my hands with the kettle, but I can hardly think, my heart fluttering as if it's poised to take flight.

"That husband never told you how beautiful you are?"

His father had. It was the way he explained why accepting me in lieu of monetary repayment of my father's debt was a fair exchange.

"You mustn't say such things." My voice quivers, fragile as a strand of silk. "It isn't proper."

Kodiak tilts his head, studying me. "Proper's a cage, little lamb. Ain't you glad to be free of it?"

His words strike deep, and my breath stutters. I should rebuke him, I know I should, yet the wild, unbidden pull of him won't allow it.

He reaches out—not to seize me, not rough like before, but slow, deliberate. The back of his finger grazes the curve of my wrist where it rests in my lap. It's fleeting, no more than a ghost of a touch, yet that small moment of contact sends a shiver sparking up my arm.

"You can call me liar, sinner, thief," he says, reaching for Joseph's tobacco pouch, "but don't tell me I don't see what's right in front of me. You're beautiful, Alice. You smile like that, and all I can think on is how to keep it there. Might spend every mile south dreamin' up ways to coax another one."

I swallow hard, and suddenly the fire, the cups—anything but him—become unbearably interesting. He rolls a cigarette, and the flames smear into a warm blur, my thoughts tripping over themselves. "You'll ruin me...words like that."

He chuckles softly, licking his cigarette shut, his tongue dragging across the paper with his eyes on me. My toes curl in my boots. *Oh my word.*

"Then you'd better stop smilin' so sweet."

I start to smile again but force it back. How cruel of him to sexualize something as innocent as a smile. Now with every expression of joy I'll wonder if I'm exciting him, if his trousers strain with it. "You are a shameless flirt, Mr. Randolph."

He leans back on his hand, cigarette smoldering between two fingers.

The wind lifts a strand of my hair, and before I can tuck it away, he reaches out. His hand brushes the hair from my cheek. A touch that lingers—not possessive, but something tender, perilous.

"You shouldn't look at me like that," I murmur, heart thudding.

His thumb grazes the edge of my jaw. "Ain't lookin' at you like that 'cause I'm a flirt. Lookin' at you 'cause I can't help it."

I don't move. Don't breathe.

His gaze drops to my mouth, but then he seems to think better of it and draws his hand back. "Best we get movin' soon," he says finally, rubbing a hand over his stubbled jaw. "Salt Lick's a ride yet, and the trail don't wait for folks to finish breakfast."

CHAPTER 12

KODIAK

Salt Lick ain't much—barely more than a spit of land for beasts. One crooked row of clapboard fronts and a church squatting by the creek. Alice takes in the dusty landscape from the carriage. Poor thing really ain't never seen much besides them few acres in Ohio, awed to death over buildings slouched in mud. She's in for a real hell of a treat where we're heading.

"Curious to name a town after a thing beasts lick," she says, with a cute little squint and her mouth pursed. "On the farm, we kept a block for the cows. They'd wear it down to a nub if we let them."

I huff a laugh. "They need it. Just like us. Wild ones'll walk half a nation just to get to salt. Hunters figured it out quick—set yourself by the lick, and supper walks right to your rifle."

Her brows lift just a touch. I can see the farm girl in her turning it over.

We rattle to a stop outside the general store. I swing down

first, boots hitting the dirt, then offer her my hand. Her fingers hesitate before touching mine, then I help her down. Reckon there's something 'bout me that still frightens her.

Can't say I blame her.

Bell over the door jingles, and for a moment, the air inside feels cooler than the street. Sunlight slants through the front windows, turning every floating speck of dust to gold. Two men idle by the firearms, quickly distracted by Alice before they catch me watching. My hand settles firm at her back. Not rough. Just there, guiding. She don't even notice, but it ain't for her. It's so folks know what's mine.

"What can I get you?" the storekeeper asks, wiping the sweat off his neck with a rag. He lingers on Alice, slow as honey dripping. Undressing her in his mind, most like. Old lech.

"Beans. Salt pork. Coffee. Smoke," I say, flat.

Alice adds softly, "Curious if you might also have a good washboard." Her lips curve polite, a small smile she don't even think twice about giving. But I think twice. I think ten times. That smile belongs to me.

The keeper nods, shuffling off, but not before appraising her once more. I feel it like a burr under my skin. Summer sun beats down, and even indoors it presses at my back, sweat dampening my shirt.

Alice drifts toward a shelf, her fingers brushing tins, her cheeks pink from the July air. She lifts her hair from the back of her neck with one hand, fanning herself with the other. She don't see what it does—how every man in this room is watching her glow against the dull heat like temptation itself.

Then I see 'em. A box o' matches with a little lamb on the box. Little Lamb Matchsticks. I'll be damned. I grab a box, give it a shake to catch her attention. "Little lamb," I say.

Alice tilts her head toward it, shy as a fawn. Her mouth twitches—sweet, quick as lightning—before she tucks it away.

When the keeper lays the washboard on the table, she thanks him with that same gentle curve of her lips. It's innocent, but my blood spikes anyway. I want iron on my hip just so I can rest my hand on it.

She pays the coin—her husband's silver, not mine—and I'm struck by a pang of hurt pride worse than hunger. I let it pass, but the vow forms clean in my gut. Next town, she won't be feeding us with another man's money. I'll win it. Or take it. Whatever it takes, she'll eat from what I provide.

Outside, I stop her on the boardwalk, catch her wrist. My thumb presses against her pulse. "Don't give him your smile," I say.

Alice blinks up at me, startled. "He was only a kind old man."

"Old men have eyes," I answer. My voice is hard, but not cruel. "Don't make yourself an easy mark. Don't need folks rememberin' your pretty face."

Her cheeks flush deeper as she presses her lips tight, but she agrees.

I release her wrist and sling the parcels over my arm. The

heat presses down heavy, but it ain't the only thing pressing. Ain't a dime to my name except for a room waiting for me down south and a sweet plan.

Though I weren't planning on having company when I dreamt it up. Can't hold up a joint with my woman in the cross fire. It's going to need some adjusting, but nothing I can't handle.

Near sundown, we pack our sundries into the carriage, tie off our horses at the rail behind the general store, and step off the street into a saloon. The air inside hits different—thick with tobacco smoke and the sour tang of beer. The lamplight's dim. A piano with only half its keys hides in the corner. Men jeer, chairs scrape. A woman's shrill laughter carries from upstairs.

Alice stiffens at my side, her skirts brushing me as she falters. The place is probably Gomorrah in her book. My hand settles at her waist, firm. Claiming. Her body don't lean into me, but she don't pull away neither.

We take a table in the back, far from the doors, where I can keep the whole room in view. She sits prim, folding her hands in her lap like we're at church.

The barkeep slouches over in his stained apron, rag in hand, studying Alice slow before landing on me. "What'll it be?"

"Whiskey," I say. "And lemonade for my lady."

Alice stiffens, blinking at me. The barkeep nods and shuffles off.

She leans in, her voice a quick hiss. "You order for me now?"

I tilt back in my chair, grin slow. "Reckon I do."

"What if I wanted whiskey?"

"Like some saloon girl?"

Her cheeks turn pink, but she tips her chin up. "Perhaps. If that were my preference, you may keep your judgments to yourself."

I hum. God I love it when she bites back. "Want me to order you a whiskey, Miss Alice?"

"No. A lemonade is fine."

"Good." My attention drifts to her lips before I drag it back to her eyes. "Suppose I could've let you order for yourself…but I like sayin' what touches that pretty mouth."

"You're a vile man." She huffs, but I catch a blush creeping up her neck. Her attention skitters to the space behind me, then to her fingernails, then a knot in the table—everywhere but where I sit.

Mmm. There's a pleasure in riling her with my wicked notions. Though best I ease off 'fore she gets too ornery.

I let the room settle in my head, figuring where the trouble would come from if it came. A couple men by the bar look our way, then don't.

She smooths her skirt. The seconds stretch.

The barkeep brings the drinks. I take the whiskey, slide the lemonade toward her. She glances at the glass, then at me. Her lips press together, a tiny line, before she lifts the lemonade and takes a prim sip like it's communion wine.

The first moan comes faint, muffled through the ceiling boards. Then another—higher, sharper. The laughter at the bar hushes for half a beat before the room rolls on like it ain't there.

Alice freezes, color flaring up her throat, right to her cheeks. She sets the glass down too fast, the base clinking against wood.

I lean back easy, swirling my whiskey slow, watching her squirm. I knit my eyebrows, tight and puzzled. "Hear that?"

She stares at the table. "I...yes."

Another moan, louder this time, with the rhythm of bedsprings groaning under it. Her fingers twist in her lap, ears red.

I bite back a grin, tilting my glass back and letting the brown liquor gather at one end. "What d'you reckon they're doin' up there?"

Scandal blazes across her face as she takes a harmless swat at my arm. "You know full well what they're doing. What kind of place is this?"

I chuckle soft. "Place like this? Saloons'll fill your belly, wet your throat, give you a game o' cards or a fiddle tune if you're lucky. Might be a hot bath in back. And upstairs..." I take a sip, let her hang on it. "Upstairs a man can pay for company."

Her mouth falls open, pretty lashes flutter. "And you, you've no doubt gone upstairs often enough yourself. Paid your coin for that kind of company."

I laugh low in my chest, shake my head slow. "Now there's where you're wrong, little miss."

She bristles, chin lifting. "You expect me to believe you haven't?"

"Believe what you want. But I ain't never paid for company." I drag the rim of my glass along my lip. "Never had a problem findin' it free."

"That's no better. Careless. No doubt you've courted every illness from here to the Mississippi."

I lean forward, elbows on the table, voice dropping for only her. "You worried for me, Alice?"

She flinches at the intimacy in her name. "I worry for myself. If you take such risks, you endanger everyone you touch."

A grin tugs at my mouth. "I ain't touched you yet."

She shakes her head hard, words tumbling out fast. "I didn't mean it like that!"

I let the silence stretch a beat, then take a slow sip of whiskey, watching her flounder.

She smooths her skirts. "And you presume much, Mr. Randolph."

"Mmm," I say finally, drawlin' it. "Don't pretend you ain't thought on it."

Her lips part, ready to protest, but nothing comes. She shuts them tight again, turns her face away. Another moan seeps down from the ceiling, and a man's grunts call after it. Alice shudders, clinging to herself, gripping her elbows like an orphan in the cold.

I lean just enough for my words to brush her ear. "That husband of yours ever make you moan like that, sugar?"

Her gasp is sharp, scandal written plain on her face, but she says nothing. I grin into my glass. "Didn't think so."

My whiskey glass runs dry, and the barkeep's quick to set another in front of me. By the time the food lands—a slab of beef and beans boiled flat—I'm halfway through the second.

Alice cuts neat little bites, chewing delicate.

"You'll starve, eatin' like a bird."

Just as she scowls at me, a shout from across the room pulls my eye—men crowding around a table, cards flashing in their hands, chips scattering cross wood. My blood warms hotter at the sound, and before I think twice, I shove my plate aside and stand.

Alice's head snaps up. "Where are you going?"

I tip my glass toward the game. "Cards. Luck's callin'."

With a wink, I saunter over and pull up a chair. The men size me up, but the dealer just grunts and slides me a hand. I peel the cards slow, hum deep in my chest, and throw in a coin.

The first round, I come out smelling like a rose. I rake the pot, chips clacking cool under my palms. The whiskey's burning warm in my gut now, loosening everything—shoulders, tongue, temper. Checking over my shoulder, Alice has left our table to stand behind me, jaw set hard enough to crack.

Shoulda let the woman order a damn whiskey. She could afford to lighten up.

Second round, I lean back in my chair, stretch my boots out long. "Reckon I got luck ridin' on my shoulder tonight."

One of the players, a farmer glistening with sweat, snorts. "See how long it lasts."

The dealer snaps the deck, cards shuffling clean, then lays 'em out one by one across the table. The air's thick with smoke and sweat. I slide my hand in close, tilt the corners just enough to take a peek. Three kings. A man couldn't ask for better.

But showing that now'd be suicide. So I let my mouth pull into a sour line. I toss a chip in with a wince, like it pains me, then slump back in my chair, all loose and defeated.

Alice leans a little closer, peeking at the cards in my hand. "But you've got three kings," she says, voice clear as a bell.

Every man at the table stifles.

I slam my cards face down, turning to her hot. "Sweet mercy, Alice—you don't announce a man's hand."

She jerks back a fraction, lips fumbling open. "Oh—"

The table erupts—hoots, jeers, men slapping their thighs, one near falls out his chair laughing. The farmer across chokes on his drink. Alice presses her lips together, trying to hold it, but then her shoulders shake and the cheerful sound bursts out anyway—bright, sweet, ringing through the room.

"I'm sorry!" she says, laughing.

"Sorry?" I growl, pushing my chair back just enough to catch her wrist. "You show a man's ass, then laugh at him for it."

With that, I tug her down into my lap. She gasps, stiff at first, but my arm hooks firm around her waist, holding her snug. Her skirts spill over my legs, her back pressed to my chest.

"There," I mutter against her ear, low enough only she hears. "If you're bound to ruin my game, might as well keep you where I can watch you."

She squirms, hands gripping her skirts like she might lift herself off. But I tighten my arm just an inch, enough to still her.

Her breath holds, cheeks flaming hot. "This is most improper."

"So's givin' away a man's hand."

That wins me another laugh, softer this time. The sound sings right against my chest where she leans, making me dizzier than any bottle could. I want another. "How 'bout I bounce you on my knee, keep you entertained while I play."

She sits up rigid, but there's a ghost of a smile on her lips. "You wouldn't dare."

I rock my knee once, subtle, just enough she feels it.

She scowls, but there ain't no true ugliness in it. It cracks into a laugh quick. A pretty, breathless sound, smothered by her hand, but it's there. Christ almighty. That sound could ruin me.

I pick my cards back up with my free hand, but it's a losing fight. Every time she shifts, it pulls me clean out the game. A player mutters about me being distracted, and he ain't wrong.

Alice tilts her head, whispering, "What do you have now?"

But she's too close, breath too warm, too soft, and it damn near does me in. "Ain't tellin' you," I growl, face schooled—though I'd be grinning like a fool if it was just her and me.

She lifts her eyebrows, mischief sparking. "Afraid I'll give you away again?"

"Afraid you'll have me stripped down to my drawers."

That does it. She bursts out laughing again, and the sound feels like heaven. I grin too, can't help it now, though I keep my face down toward the cards.

Next hand, I bet too much, too fast. One man calls, another raises. Alice squirms in my lap, and hell if I can think straight with her pressed against me like that. When the cards fall, I'm beat clean. Pot swept away.

"Damn it," I mutter, pushing back from the table.

She blinks up at me, brows knit. "Did you lose?"

I let out a humorless chuckle. "Lost near everything but you sittin' here."

I drop the last of my coin on the table for the next round of whiskey. The barkeep's quick to oblige, glass sliding my way. I take it down hard, heat burning through the hollow ache of losing.

Alice touches my arm, tentative. "Maybe that's enough for tonight."

"Not near enough," I mutter, reaching for the bottle instead of the glass.

The room blurs, edges go soft, the sharpest thing is her weight against me. I tip my head close, my lips brushing her ear as I slur, "Reckon I'd lose my shirt—hell, my boots too—just to keep you sittin' there laughin' on me."

She smells like lemon and sunshine. Goddamn, I'm a patient son of a bitch. Travelled with this woman clear 'cross hell's half acre, never stole more than a kiss. A sweet shine glistens on her neck, the hollow of her throat. Summer heat blesses me with her womanly perfume. Lamplight catches a wet bead an inch below her ear, teasing the corner of her jaw. God help me, but thinking on it's got me hard as steel. Reckon she can feel it. I can't help it. Some things can't be explained; they just are. Beasts wild roaming across the country to find salt.

"Somethin' 'bout you...a man goes mad for it," I mumble. "Like a beast cravin' salt."

Sounded better in my head.

A confused expression falls over her, and I hold her hips. Bending close, I drag my tongue slow, starting at the corner of her jaw, along the curve of her neck, taste the scent of lemon on her skin and the salt the day's heat left behind. As I taste her, I hold her firm, grinding rough against her. If she didn't feel me before, she feels me now.

She jerks, a sharp little sound tearing from her throat. Her hand lashes out, flat across my mouth, and the slap stings hot as a wasp bite. Heads swivel. A few men hoot.

"How dare you do such a thing in public?" she spits, wrenching herself out of my lap. "Or anywhere for that matter."

My grin's stupid and slow in the wake of her outrage. I rub my mouth where her hand landed, more tickled than scolded. "Ain't my fault you taste like summer."

I keep my hands where they can be seen, flat on the table.

The barkeep coughs from behind the counter. "Room upstairs if you two need privacy."

Alice stiffens beside me. "We need nothing of the sort." Her hands clutch her skirts like she could scrub away what just happened. She's scandalized near to death, and hell if I don't want to scandalize her more.

I tip back the last of my whiskey and slam the glass on the table. "Room sounds right."

Alice's head snaps to me, eyes blazing. "You—"

The barkeep's already got the key in his hand. "Two bits. Pay up or sleep in the street."

"Come on, Alice. I'm piss-drunk; you wanna see me mount up? Cain't feel my knees n'you want me to set up a tent or some fool thing?"

"You are the fool, Mr. Randolph."

"Sure as hell am. I am a fool, an' it's you who I'm a fool for."

Alice fumbles in her purse, drops the coins into his palm. She grabs my arm, hauling me toward the stairs. Small as she is, her scorn drags me up easy.

Upstairs, the hall's dim, one oil lamp flickering on the wall. Alice marches us to the door, shoves the key into the lock, kicks it open. The room's plain—iron bed, thin quilt, one chair, basin in the corner.

"Floor's yours," she snaps.

I stumble inside, halfway there on my own. "What, no goodnight kiss?"

She slams the door, spins on me. "You've had too much whiskey, Mr. Randolph. I'll not be made a fool of in front of half a saloon again. You may sleep on the floor, or under it for all I care."

I stretch out right there on the boards, hands behind my head. "Floor suits me just fine, Miss Alice."

Her nostrils flare. "I wish you would stop calling me that." She climbs into bed, back stiff, quilt yanked to her chin.

The silence hangs heavy—until a squeal bursts through the wall, followed by the thump-thump of headboard on plaster. Obscene moans roll like cows lowing on the pasture.

Alice grumbles, throws the quilt over her head.

I chuckle into the crook of my arm. "They wrestlin' steers over there?"

Her giggle is muffled under the blanket.

"Goodnight, Miss Alice."

"Go to sleep, wicked man," her voice shoots back, sharp as ever.

I rest easy, grinning. "Ain't no sleep in Salt Lick."

CHAPTER 13

By morning, I am grateful for my evening of only lemonade, while Kodiak, chastened beneath the glare of sunshine, grumbles about our modest room. He stretches, and the popping of his bones is loud in the hush.

"You sleep mighty fine, I hope, Princess Alice?"

"As well as might be expected. Thank you."

He laughs, though humorless. "Well, the floor was just dandy."

I check a smile. "Had you behaved yourself, you might have known the soft earth and the comfort of a campfire."

He does not miss a beat. "And had I left you to rot in Ohio, I'da been the one keepin' folks up last night."

The words strike deeper than they should. It is not my fault the world has contrived to trouble women with ceaseless care for safety, propriety, and virtue. Of course I must strive to prove my usefulness. I cooked for him, prepared coffee at daybreak, did what I might to ease the way. Yet no matter—I am a weight to be borne, and soon enough he will set me down and walk away.

I say nothing, wiping my face at the washstand. The boards creak as he paces.

"Come on. We best be movin'. I got business waitin' down south."

Though tempted to reply in kind, I hold my tongue. I will not grant him the satisfaction. He leads through the door, then halts at the threshold, turns and braces one hand high on the frame. The breadth of his shoulders fill the space.

I stand with hands clasped at my waist, bowing my head.

"That was me bein' a fool," he says, and leans forward, closing the distance without moving a step.

The words cause a flutter in my belly.

"That weren't kind, what I said. Whiskey's rattlin' in me, but that ain't your fault. Didn't aim to put my blight on you."

An apology—unbidden, sincere. Perhaps he saw me wince. I smooth my skirt and lift my chin. "Thank you."

He nods, then steps into the hall. His boots drag on the floorboards with less swagger than usual. I follow, unsettled in heart, though not as I was a moment before.

The air outside greets us crisp and bright, a balm after the heavy smoke of the night. "You brew a fine cup," he says suddenly, abrupt, as though the words had been wrestled from him. "Better than I ever managed."

So odd a confession—domestic, small, not his usual talk. Against my will, I smile. "That is kind of you."

His mouth tilts in the barest grin, hidden swiftly beneath his hat brim. "Don't let it go to your head."

I laugh before I think to stop myself. The sound startles me as much as him. For once, he does not try to press his luck. He only glances sidelong, and in that silence there is something sweeter than all his swagger the night before.

The road south opens wide as Salt Lick falls behind, the town shrinking to a tendril of smoke on the horizon. The land stretches in slow waves of grass and brush, stitched here and there with silver water. The red sun climbs, its warmth pressing hard upon my bonnet.

We do not speak much. His silence is not cruel; it has an ease to it. At times, he hums a tune under his breath. I catch myself watching the set of his shoulders, the line of his jaw, more than I ought. By midday the heat bears close, the horizon wavering with dust.

Suddenly he stiffens. "Keep your head down," he hisses.

My heart leaps, but I obey, ducking beneath the brim of my bonnet. A small band of riders moves along a ridge half a mile distant.

"Too neat for ranch hands, too stiff for drifters," he observes.

They wear dark coats and wide hats, their faces cast in shadow.

"Who are they?" I whisper.

His hand tightens on the reins. "Pinkertons."

The name is strange to me. "Are they dangerous?"

He snorts without mirth. "Depends who you are. They're private detectives. Rich men's hounds, sniffin' after whoever their master points 'em at. You cross a railroad baron or a bank, they loose the Pinkertons. And I crossed plenty." His jaw works hard. "Best hope them bastards ain't huntin' me today."

A shiver passes through me despite the heat. The riders crest the ridge and vanish into the shimmer of dust. He watches the horizon long after they are gone, reins drawn taut.

At length he exhales, shoulders easing. "We'll keep movin'. Country's wide. They can't cover every trail."

I nod, though unease lingers. He says little, and I do not ask. The sun drags slow across the sky, baking the land flat and still. My skirts cling to my legs, my mouth dry as dust, yet he calls no halt, only urges the horses on, mile after mile.

By sundown, my bones ache with weariness. At last the road narrows, and he draws the wagon into a thicket of trees.

"Here'll do," he says, unhitching the horses. He checks their hooves, speaking low to them, words too soft for me to catch but warm enough in tone. From time to time I glimpse his tenderness, and it is striking—that such a man, rough and ill-mannered, should be so gentle.

I climb down stiffly, legs trembling after the long day. The air cools with dusk, cicadas lifting their song. I set to work, gathering kindling, striking flint. Soon a fire glows small between us, a circle of orange in the wide dark.

"Thank you. That's a right pretty fire, Miss Alice," he says.

My back teeth clench, but I return his playful poke. "You are most welcome, Mr. Kodiak."

He smiles. "Like the ring of that."

We work around each other, a slow rhythm of yielding and leading, his hands busy with his part and mine with mine, until the camp stands ready—shelter pitched, bedroll spread, rations laid neat for morning.

Thunder rolls in like distant drums.

"Thought I smelled rain," he mutters, scanning the camp. "I'll crawl under the carriage."

The mud-spattered undercarriage is low to the ground. A man of his size could scarce fit, let alone keep dry. "There is the tent."

He turns back slow, one brow raised.

Before he speaks, I cut him short. "I suggest shelter, Mr. Kodiak. Nothing more."

He chuckles. "Why of course, Miss Alice. I would assume no impropriety."

Plainly he makes a jest of me, yet I let it pass in good humor.

When the rain comes, he joins me beneath the canvas. The drops fall heavy and warm, a summer storm soaking the world outside. The fabric sags, dark with moisture, but we are dry enough.

"Least it ain't cold," he rasps, easing down with a groan.

"I imagine that would be far worse."

"Ain't nothin' meaner than wet and cold both."

I glance toward the drowned firepit. "Would be pleasant if a fire could be brought inside."

He chuckles. "Well now, I seen it done. Not in a tent like this, but the Shawnee, they build shelters to hold heat proper. Wigwams, tight-packed with bark and clay. Smoke holes cut at the top. Dry as bone within, no matter the weather."

I study him by the lantern's glow. "You have been among the Shawnee?"

He nods, eyes gone distant. "Few years back. Took a bad break to the leg, fever after. Scout I'd worked with—he'd married a Shawnee woman—brought me in. They had no call to help me, but they did. Asked nothin' in return."

"Weren't you afraid?" The words slip out. "Of them, I mean."

He cuts me a look, firm but not unkind. "No, ma'am. They bore me no ill will. Most of what folks say is fear, or guilt. The Shawnee don't take up arms without cause. Their land's been stripped away, treaty by treaty. Hard to fault a man for holdin' fast to his own land."

He falls quiet then, not angry, only convinced.

"They liked the stars too," he says after a spell, chin tilting toward the dim patch of sky visible through the flap. "Old men would tell stories, all bound up in the constellations. Reckon you'd probably find 'em mighty interestin'."

"I think I would. I've always loved the stars. The legends behind them. I traced their patterns night after night."

"Awful lot to keep track of."

"If you track them long enough, they become familiar. Year after year, the same stars return to the same place in the sky. I suppose I found something comforting about that."

He squints upward. "When that Shawnee scout brought me in, he told 'em my name. Kodiak. One of the old men, he nodded and pointed at the sky. Said there's a bear up there, you can see him plain if you know where to look. Three hunters on his trail, never lettin' up. Every spring they rise again, chasin' him 'cross the heavens. Come fall, they wound him. His blood spills, turns the leaves red. But the bear don't die for good. Next year he's back, runnin' just the same, huntin' and hunted all over again."

Goosebumps erupt down my neck. "Ursa Major. The Great Bear."

"You heard it too, huh?" He smirks faint, like it's some private joke.

"The three hunters," I say. "Orion's belt. The bear is destined to run forever. Around and around, never resting."

The storm cools the air, the patter steady on the canvas above. I sit still, the warmth between us unexpected. "Your life sounds like an adventure."

He chuckles softly. "Fool's gambles is what it is. Only seems like adventure in hindsight."

The lantern burns low, its glow warm against the canvas

walls. I lie with hands folded, listening to the rhythm of his breath. He shifts, the canvas rustling. His nearness looms, and I can't help but lean into his warmth.

"Ever sleep out in a storm before?" he asks. His voice, rich and deep, is a wondrous thing. Capable of instilling fear or comfort. Tonight, in this tent, it soothes me.

"No," I admit. "Always there was a roof, no matter how poor."

"Roof's a comfort. But a storm in the wild, that's somethin'. Make you feel small. Let you know whatever's out there don't really give a damn."

The words tug at something in me. I live my life measured out in deeds, as if tallying the goodness I share will amount to something virtuous. It's never guaranteed my safety, and yet, here I am, with my protector, my bear, under a canvas cover, quite warm and dry.

I turn to him in the dim light. His face is sculpted in shadow, the lantern light catching his cheekbones, his mouth. I ask, "There are worse places to be than here, aren't there?"

He fixes on me and doesn't break. For a moment, neither of us breathes. My pulse beats loud in my ears. I cannot name the force that carries me forward, only that I lift my face, ever so slight, until my lips brush his.

His breath shudders, and the sound alone nearly unravels me. A man like him—so powerful and always in complete control—is made weak under my kiss. It chills me to my bones.

He does not pull back. His rough hand comes up, cupping my cheek tenderly. The kiss deepens, soft at the start, then hungry, sweeping me up tight into his arms, drawing me close, swift as the storm outside. I yield to him without thought.

The lantern flickers, shadows lashing the canvas. The

scrape of his stubbled jaw, the sound of my own breath betraying me. God forgive me, but I am only flesh.

When he breaks away, his thumb lingers at my cheek, calloused yet trembling.

"Lamb," he whispers, as though the name is sacred.

CHAPTER 14

KODIAK

No woman has ever undone me like this. I've lived too long by my own rules. Take what you need. Keep your head down and don't stop moving. But Alice makes me want things. Fool things.

Her mouth—Christ, her mouth—is softer than any pillow I've ever rested my head on. She makes the quietest little sounds, breath hitching like each kiss rattles her. Each one unchains something in me I've kept captive for years.

I pull back, and my hand slides to her throat, thumb over that wild pulse. I don't know why I do it. I'd never hurt her, but I want her to know I could. Maybe it's instinct. Self-defense for making me feel like a damn sack of nerves, knowing full well she could end me with just a look. I squeeze gently, but she don't flinch. It's her trust in me that wrecks me worse than any bullet. Don't she know I ruin what I touch?

I need her. Now.

Her bodice is a mess under my hands—too many buttons,

not enough sense left in my fingers. She don't stop me. Just watches me, eyes wide'n pure as a fawn, and hell if that don't make me burn hotter.

How's a woman manage to smell so appetizing after a full day in the summer heat, dragged through the open country? Even the salt of her sweat makes me lose myself.

I free her, breasts fair as a lily, nipples pink and tight in the lantern light. *God a'mighty.* I don't speak. Don't even breathe loud. Just look. Like some pilgrim kneeling to worship at an altar. Ain't never seen a shrine built like her, and damn, if heaven's finer than these tits, I might find God after all. I lean in and take her into my mouth.

She gasps. The sound shoots straight to the root of me. I grind against her, desperate for friction, my body raw with need. Her legs shift beneath her skirts, opening just enough. An invitation. Damn, her heat. I feel it even through the skirts, radiating up at me. The friction damn near blinds me. Nothing pretty about it, just raw hunger, my cock hard as nails and straining like I'm some kid fumbling in the dark.

We kiss, teeth knocking, messy and wet. My other hand palms her breast, squeezing rough, thumbing her nipple while my hips drive against her like I'm staking a claim. She clings to me, fingertips pressing against my ass, drawing me closer, like she wants every inch of me even through the damned cloth between us.

I can't stop. Don't want to. Every roll of my hips, I find a kind of pleasure that don't feel deserving for a poor scoundrel like me. She's making sounds, gentle and sweet, each time I press hard over that searing spot. Christ almighty, that spot.

Her mouth's slick against mine, and I picture how slick and warm she is underneath this skirt. The thoughts multiply, spinning like I'm being goddamn hypnotized. Her insides must be even more inviting than her mouth. Pious little thing like her's probably tight as a hangman's knot. I lose my breath thinking on it, thinking how I'd sink into her, stretch her, fuck her full, bury my seed dee—

Oh no. No no no no.

But that's it—that's the end of me. My body's moving by itself, jerking like a dog breeding. It hits sudden, violent. Heat tearing through me before I can hold it back. I curse into her mouth as I spill in my pants, harder than I have since boyhood. Shame and hunger twist together, near choking me.

I break the kiss, forehead pressed to hers, breath ragged. My fist knots tight in her skirts, like if I let go, I'll float away. "Alice," I rasp. "Christ. You made me spend like a damn boy."

Her lips part like she's about to speak, but nothing comes out. She's flushed deep, chest rising fast, nipples wet from my mouth. For a heartbeat she just stares, like she don't know what to do with what we've done. Then her hands slip from my hair, from my shoulders. She draws back just a little, breath ragged, and she's trembling same as me, the need clinging to her.

"God," she whispers, shifting back. Sitting up, she straights her bodice, fumbling with the fabric, covering herself. "Oh God," she says again.

Her tears come fast, sliding down her cheeks. She curls in on herself like I broke her, shoulders hunching, palms pressed hard to her face. I hear her whispering to the Lord like she needs saving from me.

Blood pumps hot through my veins like molten steel through a forge. The sound of her crying scrapes raw at me. How can she sit there carrying on like I stole something against her will?

"Hell no," I snap, harsher than I mean. My chest heaves,

mouth flying off hotter than the barrel of a spent pistol. "Don't look at me like I took what wasn't offered."

She flinches, then lifts her face. Tear-streaked, lips trembling. For a moment she just stares, and the storm outside fills the silence between us.

"I-I let you. That's what shames me." Her voice cracks, but she pushes on, desperate. "I wanted it, and I ought not to have. Don't you see? I have sinned, not you. I gave myself over to desire."

"So what? That's what people do. Ain't nothin' wrong with how you feel. I want you like I ain't wanted a thing. Say what you want, but you're mine."

"I am nothing of the sort, Mr. Randolph."

"Oh bullshit," I snarl. "Now you're startin' to piss me off."

She wipes her cheeks rough, smearing the wet across her skin. "I'll not be claimed by you."

I lean in, close enough for her to feel my breath, my voice low. "It's already passed, sweetheart. Ain't no more say in it. You're my woman, and you'll be dreamin' of me tonight, same as I'll be burnin' for you. You can try to pray it away, but you had a taste and ain't nothin' holy'll scrub it clean."

Her hand trembles where it clutches her bodice closed. She doesn't answer, only turns her face aside. Inch by inch she shifts away, rolling over to give me her back.

The tent goes quiet but for the rain on the canvas. My breath's ragged, loud in the hush.

The fabric of my trousers clings damp and wrong. I curse under my breath, fumbling for my bandana. Opening my fly, I wipe myself clean as I can. Ain't no hiding the mess, though—damp patch cooling in my britches, clinging strange. I feel like a damn boy caught dirty-handed.

I glance at her stiff back, shoulders drawn tight under her dress, fists knotted in her skirts.

Those tears, praying like I'd ruined her.

Heat and shame twist in my chest. "Yeah, you go on and pray, Alice. Pray your little lamb heart out for all I care."

We don't speak much for days. She keeps to her side of the wagon. At camp, she keeps her hands busy with cooking, mending and scrubbing our clothes. I drive and tend the horses. The silence's a weight, but neither of us breaks it. She's keeping to herself, like speaking a word is a slippery slope to ending up in my arms.

Every mile we ride, it builds. She won't dare look at me. Her laugh gone, her voice clipped to nothing but what's needed. And damn if it don't grate worse than her crying.

I catch myself stealing glances. The shape of her nose when she's staring off at the countryside. The curves of her mouth when she's stirring a pot and don't know I'm paying attention. That long hair of hers when she takes it down to brush it out. Every move she makes just feeds my hunger.

I know she feels it too, and I reckon the silence, the distance, is her way of keeping it from taking hold again.

By the third day, the summer heat's thick as lard. Sweat stings my eyes. The horses slow. When we pull up by a wide creek, the water glistens, damn near calling my name. The water's running fast and cool over smooth rock, and I make up my mind.

She wants to pretend she's some untouchable saint, begging heaven to scour me out of her veins? Fine. But I'll show her plain what she's missing.

CHAPTER 15

ALICE

We make camp. He stretches, long arms overhead, his shirt riding just enough to reveal the lean plane of his stomach. "Water looks cold," he says. "Been sweatin' in the saddle too long. Think I'll have a rinse."

He arches a brow, tugging at his suspenders with lazy defiance. "Good for the blood," he says, and strips down— boots first, then trousers, until he's bare as the day he was born.

I look away, but not before I've seen much more than I should.

God forgive me.

My soul threatens to escape at the size of him, hung thick as a beast, bold and unashamed. Stomach in knots, shame rising like steam, a traitorous thought steals through me— what would it feel like to take something so fearsome inside me? What would it do to me? Surely, it would tear my flesh, and yet I shiver at the thought of receiving it.

He wades in, the water climbing his thighs, his waist, his chest. He ducks under, vanishing a breath, then bursts back through the surface with a toss of his hair and a spray of droplets that gleam in the morning sun. He swipes water down his face, squinting against the light and dripping strands. "I reckon it'd be a finer bath if you joined me."

The Devil never rests.

"Absolutely not." My voice cracks with more urgency than I intend. "I am a decent woman."

His laugh rolls across the water as he wades a step closer, waist deep. "Come on. Creek's cool, sun's high. Slip down to that pretty shift of yours. I ain't askin' for you to go bare."

"I'll not strip down before you like some common harlot," I shout, horrified at the tremor in my voice.

"Alice, ain't nobody else here but the cottonwoods and the herons, and they won't tell a soul."

I shake my head, hugging my arms across my chest. "It's indecent."

"Indecent is livin' half a life 'cause men and preachers told you to be ashamed of your own flesh." His voice is steady, coaxing. "This is the Lord's water."

The words lodge in my chest, leaving me weak. My pulse throbs in my throat. The creek sparkles behind him like it's lit from within, and I can't help but picture myself in the water, shift floating free, his hands—oh Lord—his hands on me.

I tear myself away from the thought, heart pounding. "I can't."

He cocks his head, smile deepening. "Can't? Or won't?"

I pause. Such a beautiful day. The sun is shining. It's a gift.

It is the Lord's water, after all.

Who am I to refuse such a gift?

"Turn around."

He chuckles and turns his broad back to me. Water rolls down the ridges of his shoulders, sunlight glistening off every scar.

My hands shake as I loosen the buttons of my dress. The cotton shift clings once the rest falls away, near transparent in its thinness. Heat scorches my cheeks as I step into the creek. The frigid water bites against my ankles, then my knees, until a trapped breath shudders in my chest.

I wade deeper, heart hammering, until I'm waist-deep and the water tugs at my skirts. "You may turn," I say, though I almost pray he will not.

When he does, his expression shifts—surprise flickering through it before hunger takes over.

He comes toward me, each stride through the water deliberate and inevitable. I retreat a step, but he cages me in, the creek cradling me at my back.

I'm a fool. A hopeless sinner. Of course I know he craves me. He's told me so.

Without a word, his hand rises, brushing strands of hair from my cheek. And then his mouth is on mine, claiming, hot and deep, a kiss that turns me inside out. I gasp against him, clinging despite myself. It is too much, too soon.

I tear my mouth away, shaking my head. "I-I can't. I—"

"Tell me true, Alice. Did that husband of yours ever make you feel like this?" His palm presses at my hip, his thigh sliding between mine beneath the water.

Shame burns hotter than the sun overhead. His hand fists in my shift, dragging me closer until the fabric clings to both our bodies. "That bastard never cared if you came apart in his arms, did he?" His voice drops, coaxing, wicked. "Never had you beggin' for mercy."

My silence damns me.

Kodiak's mouth trails fire down my throat, his hands guiding me back until my spine meets the grassy bank. He lifts me onto the smooth stones, water lapping at our sides.

I should stop him. Shove him away. But I can't. The pull is too strong.

His hands are at my thighs, pushing the wet fabric higher. His mouth follows, hot and merciless, his tongue parting me. A strangled cry rips from my lips as my hands fly to his hair, meaning to push him away, but I clutch tight, pulling him closer.

"Christ, you're sweet," he groans against me. "Sweetest thing I ever tasted."

I twist, and he groans again, pleased, devouring me like there would never be enough of me to satisfy his hunger.

"God forgive me," I gasp, head tipping back.

"Don't you beg His pardon. Ain't a thing unholy in a woman bein' made to feel alive."

His hand presses flat against my middle, holding me down as his mouth torments me again. Every flick of his tongue tears me wider open, every suck draws another gasp. His fingers find me now, sliding inside with a slowness that makes my breath stutter. They move with a measured patience, stroking the tender walls within me, each glide drawing a low moan I can't suppress. The stretch is delicious, a sweet burn that fills me, his fingers thick and unyielding as they explore deeper, flexing just enough to make my hips twitch.

My hands claw at the earth, nails sinking into the mud, desperate for something to anchor me as the world tilts. His mouth returns, lips closing around my bud with a gentle suck, and I cry out, the sound raw and broken, swallowed by the creek's endless song.

His fingers curl inside me, finding a spot that makes my body buck against him, chasing the rhythm he's set, my movements no longer my own but his to command. The creek churns around us, cool against my thighs where his hands burn hot. I can't help but think of baptism, of being pushed beneath the river as a girl, the preacher promising I'd rise cleansed. But this—this feels like drowning. Like being dragged under. Held there until my last breath.

"That's it," he growls, voice rough with hunger, lips grazing the soft skin of my inner thigh. His drawl drops lower—gravel and honey. "Goddamn, look at you quiverin'." He returns to taste me, as if my tenderness is something fresh off the vine. The sound is soft suction, lush and wet, like teeth sinking into ripe fruit. "Go on now. Come sweet on me. Let me have a taste of heaven on my tongue."

His words ignite something feral in me, something that wants to break free. My thighs tremble as the tension coils tighter, a thread stretched to breaking. His mouth is devastating, teasing me toward a cliff I both fear and crave. His fingers move with the same relentless patience, coaxing, claiming, until the world narrows to the heat of his breath, the press of his lips, and the bright, dizzying edge rushing up to meet me until I'm nothing but sensation, teetering on the edge of something vast and terrifying.

Release tears through me like a ball of fire plummeting through the heavens. My back arches, a sob ripping from my throat, raw and unbridled, as my body shatters under his touch. My cries echo, mingling with the creek's rush, but he doesn't stop, his tongue stroking the soft bloom of my need through every tremor, his fingers working me until I'm limp and trembling against the earth.

He lifts his head, beard damp, mouth gleaming, a fire lit somewhere deep behind his stare.

"Look at me, Alice."

I try to turn away, but he climbs over me, catching my jaw in his hand, thumb pressing under my chin until I face him. "No hidin'. Eyes on me."

My gaze drops unwillingly, and I see him. His fist works himself slow, deliberate, every stroke dragging the skin taut over the thick length of him. He's flushed dark, the head swollen, gleaming.

The sound is the worst of it. A wet, steady slide, rough and slick at once, mingling with the lap of the creek against the bank. Each drag of his hand makes a lewd noise I can feel in my chest.

"God above," he rasps. "I'd split you in two if I slid inside right now. Stretch you till you sobbed my name." His hand quickens, knuckles brushing the damp cotton of my shift each time he grinds himself against me.

My thighs press together. He notices. There is never a detail he fails to notice. His hand hooks under my knee, jerking it open, baring me. The hem of my shift rides high, cool air rushing over skin.

"Kodiak, don't—"

"Shhh, I ain't." His eyes drag down my body, molten, devouring. "Pink as a spring rose."

I should cry out, beg him to stop, but I can't. The sight of him—hard and needy, the veins ridging his flesh, the muscles of his forearm flexing with every stroke—steals my breath.

"You'd take me deep, all of me, whether you thought you could or not. And I'd make sure you liked it."

He groans low, pumping himself faster now. The wet rhythm grows louder, sloppier. Water ripples against the bank with his rocking, as though the earth itself is keeping time.

"Don't you dare look away," he growls, his hand clenching tight around himself. "You watch what you do to me."

I clutch at the grass beside me, fingers knotting in the roots. His pace grows erratic, chest heaving with ragged breaths, jaw clenched in raw strain, a bead of sweat trailing down his temple.

"You'd take me," he grits out, almost choking on the words.

With a harsh groan, his body jerks. He spills hot against me, a guttural curse breaking from his throat as he shudders above me.

At last, his head drops, lips grazing my cheek. "Next time, little lamb…"

CHAPTER 16

ALICE

By nightfall, we make a shelter under a blanket of stars. The night is so clear the heavens glitter with promise, the Milky Way spilling across the sky like a smoke signal from some distant fire. If only I understood its message.

Since the creek, Kodiak hasn't said a word, but has not strayed from my side. He hovers in a way that feels like possession—helping me from the water, wrapping me in a blanket and wiping my skin clean of dirt and grass with the same care he might use to polish his gun. By the fire, he studies each bend and line of my hand as if measuring something he intends to keep.

We lie side by side on my bedroll, the grass cool beneath, our shoulders almost touching.

"Kodiak?"

"Yes, little lamb?"

"Where are we going? You've only said we're going south."

He turns from his back, his body shifting toward me, then

drags a thumb down my cheek. "Somethin' real important's waitin' for me in New Orleans."

"New Orleans?" I ask, sitting up some. I'd only heard about it in dime novels and gossip from travelers. I press a hand to my chest.

He erupts, his body shaking with laughter. "Ain't nothing to worry about. Don't get ahead of yourself."

He's an outlaw. What did I expect? He probably associates with the likes of whores and criminals. But even Mary Magdalene walked with sinners before finding the light.

"Do you think perhaps fate brought you to me to be healed? To put you on a faithful path so you can stop running?"

For a heartbeat, he only stares, eyes catching firelight and starlight both. Then his mouth curves into a sardonic grin. "Been runnin' all my life. Don't know about no faithful path. Only prayin' I done lately was between them soft thighs a'yours."

I gasp and bury my face in my hands. What a vile thing to say, and yet the memory of my release sends a jolt through me.

"Sweetest thing I ever tasted. Sweeter than molasses in that pot."

I shake my head. "It was carnal sin, and I will not speak of it. You'll damn us both."

His thumb drags slow along my jaw, rough as sand. "Heaven can have your soul, but your body belongs to me now."

The words strike through me, a lash of heat and fear both. "No." I push his hand away. "I was Joseph's before. His possession. His property. I'll not be that again. Not for you, not for anyone."

For a moment, he freezes and the night holds still, but then the wrinkle in between his brows relaxes. "Yes, Miss Alice."

The way he says it—not deferent, not polite, but mocking, just as he'd mocked the staff at the inn—makes a startled laugh escape me, sharp and wrong in the hush of twilight. I clap a hand over my mouth, but it's too late.

"Shhh," he scolds through a chuckle. "You make a piss-poor outlaw, laughin' loud enough to wake the dead. We're running from the law, remember? Might as well string up a lantern and wave 'em over."

My laugh dies in my throat, replaced by a crooked smile I can't quite smother. Resting on one arm, he leans in and presses his mouth to mine. His kiss is tender, breath warm. The scruff of his beard scrapes my chin, scented faintly with the perfume of our sin.

He draws back. "There's caged and there's kept. One's got bars, but the other's shelter," he says, gesturing up to the tanned hide overhead. "Protection. I ain't meant to trap you, just to keep you safe."

"For now." The words comes out cold, wounded, like a spoiled girl, injured he hadn't proposed marriage under the moon and heavens. How could I be so foolish? He's a beast. A killer. Why would I be hurt if a man like that ever left me behind? Yet the thought of being abandoned by him makes me want to cry into his chest.

"Now's all there is. A man like me never knows if he'll see another day."

I've never met a man who lived his life with such intensity he risked snuffing out his own flame. But tomorrow is not promised for any person. Surely he must have hopes. Dreams.

"Not knowing what tomorrow brings does not change what we want for ourselves."

His touch returns. A featherlight sweep of his knuckles against my cheek, and my bones turn to jelly.

"Ain't I made it plain enough?" His hazel eyes lock with mine, steady as the constellations. "I want you."

The hunger in his voice pours lamp oil on the fire already smoldering in my belly. I could lose myself in his mouth, bury my hands in that wild tangle of hair and straddle his hips like a woman possessed. I could mount him and take that monstrous thing inside. Let him buck and rut and ruin me, stealing every last trace of my virtue. Just the thought of it makes me ache. My heart erupts into my throat, and a flash of heat scalds my cheeks. I clutch the blanket and quickly wrench myself onto my side, turning my back between us. It's only temptation. It must be the Devil's voice whispering in my ear.

Inching closer, the warmth of him wraps around me, his chest meeting my back, the weight of his arm curls possessively at my waist. He rests his cheek against my hair, mouth at my ear. "The way you look at me, the way your body sang for me... Alice, you can try to fight it, but I know you want me too."

His husky voice sends a rush through me, sparks exploding in my blood like the first glints of starlight breaking through the dark.

I steel myself. "I tended to you because you were gravely injured and I was able to help. My duty was to God, as it is now. I'm flesh and blood, and I gave in to lust. But I am a decent woman, and for my sins, I beg forgiveness. It was wrong, and it will not happen again, Mr. Randolph."

He pauses and exhales a dark chuckle, the warmth of his breath at my nape. "If lying to yourself helps you sleep, Miss

Alice, you go right on and do it. But you ain't foolin' me, and I reckon that God of yours knows better too."

~

"When you run from the devil, you find him in the road."
— Creole Proverb

I THOUGHT the bustle of the Sherman Inn during the Astral Society's visits was overwhelming, but I have never seen so many people in all my life. The streets of New Orleans are swarming everywhere I turn. And the noise! Voices on every side in tongues I've never heard. My goodness, a silent moment cannot exist here. Horses clomp past, streetcars rattle on their rails, and steamboat whistles drift in from the Mississippi.

The Hotel de Chartres has six windows stacked one above the other, straight from ground to roof. Inside, the city's din fades, replaced by the roar of guests and the clatter of silverware in a French dining room that would put Mrs. Baxter's humble kitchen to shame. The ceilings soar with elaborate scrollwork I've only ever seen in the postcards Joseph's parents sent from Europe.

Of all the places I thought we might go, never did I dream of anywhere so fine as this. Kodiak and I—clad in dusty, travel-stained clothes, my petticoat wrinkled—are a tarnish on silver. No wonder he hurries us to the front desk.

"I'm told Mr. Archer arranged a suite for my wife and me," he says, his voice unusually polished. The concierge appraises us, lip curled, as though weighing whether it is worth searching his book for the name.

Kodiak clears his throat. "I know we must look a fright.

We've been upriver on the hunt and came straight here to settle in. Our valet usually tends to every arrangement. I could have him send a telegram if you require, but truly, if you'll check your ledger, you'll find it in hand."

There's no trace of his usual gruff demeanor in his lie.

The concierge's shoulders ease, his mouth now set in a polite smile. "That will not be necessary, sir."

We ride the hydraulic elevator so high I press my hand to my middle to steady the leap of my stomach. The hallway stretches on like a city block. When the porter opens the doors, I swallow a gasp. A large bed waits against the far wall, dressed in crisp white linen and a red velvet coverlet to match the chaise in the parlor. Potted palms stand beside gilt-framed paintings, and in the washroom a porcelain tub gleams, steaming water already brought to the washstand.

"How can we afford all this?" I ask, nearly breathless.

"Paid ahead," Kodiak says.

"When?" I press, careful not to raise my voice.

He sighs, scratching his stubbled cheek. "Standing reservation." His face gives nothing away; he scans the room instead. "Why don't you get comfortable. Have yourself a hot bath. I've a few things need tendin'." He reaches for his hat.

"Where are you going?" I ask, as he tugs the brim low.

He doesn't answer. The latch clicks sharp behind him.

Splendid.

What now?

I turn to the washroom. The grime of sleeping outdoors clings to me like a second skin. A bath, at least, might do me good. The porcelain tub swallows me whole. The water bites sharp at first, then eases into my bones. I scrub the grit from my hair with lavender soap until the scent fills the room.

Afterward, fresh linen and a clean dress change everything.

Lacing my bodice and smoothing my skirts, I can pass for a woman traveling properly with her husband. I sit by the window, watching the city below as my hair dries. My fingers press to the pane as a curious hunger stirs in me. In the distance, I spy the bright awnings of a market and the spires of a church. I refuse to sit idle like some caged bird. Gathering courage, I pin on my hat, draw my gloves tight, and step out of the suite. If he means to keep me cloistered, he should not leave me alone.

The streets carry me along like a sleepy river. I pass shop windows crowded with silks and boots, and salons where women sit under lamps while their hair is pinned. Peddlers wheel carts stacked with oranges, melons, and pineapples, bright as lanterns. At home, I might walk a mile and meet no more than a neighbor and a dog. Here, I can't take five steps without brushing against someone new.

I stop before a flower shop, its window so full of peonies and tulips it's like a fairytale. It's all so exciting and overwhelming, but it's tainted somehow. Fruit of a poison tree. My great adventure began by Kodiak squeezing the last breath from Joseph's throat. Maybe even poison fruit can taste sweet for a time, before it sickens you.

I wander until I find myself in a market. Rows of vendors stand in the open air, sheltered under faded canvas awnings that ripple in the breeze. A barefoot child darts between the stalls, brandishing a stick like a wizard's wand. His clothes hang off his frame, likely hand-me-downs from an older sibling.

A woman nearby calls out, "Pralines! Fresh and sweet!" Her voice carries over the bustle. On the table before her sits a basket heaped high with toffee-colored rounds studded with pecans.

It has been days of nothing but beans and jerky, and the thought of something sweet melting on my tongue makes my mouth flood. The scent drifts toward me on a warm current of buttery air and draws me closer like a worm on a hook pulling in a hungry trout.

"I've never heard of a praline before," I say.

She takes me in, head to toe, then grins. "Then you're in for a treat," she says. "Pecans, sugar, and cream made right here in the heart of New Orleans."

She lifts one delicately between two fingers and a square of wax paper. "One for two cents."

I reach for my purse, fingering through coins. Counting out pennies, I drop two in her hand, and feel a light thwack against my skirt. The boy has crept up beside me, smiling through gaps of gums and little teeth.

"Yah!" he cries.

"August!" the woman scolds. "What did I tell you about hitting people with sticks?"

He giggles and darts behind the table, pressing himself against her skirts.

"That's all right," I say. "He was probably trying to turn me into a frog with his magic wand."

"A horse," he corrects, peeking out.

"I'm sorry, ma'am, please excuse my boy. He's been beggin' his daddy for horse rides, and now he carries that stick like a crop, thinkin' everybody's part of his little game."

I can't help laughing at his imagination, though I cover my smile with my hand as not to encourage him. The woman shakes her head, her amusement edged with weariness.

"August whipped a lawman one morning, right here at my table. Didn't find it one bit funny and cost me a week's profit in fines."

I force my smile to vanish. "Oh, that's awful."

She glances down at August, who is now poking holes in the dirt with his stick. "He ought to be in school, I know. But the schools don't want a boy who can't sit still, and the parish charges more than sugar money. So he stays with me, learns numbers at the till. That's schooling enough for now."

I tuck the praline into my glove and bid them good day. August is already chasing shadows with his stick, his mother calling after him in weary French.

I linger in the square before a grand cathedral, praline crumbling sweet against my teeth. Carriages stop at the gates, footmen helping down the ladies in fine gloves and parasols. Just beyond the iron fence, children hold out flowers and trinkets. A girl no older than August offers a wilted bloom to a passing woman, who walks on without a second glance.

I turn away, praline wrapper crumpled in my glove, and let the crowd carry me back toward the Hotel de Chartres.

Using the room key from my pocket, I unlock the door and step inside. I take no more than a step before a jolt shoots through me and I freeze.

Someone stands at the window. A large man, dressed head to toe in black, broad shoulders sharp against the glass. My pulse leaps. Is this one of Kodiak's enemies, come to finish what chains and bullets could not?

"May I help you?" My voice is firm, though my heart batters against my ribs.

He turns slowly. A hush fills me where breath should be. The face is familiar—oddly familiar—and yet mismatched. Hair combed flat and shining, jaw smooth as porcelain, only a trim mustache left in place. A jacket and waistcoat hug his frame, a bowtie knotted crisp at his throat.

The outlaw is gone. In his place stands a gentleman fit for a governor's ball.

"I'm sure I could think of somethin'," Kodiak drawls, the grin all devil despite the costume.

I cannot decide what is more dangerous—the way the fabric of his waistcoat fits taut against the firm swell of his chest and shoulders, tapering to the narrow fit at his hips, or the version of him that's dressed in dust from the trail. They both tempt a woman into trouble, but I cannot decide which tempts me more.

I press a hand to my chest, my heart slowing. "Do you care to explain the change in your appearance?"

"We're goin' to the opera." He gestures toward the bed, where a gown is laid out. Pink taffeta, the corset embroidered with pearls. "Got you a dress. Lady at the boutique said it's adjustable. Some kind of ribbons or—"

"What is the meaning of this?"

"Can't a man take his lady to the opera?"

I step closer, astounded by the sharp line of his jaw. My God. I touch his face. He even smells different—clean, faintly spicy, nothing like gunpowder and sweat.

"Seein' if I caught a fever?"

"You shaved...and you've been to the barber."

"Don't clean up half bad, do I?"

"Kodiak." My mind is a blur of excitement, curiosity, and fear. "This is all so strange. Please, you'll drive me mad if you leave me to wonder."

His grin fades. "You ain't the only one nearly mad. Came back and found you gone. I thought somebody'd taken you. You don't know what that does to a man."

He steps close, the scent of spice and soap wrapping around me. "Next time you get the notion to wander, remember who you belong to, and what I'd do to any bastard tried to take you from me." He starts to set a hand on my waist, but I step back and smack it away.

"How am I supposed to know anything when you don't say a word? You disappear without so much as a goodbye, and I'm left staring at the walls like a fool. I will not be shut away while you run off to God only knows where. You can't just string me along from one mystery to the next. Now, what are you up to?"

"Little lamb, I'm only askin' you to enjoy' an evening in New Orleans on my arm. There's nothin' for you to worry about."

A PARADE of gentlemen pass in top hats, walking sticks in hand. On their arms are ladies in gowns and jewels who glide along Bourbon and Toulouse. On the brick street, the handsome theater curves around the block in Italian architecture, its facade aglow with lamplight. A banner hangs from up high. Tonight: Gounod's Faust.

We pause at the cafe adjoining the opera house. Inside, posters for coming operas line the ornate walls. The city's elite rabble and gossip over champagne, their crystal flutes glittering like the chandeliers overhead.

Kodiak plays his part well, with a genteel disposition that suits the room. He takes whiskey neat in a heavy-bottomed glass, while for me, a waiter in a white jacket sets down a dainty goblet. The drink is pale and opalescent, tinged with green, the ice sparkling like frost.

"Absinthe frappe, madam," the man says with a nod, before vanishing into the throng.

"What on earth is this?" I ask.

Kodiak smirks. "New Orleans specialty."

I nearly push it aside, though the sweetness of anise drifts up like licorice candy. I taste it carefully. The syrup and herbs dance across my tongue, and a slow heat blooms in my chest.

"It is...rather pleasant," I admit.

I cannot say if it is the bone of my corset binding too tightly or the way the allure of his darkness holds me from across the table, but I can hardly take a full breath.

"I knew you'd clean up nice in that gown," he says. "But God a'mighty, you knock the air out of me."

I smile despite myself. "It is a gorgeous gown. You have impeccable taste."

"Funny you say that. It was your taste that gave me the notion. Told the lady at the shop my woman's gown ought to be pink as a spring rose."

The words lance through me and the cafe vanishes. For a heartbeat, I see him, hand fisted tight around himself, jaw clenched as he groaned those very words. The chandelier's sparkle above me is sunlight flashing off the water. The wet clink of bar glass is the sound of his slick hand stroking as he ordered me to watch.

Wicked heat floods me, and I shift in my chair, cheeks burning, body aching, the frappe turning to fire in my chest. How can he sit there so calm, sipping whiskey like a gentleman, while I drown all over again?

"Kodiak—"

He wags a finger at me. "No, no. Not tonight. Tonight, I'm William Archer."

There's something about this man. The way he carries himself makes a longing grow in my chest. I lower my chin, peering up at him through my lashes. "And who am I?"

"Suppose that makes you Mrs. Archer."

"Does Mrs. Archer have a given name?"

He lifts his glass, takes a slow pull of whiskey, unblinking. "Depends what I'm callin' her for." His stare is dangerous and unyielding, singing through me.

I clear my throat to release the scandalous pit lodged there.

"I should hope Mrs. Archer has no need of a man's definition at all."

Leaning back in his chair, as if settling into a debate, he replies. "Ain't about definin' nothin'. Folks put too much stock in names. Say your momma had christened you Hester or Gertrude. Wouldn't make you any less of a fine temptation sittin' here before me. And my own ma, she might've called me Pope Gregory or Saint Moses for all I care. I'd be the same mean son of a bitch, my likeness nailed on walls in every town from here to California, reward stamped bold 'cross the top."

His words settle between us like the smoke drifting in the restaurant. I know it's true. He'd squeezed the last breath from Joseph's throat and then emptied his pockets without a second thought.

But he's also the man who helped me escape. Who's given me more pleasure than I've ever known, then wrapped me in a blanket and brushed the leaves and grass from my wet legs before holding me in his arms under the stars.

"And yet you've spared me your cruelty," I say, fussing with an imagined wrinkle in my lap before folding my hands neatly there, teasing. "Perhaps your reputation has been exaggerated."

He narrows his eyes at me. "Reckon I like you sweeter than I like most. Don't mean I ain't mean, just means I ain't turned it your way."

The waiter reappears, setting down a silver tray of oysters, their shells piled on ice, and another green drink waits at my elbow.

I recoil at the oysters. "They're alive."

Kodiak chuckles. "Near enough." He pushes the tray toward me. "Go on. Ain't gonna kill you."

I shake my head, queasy. "I knew of a man once who died after eating one."

He snorts. "Oysters don't travel well by wagon. These, though? Harvested 'em this mornin', most like. Don't get no fresher."

As he inches it closer, every instinct tells me no, but my curiosity gets the better of me and I lift the shell. I tip it back against my lip, the sharp tang of brine flooding my mouth.

His eyes darken. "Good girl. Swallowed it down just fine. Now, finish your drink."

Heat blooms through me, shame and want testing together as my fingers close around the cold glass. Fragrant anise slides cool over my tongue and burns me through until the crystal overhead blurs like stars.

By the time the cafe stirs and patrons drift toward the opera house, I'm unsteady, Kodiak's hand guiding me through. Inside, the house shines in marble and gold. Painted posters boast their colors in gilded frames, then drip like crushed berries staining linen.

A ticket taker floats in the archway. The crowd moves around him in a glittering stream of scales. "First box," the man says, and when his lips move, a string of bubbles escapes, rising slow as minnows through water.

We're all underneath the surface—the gaslights wavering like sunbeams through waves, gowns drifting like seaweed. The carpet breathes soft and red under my feet, velvet as a womb.

He rips our ticket.

"My darling, Gertie," Kodiak says, in that gentleman's voice he wears like a costume, pressing the other half into my hand.

Gertie. I nearly laugh, remembering the names he teased about. Had I found a name and forgotten the one I asked for? Perhaps I am no one. Or perhaps someone new.

We take our seats, so high the whole theater spreads beneath us like a pancake. The orchestra prepares below, the brass gleaming under the lights, bows rising and falling like silverware. The air squeezes my chest. I gasp. Had I been holding my breath?

"What's the matter?" Kodiak asks in a distant voice, fuzzy under the singing strings.

I hadn't noticed it before, not really—the ticket pressed in my hand that trembles when I tilt it toward the light.

Krewe of Proteus.

Some sort of parade society it seems. Thoughts spill through the words, slick as fish. I freeze at the image. A bear, drawn in black ink against the paper stub.

Below it, a single word: Callisto.

My Callisto. The one I whispered to through the telescope.

The ticket burns in my palm. I asked for signs, begged for them, and here it is: a bear made into flesh, into the man sitting beside me. Despite falling stars, learning the coincidence of his name, and his sharing the Shawnee's tales of the stars, I've resisted every fleeting clue.

But this is tangible proof. The truest evidence.

"You all right?" he asks, wrinkle in his brow.

"You're mine." I rest my gloved hand against his face, his clean shaven cheek warm through the satin fabric. "My bear. I prayed, and the stars sent you." My voice breaks as I draw back and press the ticket hard in my fist.

His lips part, eyes flutter with flabbergast, before a smile quirks up the corner of his mouth. "My drunk little lamb. Ought to strap you to your seat 'fore you try to fly."

The lights dim, and the voices fold into a hush. Curtains part, and the orchestra rises like a tide. Costumed figures surge onto the stage, painted faces beneath the flame. I try to follow, but the story swims out of reach, foreign words drowned by absinthe. The Devil's shadow looms over the stage like an anvil.

Then, warmth. Breath at my neck. The bass of his voice prickles up across my arms. "Stay put. Don't go losin' yourself while I'm gone."

I nod. At least I think I do. Or perhaps I stared. But I blink, and he's disappeared through the velvet curtain. Turning back to the stage, nuns rise from their graves, veils flapping like the market awnings in the wind. They dance in holy robes turned to sin, and my pulse quickens. The green opal spirit whistles in my veins like a harmonica. Or is that a violin, the sound distorted underwater?

Minutes pass, perhaps hours, then he's back in his chair, arm laid easy. When did he return? Had he even gone? I tug at the long satin at my forearms. My skin is too warm, the fabric too tight.

"I think my hands are growing too big for my gloves," I mutter, turning to him. "Bear, could it be that my hands are hot but my bones are cold?"

Kodiak shrugs slightly, reaches over and takes my hand in his, fingers lacing with mine. "Reckon I ought to hold 'em, then."

FRENCH OPERA HOUSE
NEW ORLEANS
Fau
Box 7
Seat 2
CHAR
Augu
Callisto PRESENTED BY THE
KREWE of PROTEUS

CHAPTER 17

KODIAK

This ain't the show I'd hoped to make, but it'll do. The open, closed, and proscenium boxes are packed tight with money, old and new. My sweet girl in her pink gown, drunker than a skunk and prettier than a rose. Softest touch I ever knew, and tonight she looked at me with tears in her eyes, damn near singing me a love song. I'll be damned if I ain't swooning like a debutante at her first waltz.

It ain't right to give a man something to live for right before he risks life and limb to secure a bag of loot. But I reckon this pot'll be 'specially sweet. All that coin will spoil my woman to death—assuming I make it out alive.

The opera's a perfect mark. Everyone here's scrubbed clean and smelling nice. Who ever heard of an opera robbery? Most men outside the law I've met on the road don't know a damn thing about this world. They hit small-time targets—cash boxes, registers, homes. Biggest they can dream up are trains and banks. But a box office?

No. This'll be another pilferage for the record books. Nobody thought one man could derail a train and run off with more money than God. Ain't nobody going see me coming now. By the time these bastards realize what hit them, I'll be long gone. Me and my woman, heading west to lay low in the mountains. I imagine Alice big and round, carrying my young. I'd get teary-eyed if I weren't on the way to knock some poor sap's lights out.

I slip away and saunter down a dark hall. The boom of the orchestra drowns each footstep, and the floor watchman don't hear me coming. I'm close enough to hit 'fore he nods at me. I tip my head in reply. My sharp smile's too pretty to suspect of anything less than complete gentility.

I trot down the stairs to the lobby. The show's well into its first act, and the lobby's near empty 'cept for a few staff who don't give me a second look. Heading toward the double doors like a gentleman after fresh air, I turn into a narrow passage where a man stands in the dim, surprised to see me but not afraid. He raises his brows, ready to be helpful.

The music swells, blaring as I say, "Pardon me. I seem to be a bit lost."

His brow furrows and he shakes his head, stepping closer, turning his ear to get a better listen. Shouldn't have turned his head. It was a mistake letting his guard down at all. Once he's close, I swing up hard, my knuckles biting between his ribs. That spot'll knock the wind out of a man every time. Element of surprise on my side, I get him around the throat, squeezing hard. He groans but can't shout—ain't enough air getting through. I hold him, pulse flittering under my palm, just long enough for him to go slack.

If my sweet woman's taught me one thing, it's compassion. Before he can wake, I take the length of cord from my coat and tie his hands. A soprano's high note hits the rafters, and the usher starts to stir. He yelps quick, but I stifle it, my hand over his mouth. I get close to his ear.

"I know you don't wanna die today, boy."

His cries muffle into my palm, breath hot and wet. I press harder, digging my nails into his cheek so he knows I bite. "I could snap your neck like a twig, and they'd come scrape your sorry ass off the lobby floor at intermission. Now you can quiet and live to see tomorrow, or you can scream, and it'll be the last thing you ever do. You gonna behave yourself, or should your ma start plannin' your funeral?"

He mumbles a pitiful, weepy plea.

"That's what I thought."

I know better, and I got a handkerchief balled in my fist. Soon as I ease my grip, I shove it in his mouth. I lay him on his belly—hands tied behind, mouth stuffed like a hog—and move on to step two.

One thing I ain't had time to do was research the lock. It's dark, but I graze the handle, feeling the escutcheon gentle for the keyhole. Cool, smooth—brass, most like. From the size and shape, I reckon it's a mortise. Ordinarily I'd carry my roll—neat little tools wrapped in leather, lost the night the Shermans stripped me to nothing—but a man expects setbacks.

I make do: a nail filed down thin, a twist of piano wire, a fat hairpin swiped from Alice.

Learned lockpicking after my pa died. Big boy like me worked muscle for a gambling den. Met more than a few outlaws with plenty to teach. Old gambler I knew was a locksmith. Said, "Crackin' a lock's like fuckin' a woman." He meant patience. "You don't force her," he'd say, lips curled like a man chewing lemon. "You listen. You take her temper. You find where she wants to give."

The nail's a poor stand-in for a proper pick, but it'll sing if you coax it right. I bend the hairpin to make a little lever, thread the piano wire through to rig tension. Fiddly work in the dark. Fingers knowing what eyes can't see. My thumb lays soft on the latch, keeping just enough pressure to make her speak without staring down her throat.

A notch here. A scrape there. Tumblers push back one by one like piano keys. Smell of old brass—dust and oil—and I half expect to hear that old gambler chuckle beside me as it clicks soft.

I don't stand there admiring my work. I push through gentle, but it don't make no difference. Soon as it opens, I got two bastards staring right at me, and they sure as hell don't wanna lend a hand. I shut the door behind me. Figure whatever's about to go down's best kept contained.

The box office is smaller than our hotel room—'bout half the size—so there ain't nowhere for them to run with me blocking the only exit. I got borrowed iron—Alice's pistol. Wouldn't be wise to use it, not unless I plan on running out of here, and I already promised that poor drunk sweetheart I wouldn't leave her behind. I rest my hand on my hip and let my face tell them what's what.

First one's brave. Comes running, swings. I jerk aside, come back with a right hook to his jaw. Soon as I hear the crack, the other one's already reaching for iron, and if he fires, this night's going a whole lot different. First one hits the floor, blood spilling from his lips. Second man's drawn, but I grab the muzzle before he can touch the trigger, catch his wrist with my free hand, and shove him back.

"You really wanna die protectin' another man's coin, you dumb son of a bitch?" I say, slamming him to the wall. He ain't in control no more. I yank the gun free and let it clatter to the floor. First man's reeling, slow to react, so I kick it away. Second one gets me good in the gut. If I wasn't nursing a wound, I'd've taken it clean, but I see white and damn near drop to my knees. He keeps coming and I block, backing off to get space. Thank whatever God Alice is always crying about, 'cause the bastard slips in the other bastard's pool of blood. That heartbeat of him catching balance gives me time to swing with all I got—right, left, jab jab jab. He hits the floor.

"Where's the key?"

"Ain't no key," he mumbles, mouth a mess of blood and loose teeth.

Gotta get them tied up proper before I start searching. Wrist to wrist, ankle to ankle, looped tight behind their backs like hogs in the slaughter yard. The first one's face is near twice the size it was when I walked in. The second's cussing steady, like a carpenter who's just flattened his thumb.

"Shut up, you stupid bastard, 'fore I change my mind 'bout lettin' you live," I mutter. "Ain't no cause for dyin' over some rich man's ledgers."

They're breathing, which is more than I promised.

The safe squats in the corner behind the desk, brass face glinting in the low light. I crouch, roll my shoulders, crack my neck. Piano wire. Nail. Hairpin.

It's so goddamn hot in here. Coats and shirts and waistcoats, goddamn. Sweat glides down my back. Music booms, drums and the crash of cymbals. Ain't the best sound for concentration, and all that punching's got my fingers tight.

If I'm gone too long, Alice might come hunting.

Then, I find it. Tumbler by tumbler. She clicks.

Inside: cash boxes tight with bills, velvet sacks of coin, ledger books with numbers I don't need to understand. I grab what I came for, stuffing it in my coat till the seams groan.

I don't linger. No time to celebrate.

I ease the door open, step back into the corridor. The usher's still there, crying behind my handkerchief, stuffed so far back he's gagging. I drag him inside to join his colleagues, then close the door.

The opera bellows through the walls—full orchestra now, some man wailing like a goat in heat. Carpets swallow footfalls. Nobody sees me. Nobody hears me. I move like I belong.

I duck into the washroom near the lobby. Small mirror. White basin. Blood on my shirt where that bastard got me in the gut. Tore the stitch. Ain't bad, but it'll leave a mark. I press a damp cloth to it, clean what I can. Wipe my brow. Pat down my coat.

Money rustles like dry leaves every time I move. Good sound. Heavy.

Back through the lobby. Dim light. Smell of perfume, lamp gas, floor wax. An usher yawns near the stairs, don't spare me a glance.

Alice waits in the booth where I left her, pretty as dawn. Pink gown wrinkled, cheeks flushed from drink, eyes half lidded and dreamy. I slide in beside her.

She don't turn right away—just hums like she's trying to remember a tune. Then she blinks slow and says, "Mmm... hands. Bear, mmm, hands?"

I pause. The hell is she going on about? Her hands?

I take her gloved fingers in mine, let our hands tangle quiet between us.

"Reckon I oughta hold 'em then."

She smiles, posture loose, and leans against me.

I sit back, breathing deep. Her hand, small and warm, in mine. Money scratching like straw under my coat. Good nights like this don't last. She leans on me, expression bright but empty as bottle glass, and I hate leaving before the lady onstage finishes her dying. But I don't wanna push my luck. "How 'bout we get outta here?"

She nods and lets me lead, even gives the empty chair a little wave.

We slip into the street where the music can't reach, and I walk with my woman back to the hotel.

CHAPTER 18

Kodiak's tall, broad figure blocks the light from the window, where the rumble of city life seeps through the glass. He's dressed like a gentleman again, though not as formal, in a crisp white shirt, waistcoat, and trousers.

The sheets beside me are rumpled and carry the faint trace of something masculine. Had we...? Surely I'd know if that monstrous thing had been inside me. The only ache I feel is the pounding in my head.

Sitting up slightly, I notice a cart beside the bed with a tray of fruit, pastries, and coffee.

His back is turned, but he glances over his shoulder with a crooked smile. "Mornin', lamb. How are you on this fine day?"

"You poisoned me."

When he moves toward a small writing desk, the light from the window blinds me. Lowering himself into the chair, he lets out a low chuckle. "Now, what profit would I have in that?"

The evening is a blur of crystals and pearls. Of music. Of painted nuns whirling like specters. What on earth?

"No," he drawls. "Nothin' more than you dancin' with the green fairy. Absinthe, oysters, and opera—that's New Orleans in a night, sure as anything."

I should have known better than to trust this city. French architecture and kind folk lulled me into a false sense of safety.

His pen scratches across the page. "Had breakfast brought up, if you're hungry."

He sleeps in the dirt, swims in creeks, gets stabbed half to death in the countryside, and yet, here he is, dressed like a mayor on holiday, working at a desk in a grand hotel with breakfast catered.

"I suppose they brought hot water as well?"

"That they did."

I fling my legs over the side of the bed, take stock of the room. It's the same as before, though a large leather suitcase sits near the desk, one I hadn't noticed yesterday. "Are you leaving?"

"Not yet. Still business to see to in the city."

"Might you be so kind as to let me in on your plans, or should I expect to ask you moment to moment?"

At that, he turns—his full body this time—tweed straining at his bent knee. A leather suspender peeks out from under his waistcoat, stretched taut across his shoulder. On the desk lie piles of notes, bags of coins he's been rolling, and a neat stack of paper slips. Checks, perhaps.

"Sugarplum, it's best you—"

"Where did you get all that money?"

He exhales sharp, rubbing his palms on his thighs. "Best you ask me somethin' else."

A weight sinks into my gut.

Stupid woman. Ran off with a criminal, now you feign surprise at his plunder. And yet, as he sits there like a bank clerk with more money than I've ever seen in my life laid before him, the thought of holding my tongue is impossible.

"I thought you were a man of your word. That you'd be honest with me."

The words must strike a match in him, because he lowers his mask, brow furrowed in a flash of concern. "Alice, if you're hauled off by the sheriff, your soft hands won't sweat and your pretty face won't twitch. You can tell God's own truth that you don't know a thing of what I done without so much as a tremble in your sweet voice."

Although he has a point, it turns my stomach all the same. "Did...did anyone die?"

He shakes his head. "No. Made it nice and easy. Now that's all I'll say, and you quit askin'."

I give in with an exhale and cut across the room to the washroom and fill the tub. Perhaps a bath will silence the alarm bells. They first flared the night we escaped and have since grown too loud to ignore. Slipping out of my shift, I sink into the hot water.

What had I done but escape from one life beyond my control into another, chained to the whims of men? I close my fingers around my wrist. There's no shackle here.

What is holding me?

There's survival to start. How would I keep from starving? There are few respectable positions for a woman like me. No formal education to speak of. Without Joseph, I'd still be a poor farm girl, learning from old almanacs in my father's collection. As much as I cursed my husband, if it weren't for his wealth, I wouldn't have been comforted by the old stories behind the stars.

I suppose I could return to the inn, the story Gideon promised to tell the others offering me some semblance of protection. Though, I fear the Sherman family might assume the worst even if the law did not. They would abandon me.

No money. Nowhere to go. Nothing but a pistol to my name. Yet here I sit in a porcelain bath, pouting over my imperfect blessings.

What can I do but make Kodiak better? Perhaps I could set him on a truer path, but how? Only God knows what he's done. But whatever it was, it is over now. One cannot unring a bell.

The ideas turn over in my mind until the water cools and I emerge, wrap myself in a cotton robe, and find Kodiak at the desk logging his fortune.

"For someone who claims he keeps secrets, you're awful bold with your bounty."

He doesn't look up, writing a number down in a ledger. "Don't usually have company."

"How much is all that?"

He sighs. "Thought I told you to stop askin'."

"You did, but I'll ask all the same."

That earns me a cross expression that cracks with an amused smile. Without warning, he seizes my waist and hauls me into his lap. I yelp, steadying myself on his shoulders.

"Mouthy little brat, ain't you?" he says. "That kind of back talk just makes me want to put that mouth to better use."

I stiffen like he'd slapped me, clutching my robe shut for dear life. Good Lord above. I've never heard anything so vile. For a moment, I can't speak.

Joseph would make me do that. Said it was a husband's right. I would weep after, begging the Lord to cleanse me. And yet...for Kodiak, the thought of giving him such pleasure makes me clench around nothing, a sinful ache blooming inside.

"You mustn't say such things," I say, my protest weak.

He's grinning when he nudges the ledger, drawing my attention to it, his handwriting tidy for an outlaw. Bank notes, gold, silver—all laid out in their denominations, added up into a sum he'd underlined twice.

Three-thousand four hundred fifty-one dollars and twenty-two cents.

The staggering figure nearly chokes me. That much would buy a farm and a carriage, perhaps even a lifetime of bread and meat. For me, it brings to mind the children outside the church selling flowers. The boy at the market whose mother couldn't send him to school. Perhaps we could help. Perhaps that could be our penance.

I swallow, clutching the robe closed at my breast. "Kodiak..." My voice wavers. "What do you intend to do with it all?"

His hand stops at my waist, grin fading into something sharper. "Why are women always thinkin' there's a deal to strike?" His thumbs press into my sides, firm enough to remind me I'm held.

I sit up straighter, affronted. "Don't you dare suggest I'm one of your prostitutes. I thought only of children. The ones with nothing."

For a long breath, his eyes search mine, suspicion and something wounded flickering there. Then the hardness eases. His mouth curves again. "Only you'd sit in an outlaw's lap drummin' up a deal for charity."

My shoulders sink with relief, but then his grip tightens, drawing me closer. Kissing my cheek, he mumbles against me. "Suppose you got the notion that givin' a cut to save the world's orphans"—his breathy husk descends to a spot beneath my ear, the bass of each word humming through me, coursing with desire—"will redeem your soul for associating with the likes of me?"

He toys with the sash of my robe, mesmerized by the sliver of skin at my collarbone. Before I can answer, his lips brush that very spot, and I forget what I meant to say.

When hunger grips Kodiak, he becomes altered, unknowable, as if the wild itself had claimed him. His lips hover, exhale drifts along my collarbone as he asks, "Do you remember what you said to me last night?"

My ribs jolt. "What did I say?"

"You called me yours," he murmurs, mouth grazing higher, skimming the hollow of my neck. "Said the stars themselves sent me."

I told him?

Aloud?

He must think me mad.

I'd once read of stars imploding, their pull so fierce they devoured even light. Now, with my chest folding inward and my air strangled, I understand it. I press my face into his shoulder, as though I too might vanish into that consuming force.

"I didn't know I spoke it," I whisper into the tweed seam.

But he won't let me hide. His hand anchors beneath my chin, tilting me up.

The kiss strips me of breath, intoxicating, relentless. When he tears away, it's only to drag his teeth along my cheek, lower, tracing the line of my jaw until I shiver. I grip his shoulders, but it only drags me nearer. With one violent tug, he rips the robe open. It slides down my shoulders, baring me in the ruthless glare of morning.

I gasp, arms flying to shield myself, but he snatches my wrists. A cry rips loose as his mouth descends upon my breast, scorching, merciless, tongue circling rough and wet. The sensation sends a shiver through me.

He growls, the vibration running through my flesh. Every nerve ignites, my body betraying me in ways no prayer could forgive.

His hand presses between my thighs, parting me.

"My God, you're wet through. Burnin' for me, ain't you, little lamb?" he mutters against my skin, teeth grazing my nipple until it hardens under his tongue. "You knew the stars wouldn't waste no gentle creature on you, but sent a wild one to ruin you proper."

His fingers glide through my slick heat, circling my swollen nub with slow, maddening strokes. I arch into him, chasing more, but just as the pleasure coils tight, he withdraws, leaving me gasping and empty.

He hums thoughtfully, eyes dark as he studies where I'm open and aching for him. "You ever seen a man work a lock?"

Gazing down between my thighs, he explores me, toys with each dip and curve of my tender flesh. "Inside is a puzzle of levers and notches, spindles, and bolts."

One thick finger teases my entrance, barely breaching. I draw in a sharp breath. "But it ain't complicated if you can be patient. It's about noticin' the tension, the sound."

He pushes in slow—inch by torturous inch—until I'm stretched around him, clenching desperately. My hips jerk; a broken moan spills out of me.

All of his attention is on me, watching and listening like a predator in the brush as the broad, calloused pad drags across a hidden ridge. He crooks his finger just right, finding that secret place inside that makes stars burst behind my eyes.

"There," he rasps, satisfaction raw in his voice. He presses again, grinding that place until I buck helplessly. "Knew you carried a soft spot for me."

A second finger slides in beside the first, stretching me wider. My body tightens, every beat pounding against him. His thumb torments my pearl—light, then firmer, never steady.

He withdraws sudden, leaving me empty. Lifting his hand, slick and gleaming, he slides his fingers into his mouth. "Christ above," he groans, slowly sucking them clean. "You're sweet as honey on my tongue. I could savor you to kingdom come."

What a sinful, wicked man.

I cannot look away.

Every pull of his lips sends a fresh pulse between my legs, as if he's still touching me, and yet I ache for his touch to return.

He runs his wet fingers over my lower lip, painting my mouth with my taste, then claims it in a deep, hungry kiss as his hand hovers teasingly between my legs, not quite touching where I need him.

Then two fingers plunge deep, merciless against that hidden place, his thumb circling harder, and the pressure builds fierce, unbearable. I thrash in his lap as he presses, curls, grinds all at once, and the tension tears me apart. It is as though I'm set aflame, every thought and breath bursting into a white flare that tears through me.

"Kodiak." His name spills from my lips, wave after wave crashing through me. My thighs quake, my body wrung out in his lap, daylight blazing over every shameless sound. Kodiak steadies me through it, his breathing ragged against my skin.

"That's right, call for me. I'm only warmin' you up. I ain't even started."

His fingers ease, gentling me down, until I slump against his chest, trembling.

He gathers me as though I weigh nothing, the robe discarded. In the morning sun I'm laid bare before him, stretched across the bed. For a long moment he doesn't move. He stands over me, mapping every inch of exposed skin like a beast lingering over captured prey, choosing its first indulgence.

He has claimed me.

He is mine and I am his. It's time I surrender to it.

He undresses like a man who knows I'm watching, who wants me to watch. Waistcoat falls open, suspenders slip free from his shoulders, shirt peels back to reveal a broad, scarred torso. He shrugs it off, leaving only trousers clinging low on his hips.

I can't breathe for looking at him—the hard cut of muscle, the trail of hair vanishing beneath the cloth, the raw power in his movements. My breath falters as he pushes his trousers lower and frees himself, thick and flushed, heavy in his grip.

He stands over me, smoldering. "Open your thighs for me," he says, voice low.

Although steeped in disgrace, my longing wins and my body obeys, knees sinfully parting.

He slides down, his calloused hands spreading my thighs wider, pinning them to the sheets. His breath is hot against my skin. The morning light catches the sheen of my own wetness, and his eyes darken. "Goddamn, you're pretty everywhere ain't you," he growls, parting me with his thumbs, an outlaw's hunger lacing every word.

His mouth descends, lips brushing my tender flesh, and I gasp, my hips jerking at the first flick of his tongue. He's relentless, licking slow and deliberate. My fingers twist in the sheets, nails biting into the fabric as his tongue circles, teasing, drawing a moan I can't hold back. My body arches, bound to him, entrapped by his spell. The room spins, the sunlight too bright, exposing every shameful shudder.

Just as I feel the wave about to break, he pulls back, his lips glistening, fierce with hunger. "You ready for me, lamb?" He rises, positioning himself between my thighs, his thick length nudging at my entrance, searing and unyielding.

I know I shouldn't, that this is an unholy weakness of the flesh, yet instead of ending this madness, I utter, "I need to feel you inside me."

A wicked grin spreads across his face as he lowers himself, then murmurs at my cheek. "I'm gonna make sure you feel all of me. And I'm gonna take you slow." He pushes, and the burn makes my nails bite into his shoulders.

Glancing down at where our bodies meet, his eyes flutter. "Christ almighty, look at you, takin' me so sweet."

He swallows my gasp with a kiss, holding me wide, easing in inch by torturous inch. The furnace of him fills me, shocking, tearing through the last of my virtue until it burns out in the fire of my hunger.

When he's buried to the root, every inch of him stretching me to a brutal fullness that borders on pain, he shudders with a faint whimper. His jaw locks tight, eyes squeezed shut, veins bulging along his neck as he fights for control.

"I'm gonna give you what you prayed for, little lamb."

He begins to move.

Slow at first, hips rolling, the drag of him stoking fire through me. Each thrust is steady, claiming, deliberate, his voice rough with filthy praise. His lips find my breast, drawing hard. The glide of him aches, friction mounting with every push. The bed groans, protesting the force of our vigor. Each stroke deeper, harder. I cry out, loud and vulgar. Thin walls be damned.

He grips my throat, letting me feel his power, his restraint, thumb brushing my jaw as though to tether me even in the roughness. Perhaps I should be frightened. This brute capable of the most gruesome of crimes holds my life in his hands. But there's something in that powerlessness that sets me free, and surrendering to it, being raptured by it, I'm beyond salvation.

He shifts, guiding himself carefully, all his senses attuned to me the way he'd watched before. As he settles deeper, the violent flare of pleasure makes me wail.

"There," he says, moving again, each push wracking my body, each devastating swing precise. The rhythm builds until I'm writhing, vision flaring white.

I break, body seizing tight around him.

He bears into me harder until another wave rips me open, and another. My sobs tumble over themselves, raw, near-hysteric, as he carries me through one shiver after the next.

"Goddamn, Alice."

His thrusts turn ragged, urgent. For all his power, he's ensnared in me. Just as defenseless against me as I am from him. He groans like a man in pain given mercy. Pulling free, he spends hot across my belly, my thighs, his cry tearing from him raw and guttural. He collapses to his forearms above me, trembling, sweat dripping onto my skin.

Catching his breath, a dazzling smile emerges as his head rolls back. "Christ almighty."

His mouth presses rough to my hair, my forehead, my cheek, as if he's overcome with affection. "Stay put, sweetheart. I ain't done taking care of you." He rises, his Herculean silhouette striking against the morning light as he steps away in his bare skin. How can something so delicious—

so beautiful—be wrong? Every fear, every anxious whisper shutters itself away, leaving only the quiet, steady hum of my body remembering his.

He returns with a damp towel, kneeling beside me and gliding the cloth over my skin, erasing his mark with a tenderness that feels like worship. "You're so damn beautiful," he whispers, his voice thick with devotion. "And all mine." His touch lingers, fingertips tracing the paths he's cleaned, as if re-mapping me as his own.

He pulls me into his chest, his arms a fortress around me, and tucks a strand of hair behind my ear, his touch both gentle and possessive. "I'll keep you close, Alice. Not just tonight, but every damn night. No one else gets to hold you like this."

We settle together, the soft roar of voices and train cars outside like quiet music.

"Reckon you'll go pray now," he teases. "Beg forgiveness for wantin' me and call it a mistake." Though his tone is playful, there's tenderness underneath.

Regret blooms in my chest for having been so desperately repentant after our first intimacy, as if he were a stain on me. Perhaps that was cruel.

"I hadn't meant it that way. You mustn't believe it was you. A lady is meant to protect her virtue, and yet when I'm with you...I'm powerless against my desire."

He nuzzles closer, the mattress dipping beneath his weight. "Yeah, but powerless ain't a sin. Just means there ain't no say in it. Same as I had no say the first time I laid eyes on you."

Something deep and long-quiet inside me stirs to life.

"No say in it," he echoes. "You and me. Always was."

The earnestness in his expression undoes me, my heart swelling with a sudden aching affection for him. Perhaps I had named it sin out of fear, but fear is not faith. Faith is trust in the path laid before me. And if that path runs through his arms, perhaps I was wrong about virtue all along.

Our union occupies more of the morning than I would confess aloud. Once my body can endure no further indulgence, we are spent and compelled at last to seek some other pursuit. Kodiak proposes a breath of fresh air before his mysterious business visit. We promenade along the levee, the Mississippi rolling slow and brown beside us, steamboat whistles splitting the heat.

Ordinarily, I am occupied with the labor of running the inn. But here with Kodiak, very little is expected of me. I never understood until now how leisure—the business of being idle, of existing only to enjoy the day—could be a full occupation. This was a luxury afforded to other Sherman women, but never me. I was equal parts servant and wife. But here, I've walked without purpose, let my mind wander where it pleases. Idle hands are the Devil's workshop, and now I understand why. The Devil finds such favor among the idle because they have the time to entertain him.

Here, the streets thrum with life. Carriages rattle past and ladies step daintily along the walks beneath their parasols. Vendors call their wares, and a gaggle of ragged boys weaves through the crowd, their voices high and urgent as they cry the day's news.

"Extra! Extra! Opera holdup! Thousands stolen under their noses. Read how they done it!"

The headline nearly makes me stumble. I steal a glance at Kodiak, but his expression betrays nothing, as though the words have no meaning to him at all. While there is no doubt this was Kodiak's scheme, I was with him the entire night, his hand in mine, his voice steady in my ear.

It defies reason.

"How did you do it?" I whisper.

"I'm sure I haven't the faintest notion what you are speaking of," he replies in his gentlemanly accent, smooth as polished silver. How easily he wears it, how easily he casts it aside.

I release his hand and about-face, hurrying toward a boy with a stack of papers under his arm.

"One paper, please."

"A penny."

I give him the coin and take the sheet, the ink smudging faintly against my gloves. Ahead of me, Kodiak slows his pace, glancing back with thinly veiled irritation. Without a moment's hesitation, I unfurl the paper and see the story plain as day on the front page.

Daring Robbery at the French Opera House

The French Opera House was the scene of a daring robbery last night, the fact not discovered until some hours after the curtain had fallen. An usher, a watchman, and the box-office clerk were set upon by unknown parties and confined during the entertainment. Though no lives were lost, the men were badly beaten. Upon the alarm being raised, it was found that the treasurer's strong-box had been rifled and several thousand dollars carried off. The perpetrators made good their escape unobserved. No arrests have yet been made. The management announces a reward for information leading to the arrest and conviction of the guilty parties.

My mouth falls open. Was he two men at once? I remember his hand in mine, yet the night runs ragged in my memory, blurred by the green fairy.

He pressed the glass on me.

He wanted me blind.

The bastard.

I march up to him, paper clutched tight. Before I can speak, he holds up a hand to stop me.

"Not here," he says, catching my wrist. He steers me off the street into a narrow court—flagstones damp, an ornate fountain ticking at the basin, shutters drawn above. He faces me, smooths the corner of his mustache once, then holds himself still, boots planted.

"Look," he says, voice stripped of polish. "I told you it was for your own good not to get in deeper."

"I am already in it," I answer. "I have nowhere to go, no one I may trust. You have made me a party whether I will it or not. So tell me."

A long breath. He rubs the back of his neck, then drops his hand. "Walked in same as any gentleman with a ticket. Waited my moment. Pulled a kerchief over my face. Cleared my path of interruptions and worked the strongbox before goin' back to my seat. Simple as that." He says it as if it were as benign as visiting the postmaster to buy stamps.

"The paper said unknown parties."

"Well it was me who beat the starch out of all three of 'em, one by one. No one else. Told you, I work alone."

I draw back, hand to my chest. "You truly struck them?"

"They're breathin', ain't they?" A dry hitch of a laugh, without warmth. "Hell, Alice, I could've killed the lot of 'em. Would you rather that?"

I can only stare.

He tilts his head, the faintest curl at his mouth. "See? Mercy. That's me bein' kind."

I steady the paper under my arm. "And what business keeps you here?"

"A fence," he says. "Buys what don't belong to me, makes it pass for clean."

"And you plan to meet with this fence?"

He nods wearily, then holds out his hand to resume our walk.

I clasp my hands neat at my waist. "I will come with you."

Something in him goes very still. When he speaks again, the weariness is gone, replaced with a hard, cold edge.

"No," he says. "You will not. And don't fool yourself—layin' with me don't give you a say over my business. I take care of what's mine how I see fit. You walk in there lookin' like a Sunday school teacher, they'll see you comin' a mile away."

The words cut. My chin lifts. "Do not speak to me as if I were a child. I will not be sent off while you disappear into shadows."

His jaw knots, a vein pulsing at his temple. The mask is gone, and I see the brute the papers warn about. He crowds the space between us, driving me back a step until my spine meets the wall. He leans down close enough that his breath scorches my cheek.

"Yes. You. Will," he says, final. "You'll do exactly as I tell you—or you can pack your shit and crawl back to Ohio. Your boredom ain't my business, Alice. I done my job of lookin' after you, and you got everything you need. If that don't suit you, walk away and see how long you last."

The cruelty in it slices deep. He has never stood over me like this, never let me feel the weight of his temper turned full upon me. A cold dread spreads through me.

Pride alone keeps my spine stiff. I smooth my gloves, set

my hat just so, and incline my head as though we were polite strangers. My voice is flat, chilled. "Very well, then."

I turn and walk out into Jackson Square, where the crowd swallows me, iron balconies shadowing my path, a brass horn wailing from somewhere down the street. Chin high, steps measured, I carry on to the Hotel de Chartres.

Only when I reach the hotel steps, the noise dimming behind me, do my knees weaken. I climb quickly, clutching the banister, my vision blurred. By the time the door closes on our room, the tears I held at bay come hard and fast, spilling hot down my cheeks.

CHAPTER 19

KODIAK

Goddamn brat.

Lamb sends me stomping down Royal Street full of piss and vinegar. Now she's gonna go on her little martyr's procession back to our hotel, pouting cause I won't let her get held up in the Vieux Carré. Out here, the cobblestone streets turn to stoves with the summer sun, the stink of horse shit and tobacco thick as mud.

Can just imagine Fitz the Fence giving me a raw deal, knowing I won't reach for my gun with my lady in the cross fire. Enemies smiling 'cause now they know just how to squeeze what they want outta me. She don't get it. It ain't just her delicate sensibilities being at odds with the likes of outlaws, or that I think she can't handle herself—though, I ain't sure for that either. Showing weakness is dangerous for the both of us.

But of course she don't know that, keeping a ledger and

folding sheets at an inn her whole life. Maybe I shouldn'ta been so cold to her. But she ought to know, this ain't a game.

By the time I find myself on Fitz's street, all that dynamite in my veins done turned to kittens. Hope she ain't back at the room crying. Or worse, packing.

Fucking hell—this woman's gonna be my death.

A phonograph rasps a brass tune that carries down the alleyways. The block vibrates with merchantry—men pushing handcarts full of bananas and oranges fresh off the port. Whores lean out of windows with rouge thick as paint, fishing for sailors spilling off boats.

I pull my hat down low and push through the doors to Fitz's shop, a "general store" selling cigarettes and candy out the front, forgeries and specialized occult items out the back. A man could unload a bundle of checks for pennies on the dollar and stroll off with a human skull; all depends on what you're into, I suppose. But I ain't worried 'bout putting on no rituals, even if I lost my good sense in the stars with this fate business.

Chimes twang, and I catch a breath of the musty air. Shop full of dusty tins of smoked oysters and canned peaches been sitting for years. Old wood planks creak underfoot as I make my way to the back, where Fitz smokes a cigar and idly shuffles a deck of cards.

"Mother of God, look who's come callin'," Fitz says. Bastard always chatting me up all friendly-like before he tries to fuck me over. "What's the craic? Word all over town about the opera house. Thought it might be you. Not many men could lift paper clean as that."

I reach into my coat and set my bundle on the counter. "Ain't my business," I say. "Came with my own paper to sell. You fence it or not?" I shove it across to him.

"What have we here?" Fitz asks. "Choir music and prayer cards?"

I stay quiet, tapping my thumb on the counter as he shuffles through, muttering numbers to himself.

"Hmm," he starts. "Face value's near a thousand. Could give you forty now. Maybe fifty if you can wait for your cut."

The bastard's being cute.

"Fitz, you move paper better than any man in town. You can do better than four cents on the dollar."

He slams his hand on the counter, hot tempered son of a bitch he is. "Five cents on the dollar, Christ above. Whole city's talking about that job. I'll hang before I see a bloody penny!"

"I'm tellin' ya, Fitz. You're givin' me credit for another man's crime. Now, twenty-five cents, or I might as well feed this paper to the stove."

"Ten and not a penny more, you bloody bastard."

I thumb my coat, hand sitting on the butt of my pistol. "Fifteen and I forget the insult."

Chimes sound behind me, and Fitz leans over to get a peek, tossing a leather ledger over top of the stolen checks as if on instinct. "Be right with ye."

"We got a deal or not?" I say.

"Fine, you devil," he mutters low, then disappears to a back room. I'm grateful for the distraction that hurried our negotiations along. I look over my shoulder to see who I might have to thank for the favor and see a man lurking by a wall of tinctures and medicines that are liable to do more damage than good.

"Here," Fitz says, returning with a few greenbacks and gold coins he pushes my way. "Now off with ye, before I change my mind."

I grin, tuck the take inside my coat. "Always a pleasure."

I'm near the door when the man edges out from between the shelves. Plain coat, broad hat. Blocks me clean.

"Archibald Randolph?"

Never met this bastard, and I ain't keen on him using my name. My hand drifts toward my coat. "Depends who's askin'."

He looks me dead in the eye, voice flat. "Virgil Sherman. Says you put Joseph in the ground and run off with his wife. Says you'll pay for both soon enough." The man's mustache twitches. "You stick out, Mr. Randolph. Ain't many places Mr. Sherman don't have someone watchin'. Bellhops, porters, barkeeps—folk who don't mind earnin' an extra dollar to pass along a name."

Silence stretches. My jaw tightens, but I ain't about to give the satisfaction. I tip my hat slow. "That so? Well, don't surprise me he'd send a boy to do a man's job. You can tell Virgil I ain't hard to find. When he's done hidin', Shermans can bury him right next to his brother."

Almost before I could finish my sentence, I hear a shotgun racking and we both turn toward the sound. Fitz aims his barrel between us, as if he don't care which of us he fires at first.

"Take your trouble outside, or I'll paint the walls with your blood."

The man sneers, dipping his head as he slides past me.

I step out into the street, heat prickling under my collar. If Virgil's sending men bold enough to name me in daylight, won't take much to sniff me back to the hotel. Back to Alice.

Shit.

That thought ties a knot in my gut.

I tilt my brim low and cut through the side streets, doubling back where I can, watching every shadow, listening for every heel strike behind me. By the time I swing toward the hotel's rear, I've near worn a hole in my boots.

Once I'm back on my floor, I enter our room, careful no one's watching from the hall.

"Alice," I call, walking fast, waiting for the relief of finding her safe and sound. But all I find is the bedroom and washroom—empty.

Damnit, Alice. Where are you?

CHAPTER 20

Buttery praline sugar melts on my tongue as I watch the children dance and cheer in the square, silver dollars gleaming bright in their small hands. A mild breeze passes through, horses clomp by and a basket of flowers rests at my feet, purchased from the children by my purse.

"Now, keep those safe, loves," I say, smoothing my skirts. "Do not wave them about, lest some thief snatch them away. Take them straight home and place them into your mommies' and daddies' hands."

They nod as if making a solemn oath, then skip off, laughter echoing and fading across the square like a playground. I look down at the basket brimming with daisies, all mine now, bought at a dollar apiece. Far greater than they're worth, and yet worth every cent. The coins were taken from Kodiak's pile, true, but they were stolen long before that. A thief's spoils used to feed and clothe children. I doubt even God would frown too harshly at such an exchange.

I nearly float back to the hotel down the crowded city streets. Though a pit of fear lingers in my belly, it's tempered with the joy of young smiles. Kodiak will understand, won't he? I had sought permission—in a manner of speaking—and he seemed endeared to the idea. Twenty dollars is a small sum compared to the thousands he stole. Though there is a chance he will be cross...especially after our spat. He might think it retaliation.

I smile to myself.

Perhaps it was.

I imagine him towering over me, his chest rising with quickened breath the way it had earlier, his face close to mine with that menacing look. It's a dizzying mix of fear and something I cannot define. A knot tightens in my stomach, and yet, the thought of his voice rumbling with authority sends a shiver rushing through me, a sudden warmth blooming low within me.

Why is it that Joseph's temper often paralyzed me from daring to defy him at all, and yet the thought of defying Kodiak, a man most would agree far more dangerous, wraps my fear in glee?

When I open our hotel room door, I find him sitting at the edge of the bed, forearms on his knees as if burdened. He lifts his head, his eyebrows lifting before his expression fades to something equal parts hostility and relief.

"Where the hell have you been?"

I jerk back. We're off to a poor start. My pulse quickens and I can barely get a word out. "I...I was at the market."

"The market," he repeats with a note of skepticism.

I show him my basket. "See, I bought flowers."

He looks at them with a wrinkle in his brow. "I don't know

what you paid for that, but I could've yanked those out of the dirt behind the hotel."

The children probably had. I cannot help but laugh to myself, which only seems to make him grow colder.

"I can't have you wandering wild all over the city. It ain't safe."

"I wasn't wandering wild. I was at the market. Please pardon me for misunderstanding your concern; I thought you'd have me crawl back to Ohio."

His expression softens. "I didn't mean that. Look, we can't stay. Sherman knows we're in town."

"Oh no," I say, a flash of ice in my veins. My hand flies to my mouth. "What happened?"

"Don't worry. I ain't gonna let no harm come to you. And we'll be just fine. 'Tween the fence and what I had tucked away, we're sittin' on enough to move on, start fresh someplace else. We ride first thing tomorrow."

He proceeds to the leather bag under the desk where he'd hidden away his plunder. My mouth goes dry. I'd secured the cash box inside exactly the way I found it, but when he sits and opens it, a deep wrinkle settles into his brow, and I hold my breath.

"Somethin' ain't right," he says. He turns to me, eyes narrowed. "You been in the cash box?"

"I-I may have taken twenty dollars." The words near choke me.

Silence follows. Kodiak's jaw flexes once, then he rises, looming tall, and the pit in my belly grows larger.

"May have?"

I clear my throat. "I did."

He raises a hand to pinch the bridge of his nose, and I flinch.

"You stole from me?"

"For the children. By the church. They sell flowers."

"You stole from me to buy twenty dollars' worth of weeds?"

"It wasn't about the flowers, Kodiak. I—" My nerves flutter in my chest. "You seemed agreeable to it this morning."

He scoffs. "I told you layin' with me don't give you a say over my business."

"I know, but you had so much. I didn't think you'd miss it."

His fists squeeze hard, as if he's crushing my words to powder. "You think I won't notice when my own woman robs me? You think I'm some fool?"

"Of course not." My breath snags. "I only wished—"

He cuts me off with a shake of his head. "I don't care if you wished, prayed, or cursed—you don't ever take from me without permission, Alice." His voice drops, dangerous. "Not if you aim to stay mine."

My knees buckle and my heart pounds. *Mine.*

He straightens to his full height with a sigh and says, "You got two choices. Twenty licks 'cross your backside, hard as I can give 'em. Or four hours standin' in that corner, nose to the wall."

A strange fire licks at my insides, fierce and unbidden. I had to have known there would be consequences. If someone had taken cash out of my lockbox without permission, I'd not abide it. What wickedness compelled me to tempt the wrath of a bear knowing he may bite?

"You wouldn't." My reply straddles the line between a plea and a dare.

He steps close, towering over me. "Oh, lamb. I would. And you'll choose."

I can hardly breathe. Four hours seems unbearable. The pain would be over faster with a spanking. "Fine. Twenty."

His hand clamps my wrist before I can take the words back. In a blink I'm across his knee, skirts shoved high, drawers yanked down. The cool air sweeps gently over my bare skin, shame hotter than fire.

"Kodiak. Please—"

His palm swats down, connecting loud as a whip. I jolt, a cry ripping out of me. The sting like a brand across my backside.

"You'll not steal from me," he growls, another crack falling before the burn has faded. "I still ain't heard an apology."

"I'm sorry," I cry.

"Now count. Out loud. That was two."

His hand claps down again, harder than the first. My legs jerk, but his arm pins me tight.

"I said count," he commands.

I weep, the tears drawn out of me. "Three." The word nearly lodges in my throat. How dare he discipline me? I'm a woman, not a wayward child.

As the fourth strike lands and I call out the number, the sting radiates, not just as pain but as something else—a sudden bewildering sensation. Before I could make sense of it, his hand strikes down again. My breath catches, a flush of heat spreading through me, pooling damp between my thighs.

"Alice, if you forget to count again. I'm adding twenty more."

"Five," I whimper, pressing my thighs together. The humiliation of being bent over, the bite of his hand, the stern authority in his voice, all twists together.

Another hit and my body jolts. "Six." The room whirls around me. I cry, gripping the sheets for dear life.

By ten, I'm fighting against my mind, tempted to idle, to freeze in the sensation of it, but the fear of more punishment reinvigorates me, forcing the next number past my lips. I'm gasping, sobbing. By twenty, I wilt over his knee, body shaking with something more than anguish.

His broad palm soothes then, caressing my backside in slow circles so gently I nearly moan. Hauling me up, he cradles me on his lap like I'm fragile after all. The air is too warm, his presence too close, and when I shift, a slick sensation makes me bite my lip, startled.

His calloused thumb sweeps away my tears, his lips press against my temple.

"Ain't the money, lamb," he says somberly. "Hell, I'd shower you with gold if you'd only asked. It's trust I want." He reaches into his coat and pulls out a thick roll of bills, gently pressing it into my trembling hand. "Take this. Feed every damn orphan in New Orleans if you want. You run out, you ask me for more. You steal again, we're done. Understand me?"

I nod, cheeks wet, body shaking from the sting and the want it ignited deep inside me.

"Need you to say it."

I answer, breath hitching. "As long as I am yours, I won't take without asking."

His mouth curves into a sly grin, and he pulls me closer, tightening his hold around me.

God help me, I've never wanted him more. I swore I'd never belong to any man again, not after Joseph. Yet here I am, aching for the very thing I swore to despise. He is an outlaw, thief, and murderer, and yet, I trust him when he says he wants only what is best for me. And though I once prayed never to be possessed, the thought of being his and his alone sets my soul on fire.

CHAPTER 21

KODIAK

A spanking ain't one of the consequences I'm used to handing out. Traveling in the company of a lady is proving to be more difficult than I'd surmised. Knew she was pure—hell, it's one of the traits that made me most fond—but I ain't expect the things that come along. She builds castles in the air, getting romantic ideas 'bout everything. She's gonna save the world's children. Put an outlaw on a holy path. Reckon she don't even know real danger. Otherwise, I'd bet she wouldn't make the mistake of stealing from the likes of Kodiak Randolph thinking she's getting some kinda Robin Hood justice.

We're skin to skin now, all the fight wrung out, her breath soft where it fans across my chest. I brush a few strands of hair from her cheek, watching her lashes flutter like she might drift off but won't dare just yet. Had to discipline her, but now her skin holds the flush from showing her my kinder side after. Hadn't needed words to make it right. She'd understood me just fine when her legs wrapped around me, moaning my name like a prayer.

Now, she's curled in tight, my arm around her, holding her close. We'll be leaving at first light, and the thought of one of Sherman's boys busting in guns blazing keeps me alert. If it were just me, I'd sleep as sound as I usually do with a rich bounty on my head, pistol at my side, rifle cross my chest. But Alice?

When I think of losing her, it's like all my insides collapsing, heart racing, mind a swirl of fear. Ain't right. But I can't help it. Of all my ill-got gains, she's my most treasured. Now I'm wearing my heart raw outside my chest. The panic that goes along with that makes me hold her tighter.

"Bear?" she whispers in the dark, sweet as can be, head resting on my arm.

"Yes, lamb?"

"I know you said it's dangerous to stay, but...Sherman has eyes in every city. It wouldn't surprise me if they had already notified all of their hotels to be on the lookout."

"You're right 'bout that. But don't lose sleep over them. Long as you're with me, I'll keep you safe."

She nuzzles closer, her arm draped over me, wrapped in a sheet. "Well, I wonder what we have to gain by running? If we're just as endangered anywhere as we are here, maybe we should stay."

I stroke her hair, smooth as silk. "Ain't about runnin', but a man like me can't linger anywhere too long. Long as you're movin', you're stayin' one step ahead."

"When do you ever rest? Put down roots?"

The question hits me in a way I ain't expect. Never bothered me before. Just was. But I can hear the disappointment in her voice, and it's like a jab to the gut.

"Man like me don't put down roots."

Her finger traces shapes on my chest, pondering what that'll mean for her, most like. And for the first time, I ponder it too.

When I think of Alice and how the stars brought us together—if you put stock in such a thing—I conjure a picture of her, my young at her breast, sitting in a rocking chair at the hearth without a trouble in the world. But it's a picture that can't be real. I've been building a castle in the air myself, fool that I am.

But holding something so precious in my arms, I can't stand the thought of letting it go.

"Maybe you could one day," she says. "Somewhere far away, in a small town."

"Suppose one day, maybe. Truth is, ain't never dreamt of such things. Hope's just a rope for hangin' yourself."

She looks up at me, wrinkle in her nose. "What an awful thing to say."

"It's true."

"Perhaps with that attitude it's true, but it does not have to be. Sure, hope alone is something, but it doesn't do much alone. Hope and action together, well then, you might have a chance."

I press a kiss to the top of her head. Part of me wants to believe, the other part thinking of the roses and butterflies that live in that pretty head of hers.

"What would you have us do?"

She sighs and clicks her tongue, like she's struggling to decide whether it's safe to speak her piece.

"Go on," I prod.

"If we run, they'll keep chasing us. But if we stand up to them, maybe they'll leave us alone."

I exhale slow, studying her in the dark. "You say that like it's simple. Like the Shermans are just some school bullies needin' a good wallopin'."

She doesn't flinch. Just lifts her head. "I'm only suggesting we send a message. Something that embarrasses them. That makes people think twice about staying in one of their hotels. Not with guns, but something clever."

There's a pause while I stare, trying to figure out who's this *we* she keeps talking about and decide if she picked up some crazy pills at the market earlier. But it seems like she's already given it a lot of thought and curiosity wins out.

"You have somethin' in mind?"

She shifts, half sitting now, hands folded politely in her lap, like she's excited to recite a poem. "There's a Sherman Hotel here in New Orleans. All their hotels encourage guests to store their valuables in the hotel safe behind the front desk. The inn would protect stocks, bonds, cash, jewelry. We'd take an inventory each evening before locking it for the night."

I think back on the night she made me leave empty handed and squeeze my eyes shut. All that loot, left behind. This woman will be my death.

"What if someone broke into their vault? Took valuables. If brazen enough, it may even make the cover of the paper. People wouldn't feel safe staying there anymore."

I stare at her, jaw slack.

"You're talkin' about robbin' the Shermans?"

Her chin lifts, just slightly. "Don't mistake my manners for weakness, Mr. Randolph. I may not believe in theft, but I do believe in self-defense. Besides, the Shermans carry insurance. The guests will be repaid tenfold."

I run a hand over my face. "You know how hard it'd be? They got men, steel doors, watchers on every floor."

"I imagine you've broken into worse."

"I have. But not with someone like you taggin' along and not without spillin' blood."

She leans in then, her breath warm against my throat. "I know all of the Sherman hotel policies. I could pose as a guest. We're not allowed to let guests into the vault, but once an important member of the Astral Society had brought along a large meteor specimen to present to the other men. It took a porter and two hands to move it. The man was a pest and inquired about it each evening. We couldn't very well drag it out to the front desk, but because of his status, the man was allowed in the vault with an escort supervising. What if I posed as a guest? Checked in an item too large to easily move?"

I pull back just enough to look her full in the face. The words I hope to find are lost in a storm of shock, and all I can say is, "Well, I'll be fucked sideways."

She gasps, shoving against my chest. "Archibald Randolph."

Laughter spills out of me, and I don't mean to be cruel—hell, it's a good idea—but I'd be damned before I put her in harm's way. I sweep a weft of hair from her face.

"Criminal mastermind that you are, by God. I'm pleased you'd like to lend a hand, but there ain't no way I'm puttin' you in that kinda danger."

She sits up straighter and smacks the bed. "I'm *in* danger, Kodiak. We are both in danger as long as the Shermans are after us."

"And you think lightin' the dog's tail on fire's gonna help that?"

"I cannot imagine running for the rest of my life."

"It won't be forever," I say, knowing full well it ain't true.

That seems like the end of it. She sinks back into bed and

we settle in. I'm nearly asleep when she says, "Are you not worried your enemies will take your retreat for weakness?"

"Is that a fancy way of callin' me yella?"

"I would never say such a thing. But the Shermans...they would."

Is she razzing me? I never met a dainty thing like her find a bear to just poke and poke. "You want back over my knee?"

Her hands slip under the covers, gliding over my chest, and my bones turn to jelly. Damn woman knows how to work me over good.

"You know there are only so many roads out of New Orleans," she murmurs. "The Shermans could surveil on the trails. Lawmen too. If we leave now, they'll be watching. Once we're in open country, there won't be crowds or city noise to vanish into. Just us and them."

I let out a long breath. Hell, I know she's right. I hate that she's right. Running now, tail between my legs, makes me look weak, leaves us exposed. Standing our ground with a trick like she suggests might just work. Make us a little richer before we move on if nothing else, I suppose. But I don't like the notion of my woman being in the middle.

"If we do this, we find a way to get you out before any guns are drawn. Leave the vault to me."

CHAPTER 22

In preparation for my role, I develop a character. Someone important. Trustworthy.

"What about a princess?"

I catch Kodiak mid-yawn before he answers with a sleepy, "Princess of what?"

We're in bed, having spent the morning expressing our fondness of each other. Kodiak's arm curls lazily across my stomach, warm and possessive. I trace idle circles along the inside of his wrist, and for a moment, we are nothing but two souls basking in borrowed time—no ledgers, no errands, no titles. I relish in him, and him in me, like a long bath or an unhurried conversation.

The sun cuts through the curtains, half open, our spent breakfast littering a nearby cart.

I think of a place. Somewhere imagined but real enough to be possible.

Sitting up, sheet clutched to my chest, I offer a suggestion.

"Princess Callista of Mizarra." Like Callisto and the star Mizar. Perhaps the connection will offer good luck.

"Where the hell's Mizarra?"

I shrug. "Nowhere, I made it up."

That earns a handsome smile, and I've half a mind to mount him again.

"What's Princess Mizarra doin' in New Orleans?"

"Princess Callista," I correct him, "is in exile. You see, the Merak have invaded her small mountain kingdom."

He teases the edge of my sheet with this finger, considering it a moment. "How do you intend to make these folks believe you're royalty?"

As an innkeeper, I'd seen that the most important guests are often accompanied by large entourages. A lady of status would not travel alone. She would at the very least have a maid or a chaperone attending to her. Perhaps a princess in exile lost her chaperone during her escape. Quite tragically. Captured. Or killed.

Gold certainly speaks the loudest of someone's status. That and an abundance of things. Her luggage should be a porter's worst nightmare—trunks, crates and valises. Racks of gowns and luxury goods.

"Fancy letter might do the trick," Kodiak offers.

Of course. The Astral Society would send letters in advance of their visit, explaining why doctor so-and-so should be treated with the utmost respect and receive the best suite available.

"Yes, Her Highness Princess Callista of Mizarra is traveling abroad under the protection of her family crown. In secret. It is of the utmost importance her presence there not be announced."

He nods in agreement. "Know a fella that could make somethin' like that look real official."

An effervescence bubbles up inside me. This plan seems to be coming together nicely.

Over the next week, we map it all out—from our telegram announcing the Princess's arrival in advance, to our escape plan, down to the local events calendar to pick a date where we'd expect the hotel to be most busy. Kodiak takes care to leave the thievery to him. When I request to visit with my beloved country's precious artifact, I will be just as surprised as their poor clerk that an armed man has taken this opportunity to empty the vault.

When I arrive at the Sherman Hotel New Orleans, I join the end of a long queue snaking through the grand lobby—all gilded trim and high ceilings, with chandeliers dripping crystal like champagne caught mid-fall. Velvet armchairs line the edges, and a massive oil painting of some bewhiskered general looms above the fireplace, judging us all with eternal discontent.

I wait alone, weighed down by gold, sapphires—jewels Kodiak assured me he secured by legal means—and the smothering embrace of silk and velvet, my bodice pinched so tight I feel faint. The heat of the day clings to the marble floors, and sweet tobacco smoke lingers in the air.

At the front desk, a man in linen pleads his case while a flustered gentleman in a waistcoat and spectacles fumbles through papers. I shift my weight, corset biting deeper with each breath.

"My apologies, sir," the clerk stammers. "We seem to have misplaced your luggage. However, I assure you I have our best porters searching for it, and I'm quite confident it has not left the hotel."

The man barks back, his voice loud enough to make several heads turn. The clerk shrinks further, his composure unraveling with each syllable.

I scan the room and catch sight of an elderly watchman leaning against a polished pillar near the entrance, absently jingling his keys, gazing out at the carriages passing along Canal Street. I clear my throat delicately and raise my hand in a subtle wave. He perks up at once, his smile warm, posture stiffening as he approaches slowly.

"What can I do for you, Madame?"

I tilt my chin toward the front desk. "Sir, it seems there may be trouble there. Perhaps you could assist so that this queue might move along?"

He listens for half a moment, frowns, then hurries toward the scene, the brass buttons of his uniform gleaming under the sunlight streaming through the stained-glass transom overhead.

Behind me, porters strain under the weight of trunks filled with carefully selected river rocks, sweat beading along their brows. Crates groan on creaky carts, and racks of velvet gowns —all of which Kodiak promised were paid for—sway with each step.

The line inches forward. I take one elegant step.

"Madame!" a voice rings out, urgent and reverent.

I turn, heart fluttering. A man in formal dress hurries toward me, breathless. "You must be Her Majesty, Princess Callista of Mizarra."

I cast a glance around the glittering lobby. "Shhh," I murmur, leaning close. "You mustn't announce my presence here."

He recoils with theatrical guilt. "Forgive me, Your Highness." He bows deeply, the seams of his coat straining. "Please, Madame, come with me."

We abandon the line of commoners and glide across the marble floors toward the elevator, passing a gilded staircase wrapped in red carpet like a tongue, curling toward a mezzanine of stained-glass windows and heavy drapes.

"Wait," I say, stopping short. "There's a very important item with me. I need to ensure—"

"The artifact, Madame. We've arranged for it to rest secure in our vault."

"Wonderful. It is one of the few heirlooms the Meraki people did not destroy during the war of Cassiopeia," I say, drifting off script. "You see, my great-great-grandpapa commissioned the Bear Throne. Ebony, imported from Madagascar. Inlaid with sapphires. Priceless."

It's as if I've recited scripture. "Goodness, Madame. We are so honored to protect it." His voice lowers. "Forgive me, but... are you traveling alone?"

Footsteps echo behind us. I inhale sharply—planned, but jarring nonetheless. "No, monsieur. I mean...yes. My lady maid was"—I reach for my kerchief and blot away nothing from the corner of my eye—"captured."

"Oh my," he gasps, one hand to his chest. "Shall we send someone to assist with your luggage?"

My stomach tightens. I imagine a porter prying open a trunk to find nothing but stones. "No, thank you. I must learn to carry on alone."

The elevator opens with a soft chime, its golden grate folding aside like a curtain before a royal entrance.

"Very well then," he says. "Please allow me to help you to your suite."

CHAPTER 23

KODIAK

I make it to the Sherman hotel on foot, damn near walking in circles, taking a path twice as long just to keep eyes off me. Sherman informants prowl the alleys, but their own hotel? What kind of fool would cross them then step through their gilded doors?

Turns out, I'm that fool.

Got on my Sunday best—shirt, waistcoat, trousers, derby pulled low. I whistle a tune like I own the place and stroll in under the glare of that damn painting in the lobby—some mean old general staring down from a gold frame big as a coffin. The marble under my boots is polished to a mirror shine. Whole damn lobby looks like the inside of a jewelry box, all velvet chairs and carved columns, every corner reeking of perfume and money.

Place like this, you'd never guess Alice was once a Sherman wife—least not the way they had her slaving in that country inn. I'm starting to think Joseph was the black sheep of the family, and his brother Virgil's the one wearing the trousers. I tip my hat to the watchman half asleep by the pillar and head straight for the elevator—brass gates, slow as honey. Ride it to the top.

Alice left her door open a crack. Inside, she's twisting like she's caught in a snare, hands behind her back.

"Oh, thank goodness. Could you please help me out of this corset?"

"Of course, your majesty."

Hooks, buttons, ribbons—fortress tighter than a vault. I've broken into banks with less trouble. Once I get her loose, she near melts, breathing like she's just remembered how.

After, I haul the trunk into the washroom and dump it quiet, stacking those river rocks in the tub one by one. We gathered 'em ourselves, days back—boots in the mud, laughing like we weren't planning a crime.

We wait for nightfall, when the hustle downstairs dies down. I go first, dressed in black from crown to cuff, hat pulled low, bandana in place. I move quiet, sticking to shadows.

The lobby's different at night—same chandeliers, but now they burn low and gold, casting soft shadows across all that polished stone. Piano drifts in from the parlor, mixed with clinks of glass and low laughter from the bar.

I wedge myself in a stairwell, keeping to the dark, hand on my Colt, knife strapped tight. I pray I don't need either. Not for my sake—for Alice's.

And then she comes.

She don't walk—she glides, floating across that marble like some temptress made of magic. Her satin robe clings to every sinful curve, the slip beneath near see-through, shadows drawing maps of what should stay hidden. Her slippers whisper against the stone, hem swinging high enough to flash pale ankle and a promise of more.

I swallow hard. God help me.

She approaches the front desk like a vision, voice all soft and trembly. "Monsieur, forgive me for troubling you at such an hour."

The night clerk damn near falls over himself. Middle-aged, balding, probably hasn't seen a woman like her outside a dime novel. "Not at all, Madame. How may I assist you?" he asks, all nerves and sweat, Adam's apple bobbing like he swallowed wrong.

Alice lowers her lashes, eyes glistening like she's been crying. "It is only that I cannot sleep. My nerves, you see. My family's treasure is here, under your care, and the thought—" She dabs her cheek with her kerchief, just so. "The thought of it locked away, beyond my reach..."

We'd talked about her being distressed, but I could do without watching the damn flirtation.

"Oh, Madame," the clerk blurts, leaning in closer. Too close. "You mustn't distress yourself. The hotel vault is secure. Nothing could happen here."

She sniffles pretty. "You are kind, monsieur. Truly. But my grandpapa—before the Merak assassinated him—told me to keep it always in sight. And now I am so far from home, with so few comforts. If I might only look upon it, just for a moment, I should rest easier."

The clerk hesitates, fingers twitching atop the counter, sizing her up her like he's weighing more than just hotel policy. Alice presses her kerchief to her chest, eyes big and glistening, voice all sugar and sorrow. He nods.

"Oh, monsieur, you are as generous as starlight on a dark night."

Starlight. That's the signal.

His smile spreads slow, like varnish on pine. "I'd consider it my honor to be of personal assistance, should Your Grace require anything else…later this evening," he says, leaning forward. "Perhaps a nightcap?" He sways back and his tongue wets his lip like he's savoring the thought.

That son of a bitch.

I shift in the shadows, hand tight around my Colt. Blood jumps hot. I slip from the stairwell, keeping low as he fumbles with his keys. Alice trails after him. The sway of her ass in that satin should be punishable by law.

By the time the vault swings open and they're inside, I'm at their backs.

"Evenin', folks," I bark, cocking my pistol in the air.

The clerk jolts pale, mouth open. Alice gasps, clutching her robe shut like a scandalized maiden. "Mercy! Please don't shoot!"

"Do as I say and nobody gets hurt," I rasp. I flick my attention to her robe before adding, "Though that chamber-wear's indecent as sin, lady. You ought to show some modesty."

Her kerchief trembles at her cheek, eyes wide for the clerk's sake, but I catch the twitch at the corner of her mouth.

The vault's lined wall to wall, drawers and steel strongboxes stacked high, shelves loaded with ledgers and pouches. Jackpot.

The man looks back at me, lips quivering, waiting on orders. I point my barrel at him, finger teasing the trigger.

"Open 'em. Start at the top."

His hands shake so bad the keys near spill. He gets one turned, drawer screeching wide, bundles of notes fat and green staring back.

I retrieve a canvas sack from my coat and toss it at his feet. "Empty it in the sack."

He hesitates, jaw working like he might argue.

I press the pistol to his head. "If you're thinkin' on takin' a stand, don't," I growl. "Ain't no glory dyin' over another man's money. Now move."

That seems to motivate him. He shovels fast, bills scattering across the floor, and I ease off some, lest the fool piss himself. Alice presses her kerchief to her cheek. "Please don't hurt him."

I cut her a look. "Suppose you hope to give this clerk a thrill dressed like that in your night-clothes."

He flushes red, near drops the lantern, scrambling for the next drawer. Velvet pouches heavy with coin, gilt-edged stock papers—all of it goes rattling into the sack.

"Hurry up, stupid," I snap. "If you're dilly-dallyin' till the law gets here, ain't nobody comin' and you ain't gonna be alive to greet 'em if they were."

He speeds up, drawers banging, shelves stripping bare one by one. The sack swells fat, clinking with gold, rustling with paper, near to bursting.

I jerk my chin. "Down. On your belly."

He crouches to the floor, hands trembling.

Alice moves to follow.

"Not you," I say, grabbing her by the arm and raising her up. "I may be a mean son-of-a-bitch, but I'm a gentleman. Now get the hell out of here, go on upstairs, and for God's sake, put some damn clothes on. And don't go looking for the law unless you want your little friend here to get a bullet between the eyes. We understand each other?"

Her brows lift. For half a heartbeat, I catch the ghost of a smile before she masks it with a tremble. "Yes, monsieur."

But she lingers, turns back. "Please, monsieur, the Kingdom of Mizarra is at war. If my presence here this evening makes the news, surely the enemy will find me."

The man nods quick, pale as a sheet. "No, Madame. I won't say anything. You were never here. I swear it."

"Thank you," she says, then sweeps out, robe swishing like sin.

I tie the clerk fast, wrists behind him, gag tight between his teeth.

Sack slung heavy over my shoulder, I follow Alice's path back into the dark.

I haul the sack up the stairs, near dragging with the weight of it. By the time I reach her floor, my shirt sticks damp at the back. Alice's door cracks open just as I round the corner in the hall outside. She's already there in her gilded suite, cheeks flushed, robe tied closed.

Inside, the trunk I emptied of rocks sits at the foot of the bed, waiting for our take. I drop the sack in and close the lid. Set my hat on the dresser.

Alice smooths her robe. "That went well."

I give her a stare from hell, raking my fingers through my hair. "You walked out there half dressed."

She blinks, all innocence, fighting that damn smirk again. I close the distance, hands clapping hard to her waist. "Slip's damn near see-through. Huggin' every curve. That bastard's ears turned red as a beet, and I near put a bullet in him for starin'."

Her lips twitch, but she bites it back. "It worked, didn't it?"

"It worked, but you put yourself on display to do it, and that's a line you don't cross without payin' a price."

A flush creeps down her throat. "Kodiak—"

I sit on the bed and haul her across my lap in one motion, robe sliding with a hush against me. Heat from her thighs sears through my trousers.

"You knew what you were doin'—paradin' yourself in front of that man, lettin' him near choke starin' at you."

Her answer comes muffled in the covers. "It was part of the act."

I yank up her slip, baring her pale flesh. One hand covers her mouth, and the other comes down powerful, the crack of it filling the room. She jerks, her wet, muffled cry dying in my palm. The way the sound hits my ears near sounds like pleasure, but I reckon she's just gritting through the pain. Another swat, harder. Satin slides higher, bunching around her middle. "You belong to me, Alice. Not to some clerk watchin' what's mine."

Her hips shift, the heat of her exquisite against my palm, and something bursts wide open inside me. I swing my hand harder. Her moan, sweet and shameless, is unmistakable.

"You like this," I mutter.

"No," she whispers, bashful voice trembling. I bring my hand down again, harder, and I swear that woman purrs.

"Christ almighty," I growl, breath catching. Her words lie, but her body tells the truth. Each swat leaves her shaking, legs parting, body arching like she's begging for more. The feel of her burning for me under discipline meant to humble her nearly undoes me. I reach between her thighs, fingers gliding between her folds, and find her ready for me.

She hums, lifting her hips into my touch.

I tease her, finger barely touching her damp heat. "You're wantin' this," I whisper, half disbelieving, half burning, full-on iron-hard with need. "Damn you, Alice. You wanted me angry."

"Bear. Please."

"Please what?"

My hand cracks down again, harder. She gasps.

"You like me punishin' you," I rasp, each word landing like a brand.

Smack.

"You like me ownin' you."

Smack.

"But that ain't near enough, is it?"

Her sobbing breath is answer enough, but I press, voice hard at her ear.

"You don't just want my hand, lamb. You want to take me so deep you can't think straight—want me fuckin' you so hard your prim little prayers die in your throat."

She whimpers, the sound choked and desperate. "Yes. Please, bear."

I move her from my lap, lifting her into bed. "All fours."

She does as she's told, waiting for me, looking over her shoulder. Slip bunched at her waist, satin straps slid from her shoulders, hair wild, lips parted. Her breasts spill from the top of her slip, nipples tight. I might die if I don't have her now.

I toe off my shoes, unbutton my trousers, and shove 'em down just enough to drive into her with one hard stroke. She cries out—half pain, half pleasure—clutching at the sheets with white-knuckled fists. My jaw grinds, a growl breaking loose from my chest as I claim her.

She arches, whimpering, pushing back to take me deeper. Her body shakes under each thrust, her cries stoking me hotter, till I'm blind with want.

"You're mine," I roar, driving harder. "Say it."

"I'm yours," she sobs.

I slam deeper, forcing the words out of her. The sweet thick of her perfect ass glowing rosy from my punishment, bounces with every swing.

Her head tips back, a cry spilling free, desperate now.

My grip fists in her hair, hauling her head back just so I can see her face—mouth parted, tears streaking her cheeks.

"You don't know what that does to me," I rasp, yanking her closer, hand to her throat. Her back's to my chest when I crush my mouth to hers. It's clumsy, crooked—more teeth and breath than anything, like we'd sooner devour each other than kiss.

I shove her forward, her face pressing into the pillow as I crouch down over her like a beast—feet planted wide, knees bent—using my whole damn body to hammer her soul to mine. The wicked noise, that rhythm of us colliding again and again, of her taking me, filthy as sin. Nothing holy about the way I worship her.

Her body shatters first with an ardent wail, gripping me in waves so fierce I near see stars. I hold on, riding every one until I can't hold back no more. The world narrows to her heat, her voice, the velvet feel of her taking me, and I give in, spilling inside her and claiming her as mine in every way a man can.

My blood roars, possessive and wild. For a moment, I can't move, the rush leaving me in a daze. When I finally ease away, she gasps, thighs pressing tight as if to hold me in. But there it is—my essence trickling from her. I freeze, captivated by a savage hunger.

That's mine.

I haul her up, gathering her against my chest. She's limp, hair wild, lashes wet, lips parted soft. My lamb. My death. I press my mouth to her temple. God help me, I'd burn the world to keep her like this.

I smooth her hair back. "Next time you want a spankin', lamb, just tell me. You ain't gotta rile me half-mad first."

Her lashes flutter, a hint of a smile curling at her mouth. "Where would the fun be in that?"

A laugh breaks out of me, and I squeeze her hip. "I'd put you over my knee again if I didn't think you'd enjoy it so much."

She burrows closer, humming soft against my collar. And I swear, the danger ain't in the law, or the Shermans, or the hangman waiting down in the gallows. The danger's here, in my arms, in how much I need her. Like air, like water. Don't know how I'd go on living without her. The thought of not having Alice by my side feels like death itself. I press a kiss to her hair.

"Christ almighty, woman. I'm so gone on you."

She giggles, but I ain't kidding. "I mean it, lamb. I ain't used to needin' anybody. But I need you. I'd ride through hell if I knew you were waitin' on the other side."

She pulls back, fingertips brushing my jaw. "You need me?" she whispers. "Then don't ever leave me behind, Kodiak. Not for the law. Not for anything."

"Never would." I take her hand. It's a promise, like signing my life away with a kiss to her knuckles. "There ain't a place on God's green earth you could go that I won't follow."

Her eyes shine in the low light—not just soft, but wet—and she don't try to blink it away.

"Then we're agreed," she says, voice a little shaky. She lifts my hand to her lips and kisses it, right over the scar across my knuckles. Like she's signing the same promise I just made.

Right then, I know—whatever comes next, hangman or hellfire, we'll meet it together.

And then she shifts, glancing past me at the trunk sitting

neat at the foot of the bed. The one now fat with the Shermans' fortune. Gold, bonds, jewels, all boxed in their fine leather, not ten feet from where we lie.

"We did it, bear. And tomorrow morning, their own porters will carry it right out for us. Isn't that delicious?"

"Damn right," I mumble against her hair. "Then on to the next."

CHAPTER 24

ALICE

A hard knock jolts me awake.

Kodiak hears it before I do. He is already up, reaching for his pistol, naked as the day he was born. "Ask who it is," he hisses from the threshold between bedroom and washroom. I slip into my night-robe and tie it shut, fingers clumsy.

"Who is it?" I press my ear to the door.

"It's me. Byron. From the front desk."

Mercy me. He has a name.

"At this early hour? What is it you seek?"

"Please, my apologies, Madame. I just spoke to a detective. I would not trouble you were it not urgent."

For pity's sake. I glance at Kodiak in the shadows.

"Hell no," he rasps.

But what's happened? What do the detectives know? Perhaps he has information we might need. My hand goes to the lock. I ought not. And yet. The metal turns under my thumb.

I open the door and Kodiak sighs, retreating back into shadow.

Byron smiles too wide. "Princess," he whispers. "A watchman found me and summoned the police. I told them a great brute forced me at gunpoint to open the vault, then fled with the lot. I never breathed a word of you. Not one."

Relief loosens my chest, though what is the urgent matter he spoke of? "You have been discreet, Mr. Byron. For that, I thank you."

He pushes closer, and I stumble back a step. "I could have spoken your name, and by morning every paper in the city would print it. Yet I held my tongue for you because you're here, all alone. Vulnerable." His fingers brush my sleeve as he steps closer. "Surely you might recognize my devotion."

I draw back, spine stiff. He's here for his reward. To trade his silence for my bed. "You mistake the matter, sir."

He catches at my sleeve, boldness rising. "Only a token," he pleads. "A kiss, for my silence. For all I've suffered this evening on your behalf, you owe me that much."

"Release me at once."

"Princess, please. Just one kiss."

His hands grip my waist, and though he asks for a kiss, his fingers press against the knot of my robe. He forces me back until my legs touch the bed. I jerk my arm free, heat flashing my cheeks. My pulse races, not for me, but for the danger I know lurks in the dark. For the unbridled violence Byron invites upon himself that I'll soon witness.

He presses closer, breath hot at my temple, hands rising to my breasts. "Princess, after all I risked for you. Please, do not be cruel to—"

The door clicks shut behind him. He pauses at the sound.

"I got cruel for you waitin' in this hand," Kodiak growls.

Byron jolts and spins around. Kodiak stands in the gloom, pistol set aside, hunting knife glinting in his fist, broad, naked, and menacing. His chest heaves with quiet rage.

Byron reels back, attention flicking between Kodiak, me, and the door—latch, hallway, escape. "That voice," he croaks. Recognition floods his face pale.

"Evenin', Byron, think the Princess told you to leave her be."

"It *is* you. Good God...you're the outlaw." He turns to face me, the pieces settling together into the puzzle. His brow furrows at me, seemingly betrayed, as though I'd owed him honesty. "Both of you. The detective will know. I'll tell him. I'll—" His gaze skitters down Kodiak's body and snags there. "Y-you're naked."

Kodiak takes a step closer, then another, the knife catching lamplight. His voice drops to a lethal hush. "Puttin' hands on what's mine is the wrong move to end a life on."

He cowers back. "Oh hell." Byron bolts for the door with a ragged shriek.

Kodiak is already moving. He drives a shoulder into Byron's ribs, grabs his legs, lifts, then slams him to the floor. Byron hits hard, the breath jumping out of him. Before he can draw it back, Kodiak is astride him, thighs like iron cable. His manhood hangs heavy as the knife hovers at Byron's throat. The violence and flesh together is a grisly sight, and yet I cannot look away.

"Please," Byron gasps.

"Bear," I beg. "Don't hurt him."

Kodiak doesn't look at me. "Sorry, little lamb, but he dies

here. He laid hands on you and threatened us with the law. That's two sins too many. Say your prayers, boy."

Byron writhes, pinned, mouth gaping. "No! Please! I'll keep your secret. I swear it!"

"I reckon I ought to let you run just to see how far you get," Kodiak says, pressing steel to skin. "But I heard you right the first time. Men who run their mouth to the law don't live long."

"Have mercy!" Byron's voice cracks. His eyes find mine, wild, beseeching. "Please, tell him!"

"She don't answer to you," Kodiak snarls. The knife glides, fast and sure. Crimson wells.

I clap a hand to my mouth and stumble back, bile climbing my throat. "Kodiak, no! Stop, please!"

But it's too late. A wet, terrible sound fills the room. Byron convulses and gurgles, his pleas drowning in blood. It spills over Kodiak's hands and sheets the floor in pools of red. Kodiak stays crouched over the body, chest heaving, knife dripping blood like syrup.

"Sweet Lord above," I whisper, tears hot on my cheeks. "You killed him. You—"

"He laid hands on you," Kodiak says, rising to his feet. "He came up here to collect on his kindness, and had I not been here, he woulda forced you down. He was already dead the moment he stepped through that door."

He wipes the blade across his thigh, streaking himself in the blood of the kill. His chest is slick with sweat, muscles taut, his body still humming with rage. Naked, terrible, smeared in gore. And—God help me—the violence has stirred him, his length not full but swelling, thick and dark. Proof his body had found delight in blood makes me tremble, ashamed.

Have I become wicked as he is, to want him when he

delights in another man's death? To find comfort, even desire, in the violence he commits for me, when in truth I am at the center of it? I matter more to him than mercy, more than another life. I shake my head, shuddering, words tumbling ragged from my lips.

"What have I done? You're...you're a monster," I whisper. Terror grips me and I scream. "You're a monster!"

Kodiak surges up. In one stride he is on me, his bloody hand clamping over my mouth, copper and iron in my nose.

"Quiet," he breathes at my ear, hot and ragged. "You'll bring the whole house down on us."

I tremble in his grip, pulled between horror and the shattering truth that this man, this beast, would murder the world to keep me his.

"Alice," he whispers against my ear, as if to soothe me. "He laid his filthy hands where they don't belong, threatened us both. Far as I'm concerned, that's as good as drawin' iron."

I'm numb.

The clerk's body empties his veins onto the floor, and I fear I've woken in a nightmare.

CHAPTER 25

KODIAK

She thought she loved an outlaw till she saw what an outlaw was really about. It's the only explanation I have for the silence. The distance. Truth is, I feel a fool. Shoulda known better than to believe a soft, pious thing like her wouldn't be horrified by the likes of me.

Hope is a rope to hang yourself, and I'm long gone.

She don't say a word while I tend the mess I made—just curls up in bed crying while I drag the poor bastard to the washroom. Not worth the trouble of hauling his bones out, stirring a ruckus, drawing more attention. Best we leave him for the law to find.

"Come on," I say. "Get dressed. We're goin' now."

Wash water runs red. I scrub, slip back into my gentleman's suit, and scrawl a note.

PRINSESS IS DED.

Figure it'll throw them off. Buy us time, hunting assassins from a kingdom don't exist. Poor desk clerk casualty of a war that never was. I shoulder the bag, coat heavy with gains, and creep down the stairwell, Alice trailing behind like she wants us both to hang. Can't even hiss at her—the whole place echoes—so I stand at the bottom, watching her drift down like a ghost.

Horse and carriage wait in the alley, but my gut says no. My gut ain't been wrong yet. Sun's hid but rising soon. We need distance, and Alice's warning rattles me: only so many roads out of New Orleans. Sherman's men will be watching them all, sure as the vault was robbed. Virgil will see the wire by afternoon and know it was me. I almost laugh thinking on his face. But we got to vanish, not trot the open country in a carriage they might have seen.

Then the answer comes—a screech and a bellow, like a cow caught in a church organ. Lanterns glow yonder at the wharf. A ship.

That's it.

"Don't go nowhere," I say, dropping our haul at her feet. "I'll be right back."

She don't look, just folds her arms. I got no time for pouting. This was her idea anyhow, and I'm the one keeping us alive. Had she not come down half-naked, maybe the bastard wouldn't of thought he'd be getting lucky.

I run back up, grabbing luggage, dumping stones out on the floor. Patting Byron's pockets, I find a pocket watch, a chewed pencil, and a few coins. I take them and head back down. Alice stands in the street looking hollow, arms crossed, treasure at her feet. Ain't no one around 'cept gulls and a roaming cat.

I split the haul between two bags, cinch them tight.

"Come on," I call.

She don't answer. Just follows, broke inside.

Seems she liked a taste of danger, a rough word, a hand on a pistol. But blood's too ugly. Too real. Naive little thing. Don't know nothing 'bout honor—the only thing worth a damn to an outlaw. She don't see how that boy crossed every line 'cept spitting in my face. Out here, the weak don't last. A man who don't demand respect won't never know peace, won't never hold nothing safe, 'less he's willing to die for it.

"Look alive, Alice," I say, quickening pace toward the wharf, half a mile south. Dawn paints the sky. In the faint light, the gangplank shows, crew working at the landing.

We pass a shed with a placard:

MORGAN LINE — GALVESTON, SABINE, AND INTERMEDIATE PORTS

Texas.

At the gangway, a purser waits with a ledger open. "Name for the book?"

"Byron," I say. "William Byron, and my wife, Mary."

"Saloon or bunk? Bunk's cheaper. Meals with saloon only."

"Saloon," I say, counting my coins. "Private." I pull a double eagle and lay it down.

The purser bites it. My jaw tightens. "I look like a cheat to you?"

He glances at the dented rim. "Company policy," he says, tearing a ticket, scrawling the dead man's name, handing me the stub. "Steward'll show you. Mind the step."

I pocket the ticket and step aboard.

CHAPTER 26

ALICE

The steamer line's "first class" is no bigger than a closet, a berth chained to the wall made up in white sheets, with iron bars along the side to keep a body from rolling out.

The sun rises as we depart, a fire burning over land that follows though the shore shrinks away. It will be two days to Galveston, and while I am relieved to put miles between me and the site of my worst sin yet—revenge, robbery, a life taken —the distance has not unencumbered my soul. My stomach sours, though I cannot say if it is the gulf waters or the weight of my sin.

I have never ridden a steamship before, nor any ship at all. A farm girl from Ohio, I have scarcely seen a lake, much less the boundless blue stretching in every direction off the deck's edge. My only escape from Kodiak is to idle along the first-class promenade, and after finding our room, I do just that.

A gong sounds, announcing breakfast. The saloon fills with the smell of coffee, bacon, and biscuits. Long tables draped in white cloth stand ready, chairs fixed to the floor and upholstered in damask brocade of red and gold. I am admiring the fabric when a firm grip seizes my arm.

"You ain't dinin' alone, and you damn sure ain't dinin' with nobody else."

Kodiak pulls me to a pair of seats at the far end of a table. I stand behind my chair, clutching its carved back like a cat clinging to the mouth of a well. His glare holds none of the warmth it once had.

"Sit," he growls.

With a sigh, I turn the chair on its swivel and sink into it, folding my hands on the table, refusing to acknowledge his presence. Perhaps I will let my plate go untouched from here to Galveston. Perhaps I will never eat again.

An older couple lingers nearby. With the room filling, they claim the remaining seats, the woman beside Kodiak and the gentleman beside me.

A steward arrives with a tray, setting cups before us, pouring steaming coffee into china. Another follows with baskets of biscuits and plates of bacon, ham and eggs, laying them out with haste. The smell turns my stomach, though my mouth waters all the same.

"Good morning," the man says. "Are you bound for Sabine?"

"Galveston," Kodiak replies, his gentleman's mask firmly in place.

"Splendid," the man says. "I'm Heathcliff Taft, and this is my wife, Desdemona."

"My father founded a theatre company," she beams. "Lovely to make your acquaintance."

Kodiak clears his throat. "You as well. I am William Byron, and this is my wife, Mary."

I tighten my jaw, breathing steady through my nose. The old woman studies me as if to read my secrets.

"Forgive her quiet," Kodiak continues smoothly, "Mary has been in delicate health. We are traveling to Galveston to consult a physician who specializes in nervous disorders. The change of air, it is hoped, will do her good."

"Oh dear," Mrs. Taft says, lifting a hand to her lips. "How dreadful. Our son has troubles of his own. His wife passed not three months ago, delivering their youngest. We are bound for Sabine to help him with the children."

Mr. Taft nods gravely. "Three boys, all under ten. He has his hands full now. We mean to do what we can. No child should grow up without a mother's care."

Kodiak's fork stills where it hovers above his plate. His jaw works once, his eyes dropping to the table. He clears his throat roughly. "Cruel world. No sense in it." He forces a thin smile and shifts the subject, asking after the weather on the coast.

The Tafts follow politely, though Desdemona lingers on me as if she hears words I have not spoken. I sit stiff, heat prickling my cheeks. To feign sorrow so neatly, to mimic grief for strangers' approval—damn him. If they clap for his performance, let them. I know better.

Mrs. Taft tilts her head, concern knitting her brow. "My dear, you've not touched a thing. You're far too thin, you must eat."

My fork lies idle beside the plate. I feel the heat rise in my cheeks but keep my hands folded tight.

Kodiak doesn't so much as look at me. He lifts his cup, his voice smooth as ever. "Her appetite comes and goes. Nothing to be done but wait it out."

Mrs. Taft sighs, dabbing her lips with a napkin. "The sea air may do wonders yet."

His words are silk to them, but to me they're a knife—his way of saying, fine, don't eat. Calling my bluff before strangers. If I take a bite now, I lose. If I don't, I sit starving as they all dine. I stare at the damask cloth until the red and gold blur together, my hunger twisting like a kite taken by a strong wind inside me. He doesn't care if I waste away. Perhaps he would rather I did.

By evening, the ship rocks steady beneath us, lanterns swaying in the narrow passage outside our cabin. The berth creaks as I sit with arms folded, stomach hollow, head aching from hunger and pride.

Kodiak leans against the wall, studying a map of Galveston. My stomach groans. He smirks. That's my last straw.

"I suppose my hunger amuses you. You'd have me starve."

He doesn't look at me, instead returning to whatever he was doing with the map. "That was your choice."

"How could you eat? How can you live with yourself having not a day ago relished in a man's blood?"

"Ate well. Food's delicious, thanks for askin'."

My lips flatten and my fists tighten. "Of course. Because you are a monster. Have you no conscience?"

He shakes his head wearily and sighs.

I'm tired of being silent. I raise my chin. "Of course you do not. What a silly question. You are a hollow mask. Soulless. Shameless. You put on an accent, a persona, like an ordinary man tries on a coat. You feign emotion. Even that little act at breakfast, voice breaking—as if you were capable of feeling anything at all. You may have fooled them, but not me."

He squeezes the map, crushing it into a ball in anger. The paper crumples in his fist, veins bulging in his forearm. He stares at me, chest heaving. For a moment, I see something raw in his expression—shame, sorrow, I cannot tell—but then it hardens into ice.

"You think I ain't got feelings?" he rasps. "World beat the softness outta me when I was a boy. What's left is what you see. A man who survives and protects what's his."

My throat tightens. And then I hear them again—their voices from the breakfast table. Three boys, all under ten. No child should grow up without a mother's care. Their son's wife, dead in childbirth. The children she left behind. That was what drew the flicker from Kodiak, what cracked his mask.

Perhaps it wasn't a lie.

"Felt somethin' for you, and now I feel a goddamn fool. Thought you were sweet. Gentle. Pure goodness through and through. But you ain't. You're a brat. An ungrateful one at that." His eyes flash, wild and wounded. "You sit there callin' me a monster, when the only monster in that room was the bastard you let in. You think he came up with his hat in his hand? You think he'd have left without takin' what he wanted? I saw it in him. I know men. I know that look. He wasn't leavin' empty-handed."

He jabs a finger at me, words spitting like lye. "And I put him in the ground for it. For you. For us. And what do I get? Not gratitude. Just you starvin' yourself and callin' me a devil." The paper tears in his fist, and he throws the shredded ball aside. With that, he storms out, slamming the door behind him, leaving me to sit with the blister of his words.

Perhaps he's right, and I judged him too harshly.

Perhaps he spared me a worse fate.

Though he must know killing was a gruesome act to witness. How can I bless the hands that so easily spilt blood?

And yet, I sail under a ticket scrawled in a dead man's

name nevertheless. I am just as damned as Kodiak, and yet, I offered him no grace. Worse, I was cruel.

I must make it right.

CHAPTER 27

KODIAK

Nobody's ever talked to me like that and lived to tell it. I'm a bull, seeing red, charging straight to the saloon. Ain't no proper saloon neither, but a first-class joint—no arguing, no fighting, just men with their brandy and the air thick with cigar smoke. Ain't half bad, 'less you're looking for trouble. Tonight, I'm hiding from it.

If I'd stayed in that cabin with that ungrateful brat, I'd have hurt her, and God knows I couldn't live with myself if I did. If nothing else, I'm a man of my word. I swore I'd protect her— even if that means protecting her from me.

What happened to that angel who fussed over me? Tender hands, soft voice. Now it's nothing but complaints. Guess I shielded her too well. All I ever been is good to that woman, and she's got the damn gall to call me a monster. Say I don't feel nothing.

I know what I felt when that son of a bitch laid hands on

her—pure rage. Fact I gave him a chance to square things with God 'fore I cut him ear to ear was a mercy he didn't deserve.

I belly up to the bar, order a whiskey neat. Ain't five minutes past with me sipping slow 'fore I hear it: "Mr. Byron."

Damn near ignore it till I realize it was meant for me. Turn, find Taft sitting at a table with a few other men. I lift my glass, give him a nod, and face the bar again. Sometimes a man just wants to drink alone.

Truth is, that's the way I prefer to drink. Alone. And it ain't no wonder. World's gone soft. Men hide behind the law like a mother's skirts. Used to be you stood your own ground, settled your own scores. Now they whimper at a curse word, running to the law like babies. A man like me can't even lay low no more. Now, some clerk taps a key in Kansas, and every badge from here to Texas knows my name. Shit just keeps getting worse. Yet, here I am, wishing on a star, hoping for a blessing like a damn fool.

Bottom of the glass comes quick. Then another. Then another, till the smoke thins and Taft's crowd starts drifting out, laughter trailing after them, all rosy-cheeked from port wine and parlor talk.

"Mr. Byron," Taft calls again. He's on his feet now, standing beside me, hand clapping my shoulder. "You should've joined us. We were playing whist, singing a bit. Even tried a hymn or two."

He's jawing on, but I ain't hearing it. My attention's on the bastard lingering by the door, shaking hands, smiling polite, uniform cut neat as a banker's.

Hired gun.

Pinkerton.

My heart kicks hard against my ribs. That's a wolf sniffing for blood.

I force myself back to Taft, smoothing my face, settling my voice into that false civility I wore at breakfast, though my tongue's a little heavier now than it was then. "Cards and hymnals?" I say, trying on a chuckle as if I wouldn't rather sit on my spurs than spend an evening singing hymns with them. "Sir, I'm afraid I'd spoil the harmony."

Taft laughs, squeezes my shoulder like we're old friends. "Nonsense, Mr. Byron. You'd have fit right in."

I raise my glass, tip it polite, every inch the man I ain't, while inside I'm coiling tight as a spring. All the while, that Pinkerton's focus sweeps the room again, and I feel him stop on me. Turns my blood to ice.

One of the downsides to being built like me is I can't vanish. I could be wild haired and dusty from the trail, or dressed polite, don't matter. I stick out same as a black bear in church. That Pinkerton's studying me like he's already matched my face to a poster. Pinkertons don't let go once they catch a scent. They'll trail you 'cross three states if they need to. And I ain't some small-time gambling cheat they'd pass by. No, I'm the kind they'd dream of catching.

"Another round?" Taft asks, flagging the barkeep.

"Kind of you," I say, laying the drawl on, "but I'll see myself retired. Early breakfast, you know."

"Ah yes, yes." He pats my shoulder again, like he owns me. "Discipline. A fine trait in a man."

Discipline, hell. Takes all I got to walk slow, calm, when my blood's pounding to bolt. I nod polite, drain the dregs of my whiskey, and set the glass down careful. My hand don't shake, though I can feel the tremor in my bones.

As I step away, I can feel the Pinkerton's scrutiny hook me again, lingering long enough to set my teeth on edge. I don't meet it. Just tip my head, gentlemanly as can be, and stroll out quiet, same as any other man full of whiskey and weary of company.

The hallway's cooler, quieter, though my pulse don't settle. I walk steady, making sure no one's following. Each door I pass, I expect to hear boots behind me, feel a hand on my shoulder, a voice calling me out.

But none comes.

At last I reach our cabin. Hand on the latch, I glance back once more. Hall's empty. I slip inside. Alice sits up when I ease through the door, lamplight catching her hair loose around her shoulders.

"Where have you—"

I shut the door soft, lift a hand to cut her short. "Not now." My voice comes out low, rougher than I mean, but my chest's hammering like I ran a mile.

She studies me, cautious. "What happened?"

I cross the cabin, set my hat on the peg, blood running hot. "Nothin'," I lie. "Just had a drink."

Her brow furrows. "You've had more than one."

"Don't start." I pinch the bridge of my nose, trying to will the tightness out of my chest. "Place was thick with men laughin', singin'. I weren't fit for it."

"Then why go?" she asks.

"Why stay here where I ain't wanted?"

She don't flinch, though her hands knot in her skirts.

The ship's timbers creak, water slaps the hull. Finally, I drag a chair close to the bunk, drop into it heavy, elbows on my knees, head bowed. Her hand rests on my neck, warm and steady. For a breath, it quiets the storm inside me.

I look up at her. She tilts her head, studying me. "You look tired," she says. Then, after a pause, "Do you mean to wash before bed?"

I drag a hand over my face, shake my head slow. "Ain't thought on it."

Her lips curve the faintest bit. "Then let me think on it for you." She rises, moves toward the basin. She freshens the cloth, wrings it, then turns back to me. "You'll need to take that off," she says, nodding at my shirt.

I grunt, but I don't argue. Fingers work at the buttons, my hands clumsy with whiskey and nerves. She steps close, brushing mine aside, finishing the job herself. Each button slips free under her touch till the shirt hangs loose, sliding off my shoulders. She lays it over the chair back, neat as can be.

She works the cloth slow over my neck and ears, gentle like she's tending to a pup or something precious. It'd make me sick if it didn't feel so fine.

"Always fussin'," I mutter. Though my voice is rough, ain't no bite in it. She works down across my chest, over the scars and dirt, rinsing and wringing, coming back again. Each pass slower than it needs to be, her breath soft.

By the time she drags the cloth low over my torso, lingering at the waist of my trousers, she asks gently, "Do you want me to stop?"

Hell. I couldn't say yes if my soul depended on it.

I lean back in the chair, chest heaving. "Go on, then."

She works the button loose, then the next, drawing the fabric open with careful fingers. The trousers slide down enough for her to reach me proper. She takes up the rag again, freshens it in the basin, and kneels at my side. Starts washing me low, thighs first, then hips. Then she slides higher, to the root of me, wrapping me gently in that warm cloth like it's part of her duty.

I'm already standing hard. Every pass lingers longer than it ought, the rag stroking up and down my length, soap and water slick between us. She keeps her head down like she's intent on the work, but her hand's steady, and it ain't no mistake what she's doing.

A broken groan rumbles out of me. I settle back in the chair, jaw tight, fighting to breathe as she strokes me. She pauses only to rinse the rag, wringing it clean, then wipes me careful, clearing away the suds. No hurry in her, no shame neither, just that calm, dutiful touch.

And then the rag slips from her fingers, falling back in the basin with a splash. She stays kneeling, both hands on me now. Her eyes' lift at last, steady on mine, and before I can draw breath, her mouth closes over me.

Warmth seizes me the instant her lips close over the head, tongue circling like she means to taste every bit. My whole body jerks, a curse torn out low. "Christ."

She takes me slow, careful, sinking inch by inch, her lips stretched tight around me, every nerve burning. The room narrows, and there's only the wet pull of her mouth, the way her tongue presses against the underside.

I grip the chair arms hard, fighting the urge to seize her hair and drive myself deep. My hips twitch anyway, but she don't flinch, just hums low in her throat, and the vibration near makes me whimper.

Her hands keep working what her mouth can't take, stroking the rest of me steady and firm. She pulls back, breathing soft through her nose, then sinks down again, taking more this time, her throat tight and hot round me.

"You'll finish me fast if you keep lookin' at me like that," I rasp.

She don't ease off. Every time she pulls back, it's only to sink deeper, her lips sliding lower, till I'm damn near buried. Her hand grips the base, stroking the length in time with her mouth, each pass slicker, harder, till I'm cussing under my breath.

"God almighty," I snarl, my hand shooting to her hair, rough, holding her steady. My hips jerk, driving me deeper, but she takes it, humming low, eyes locked on mine like she wants to see every damn second.

The obscene sound of it, breathy and slick, fills the cabin, drowning out the creak of the timbers. My thighs quake, blood roaring in my ears, every muscle strung tight enough to snap.

"Alice," I grind out, voice ragged, "I'm close."

But she don't stop. She works me harder, faster, and the fire rips through me sudden and violent. A groan tears from my chest, guttural, raw, as I spill into her mouth, pulsing hard against her tongue. My body bucks, shuddering, and I hold her there, rough hand tangled in her hair.

When it's done, I slump back in the chair, chest heaving, sweat running down my temples. She pulls off slow, lips glistening, and wipes her mouth with the back of her hand. Rising smooth, not a word passes between us, but I reckon this was some kind of apology.

If this is how she says she's sorry, hell, I hope she keeps finding reasons to cross me.

She dresses for bed in silence, the room warm with lamplight, and we climb in close. The thought of that Pinkerton slips clean out of my head. The law can hunt tomorrow.

CHAPTER 28

ALICE

"Bear?" I whisper. We're pressed close in the narrow bunk, my back to his chest, the iron rail keeping us tucked together. The heat of his body envelopes me and soothes every raw nerve that had been frayed between Ohio and this ship. Though, there was that look. Kodiak's momentary pause of barely contained emotion. I had meant to ask about it before he stormed out, but the question lingered.

"Yes, angel?"

"The Tafts. What they said at breakfast about children growing up without a mother's love. It seemed to trouble you."

He exhales deeply, weariness in the sound. "Why'd you have to bring that up now?"

I roll to face him, the lamplight faint against his handsome features, the shadow of his beard making his cheek rough. "Because I wish to know you. Truly."

He makes a gruff sound. "Ain't nothin' to tell. What do you want me to say?"

"What was your life like? As a boy?"

He shrugs and offers a clipped, "I was a boy, now I ain't."

"Kodiak, please." I soften my tone, careful but insistent. "Didn't you have family? Randolph, that is your true name, is it not?"

The name. I had heard it before: Randolph, an old Virginian family. Tobacco planters and politicians. A dynasty that can be traced back to the founding fathers.

"Yeah, so what?"

"You are from Virginia, then?"

"Yeah, but it ain't what you think. I'm from a broke line. A line of drunks and gamblers who squandered away their fortunes and good name." He lets out a humorless chuckle. "Funny thing, though. All them years sittin' at my old man's table, hearin' him rant about 'the Randolph name' while he pissed it away...I picked up more'n I knew. How to hold a fork. How to smile polite and talk slick."

It strikes me; the gentleman's act he sometimes wears is not a disguise at all, but an inheritance he despises.

"And your mother?" I ask gently.

"Died birthin' me."

"I am so sorry."

He shrugs, as though sympathy is wasted on him. "Never met her." His arm shifts beneath me, restless. "Why you diggin' up the past?"

"Because I want to understand you," I answer simply.

He goes still, his expression dark and distant. "My old man, he weren't just a drunk. He was cruel. Used to tell me I'd killed her, my ma. Said I come into this world cursin' it. And I believed him. Every damn word."

My hand reaches for his, but he does not return the grasp.

"When I was thirteen," he continues, flat and unflinching, "he put a pistol in his mouth and pulled the trigger."

My throat tightens. I can scarcely breathe.

"His people wrote after. Said they'd take me in." He snorts with disgust. "Sit me at their table, feed me on pity while they whispered I was bad blood. I weren't about to bow my head for that. I'd sooner starve on my own terms."

"What did you do?" I ask softly.

"Walked away. Left it all behind."

The silence between is broken only by the creaks and groans of the ship.

I lay my palm against his chest, feel his heart thundering beneath. "You did not deserve such a burden," I whisper.

He lets out a mirthless laugh. "Deserve got nothin' to do with it."

I watch him in the dim light, struck by the contradiction: a man who can sit polished before strangers, all manners and bearing, yet carry such darkness inside. The mask is not counterfeit but inherited, a legacy of gentility calloused into armor.

"There's somethin' I gotta tell you," he says, his serious expression making my pulse hitch.

"What is it?"

"I seen a Pinkerton in the saloon. Pretty sure he saw me too."

"A Pinkerton?" My breath catches. Dear God.

His voice goes cold. "I'll handle it."

I know what that means: violence, blood, an end I cannot stop. My mind whirls. We are on a ship. There's nowhere to run. If that man goes straight to the captain, or to the purser, a single word from him and every officer will be set on us. They can lock cabins, hold us at port, send a telegraph ahead. In hours—less if he hurries—men in authority will be waiting at the dock.

No one knows us by name. Not our real names. To all aboard, I am Mrs. Byron. But perhaps...

If all of his crimes are known, then it's possible the Pinkerton believes me a hostage. An unfortunate woman found in the company of an outlaw. That is the tale he might accept readily. A frightened lady, begging for rescue, will lower some cautions and might draw the Pinkerton into letting his guard down. Might he tell a victim where he lodges? Where he intends to make his next inquiries? Or at least show himself moving toward the captain's office?

"Kodiak," I say. "If he's seen you and does not yet speak to the captain, we must keep him from having the chance. He can put men to watch every exit before dawn. He can send word ashore. We cannot let him do that."

"I know. I said I'll handle it."

"How?"

He snorts. "I was thinkin' on it when I got back, but then you went and scrambled up my brain. I ain't exactly worked it all out yet."

"What if I speak to him?"

"And what, beg?"

"No," I say. "Well...in a sense, maybe. As far as the authorities are concerned, I've been kidnapped."

He nods, his eyes narrowing.

"What if I approached him, asked to speak in private. Perhaps he'd lead me to his cabin, or some other private place where you could follow undetected."

For a moment he only studies me, pensive. "Lamb, you know damn well when I say I'll handle it, I don't mean askin' nice."

A pit opens in my belly. "I know."

"First thing—we find out if he's alone. Pinkertons travel in pairs more often than not. You'll know 'em dressed fancy, flash of a tin badge on a coat. But more than anything, they're always watchin'. If one goes missin' while another's aboard, best believe no soul leaves this boat till they got answers."

I nod, dread coiling in my chest. Oh God. How many dead men will we leave in our wake?

"Problem is," he says, jaw tight, "I don't want to give him a chance to spot me again and confirm his suspicions. I can't leave this room till we got a plan firmed up."

Just like that, the reality clicks into place.

"So I'll need to investigate on my own?"

"Afraid so, sugarplum."

I press my lips together, trying to contain the shake in my chest. They could take him from me—drag him in chains, hang him for everything he's done. I'd never again feel the warmth of his touch, the shelter of his arms. If stepping into danger is the price to keep him free, then I will pay it. Without hesitation.

In the morning, I dress for breakfast while Kodiak stays behind, laid out in our bunk, watching me. We're set to reach land today—God willing. My job is simple: make sure we get off this ship together. And free.

I'm nearly at the door when he stops me, pulling me back, his hands resting at my waist.

"Whatever happens," he murmurs, "you're my greatest adventure of all."

It stabs me right in the heart and twists. I can't breathe.

"Why would you say such a thing?" I whisper, shoving him gently, a sting rising.

"Because I still can."

I draw in a breath and hold it, then let it out slow.

"It's goin' to be all right, lamb," he says, his hands gliding down my arms. He leans in, presses his mouth to mine, and I savor his taste.

Lord above, help me—I've lost all sense of up and down, right and wrong, for loving this man. But no one, not in all my life, has ever looked after me the way he does. No one has ever fought to keep me safe, no matter the cost. Though he is brutish and brash, he is mine—and I am his.

If we're truly bound by divine design, then surely all will be well.

I step back and smooth my skirts. It is simply breakfast. Perhaps this Pinkerton never noticed Kodiak after all. Perhaps it was only paranoia.

"Wait," he says. He crouches beside the bag, rifles through it, and rises with the hunting knife in hand. "Take this."

The knife. The one he used to kill the hotel clerk, but now in a leather sheath.

"Why are you giving me this?"

"In case you need it. I pray you don't."

"You pray?"

"For you, yes, I do."

I stare at it—dark-bladed, bone-handled, pregnant with the memory of the man he killed with it. It's too big for a pocket, too brutal for subtlety.

I lift my blouse and reach for a stocking from the trunk. He doesn't look away, and I don't ask him to.

"Tie it tight," he says.

I loop the fabric around my ribs and knot it twice, anchoring the knife so it rests along my side. When I lower my blouse, I feel it there with every breath. It presses cold against my skin, an unforgiving weight. A reminder.

Kodiak reaches for me one last time, his fingertips brushing my wrist like he's memorizing the shape of me. There's no jest in him now, no shield of bravado.

"Whatever happens out there," he says, "you come back. That's the only thing I care about. You hear me?"

I nod, not sure I can speak. My throat is too tight. My body too aware of the blade at my side, the finality in this goodbye, the storm waiting just past the dining room doors.

I turn toward the door, hand on the latch. The ship sways gently beneath my feet as I step into the corridor. I do not look back.

The dining room bustles loud as ever, first-class passengers laughing with their new shipboard acquaintances. I, however, have no interest in chatter. I skim the room, searching. Kodiak had described him—a red vest, a matching tie—but he's nowhere in sight.

I hover near the doorway, unwilling to sit. The room presses in: the scrape of cutlery, the clink of porcelain, the mingling smells of coffee and fried ham.

"Mrs. Byron," a voice chimes.

Mrs. Taft sweeps toward me in all her silks and pearls, smiling as though we were fast friends. Her gloved hand touches my arm. "Where is your darling husband?"

"He's not feeling well," I say, careful, cautious.

Mrs. Taft's face brightens with surprise. "Why, how splendid to hear you speak at last! Only yesterday, your husband said you were stricken with nerves. And yet here you are, so composed. How well you seem today."

I force a smile, though my throat is tight. "Yes...much improved."

"Oh, but how dreadful for him," she goes on, slipping her hand through my arm. "You mustn't sit alone. Come, join us." And there he is. Vest. Tie. Glinting badge. Sitting beside Mr. Taft, as if the whole arrangement had been staged. As if he'd been waiting for me.

A chill grips my spine as I lower myself beside Mrs. Taft.

Mr. Taft beams. "Good morning, my dear. Have you met Mr. Pennington?"

"I haven't had the pleasure."

Mr. Taft seems just as gleefully surprised to hear me speak.

"Good morning," Pennington says, his expression polite, unreadable.

Mrs. Taft fans herself. "Mr. Pennington is a detective. How thrilling to have him aboard with us."

I swallow hard. "Thrilling indeed. What sort of cases do you handle, Mr. Pennington?"

"All manner of criminals. Often men who have taken what isn't theirs," he replies.

My throat tightens, but I laugh lightly, as if he has told a clever jest. Harmless, Alice. Be harmless. A silly wife with no notion of the world beyond her teacup.

"My husband would be delighted to hear your stories," I say smoothly, "though he is sadly confined to our cabin this morning."

Pennington does not give anything away. "I should very much like to meet him."

My blood runs cold. Every word I speak binds me tighter to Kodiak's lie. To play the dutiful wife is to shield him, but to shield him is to damn myself beside him. This was not how I'd imagined this playing out.

Pennington studies me as if searching for a lie. "And where is home, Mrs. Byron?"

"Ohio," I say smoothly. "Cincinnati."

"Ah. A fine city." He sets down his cup. "And yet you boarded at New Orleans?"

I force a smile. "We've family there. My husband wished for me to meet them."

His expression remains mild, but his eyes sharpen. "And how long have you and Mr. Byron been married?"

"Three years," I say, the lie slipping out silky smooth. My hands tremble beneath the table.

"Three years." He repeats it softly, as though testing the words.

Mr. Taft chuckles, dabbing his lips with a napkin. "Your husband is a large fellow, quite a presence. Why, Mr. Pennington here was asking after him only yesterday."

My fork slips against the china, the scrape far too loud in my ears. I school my face into a polite smile, though my pulse is a drumbeat in my throat.

Pennington inclines his head. "Yes. Hard to miss a man like him on a vessel like this." He leans back in his chair. "What line of business is he in, Mrs. Byron?"

The room seems to hush around me. Every path feels dangerous—too plain, too evasive. My palms sweat against the napkin in my lap.

"He manages accounts," I say. "Trade matters. Boring things, I fear."

Mr. Taft chuckles. "Ah, numbers. Not so boring when fortunes are at stake."

I set the cup down. "And you, Mr. Pennington? You must forgive me; I've done all the talking. What brings a detective aboard this ship?"

His eyes narrow a fraction, though his smile holds. "My business is varied. Merchants. Banks. Rail men."

"You must travel constantly. Do you have family aboard, or are you alone in your work?"

His pause is slight, but I catch it. "Why do you ask? Do I seem in need of company?"

Mr. and Mrs. Taft laugh, delighted, but my stomach knots. He hasn't answered at all. Only reminded me that he sees through me.

I fold my napkin in my lap, unfold it, fold it again, fighting to steady my hands. "Forgive me," I say with a small laugh, feigned and fragile. "I suppose I was only making conversation."

"Of course. Idle talk helps the voyage along," he says. His spoon taps once against the rim of his cup. A delicate sound, though it makes me flinch. "And what does Mr. Byron call his business? You say he manages accounts. With which firm?"

The air drains from my lungs. "With several. He is... independent."

"Ah," Pennington says softly, as though the answer amuses him. "Independent. Then he must be quite capable with numbers. I wonder, did he study for it? At a university perhaps?"

"No. His father instructed him."

"Indeed?" His eyes sharpen.

The room sways, the chatter of the dining hall fading to a dull roar. I want to flee, but Mrs. Taft's hand rests lightly on my arm, pinning me in place as surely as a shackle.

She dabs her lips with her napkin. "Mr. Pennington, you do ask the most questions. Like a true detective at his work, never content until every fact is laid bare."

Mr. Taft joins her with a genial chuckle. "Yes, sir, one might think you were interrogating the poor lady."

Pennington's smile doesn't waver. He turns his cup slowly between his fingers. "One never knows who they may meet, Mr. Taft. Or what small detail might serve to turn over a stone in some larger matter. Every conversation can yield a clue, if one listens closely." His gaze fixes on me. "For instance, perhaps you recall, Mrs. Byron, a case that made the Ohio papers. A murder and a kidnapping at a roadside inn."

The room spins. The din of cutlery and laughter fades to nothing. My arms go numb, blood rushing in my ears. He knows. God help me, he knows. Or suspects enough that it will not be long before suspicion becomes certainty.

I manage a smile, brittle and weak. "I'm afraid I do not keep up with such dreadful things."

"Of course not," he says softly, as though humoring me. The weight of his stare tells me otherwise.

I lower my head. My plate is blurred, unrecognizable. All I can think is that he will not let us walk free from this ship. Desperate to move, to flee, I force myself calm. A hasty departure would mark me worse than any lie I have told.

Mrs. Taft prattles on about the ship's arrival, about Galveston's promenades, about the weather. God bless her chatter for filling the silence I cannot.

But Pennington is steady as a hunter. His cup sits untouched now, his hands folded as he analyzes my every move. My body trembles, and I struggle to steady it. If I stay, I will break. If I leave too suddenly, he will follow. I need a reason.

I dab my lips with the napkin and force a small, apologetic smile. "You must excuse me. The room is rather warm."

Mrs. Taft squeezes my hand. "Of course, my dear. Do go and rest. I shall send a tray up for your husband."

"Thank you," I say. My legs are heavy as lead as I push back my chair. I do not look back, but I feel him rise. The weight of his gaze clings to me like a shadow.

I walk with measured steps toward the door, every muscle screaming to run. The roar of the dining hall fades as I pass through the doors into the open corridor.

"Mrs. Byron."

His voice is low, only for me. Not polite now, not conversational. A summons.

I turn to find him standing a few paces off, badge glinting in the daylight.

"A word, if you please."

A scream claws at my throat, but I choke it down. To run, to refuse, would damn me on the spot. Kodiak waits in our cabin—I ache to bolt to him—but instead I lower my head, my voice calm though my insides quake. "Of course."

He leads me down the aft passage, his manner courtly, almost mocking. A narrow door opens into a writing room, empty and cool. When it shuts behind us, the hum of voices dies away. We are alone.

I turn to face him, pulse hammering. "What is it you want of me, Mr. Pennington?"

His gaze sharpens. "Truth, Mrs. Byron. Only truth."

My fingers knot together, white at the knuckles. "And what truth is that?"

He studies me, head slightly tilted, as though measuring how quickly I'll break. "That your husband is not the man you claim. That you are not the wife you pretend to be."

The dam bursts. Tears spill hot down my cheeks, and I bury my face in my hands. "I-I was frightened," I stammer, sobs breaking through. "Ashamed. I couldn't cause a scene in front of the Tafts. They're such kind people—Mrs. Taft especially—and I didn't want her to see…"

His expression shifts, a shade of relief crossing it. "So. You *are* Alice Sherman."

I clutch the back of a chair. "How do you know? How can you possibly know who I am?"

His mouth hardens. "Your kidnapping has been shouted across every Pinkerton office between Cincinnati and New Orleans. The Shermans want you home."

My stomach twists. To them I was nothing but a farmer's daughter. Chattel. And now they cry for me only because it suits their honor.

Pennington presses on, relentless. "As for the man you call your husband—Archibald Randolph. Known as Kodiak. He is a thief, a murderer, a marauder of trains and homes alike. There are families who will never sleep sound again because of him. There is blood on his hands in three states. He will hang," Pennington says flatly. "On that you may depend. And you, Mrs. Sherman, you will be returned to Ohio. Where your family waits for you."

"Then…you mean to take him before we make land?"

"When the time is right," he says evenly. "If he is cornered too soon, others may be harmed. I will go speak with the captain now. He'll see to it no one leaves this ship until the outlaw is in custody. He will be brought ashore in irons."

The words make my stomach lurch. Ashore. In irons. Galveston will not be freedom but a noose. I let my voice tremble, feeding his certainty that I am weak. "And what of me?"

"You need not fear," Pennington replies, softer now, almost

reassuring. "The moment you are free of him, your ordeal will be over. You will be restored to your people."

Those are not my people. The Sherman's were never my people. Not Joseph or any of his ilk. My own family sold me to save themselves, and for years I excused them. They were never my people either. Kodiak has shown me true love, and if Mr. Pennington leaves this room, Kodiak is as good as dead.

"Oh," I say, feigning relief. "Thank you, Mr. Pennington. Thank you."

He nods once, stiff and proud. "I will notify the captain now," he says, turning away.

I cannot let him go. Not with that promise. Lord forgive me. My hand slides to my waist, prying under my blouse. Unsheathing it from its buckskin sleeve, the knife is cool in my palm. My hand shakes, but I step forward, blade hidden at my hip.

"Mr. Pennington."

He pauses, then looks back. The polite mask remains, but curiosity and a sliver of caution sharpen his face. "Yes?"

For the barest instant, I see another path—confession, mercy, surrender. But it vanishes as quickly as it comes. If he leaves this room, Kodiak is finished. We are finished.

I raise the knife, hands trembling around the bone handle, and drive it hard into his heart.

His breath bursts out in a ragged gasp, eyes wide with shock. His hands clutch mine at the hilt, not pushing me away, not yet believing.

"Lord forgive me. I'm sorry," I whisper, tears streaming. "So truly sorry. But I cannot let that happen."

The sound he makes is soft, almost a sigh, as his knees buckle.

I stagger back, the knife slick in my hand, my heart hammering louder than a gun.

Kodiak is mine. And for him, I will damn myself.

CHAPTER 29

KODIAK

Alice crashes into the cabin, near falls against me. Her hands are slick with blood, chest heaving. The knife I gave her hits the floorboards with a clatter.

I catch her by the shoulders, hold her up, but my gut's already turning.

"What happened? Who did this?"

Her lips shake. "I did." The words spill out, small and broken. "I killed him."

This ain't her blood. For a heartbeat I just stare, waiting for her to say something else. Something that makes a lick of sense. But she don't. Tears stream down her face, her whole body quaking like she might shatter in my hands.

"You killed the Pinkerton," I murmur, more wonder than question.

She presses her face to my chest, sobbing. "I had to. He knew everything. Knew who I was. Who you are. He was going to tell the captain. He was going to take you."

Her words tumble out in a flood. I wrap her tight, stroke her hair, my heart pounding like a war drum. She's never hurt a fly in her life, and now she's cut down a man. For me. For us. There ain't no greater proof of love than this, bloody and terrible though it is.

I kiss the crown of her head, breathing her in even through the copper stink clinging to her.

"Lamb, listen, you done what you had to."

Her sobs ease just enough for her to lift her face. "He's in the writing room. Slumped over. I just ran."

"Then we ain't got time to waste." I cup her cheek, make her meet my eyes. "You're mine, Alice, and I'll see us both off this boat, no matter what it takes."

I leave her in the cabin with orders to clean herself up proper, bolt the door and not open it for no one but me. The passage is quiet as I walk, ship groaning, daylight too bright, too exposed in the briny air. I push into the writing room and shut the door behind me.

The Pinkerton is slumped on the floor, head lolled to one side, waistcoat soaked black-red. His eyes stare glassy past me, like he still don't believe what hit him. Hell, I can't believe it either. I check his throat, though I already know. A shiver runs through me, not from death but from the thought of her putting that blade to him. She saved me.

But now I gotta save us.

Can't exactly drag 'em out. Nothing like getting caught carrying a dead detective. They'll hang me right off the side of the ship. Maybe...

What if I could hide him real good?

I grab him by the lapels, hauling him up, all dead weight. He slides, head knocking the desk with a crack that sounds like a gunshot, knocking over a jar of ink. It paints a black streak across his cheek and crashes to the floor. I freeze, breath caught.

Footsteps in the corridor. Slow. Stop right outside the door.

My heart hammers. I crouch low, keeping one hand clamped on his coat, other hand reaching for my revolver. A shadow cuts across the strip of light under the door.

A man's voice, faint but clear: "You hear that?"

"What?" another man says.

"Door's shut. Thought it stayed open during the day."

A chuckle answers. "Maybe someone's writing something private in there. Come on, leave it."

"First-class folk just like to hear their own words scratching paper."

The footsteps move on. Fade.

I let out a slow breath. Christ almighty. Work faster.

I drag him 'cross the floor, fixing to get 'em close to the settee shoved against the far wall, burgundy velvet cushions faded, a drapery hanging loose over the window behind. Better than leaving him there than sprawled like a gutted hog.

"Come on, you rat bastard," I mutter.

I wrestle him down the gap between the settee and the wall, shoulder jammed to keep him from sliding back out. I curse and shove harder till he disappears into shadow. The velvet drapery hangs heavy, thick as a horse blanket. I yank it down from the rod, fling it over the heap he makes. A dark bundle now. Maybe a steward'll think it's extra bedding, maybe they won't look twice.

I wipe my palms on my trousers, strain to hear. Only the creak of the ship now. Rush of wind. One last look—just a heap of shadows in the corner. Passable.

My pulse beats in my ears as I ease the door open, peeking out. I near choke. Breakfast's letting out, and the passage floods with ladies in lace, gents in fine coats, children darting between skirts. Laughter, chatter. Too many eyes. I draw back a fraction, keeping my hand on the knob, fighting the urge to slam the door shut. That'd be worse. Louder, drawing attention.

A pair of women stop close by, fussing with their shawls, blocking the way like a barricade.

Now.

I slip out, force my face blank, steady my breath. Just another passenger, nothing out of sorts. Slipping into the tide, I let the crowd swallow me.

"Mr. Byron!"

Shit. I recognize Mrs. Taft's voice as it cuts through the crowd, shrill as a bell. I turn, teeth hard together, praying my face don't show a damn thing. She's waving a silly lace handkerchief, her husband lumbering behind her like a horse in a waistcoat.

"There you are," she trills, hurriedly weaving through the other first-class passengers. "Why, your wife told us you were ill."

"Feeling better by the hour," I say. My voice don't shake, thank Christ.

Mrs. Taft beams, reaching for my arm. "Then you'll join us for a stroll on deck? The sun is glorious." Her gloved hand hovers close. Too close. I swear the stench of that Pinkerton's gore hangs on my sleeve.

Behind her, Mr. Taft booms, "Come on, man, a little air will do you good."

Every second I linger is a noose drawing tighter. The Pinkerton's lying cold just yards away, and these two stand here, wanting me to walk polite into daylight.

Suppose it don't hurt to blend in with ordinary folks right about now.

Mrs. Taft latches onto my arm before I can sidestep, silk glove cool on my sleeve. The patch of blood under the cloth, tacky even now, sticks to my arm against her pressure. If she squeezes harder—Christ.

"The sea is so calm today," she says, steering me toward the companionway. "You'd never guess we were moving at all."

Mr. Taft chimes in at my other side. "That's the mark of a fine vessel. I heard the captain say we have made excellent time and should be in Galveston in just a few hours."

Good. That's good. We can survive a few hours.

We step out onto the deck, sunlight sharp, air heavy with damp. The horizon stretches clean and endless. Mrs. Taft chatters on, pointing out gulls, sails, the sparkle of the water. Her perfume curls sweet around me, covering the scent of the kill. She leans closer, patting my arm.

"And how is your dear wife faring? She seemed well at breakfast."

"She is. Much better, I think."

Mr. Taft claps me on the back. "Fine woman, your wife. A good match for a strong fellow like you. Pennington said as much himself yesterday."

My gut lurches, but I school my face blank. "Pennington?"

"Detective fellow," Taft says. "Sharp as a tack. I dare say he's the sort of man who notices everything."

Bet he ain't seen Alice coming, I think, and damn near crack a smile.

Mrs. Taft fans herself with a giggle. "Why, Mr. Byron, you must have met him."

I shake my head like I've missed the obvious. "Can't say I

recall the name. Perhaps I've been too long cooped up in our cabin."

Mr. Taft roars, amused. "Well, you'll make his acquaintance soon enough. He makes it his business to meet everyone."

His cold, dead eyes laid on me just a few minutes ago. "I look forward to it."

We stroll past children playing with hoops, women trailing parasols, uniformed crew walking with ordinary purpose. I keep my shoulders square, my pace easy, though sweat prickles under my collar.

Mrs. Taft prattles on about Galveston—its promenades, its society, how much she wishes us to visit them in Sabine so she can introduce Alice at some garden party. "A woman with such poise must be the jewel of Ohio."

"Ohio?" I ask. The word damn near stops me cold.

"Why yes. That is where you and Mrs. Byron are from, is it not?"

"Oh, yes. Of course."

Why would Alice tell them we were from Ohio? Christ almighty. If they do a little digging won't be hard to see that missing woman from Ohio looks an awful lot like Mrs. Byron. They'll know we're in Galveston.

It takes a special kind of screwing up to burn a new city before ever setting foot there.

I clear my throat. "I wonder if I've pushed myself too soon. You'll forgive me; I think it's best I continue to rest."

"Oh dear," Mrs. Taft says. "Please do rest, and send your dear wife our regards."

As she rests her hand on my arm, I notice a bit of blood on her white glove.

Jesus H. Christ.

"Of course," I say. I tip my hat, give them the smile they want, and step back from the rail. I move quick, sly, back into the flow of guests, but I'm taller than almost every son of a bitch out here. Picked the wrong occupation when I can't help but stick out like a gopher from a damn hole.

Just make it back to Alice. Lock the door. Wait for land.

I round the corner of the deckhouse—and near freeze.

A man stands by the rail, bowler hat low, cigar smoldering between his teeth. Badge glinting faint at his vest. Goddamn Pinkerton.

His hand flicks open a silver watch. He checks the time, snaps it shut, scans the deck.

Waiting.

Waiting for Pennington, most like. I knew those bastards never travelled alone. How many of them are here? My gut knots. Lord above, we ain't ever getting off this ship.

I duck my head, keep my stride steady, though every nerve screams to turn and bolt. Just a husband going back to his wife. Just another passenger.

But when I pass him, his eyes flick up, meet mine. Sharp. Measuring.

The weight of that stare clings to me long after I've walked on.

CHAPTER 30

Lord forgive me.

I scrub the blood out from under my fingernails, rinse it from the seams of my dress. Dear God, how could I have done this? Killed an innocent man who never raised a hand against me.

The room whirls. I move through it in a nervous haze, my heart hollowed out like a cored apple. What now? What will become of us?

I want life to be simple again. Even when the waters were cruel, I knew how to keep my head above them. Now I am drowning in Kodiak's world, the sting of salt and sea in my lungs, and I cannot tell if I am fighting the current or letting it pull me down.

What is the lesson, Lord? Why was he placed in my path?

I pace the small room, cold hands rubbing one another raw. Where has Kodiak gone?

Perhaps he's only a step away, only a breath beyond the door, but the thought gnaws at me: what if he is farther? What if he has decided I am too much trouble, too much risk? What if he lets them find me?

I listen against the door, straining. Footsteps, chatter. Ordinary shipboard sounds. Nothing of alarm, no shouts of murder. That should ease me. It does not.

He would have taken Kodiak. Better my soul be damned than leave him to the rope. And yet, what of me? What will they do if they discover me? Send me back to Ohio. Back to the Shermans. Back to that inn that was my prison long before Kodiak was carried through its door.

In Ohio, I would no longer be just an innkeeper's wife. I would be a scandal. They'd look at me with those judging glares, weighing whether to call me whore or conspirator.

Perhaps they'd be right. Perhaps I am both.

But I would rather swing from a gallows beside Kodiak than rot in their parlor, paraded as their wounded bird until the pity turned to scorn.

The ship creaks. Somewhere far down the hall, a child laughs, and the sound is so bright, so alive, it stabs through me. Life is carrying on, as if I did not stain it with evil.

I clean the basin twice, though no blood lingers. Scrub at the floorboards until my knees ache, though they were never marked. The knife I wrap in my shawl, binding it tight as though I could smother its memory.

My gown folded, his coat laid atop, boots polished. I stack it all by the door as if there is no question, no possibility but one: we will leave this ship together when it docks. Step onto Galveston's soil as man and wife.

The lock clicks.

Kodiak slips inside with a sigh. "There's another one."

"Another—"

"Pinkerton. Looked to be waitin'. We got a few hours to

port, then when that Pennington don't show up, they'll be investigatin'."

This is it. The end of the road.

Kodiak sinks onto the edge of the bunk, staring at the floorboards like he might burn a hole through them. "We'll lay low. Soon as they drop the gangplank, we blend into the first-class crowd best we can. Lord knows rich folk don't take kindly to bein' held up, 'specially if they think they're bein' accused of a crime. Steward won't risk stoppin' a lady in silk. All we need's a little luck, a steady walk, and for you to hold your chin up like you was born in a pile a'gold. You do that, and we'll step on Galveston soil with pockets full and a whole new life waitin'."

I try to believe him. To let his certainty soak into me. Though hope is brittle, I nod anyway. Because what else is there? We will walk off this ship together—or not at all.

The air changes before the harbor comes into view. It's charged now, like static, clouds above threatening a downpour as first-class folk make ready to disembark. Kodiak and I wait in the cabin until the last possible minute.

When he finally nods, we gather the bags. They're heavier than sin. My arms ache before we even reach the passage.

"Head high," he instructs. "Don't you falter."

The staircase down to the main deck feels endless. A tide of silks and fine hats presses around us, and I try to mimic their ease, their polish, but sweat trickles down my back.

Then I see him. The Pinkerton by the gangplank. Bowler hat, brown coat, eyes sharp as he watches each passenger descend, his thumb brushing the silver watch in his vest pocket. Waiting.

Waiting for us.

The crowd slows, clusters. A steward murmurs apologies as

he checks tickets, his voice thin against the swell of passengers. The Pinkerton scans every face, lips set in a grim line.

Kodiak's hand brushes mine—barely a touch, but enough to ground me. His whisper is hot at my ear. "Easy, lamb."

My heart thunders as we inch forward. Every step a lifetime.

Ahead, the Pinkerton leans toward a gentleman, asks a quiet question, then lets him pass.

We're three paces away. Two. The gangplank is there, sunlight glaring off the water, freedom close enough to taste.

The Pinkerton's eyes cut to mine. Hold. Narrow. He steps forward, blocking the way.

"Ma'am. Sir." His voice is polite, but firm enough to freeze me where I stand. "If you'll pardon me, your baggage, please."

Kodiak's grip tightens on the handle of his case. The air hums between us. This is it—the choice. Hand it over and be undone. Fight and damn everyone in sight.

Kodiak straightens, a bear rising to its full height. "You best mind yourself. I don't answer to hired men. Nor does my wife."

A ripple passes through the line of passengers. Heads turn. Hisses prickle the air. Kodiak's chin lifts a fraction higher, disdain cutting sharp across his face.

The Pinkerton doesn't flinch. His eyes flick from Kodiak's hand on the case to my face, then back again. "Sir," he says. "Your name."

Kodiak's jaw hardens. "I'm not obliged to give it."

"Travelers of interest match your description," the man goes on, hand close to his coat. "I'll need to search your luggage."

"No, you won't," Kodiak answers, loud enough to feed the

crowd eager for spectacle. The Pinkerton's hand drops to the pistol at his hip, resting the heel of his hand on it.

"Mr. Byron!" Mrs. Taft sweeps forward, pearls flashing, indignant as a queen. "How dare you!" she says to the Pinkerton, planting her hand firmly on Kodiak's arm. "This man and his wife are friends of ours."

The Pinkerton's eyes slide to her hand. To her glove. White silk, marred by a faint smear of brown-red.

Blood.

"Madam, where did you come by that stain?"

"What stain?"

The Pinkerton reaches for her, taking her wrist and twisting her arm slightly to give her a better look.

She stammers. "I-I cannot say. Perhaps the dining room, perhaps—"

He interrupts her. "Madam, please step aside." He turns to us. "You step aside as well, please. I'll need to speak with you all privately."

Kodiak squares his shoulders. "We're disembarking, same as anyone. We've nothin' to say, in private or otherwise."

The Pinkerton tips his head at a steward. "Bring me their bags."

The steward hesitates, glances at us, then reaches for the case in Kodiak's hand.

"Wouldn't recommend it, boy," Kodiak growls, voice dangerous.

The steward startles, but the Pinkerton presses. "It will be returned once I've inspected it."

That's when Kodiak moves. One hand seizes the Pinkerton's pistol, the other drives his shoulder forward, twisting the man off balance. Before anyone can gasp, the barrel's pressed to his temple.

The Pinkerton's eyes widen.

A shot splits the air like cannon fire.

Gore sprays across the steward's coat. The Pinkerton crumples sideways, skull shattered, the echo rolling through the ship's timbers. For a heartbeat the deck freezes, stunned into silence.

Then the gates of hell burst open.

Screams. Shrieks. Parasols scatter. Men shove their wives behind them. Children wail. A gentleman vomits into the sea. Mrs. Taft stands perfectly still, expression frozen, silk hat spattered with blood.

Kodiak shoves the smoking gun into his waistband, seizes me hard by the arm, and drags me through the chaos.

"Move!"

We plunge into the sea of first-class passengers. They claw at each other, scrambling for distance from the corpse. I stumble, clutching the satchel to my chest. It's heavy, so heavy. The steward slips in blood, and Kodiak kicks him square in the chest, toppling him into the rail.

Every officer's whistle shrieks at once, the shrill blasts cutting through the panic.

"Stop them! Stop the shooter!"

But Kodiak is already angling toward the service stair, the narrow iron flight meant for crew. He barrels down, dragging me with him, boots pounding, shouts echoing above.

A shot rings out, then another.

Wood splinters near my shoulder. My scream catches in my throat.

"Keep low!" Kodiak snarls, shoving me ahead.

We burst into the lower deck, the stink of coal thick in the air. Dockside ropes are already being thrown ashore. Dockhands shout; whistles blow; chaos reigns above us.

Freedom gleams just ahead.

"Almost there, just—"

A bullet rips past, biting into my side. I stumble, blood warm at my hip.

Kodiak catches me before I fall, hauling me tight against him as he runs headlong for the gangway. My knees buckle. The satchel slips in my grasp. I clutch harder, knuckles white, but my strength is leaving me. The bag drags me down with its weight, like an anchor pulling me under.

"Bear," I gasp again. "I can't—"

Eyes wild and blood streaking his face, he notices the crimson staining my gown and he makes a quick decision. "Drop it," he orders.

I shake my head, tears spilling. "No. We came this far, we—"

"Drop it, goddamn it!" His voice is a whip, fierce and final.

I let go, and the satchel strikes the dock with a hollow thud, bursts open, and gold scatters like embers from a fire. Coins roll wild, jewels skitter across the planks. Hands dive for them—porters, passengers, and strangers scrambling like rats.

I sway, breath shuddering in my throat. Kodiak hauls me up into his arms, cradling me against his chest. Behind us, the fortune vanishes into grasping hands, gone as if it never was. Ahead, only the open dock, the sun blazing cruel and bright.

"Hold on, lamb," he growls, barreling forward, voice raw with something I've never heard in him before—fear. "Ain't no gold in this world worth losin' you."

We hit the gangway at full tilt. Dockhands scatter, dropping coils of rope and crates as Kodiak barrels through. Blood drips from my side, hot down my skirts, but he doesn't slow, doesn't falter.

Someone yells, "Catch the outlaw!"

Pistols crack, shots raining down from the rails.

Kodiak clears the gangway in three strides, boots hitting Galveston soil with a thunder that rattles through me. He scans once, sharp as a hawk, and spies a carriage horse tied to a post. The horse rears at the noise, the whites of its eyes flashing.

Kodiak's already moving, barreling toward the animal, brushing men aside like they're no more than stalks of tall grass. With one savage wrench, he rips the reins loose, vaults onto the beast's back, and yanks me up in front of him.

Pain sears through my flank as I'm hauled across his thighs. His arm locks around me, an iron band.

"Hold on," he cries.

Gunfire cracks from the wharf, bullets sparking off crates, tearing through canvas. Dockhands duck, women shriek, men scatter in every direction. The horse bolts at the sound and rips down the wharf, knocking over barrels and baggage. Briny wind whips my hair across my face, stinging my eyes.

At our backs, whistles sing, and we leave the port a kicked hornets' nest of fury. Ahead, the wide street gapes open, lined with carriages, wagons, and startled townsfolk diving for cover.

Kodiak's voice rumbles against my ear, fierce and raw. "Don't you quit on me now, lamb. You hear me? You keep breathin'."

I clutch at his arm, slick with sweat and blood, and try to answer, but the words won't come. The horse's muscles band and strain under us, every tromp lashing my wound, but I cling to Kodiak, the only thing keeping me from descending into the abyss. The world blurs, bright sun flashing, shadows strobing past as the horse flies beneath us. My fingers slip on Kodiak's arm, too slick, too weak.

"Stay with me!" His chest hammers against my back, every breath of his ragged and fierce.

Mine come shallow, broken. My skirts cling heavy, wet with blood. The air tastes of iron. I try to lift my head to answer him, but my vision spins, dark pressing in from the edges.

"Kodiak," I breathe, barely a whisper.

His arm tightens, crushing me close, his voice breaking rough as I've never heard. "Don't you dare leave me, lamb. Don't you—"

But I'm already plummeting, sinking into the dark. Away from his voice, his heat, the charge of hooves. The last thing I feel is his grip, fierce and steadfast, the last sound his roar—half prayer, half curse.

Consumed by endless black.

CHAPTER 31

KODIAK

The wind whips by, shouts and gunfire warring behind us.

In my head, there's my pa sayin', "You are a blight." Voice steady as a minister even with the whiskey. "This—our present ruin—is your doing."

This sweet woman suffered all her life, just for me to show up and finish the job. Should've done her a favor and let the fever take me. But I did what I always do—took what I wanted, because I needed it, and damn everything else. I needed free, so I made her complicit in my crime. I needed coin, so I dragged her along, got her thinking up heists of her own. Now look.

Christ almighty, she's white as a ghost.

"Stay with me!"

My lungs can't draw enough air. My heart's beating so fast, it's pounding my breath clean out, and I can't catch up. Lord above, her skirt's more blood than cotton.

"Kodiak," she whispers, so soft I barely catch it.

"We're gonna get help, all right? Just stay with me."

Goddamn it. I don't know Galveston worth a damn. Streets twist. Signs blur.

Doctor. We need a doctor.

Docks are docks. Sailors bust bones same as outlaws, and every port keeps a surgeon close by. So I drive the mare through the port road, praying I find what I'm looking for. I lean low, heels to the mare, and follow the masts rising above rooftops.

Then I see it: big brick walls by the wharf, flag snapping above, white cross painted bold on the lintel. Marine Hospital. No mistaking it.

A wanted man, a bloodied woman, in a federal hospital. Guards. Military men. Telegraph right there. Might as well walk to the gallows myself. Feeling the life draining from the only woman I ever loved, I just might. I haul the reins, near spill off the saddle with her in my arms, and shout before my boots hit stone.

"Doctor! She's bleedin' out!"

Hands reach. Voices call for stretchers. I lay Alice down gentle as I can, her breath fluttering like a candle. They take her through doors smelling of carbolic and boiled linen. A surgeon in a stained coat snaps orders.

"You her kin?" he demands.

My mouth goes dry. In my heart, she's mine. Ain't no say in it. Stars decided long ago. But say yes, and I damn her. Say no, and they treat her like a stranger and start asking more questions.

The men we ran from saw her go down like a bloody rag. They'll follow that trail. It's only a matter of time now.

"No," I blurt, then catch myself.

You are a blight. The words land like fists, blunt strikes near taking me to my knees. Pa was always right. Maybe the clean thing to do is the one thing I never could—let go. Tell the truth, and the house'll move. Deputies. Pinkertons. But she'll be in the right hands. She'll have a roof. She'll be safe.

She'll be away from me.

God help me. Even a lowlife like me knows to put a bullet in a mare with a broken leg. Especially when it pains you. It's a kindness, and after all she's shown me, it's the least I owe her. My best days are behind me. My lamb. Waking beside a damn angel. A sting I haven't known in years rises to my eyes. I stuff it down.

Enough.

Things are, then they're not. Just the way it is.

"'Fore she blacked out, she said her name's Alice Sherman. Kidnapped a month back in Ohio. Found her near the port, brought her here. I ain't got no coin, but there's a reward on her, I'm sure. You'll want to tell the sheriff."

The surgeon's jaw tightens. "Sherman? You're sure?"

"Sure enough." I spit the truth raw. "Give her every stitch and care. That's all I'm askin'."

The nurse and doctor study my hands. The black of blood under my nails. The stink of gunpowder rising off me.

"We'll take it from here," he says.

Before they take her, I take her hand—brief as a struck match. Her fingers are cold.

"You'll be home, lamb."

"And your name, sir?" the nurse asks.

"Ain't got one."

I turn to go, but two men are standing in the way.

"Sir," says one—orderly, maybe. "We need you to come with us."

I look back. Alice is being wheeled away quick.

Ought to run. Ought to carve freedom out of these boys. But how's a man pray for a miracle while spilling another man's blood? No, I think it's time me and the man upstairs get square.

I go easy, you save her.

Forgive her for what she done for me.

Wipe the slate clean.

Give her the life she deserves.

With a nod, I make peace with it and hold up my hands. "Don't want no trouble."

I'll put up my end of the bargain.

Now God better take care of His.

ONCE THE GOVERNMENT'S dogs got their teeth in me, Uncle Sam tipped his hat. *"Well, hell. Didn't even have to chase you far. Federal courthouse is just down the street."*

Thanked me for delivering myself to Galveston. They ain't need to do much once the local sheriff and the Washington men quit bickering over which one of 'em would have the pleasure of tightening a noose around my neck. Trial or no, I've never seen a jury do more than nod toward the gallows.

It ain't the rope that keeps me awake. It's Alice. Her hand on my chest, her scent—rosemary soap. Beat the hell out of the fish and brine, filth and shit stinking up this cage by the gulf. Gangs of men in the county jail all snarling at each other like penned dogs, rattling chains and coughing up blood. I miss the way Alice made the world quiet. I don't know if she's alive. Part of me don't even want to, 'cause if the truth's too dark, it'll gut me worse than their gallows.

If she's gone, if hell's a lie and death is just another trail, maybe when they drop that trapdoor we'll find each other again. But if she's alive, well, I'll die happy knowing it was worth it.

In the morning, it's, "Eat up, outlaws," and a guard slops beans into a communal tin pan, with a side of rancid meat and moldy bread. Dine on the floor of a cell with a bent spoon, if I'm lucky. Four of us in a cell. Being the biggest and meanest makes living a little easier, unless someone wants to make a point and I gotta put 'em in his place. Ain't come to blows with no one here, but I come close.

"On your perch, jailbird. Charity lawyer wants a word."

Oh, lucky day. Judge saddled me with some penny lawyer don't give a damn whether I swing. I stretch as the guard opens up my cell, deputy waiting to take me wherever the hell it is we're going. I step out, holding out my wrists.

"No shackles," guard says. "Takin' you to an office down the hall."

I shrug. Makes no damn difference to me where I go.

"Come on, outlaw," deputy says and walks on, hand on his iron. Looking at a man like that, with his government gun and uniform all picked out for 'em, makes my mouth sour. Tall, lanky cocksucker, not an ounce of muscle on him. Take that shiny badge away, take the gun, let us settle things like nature intended. Wouldn't last two minutes with me 'fore I knocked his head clean off his shoulders.

Now he leads me down the hall, all puffed up 'cause the law deputized him important. He opens up a door to a small office, stacks of files piled up high. Smell of coffee makes my stomach tug. Alice brewed a fine cup.

Don't make no sense how fast that thought tries to choke me where I stand. Blight, I am, poisoned the purest thing I'd ever known. Now I got some pole-thin penny lawyer standing at attention, ascot round his neck, hair slicked back with silver streaks at the sides.

"Mr. Randolph," he says, extending a hand. I look at it and back at him like I'd sooner wipe my ass with a cactus than shake his hand. He draws it back, swallowing hard. "Right. Please have a seat."

He pulls out my chair like he's courting me and skitters around to the other side. If I had a chance in the dark of getting free, I'd watch it burst into flames in this bastard's hands.

He sits, clearing his throat. There's a stack of papers on the table in front of him, and he looks 'em over.

"Mr. Randolph, my name is Henry Wallace, Esquire. The court has appointed me to aid in your defense, as is your right," he says. "You've been accused of one count of kidnapping and carrying away of a citizen across state lines against her will. Five counts of murder in the first degree." He flips a page. "One count of train robbery, said robbery being committed against the mail and passengers in transit. One count of willfully derailing a train. Destruction of railroad property. Horse theft, arson, and escape from lawful custody."

He pauses to take a breath, then clicks his tongue.

"Assault upon a law officer, and two charges of attempted murder on survivors. That's the whole bill, as the grand jury handed it down."

"Guilty as charged," I say.

He nods like I just told him I was born on the moon.

None of this matters a lick to me, so I ask the only thing worth knowing. "Alice. You know if she's all right?"

He blinks, pen frozen. "I'm sorry... Alice?"

"Alice." I lean forward, wrists on the table.

He flips through his papers for a clue. "I don't believe I'm familiar with anyone by that name."

The room shrinks. For a second I don't hear the jail, don't smell the coffee, don't see his stupid ascot. Just the sound of my knuckles cracking.

"She's the woman you're saying I kidnapped," I growl.

"Sir, I-I'm just your attorney. I have no knowledge of—"

My chair scrapes back, hands curl on the edge of the table. One hard move, and the law would have a reason to make this hanging quicker.

"Mr. Randolph," he says, voice high now, "I'm only here to—"

I shut my eyes, counting slow.

CHAPTER 32

ALICE

Bear and I lie in our bunk. The groan of the ship keeps time along the passing hours. His chest rises and falls against my back, one arm slung heavy across my waist. "Texas is wide," he says, his breath warm against my neck. "Plenty of land to claim. A haul like this will set us up right. Build a house somewhere nice. Quiet."

"With cattle?"

"With cattle. Or hogs."

"We can have both."

"And chickens," he adds. "Live off the land."

"That would be nice. But we need to make it off this ship first."

"We'll make it off this ship," he says. There's no doubt in his voice. His arms tighten around my middle.

I shift to face him, the wood beneath us creaking. The lantern in our tiny room casts just enough light to catch his features—the stubble that roughens his jaw, the pale scar that splits his eyebrow, his eyes—gold, green, something in between. One of them has a fleck in it, like an ember.

"What are you lookin' for?" he asks, curious.

I rest my hand on his cheek, letting my thumb graze the edge of his mouth. His skin is warm, and I can feel the slow beat of his blood under my palm.

"Just learning you, I suppose."

He doesn't speak, and I don't need him to. The ship sways beneath us, a slow cradle rocked by rough water. Somewhere, men murmur through the walls. One laughs too loud. Another coughs. But in our little bunk, it's just us. He smiles that slow, reluctant smile that only shows on one side.

"Ain't much to see."

I start to speak, but he catches my hand and kisses the heel of it.

His hand finds my hair and brushes it back behind my ear. "You look at me like I ain't half bad."

I shift closer, touch my forehead to his, thumb tracing the edge of that scar above his eye. "You don't have to be bad," I whisper. "There's goodness in you. I see it."

He huffs. Not quite a laugh, more like disbelief. "Don't tell nobody," he murmurs. "Wouldn't want word gettin' out."

The ship groans. His thumb brushes along my ribs with a tender rhythm.

"Sleep," he says, barely audible. "I'll keep watch."

I close my eyes, steadied by the rhythm of his inhales and exhales, until the night melts into day.

Pain.

Searing pain. It radiates from my hip, deep and jagged, like something hot and wrong is lodged beneath the bone.

It's bandaged. Why?

I try to breathe, but drawing in air is a labor in itself.

The ceiling is high and yellowed, wooden beams crossing overhead like ribs. A single oil lamp flickers in the corner. A woman's voice sounds, faint behind a wall. Boards creaking above, as if someone's pacing.

The sheets are coarse. My skin sticks to them.

I try to turn my head, and a bolt of pain shoots through my spine. My breath hitches.

"Bear?" His name barely escapes my lips. The memory clings to me—his arms around me, the sway of the ship, his voice whispering, *Sleep. I'll keep watch.*

But the bed is too wide. The room is too cold.

He's not here.

Where has he gone?

The memory floats just out of reach. I try to remember his voice clearly, but it slips sideways, muddied by pain and the weight of whatever happened next.

Did we make it off the ship?

We must have.

My eyes open again, lids heavy. A figure moves near the door, shape blurred by the lamp's low flicker.

"You're awake," a woman says. Her dress rustles as she crosses the room. I catch the hem of a gray skirt, the edge of an apron. A basin in her arms.

"You'll want to stay still." She sets the basin on a table I hadn't noticed. "You've torn the stitches once already."

"Where—" My throat rasps. I try again. "Where is he?"

She doesn't answer right away, just pours water into a chipped enamel bowl. The scent of carbolic soap curls through the air.

"You'll need broth. Something soft."

"Where is he?" I ask again, louder now.

She looks at me. Older, lined face full of pity, like she's seen too many women wake up asking the same question.

"I don't know who you mean," she says.

The light is sharp now. Not the flicker of a lantern, but sun, high and intense, pouring through the window. It's midday. I must've slept through morning.

The nurse dips a cloth in the basin and pats my forehead with it. Her hands are efficient, impersonal.

"Who brought me here?" I ask.

She glances at me, then back at her work. "I couldn't say. You were brought in some days ago. Carried in unconscious."

"How many days?"

She doesn't answer right away. Wrings the cloth out. Folds it over. "Four. Maybe five."

My heart kicks in my chest. Nearly a week. A floorboard creaks. A shadow moves behind her. "No. No. How can--"

"Shhh, shhh. It's all right."

The voice crawls in like a draft under the door. Soft. Familiar.

I know the voice before I see the face.

Virgil.

Hat in hand, his hair is neatly combed, and the only sound he makes is the click of his shined boots. He draws the leather from his hand slowly, peeling off his gloves.

"Well," he says, smiling faintly, "you are awake." He approaches with the calm of a man who owns the bed, the room, and the land beneath the building.

"You gave us quite a fright," he says, settling into the chair beside me. "We had the entire country searching for you. Notices in every rail town between here and the Lakes. Pinkertons, private agents—we spared no expense. And now," he continues, folding his hands, "we've found you. In Galveston. In the company of the man who killed my brother."

My stomach tightens, but I say nothing.

"You were unconscious when he brought you in. Curious, don't you think? An outlaw carrying his victim into a hospital at such great personal expense?"

He lets the question linger.

"One might almost mistake it for concern. Of course, no one is making assumptions. Not yet. These are complicated matters. Emotions. Fear. Confusion." His voice gentles. "You were taken. You were grieving. You lost your husband under violent circumstances, then vanished without a trace. That is a tremendous burden for any woman."

I turn my face slightly toward the window.

"But now that you're safe, the proper course can be set. Justice can be served. Joseph can have peace. And so can you." He leans forward just enough that I can feel the shift in air, the nearness of him. "The trial will be soon," he says, lower now, almost private. "You'll be called to speak. All I ask is that you tell the truth, Alice."

A trial? If there's to be a trial, that means they have him. My mouth goes dry as ash. I cannot let it show. Virgil is watching.

"I'm sure you remember what that is," he adds.

I smooth the sheet with my fingers, steadying them. When I speak, my voice is soft. "Of course I remember." I meet his eyes. "Thank you. For coming." A smile. Just enough to keep him from looking deeper.

Virgil returns the smile, polite as ever. "Of course. I wouldn't be anywhere else." He picks up his gloves but doesn't put them on. Just smooths the fingers flat against his thigh. "There will be a deposition before the trial. A statement taken under oath. It will be read before the court, alongside your live testimony. The federal prosecutors will ask for details—how he took you, where he kept you, what you saw."

He glances at me. There's nothing sharp there. Nothing overt. Just the glint of calculation.

"They'll want to know why you didn't escape. Why you didn't run when you had the chance." A long pause. He clasps the gloves in both hands now. "You were in mourning. You were taken from your home, disoriented, coerced. You were held against your will, moved across state lines by a violent man—one responsible for the death of your husband."

He recites it like a script. Polished. Unassailable.

"You feared for your life. He threatened you. You did not participate. You were forced to witness unspeakable things. You followed him only because there was no choice. That is the truth I expect you'll be telling."

I feel the heat rising behind my eyes, but I say nothing.

Virgil stands. "Because any other version," he says, straightening his cuffs, "would be unfortunate. For you. For the Sherman name. There is no public appetite for hanging a woman. Especially not one who used to sit at my family's table." He walks to the foot of the bed. Slow, composed. "What I am offering you, sister, is not protection from the law. It's protection from what the law will do to you if you defend that man."

Sister. My jaw tightens and fury brews hot in my belly. I cannot hold my tongue at these thinly veiled threats. At his revisionist history. My voice is steady, but cold. "I am not your sister. Do you think I loved your family? That I loved Joseph?"

He lets out a breath. Not quite a sigh, more like disappointment I am no longer participating in this charade.

"That's irrelevant. What matters is what the papers print.

What the jury hears. What the Sherman name can survive. Our relationship with the L&N is critical. We cannot afford for them—or any of our partners—to believe a Sherman ran off with a criminal who derailed their trains and cost them thousands in damages."

He looks at me, no softness left.

Of course. It's only ever been business.

"We will not suffer that loss because you couldn't control yourself."

The words land like a slap. Not shouted, but sharp enough to cut. I feel him waiting for something. A denial. A protest. Even tears. I give him nothing.

Let him fill the silence with whatever story he needs.

After a long moment, I hear the rustle of his gloves as he pulls them back on.

"Rest, Alice," he says, smoothing the leather down each finger. "You'll need your strength for the days ahead. There's no need to dwell on what's already decided. The truth will keep you safe."

The door clicks shut behind him.

My body is rigid. The light through the window shifts again, catching the brass bed frame and throwing a dull gleam across the floor. The nurse doesn't return. No one comes.

Just me and the pain.

Kodiak is in custody.

There will be a trial.

And he will hang.

My gut turns, and I brace against the mattress. A shiver runs up through my shoulders, into my throat. I blink hard as tears burn. I try to breathe, but my chest won't rise. It's too heavy. Like something's caved in. Like something's crushed beyond repair.

A sob tears loose before I can swallow it. It slips out sharp and ugly, then another follows, and suddenly I'm crying—quiet, violent. I clutch the blanket, bury my face in it, teeth clenched to keep from screaming. I cry until my ribs ache and my throat is raw. Until the only sound left is my breath and the madness echoing in my head.

He will hang.

Unless I do something.

CHAPTER 33

KODIAK

"**M**r. Randolph, if you intend to plead guilty, this will be over quickly. No parade of witnesses, no days of testimony. You spare the court the trouble, and you might spare yourself some additional ignominy."

I open my eyes slow. "Spare myself what now?"

"Igno— Shame, Mr. Randolph. Spare yourself the indignity of a public trial," the little man says, tugging at his frayed cuffs.

A chuckle breaks free from deep in my gut, just bubbles up by surprise. Shucks, I'd hate the world to know what a dirty scoundrel I am. I laugh a bit longer. "Mr. whatever your name is, I know you're just a 'gimme' lawyer and you don't know me from Adam, but the only thing undignified in my book is livin' by the government's standard. Ain't a lick of shame in bein' a man. I did every damn thing those papers said I did, but if you say a goddamn thing besides not guilty, they'll have another charge to add. If the government wants to see me swing, they're gonna have to earn it."

The lawyer clears his throat, straightening papers that don't need straightening. The office goes silent save for the tick of his watch. He blinks. "Very well. I will prepare for trial. I'll do what I can, but the pace is extraordinary. I've seen men sit six months in the county jail waiting on an indictment. In your case, the court has moved in a week's time. Federal prosecutors, Pinkertons, the railroad company—they all want blood. They want to make an example, and they want it quick. Mr. Randolph, this does not look good."

I nod. "Knew it weren't good comin' in here. Damn sure knew it soon as you opened your mouth."

He sighs, his shoulders sloping. "Mr. Randolph, is that really necessary? You've made your threats and landed your insults. Do remember who is tasked with defending you. Now —" He clears his throat. "The court will convene in Galveston proper. You'll be arraigned before Judge McKinnon. A jury will be drawn from the county rolls—shopkeepers, dockmen, farmers—all of them acquainted with the headlines. Every one of them will know your name before they hear it read."

He glances at me over the stack of damning words. "That's the other matter. The courthouse will be rife with reporters. Sketch artists. A photographer or two. With the attention you've garnered, I expect they'll come from far and wide."

I huff a laugh. "Well, I'll be damned. Thought it was just Jesse James who got all the ink. Guess I oughta thank the railroad for free advertisin'."

"Do not be flattered. As I said, you have the attention of important men who want to see you pay with your life. Now, the prosecutor will lay out the bill of indictment and then he'll begin calling witnesses. Railroad men, law officers, perhaps even passengers who lived through the wreck."

I lean back, squinting at him. "And Alice?"

His brow furrows. "Who?"

"Christ almighty." My palm hits the table hard enough to make his inkwell jump. "The woman I kidnapped. The one in your own damn papers. Keep up."

He blinks, his hand trembling as he straightens his collar, "Yes, of course. If she is available and can be located, she will be summoned. A victim's testimony is considered paramount."

"She was at the Marine Hospital, last I knew."

He straightens with a sniff. "Well, then assuming she is alive, the prosecution will do everything to bring her before the court."

The air goes heavy. I sit forward, knuckles pressing white against the wood. "Assumin'," I echo, the word sour on my tongue.

He shifts in his chair, fingers drumming once against the table, eyes darting to the door where the guard waits just outside. "My duty is to inform you how the law will move. Once I know who the government plans to call, I will let you know."

A litany of images kicks in, one after the other: her white skirt gone dark with blood, the way she breathed shallow when I laid her on that stretcher. If she's alive, if they drag her into that courthouse, she'll have to testify.

Will she hate me for getting her shot, for leaving her in that hospital? Maybe. She's got every right. The law will want her to say I stole her clean from her home and never let go, that I crossed state lines with a rope around her wrist.

Truth is, I don't give a damn what she says about me. If she turns up alive, she can call me a thief, a murderer, a monster— every foul name under the sun. She can lie through her teeth if it buys her a life. Long as she's breathing, long as she gets to walk free and find quiet somewhere, I'll take it.

If the jury hears her curse my name and damn me six ways, I'll nod along. If it keeps her outta the fire, let 'em string me up twice. All I want—Lord, all I ever wanted—is for her to be safe and to forget the blight I laid on her.

I drag a hand down my face, come back to the room.

"You may take the stand yourself or you may remain silent and let me argue," the lawyer drones.

"I ain't sayin' nothin'."

He nods agreeably. "I believe that is a wise decision. You have a temper, Mr. Randolph, and the prosecution would delight in drawing it out before the jury. One angry outburst, and they will have you painted guiltier than you already stand. I will argue the insufficiency of evidence, the unreliability of certain witnesses, the—"

"Not Alice."

"What do you mean?"

"You ain't gonna shove her in the dirt. If she says what keeps her free, you let her."

He runs a hand through his hair, uneasy. "I will not intentionally subject a victim to needless humiliation. That is unbecoming of any counsel. But you must understand that my obligation is to your defense." He reaches for his pen, scribbles a note. "I will notify you of any summons. I'll also send for the Marine Hospital records and speak with the clerk. If she is there, we will know."

A boot scrapes in the hall. A knock on the door.

The lawyer folds his papers. "Very well. I shall prepare accordingly. "

They lead me out then, the deputy's hand at my elbow, the corridor smelling of spilt coffee and stale tobacco. My mind is already back with her.

The thought of laying eyes on her again fills me with a

hope I'm tempted to tamp down. Won't dare dream on it. But if I do see her, I'll tell her true. Loving her was the only thing I did worth a damn.

CHAPTER 34

ALICE

J ust a fortnight after Virgil's visit, the carriage sets us down on Tremont Street at the foot of the federal courthouse. The stone columns rise tall as oaks, pale against the Gulf sky. My hip aches, but I can manage. The bullet passed clean through the fleshy part, sparing the bone, but it sliced a minor artery. The doctor said it was a miracle I survived, given the blood I lost. Had Kodiak not carried me to the hospital when he did, I'd have perished for certain. Now he's locked in a cage, facing certain death, and I cannot allow him to trade his life for my own.

Virgil nods at the marshal who meets us at the door and steers me across the vestibule. The air smells of ink and cigar smoke. Clerks hurry up and down the marble hall, folders clutched in their hands, the echo of boots clapping under the vaulted ceiling. Brass lamps flicker. Portraits of men line the walls, stern faces fixed in gilt frames.

Will he be here? Nothing would give me more peace than

to look upon him. If I could see him, speak freely, we could stage a plan.

We pass open double doors. I catch a glimpse of the courtroom—polished benches, a high wooden rail, the judge's chair looming above like a throne. The marshal presses onward, up the stairwell. Judge McKinnon's chambers are paneled in oak, heavy curtains drawn against the sun. He sits already at his desk, round spectacles perched on his nose, a cigar smoldering in a tray beside him. The US Attorney rises politely, and a stenographer shifts, hands poised on his keys.

No Kodiak.

The judge looks me over like a stack of canned goods at the general store. "Well, Mrs. Sherman, I expect we'll have this villain's neck stretched in short order. Men who lay hands on women such as yourself don't deserve another sunrise."

The marshal guides me to a chair. I sit, folding my skirts tight, my pulse a drum in my throat. My voice is meant to be sworn, measured, captured in neat little lines for the record. But all I can think, staring at the judge's blunt certainty, is how every stone in this house has been stacked to see Kodiak condemned.

And if I mean to help him, I will have to find a way inside these walls.

The US Attorney speaks. "Would it please the court to set the trial date in the next week or two?"

A clerk clears his throat. "Mr. Randolph's attorney has not yet arrived."

For a heartbeat, I imagine Kodiak in the doorway—eyes wild and burning, blade in hand ready to deliver retribution—but there's nothing. Just the hush of the room and the judge watching everyone, as if he can read our intentions by our faces.

Judge McKinnon looks over his spectacles. "Where is counsel?" His voice is a gavel unto itself.

The US Attorney shakes his head. "I do not know, Your Honor. The government is ready to proceed, however."

"Given the gravity of the charges—and the public interest—I ask the court to set the earliest practicable date," Virgil says.

"And who are you?" the judge asks.

Virgil straightens his posture. "I am Virgil Sherman, Your Honor. Of the Sherman Hospitality Company. My brother Joseph was murdered by this Randolph beast. My dear sister-in-law Alice," he says, tipping his chin toward me, "was kidnapped. Defiled and forced to witness truly gruesome atrocities."

The judge nods, his expression softening from offense to sympathy. "I see. Mr. Sherman, the wheels of justice do not usually move so swift, but I can assure you, holding this criminal accountable is the message we need to send to all outlaws like him."

"Hear, hear," says the US Attorney.

A knock rattles the chamber door. It opens before anyone answers, and in stumbles a thin man in a crumpled waistcoat, hair slicked flat in streaks that don't hide the sweat at his temples. "My apologies, Your Honor," he says, fumbling with a stack of papers that spill to the floor. He drops to his knees. "I was told the deposition would be held at the US Attorney's office," the lawyer mutters, as he gathers his papers. "Not here before Your Honor."

"Well, you're here now, counselor. Do try to keep up. Your name please?"

"Henry Wallace, Your Honor. Appointed counsel for Mr.

Randolph." He smooths his papers on the conference table, though half of them are bent and smudged.

Virgil's mouth twists, but he says nothing. The US Attorney lifts his brows, barely hiding his satisfaction.

The judge exhales, weary. "Mr. Wallace, the government has already moved to set an expedited trial date. We were about to begin the deposition of Mrs. Sherman."

Wallace frowns, blinking hard as he flips through his rumpled stack of papers. "Your Honor, I— Pardon, but is this a deposition or a pretrial conference?"

"It's both, counselor. Given the urgency of the matter, the court is choosing efficiency."

Wallace opens his mouth again, flustered. "But I was not informed—"

McKinnon cuts him off with a sigh. "Mr. Wallace, if you plan to object to every formality, this will take all day. Sit down and allow the record to proceed."

"Y-yes, of course." Wallace sways a little as he lowers himself into a chair. His pen rattles in his hand. "I will, ah, do my utmost to see that my client's interests are preserved."

The US Attorney clears his throat, ready to continue as if nothing has changed.

I press my hands together in my lap, tight as a knot. This is the man meant to defend Kodiak? Late, rumpled, and meek.

Virgil rests his hand on the arm of my chair, fingers firm, guiding me forward. "It is time, Alice."

The clerk lifts the Bible. "Please stand, Mrs. Sherman."

My hip throbs. The chair feels too deep, my skirts too heavy. I brace a hand against the armrest, try to push myself up. Pain shoots through me, sharp enough to draw breath from my throat. For a heartbeat, the room blurs, wood paneling and brass lamps swimming together.

Virgil is on his feet at once, hand firm beneath my elbow. "Steady, sister," he murmurs, voice pitched for all to hear. "She is still convalescing, Your Honor. A miracle she survived at all."

The judge nods gravely, as though Virgil himself has been my nursemaid. "Yes, yes, take your time. We understand."

At last I make it upright, my weight heavy on Virgil's arm. The clerk holds out the Bible.

"Do you swear to tell the truth, the whole truth, and nothing but the truth, so help you God?"

"I do," I say, though my voice is thin.

The US Attorney rises with his notebook. "Mrs. Sherman, thank you for your courage in coming here today. I will begin simply. You were married to Joseph Sherman, is that correct?"

"Yes," I whisper.

"And it is true that your husband was killed by Mr. Randolph, and that Mr. Randolph took you from your home in Ohio?"

"Objection." Mr. Wallace coughs, clearing his throat. "Objection."

"This is a deposition, counselor. Overruled. Your objection will be preserved for the record."

Wallace raises a finger. "But I didn't—"

"Answer the question, Mrs. Sherman," the judge commands, cutting him off.

Virgil's hand tightens on my arm; a subtle reminder, a warning.

"Yes," I say, though the word tastes like bile.

The stenographer's keys clatter, etching my lie into the eternal record.

Across the table, Wallace scribbles something crooked in his notes, clears his throat like he might speak, then thinks better of it.

The US Attorney paces slowly, one finger marking his page. "Mrs. Sherman, can you describe the circumstances under which you were taken?"

My pulse quickens, the memory of that night a whirlwind. Joseph's limp figure slumped in Kodiak's lap. The road unraveling beneath horses' hooves.

Virgil's threat needles me from too near, the faintest tilt of his head warning me which lines to walk.

"I was taken from my home," I say at last.

The prosecutor nods, satisfied. "And you did not go of your own choosing?"

Silence hums heavy. My fingers knot in my skirts. I could tell them the truth: that I had a choice, that I chose to follow. That what bound me to Kodiak was not rope but will. Desire. But that truth is a gallows not just for him, but for me. He'd insisted upon this from the beginning—if we were ever caught, I was to say I was kidnapped.

"I did not go of my own choosing," I repeat, softer.

The stenographer's keys clatter, fixing the lie in iron.

The US Attorney presses gently, almost tender. "During your captivity, were you subject to violence, to threats?"

My hip throbs where the bullet tore me open. Not his fault. Not his hand.

But their judgment expects it.

"There was...violence," I say. The word rings false in my ears.

The prosecutor's brows rise in sympathy. "Against you?"

The room waits. Virgil breathes steady beside me.

"No," I whisper. "Never against me."

The room holds its breath. The attorney's smile falters. Virgil's fingers dig sharp into my sleeve.

"But you witnessed violence?"

"Yes." That, at least, is true.

The US Attorney goes on and on, hours of questions—about the inn, Joseph, the Pinkerton deaths aboard the ship. By the time he stops asking me questions, my stomach is raw with acid.

"Your Honor," I say, my voice quieter than I intend. "Might I excuse myself a moment? I-I need the facilities."

McKinnon waves his hand like I'm nothing more than a buzzing fly. "See to it, Marshal. We will resume when she returns."

Virgil rises too quickly, his hand already at my elbow. "I'll accompany her."

"No." The word leaves my mouth before I can temper it. His eyes narrow, but I steady myself. "Please. I only need a moment."

The judge doesn't even glance at him. "Marshal, take her. Return promptly."

The marshal nods, but he doesn't grip my arm the way Virgil does. His pace is slower as we descend the hall, my steps uneven. The courthouse here is quiet, but the noise of the vestibule carries faintly—boots striking marble, clerks calling to one another, typewriters chattering from open offices.

We pass the courtroom doors again and I slow, feigning a wince at my hip. "Might I pause?" I ask, breathless.

The marshal obliges, waiting by the door as I rest my hand on the frame. Inside, the benches stand polished and empty, the judge's chair looming high above the rail. Light pours through tall windows, gilding every brass fitting, every carved panel of oak.

This is where they mean to condemn him.

I make myself memorize it—the rail, the jury box, the doors where prisoners are brought in chains. My mind counts paces. I note the galleries above, the stairwell beyond, the side hall where witnesses will be kept before they're called. Every stone in this place is against him, but stones have cracks. And if I mean to help Kodiak, I must learn where they are.

The marshal clears his throat softly, motioning onward. "Restroom's this way, ma'am."

CHAPTER 35

KODIAK

Two marshals—one on each side, revolvers heavy on their hips—march me in early, irons clinking at my wrists. They plant me at the defense table and leave me under watch. In the jury box, benches stand empty, sunlight pouring through the high windows, cigar smoke and coffee smells both clinging to the oak paneled walls.

Wallace stumbles in a few minutes later, hair wild, coat crooked, reeking faintly of whiskey. He drops his papers on the table with a slap and sits like he's run a mile and already lost the case. Christ almighty. This is the man meant to save me.

The bailiff calls, "All rise," and the room shuffles to its feet. Judge McKinnon takes his throne, robes trailing, spectacles perched sharp on his nose. "Bailiff," the judge starts.

"Your Honor," Wallace shouts, startling even me.

He scrambles up, wiping his fingers across his brow. "Your Honor," he says again, voice breathless. "I'd ask the court to consider—erm, if it would please the court—that Mr.

Randolph's visible shackles be removed while proceedings are underway. It's prejudicial for the jury to see irons on a man at counsel's table. The presence of shackles begs the question of guilt before any evidence is heard."

The judge blinks at him, then at me. "Is that your request, Mr. Randolph?" McKinnon's tone is weary.

A dozen things want to fly out of me—anger, pride, the urge to spit—but I keep my jaw nailed shut. I nod once. "Yes, sir."

The US Attorney pounces before the clerk can finish penciling the remark. "Your Honor, with respect, this is a dangerous man. I protest for the safety of the court and the public." He looks to the gallery as if to find applause.

I glance quick at the door. There are men—more than I thought. Faces I don't know. Plain suits and uniforms. A marshal's flat badge glinting under a vest. They're spread: two at the double doors, one by the jury, another near the judge, one close to the side door.

Wallace swallows. "We'll accept marshals close by, Your Honor. We merely ask, let my client sit before you as a man, not a caged animal. The prejudice is enormous, and it strikes at the very fairness of the proceeding."

I can tell by the judge's face he hears the law in it, not the whiskey.

McKinnon steeples his fingers and regards the room. "Marshal, is the court's security sufficient to permit removal of visible shackles while keeping the defendant under guard?"

The marshal near the door steps forward like a soldier, square and steady. "Your Honor, there are ten men on duty inside and ten outside."

The judge nods, seemingly satisfied that I'm sufficiently outnumbered. "Very well. The Court orders the wrist shackles removed for the duration of the day's proceeding." Then mutters, almost under his breath, "Ain't gonna make a difference."

Wallace sits back down.

I'll be damned. The bastard actually did something right.

The judge calls for the jury, and they file in like a line of ants. Shopkeepers and dockmen with stiff collars, farmers with sunburned necks, all of 'em sneaking glances at me like they've already read the verdict in this morning's paper.

McKinnon rattles through the charges—murder, robbery, derailment, kidnapping. Etcetera, etcetera. Each word hangs like a block around my ankles 'fore I'm tossed in the Gulf.

Then the US Attorney rises, tall and cocky, voice smooth as a fiddle bow. "Gentlemen of the jury, today you will hear a case that strikes at the very heart of our civilized nation. The defendant, Archibald Randolph, known as 'Kodiak' for his size and brutality, is a ruthless outlaw who has left blood on every road he's traveled. But this case is not just about railroads and stolen payrolls. This case is also about a woman. A virtuous and dutiful wife, torn from her home, carried across state lines, made to suffer as the prisoner of this man."

The jurors mutter with disapproval, shifting in their chairs.

"And you will hear from Mrs. Alice Sherman herself, the widow of Joseph Sherman, who was murdered in cold blood."

The words rip through me like a .45 slug. My head snaps up.

Alice is alive.

For the first time since I made my bargain with God, something like gratitude blooms in my chest. I don't hear the rest of his speech. Don't hear the threats or the curses he lays at my name. All I can think is that she made it. She'll be here.

God help me, I can't stop the smile tugging at my mouth.

The jury don't miss it. They catch my grin. Half of them whisper to each other, and the other half got their lips curled up in disgust. To them, it ain't the kind of joy that hits a man when he knows the one he loves draws breath. Far as they're concerned, I'm positively tickled by the memory of making that woman suffer.

Wallace nudges me, sweat shining at his temple. "Don't smile," he hisses. "For the love of Christ, don't smile."

I drag my jaw shut, but it's too late. The damage is done. They've already got their story.

The US Attorney presses on, painting me more like Lucifer with every breath. "This trial will show you the defendant's callous nature, not just in what he has done, but in the cold indifference with which he carries himself, even here before the bar of justice." His hand sweeps toward me like I'm a carnival display. "You've already seen it. That is the face of a man without remorse."

The jurors' scrutiny burns through me. My blood boils under the heat of their hatred, fists clenching under the table, but I choke it back. Don't give him what he wants.

Finally, he closes his book with a snap. "When you have heard all the evidence, gentlemen of the jury, we will ask you to return the only just verdict: guilty on all counts." He nods to the judge. "Thank you, Your Honor."

The judge turns to Wallace. "Defense may proceed."

My lawyer clears his throat, stands too quick. "Gentlemen of the jury, my client, Mr. Randolph, stands accused of grave offenses. Very grave. But I ask that you remember the burden lies with the—" He stops, face turning green. Looks like he's holding down a belch or wrestling with his breakfast. With a pause, he seems to get a leg up on it and composes himself.

"With the prosecution. You must weigh evidence. Not

sentiment, not sympathy, not stories." He wipes his brow, blinking down at his bent notes. "You will see that much of what is presented will not withstand the light of reason. Witnesses may contradict themselves. Memories fade. And above all, there is doubt," he says, wagging a finger. "Reasonable doubt."

That's it. That's all the poor bastard's got. He sits, shoulders slumped, while the US Attorney writes something smug in his notebook.

The judge calls the first recess. Marshals step in close to shackle me again, irons rattling as I rise. The jury files out slow, staring, weighing me like meat on the block.

But all I can think, through the stink of sweat and cigars, through the clatter of boots and chains, is Alice is alive.

And soon, I'll see her.

They bring the jury back right after lunch. Sunlight catches dust in the air. The judge sets his palms on the bench, and the US Attorney rises, buttoning his coat.

"The government calls Mrs. Alice Sherman."

The room shifts, seats creak, jurors bend their necks. I hear the scuff of her skirts before I see her. Then she steps through the partition, slow, careful, a marshal's hand hovering at her back.

God almighty.

She's pale as milk, thinner than when I last held her, moving with a limp where the bullet tore her. But she's upright. Breathing. My chest tightens until it near breaks.

Every head turns. Men on the benches nod to themselves, eyes soft with pity. To them, she's the picture of virtue wronged, a lamb carried off by the predator now at the defense table. They don't see the fire I know burns in her. How we burned for each other. Always will.

She fixes forward, jaw set, as the clerk swears her in. Her hand shakes a little as it rests on the Bible.

"Do you swear to tell the truth, the whole truth, and nothing but the truth, so help you God?"

"I do." Her voice carries, soft but steady, enough to fill every ear in the room. I drink the sound in like a man dying of thirst.

The prosecutor smiles. "Mrs. Sherman, thank you for your courage. Please, tell the jury who you are."

"My name is Alice Sherman. I was the wife of Joseph Sherman."

The prosecutor paces. "And can you tell us what happened the night your husband was killed?"

The jurors lean closer, eager for her words, for her pain.

And I sit shackled, heart hammering, waiting for her to speak—for her to damn me, or save herself, or both.

She lifts her eyes at last.

Across the gulf of oak and polished brass and fancy law books, her gaze finds mine. Everything else drops away. It's just her.

Alive, whole enough to stand, her hair pulled back neat, though I can see the tremor in her lip. The sight of her hits me so hard I forget how to breathe.

And then it comes. Hot, uninvited, burning my eyes before I can stop 'em. Christ, I thought I was clean out of those. One slides down my cheek, and I don't even bother to wipe it away. Let 'em see. Let 'em think it's guilt or shame. They can call it what they want.

She sees it. I know she does. Her lips part, just barely, like she wants to speak. I inhale deep and slow, big enough for her to see, then exhale calm and easy. She does it too, and I nod my head. Just once.

It's all right.

That's what I want to tell her. It's all right. You do what you have to. Say what they need you to say. Save yourself. I already got all I need.

The jury's watching her, hungry for tragedy, but she keeps her eyes locked on me a heartbeat longer. Her chin trembles. She looks down quick, like she's afraid the room will see too much.

The marshal beside me shifts his stance. The US Attorney clears his throat, starting in on another question, but I don't hear a damn word.

Because that look—that one look—was enough.

She's alive. She knows I ain't angry. And if this is the last time she ever sees me breathing, she'll know I died glad for it.

The government feeds her questions, but I ain't listening to him. I'm watching her. My beautiful lamb.

Alice walks a tightrope, every word measured. Then—

"And when we departed New Orleans, I remember the sky. I remember it was near dawn because the starlight was remarkable. Starlight, bright enough to see the waves."

Starlight.

The word drops like a stone in my gut.

I remember that morning—it was foggier than hell, couldn't see nothing but gray. But that night in New Orleans when we cracked the hotel vault, she'd said starlight when it was time to move. It was our signal. Our go.

Why would she say it now?

I glance around the room. Two marshals by the double doors at the back. One planted near the jury box, another between the judge's bench and the side door. One beside me, hand resting easy on the butt of his Colt. Five inside. Gotta be more in the hall based on the marshal's estimate, maybe more outside.

I look at her and her eyes are on me, hand to her chest. She turns her head slightly, eyes darting to the side door, before she closes them, wincing as if in pain.

The US Attorney asks another question I don't catch.

Alice sways a little, color draining from her face.

"Mrs. Sherman?" he prompts.

She presses a hand to her temple. "Forgive me. I'm— I've been in hospital and...I-I'm not feeling well."

The judge starts to say something, but it's too late. She crumples like her bones have given up. The gallery gasps, and everything snaps at once. The marshal beside me jerks toward her, his hand leaving the grip of his pistol.

And that's all I need.

My hand's fast. I wrench his Colt from its holster and fire point blank. The shot cracks like thunder, echoing off marble. The marshal drops, smoke filling the air, screams breaking loose from the gallery.

I shove the table aside and run for the side door. The marshal near the judge draws, fires, misses, round punching into the wall by my head. I pivot, squeeze the trigger twice. He falls back into the curtains, blood blooming dark down his chest.

The courtroom is chaos: jurors diving for cover, papers flying. The judge yells something, pointing in my direction, his voice drowned by the ringing in my ears. I reach the side door and shoulder it open, the hinges shrieking.

The hallway's ahead, bright and open. One guard posted, running to the opposite door, but that ain't where I'm headed. The walls are paneled in glossy wood, and against an oak rail by the door sits a box of matches—a lamb on the front. Little Lamb Matchsticks.

Salt Lick. I bought these once because of her. Thought it was funny.

Old man behind the counter couldn't quit staring when she smiled.

I grab the box, shove it in my pocket. Ain't got time for more.

In the smoke and shouting, I catch one last glimpse of her on the floor, eyes open, watching me go. My God, I love that woman.

I spill into the main hall. Men turn and shout. The sound catches in my ribs—metal, breath, the slap of boots. Outside the side door, the courthouse narrows into a service lane and a low stretch of yard before the street. It's worse than I thought.

Six men rush the exit like a net—marshals and sheriff's deputies, all with faces set like hammerheads. No escape. Two of them level Winchesters, but most of them wear Colts in plain leather. One's got a shotgun cradled across his chest. They move quick, closing in on me.

Son of a bitch.

No time to think. I swing my weight shoulder-first into the nearest man. He goes down grunting. A Winchester kicks, and the roar cracks past my ear, damn near blowing out my eardrum. Hot air burns my cheek. I grab the fallen man, wrench his pistol free, and fire twice. One goes down on his knees, another folds to the curb.

A carbine butt slams into my shoulder, knocking me sideways. Pain blooms, searing, but it's the kind I can swallow. Don't stop me.

Marshals circle, voices barking commands I don't bother to hear. I duck behind a stone buttress and return fire with the stolen Colt. The law answers in thunder. Winchesters bark from the yard, slugs blast from the shotgun and throw grit into my face. A deputy in a gray coat takes one in the leg and goes down with a howl. Another fires high, the ball tearing the plaster over the courthouse door.

I keep moving, using the angle of the walls, trading shots. The world narrows to breathing and the taste of iron in my mouth. I see one of them leaning out from behind a pile of crates. I don't aim. I shoot the crate where his head just was. He falls anyway.

The yard is a battlefield of smoke and splintered wood. The nearest marshal—ugly bastard with a badge at his vest—cocks his rifle and takes aim. I hurl myself at him, wrap my good arm round his throat and wrench the gun free. It's heavier than I expect. Kicks like a mule. I shoot once, twice. He spasms and rolls.

The street is right there. A block of riders crowd the curb—more marshals, maybe Pinkertons, some in plain suits. I taste tar and the salt of the Gulf wind. A chestnut mare is hitched to a delivery wagon. Its driver slumps where he sat—caught a stray bullet, most like. I snatch the reins, swing my leg high and hard, and find the mount more willing than the men lining the curb.

The world blurs with too much information. They fire after me. Pain slices across my ribs, just a kiss of lead. One round bites into the horse's flank. The animal screams and lashes, bucking me, but I hang on. Another round slams into the wagon wheel and splinters wood to dust. I drive the mare into the street, using her panic as cover. Men scatter, shouting. I don't look back.

Weaving through alleys, the mare's feet slide on wet stone.

Blood trickles warm where the cloth is torn at my side. I slap at it, taste copper, and force my jaw shut. I pull her to a low, sheltered courtyard, slide down, and press my palm to the wound. I listen. A dog barking, a cart's axles creak. No heavy boots. Not yet.

I think of Alice on that floor, her eyes on me as I ran. For a stupid second, I let a laugh leak out. Goddamn.

I look up at the sky, a slice of pale blue cut thin between rooftops. My hand shakes against the hole in my side. "Know we had a deal." My voice rasps out like gravel. "I said I'd go easy. No blood. No running. You keep her breathing, and I'd walk quiet into the noose." Another laugh slips out, this one sharp and humorless. "Well, You did Your part. She's alive. She's standing. Guess that makes You the only one of us can keep a promise."

I drag my sleeve across my mouth, taste the copper on my tongue. "Me? I broke it soon as she looked at me. Soon as she said that word." I draw a ragged breath. "I'm sorry for that. Sorry I'm the man I always was. Guess You knew what You were gettin' when I prayed." I press my palm harder into the wound, grit my teeth. "But You keep her safe, Lord. Whatever happens next, keep her safe. I'll pay the rest."

The matchbox.

I reach for my pocket, pulling the matchbox out. Running my thumb over that lamb, I think of Alice falling limp–the risk she took today for me. Lord, I hope they don't make her pay for what happened in there. I slide the box open and inside there's a scrap of paper tightly folded, small as a thumbprint. Unraveling and flatting it across my palm, I see it's a note.

My bear. My starlight. Return to me.

I press the paper to my lips before I can think better of it, breathing her name into the creases. Blood wet at my side, eyes on the horizon.

"All right, lamb," I whisper. "I'm comin'."

CHAPTER 36

ALICE

"You understand, Mrs. Sherman," the US Attorney says, "if he's found, you'll still be essential to the case. More charges will follow."

I nod, tell them what they need to hear. They write it down. The more time passes, the more the day starts to sweep itself away—clerks close their ledgers, the courthouse hushes to a quiet drone—the more I allow myself what I ache to believe: that silence means he's out there, alive and moving.

They call it a day. In the hotel lobby, Virgil watches me with the look of a man who has caught a thief at his table. He accompanies me upstairs and orders tea to my room. When it arrives, we sit in a small parlor there.

"I suppose," he says over his tea, "that fainting in court was rather convenient, wasn't it? To collapse like that right as the defendant runs." He lets the words stew. "You must understand how it looks."

I say nothing, but Virgil does not wait for my answer in any event.

He rises, and something in him bursts and spills out like a broken spigot. The gentleman drops away in one motion. Grabbing my wrist, he snatches me so hard my cheek catches in my teeth. I try to pull back. He flings me across the settee as if I were a sack of flour. His palm comes down on my cheek with blind, burning force. Pain surges, and a shocked yelp escapes my lips. My hands fly to my face, hot and stinging under my palm. A metallic taste rises. I've bitten my own cheek.

The lamps buzz, the clock on the mantle ticking.

Virgil's face is a dark thing in the light. "You did this on purpose," he hisses. "You set him free. You set him free, and you fell in love with him like a fool."

He comes again. I do not fight well; all I can do is hold up my arms in an attempt to stop his blows. Each one lands—hard—against my arms, my ribs, my middle. I think of Kodiak and how he'd protect me if he could. How I wish he were here to stop this.

When he stops, it is because he wants to. He breathes hard, brushing at his cuffs as if to rid them of my scent. "You will tell no one you did this," he says, as if I alone could stain him now. "And you will pray I find him. I will not ask the law to take him. I will find him myself. I will find him, and I will make him pay. Even if I have to kill him with my own hands."

I taste copper, and a small part of me thinks of Kodiak and smiles, though the smile is cracked and wet with blood. I picture Kodiak's laugh—the cocky sound of a man unafraid of death—and I laugh too.

"Do what you must," I say.

He glares with disgust, standing a moment as if debating

whether to beat me again for my insolence, then thinks better of it. He leaves me there with my palm pressed to my mouth.

I wander to the window and open the curtains. The stars over Galveston twinkle with infinite light and distant promise. The heavens helped us find one another before; what is destined cannot be broken, no matter how hard Virgil or Pinkertons or government men may try.

The train ride north is punishing. My body aches from what Virgil did, though the bruises hide well enough beneath my collar and sleeves. He doesn't speak to me the whole way. He reads his ledgers, checks his watch, and folds his handkerchief into smaller and smaller squares.

By the time we reach Ohio, the sky has gone pale and the leaves have begun to rust with red and orange. The inn is quieter than I remember. The road to the house is the same—gravel crunching under the carriage wheels, pines bending over the drive—but everything feels smaller now. A place I outgrew.

Virgil steps out first. He helps me down—not out of kindness but habit. There's a man waiting by the porch, broad through the shoulders. I look twice. He's tall and broad like my Kodiak. The reminder that my bear is somewhere out there surviving without me turns into a lump in my throat.

"Mrs. Sherman," the man says warmly. Up close, he's nothing like my Kodiak—his face drawn tight at the center, every feature crowding the next, as though afraid of being left out.

"Name's Mr. Collier. New owner of the Collier Inn." His voice is deep and rough.

Virgil clasps Collier's hand firmly. "Ah, Mr. Collier. We have documents to settle. Please wait until the ink dries and the funds clear before removing our family name from the sign, will you?" He says it half serious, half in jest.

"You've sold the inn?" I ask.

Virgil turns to me. "Under my leadership, the Sherman portfolio has shifted focus to luxury hotels in major cities. Now that Joseph's gone, we've no use for a country inn. But Mr. Collier's been of great help. He's kept the house and the accounts in order while this messy business with the outlaw gets settled. I'll be returning to Cincinnati tomorrow—too much work to attend there to linger here. Collier will see you're settled."

Virgil turns back to him, offering another handshake. "Mr. Collier, thank you for your assistance and charity. Mrs. Sherman may no longer be a member of my family, but she is a loyal employee. I'll return in a month's time to settle things."

He says it like a kindness. Like he's done me a favor. He doesn't meet my eye again. He leaves, his carriage rattling back down the road.

Collier scans the yard, then turns to me. "Mrs. Sherman, you're even lovelier than Virgil promised," he says.

My few belongings rest in a valise at my feet, and my insides draw tight—a slow, spiraling knot. I lower my gaze to my shoes, willing myself not to flinch.

"Virgil tells me you were once married to his brother, lived in the main house. I should warn you that you'll find things different."

"How different?" I ask, my voice small.

He gestures toward the rear of the property, where the narrow servants' wing juts off the main house. "You'll be housed there. Modest but sufficient. The housekeeper's quarters are already occupied."

I blink. "The servants' wing?"

"There's no need for you to rattle around the master's rooms anymore. I've taken that as my residence. The staff can use the help—cooking, cleaning, mending, laundry. You'll earn a modest wage for women's work. Better than charity, I'd say."

He says "women's work" like it's a silly thing.

I stand while he gives instructions to a maid about supper, my hand on the porch rail, my hip tender where the bullet found me. The place I once walked through as mistress now belongs to a man who buys and sells homes like ledger entries.

I find my bedroom in the servants' wing, apart from the main hall down a long corridor. There the walls are plain plaster, stained with years of touch. A row of small windows are set high, meant to let in air but not a view.

The bedroom itself is no bigger than a pantry. Just enough room for a narrow iron bed, a chipped washbasin, and an old dresser that tilts from the loss of a leg. The walls are close, made closer by the sloped ceiling that angles low on one side.

There's no lock on the door, just a hook latch from the inside. Still, it is quiet.

That night, when the lamps burn low, I sleep—peaceful enough, knowing somewhere out there my Kodiak is alive.

Morning comes, gray and cold. The air smells of coal and soap—lemon now, not rosemary. I move slow, careful not to wake the ache beneath my ribs or the deeper pain along my hip. Every motion reminds me of what Virgil's temper can do.

The servants' bell clangs from the kitchen below. I've rung that bell a thousand times in another life. Now it calls me. I pull my shawl tighter and make my way down the back stairs, one hand on the rail. The house hums—clatter of dishes, whisper of women's voices, creak of busy footsteps. They're all here: Mrs. Baxter at the stove, Mira sorting linens, Fred beside the pantry, chatting before taking inventory. They look up when I enter.

For a heartbeat, no one moves. It's only been a few months since I've seen them, and yet everything feels so different.

Mrs. Baxter sets her ladle down. "Miss Alice," she says softly, unsure if she may still call me that. Her eyes glisten as she wipes her hands on her apron.

"Mrs. Baxter," I manage. The name falters in my throat like cracked glass.

She embraces me and my arms wrap around her. Behind her, Mira ducks her head to hide a smile. Then footsteps.

Mr. Collier appears in the doorway, ledger under his arm, expression unfeeling. "Mrs. Sherman," he says, the title a mockery now. "The breakfast service is delayed. Kindly make yourself useful with the washing until the others finish. We'll discuss your duties afterward."

I bow my head. "Yes, sir."

The others go still again. Mrs. Baxter whispers, "Don't mind him. He's a brute and we all know it."

"I'm fine," I lie. "I'm only grateful to see you all again."

"Ain't right, what they've done. Not a bit," she snorts.

"Enough," I murmur. "Please."

I move to the basins. My hip protests, but the water's warmth is mercy on my hands. I scrub until the ache dulls to something I can live with.

By midmorning, the sun peeks weakly through the kitchen window. The door creaks open and a small shape hovers there, shifting from foot to foot.

"Miss Alice?"

I turn. Gideon stands in the doorway with the same mop of hair and eager eyes. For a moment, everything inside me softens.

"Gideon," I whisper, voice catching. "Look at you. I'll have to let out the hem at your ankle again."

He grins wide. "Been helpin' in the stables. Mr. Collier says I'm near strong as a man."

I smile for real then, though it hurts my split lip. "I don't doubt that."

He steps closer, uncertain. "I'm real glad you came back. It was awful without you." His brightness chases some gray away. "You'll stay now, won't you? Things'll be better with you here."

I reach out and brush a curl from his forehead. "Mind your work, sweetheart. Don't let Mr. Collier catch you idling."

He nods solemnly and trots off.

For a long while, I stand with my hands in the wash basin, staring out at the gray Ohio sky. For the first time since I came back, something like warmth finds me again. Come afternoon, I hang clean linens on the line. My hip protests, but I grit through it. The rhythm—shake, pin, reach, repeat—keeps my thoughts from wandering too far. I pin the last sheet, its white hem flapping against the wind.

Bootsteps crush the gravel behind me.

"Afternoon, Mrs. Sherman."

I turn. Mr. Collier stands a few paces back, hat in hand, sleeves rolled just enough to show he's been across the grounds. His smile is thin. Forced.

"Afternoon, sir," I say, adjusting a clothespin.

He watches the sheets sway. "Suppose a woman like you never figured you'd be the sort to take up washing."

"Truly, it's not so different than before," I answer. "Only I sleep alone now." And I'm better for it.

He gives a short laugh, low in his chest. "Reckon we've that in common, then. Seems odd a Sherman woman would be getting her hands dirty."

I shrug. "I knew nothing else."

"It's not right if you ask me. Wealthy man like Joseph ought to have spoiled you. You were the woman of the house. A pretty lady like you, kind and proper. You deserve a softer life."

I offer a weak smile in return but don't reply.

He steps closer, close enough I can smell tobacco on his breath as he fills the silence. "Lonely business, running a house," he says, eyes moving along the line of laundry.

I keep my hands moving, folding a corner of a pillowcase. I offer a polite reply. "It must be odd to step into a place left behind by us who once called it home."

He watches me a long moment, squinting against the sun. "This is still your home."

"Only because I've nowhere else to go."

"Then you ought to make yourself comfortable." His voice drops. "No sense living like hired help when there's a bed in the main house." He studies me another moment, head tilting. "You ought to know, the servants hold you in high regard. Makes things easier if you and I see eye to eye. Harmony in the house, that sort of thing."

"I believe I understand your meaning," I say, voice flat.

He steps closer, close enough that the line flutters between us. "Seems you and I, we're both without family now."

"Why are you without family?"

He teeters back, shoving his hands into his pockets. "Always favored soft women. You know—high society-like. But they turn their noses up at a working man like myself. Well, I may have made my money with my hands and not business, but it's wealth all the same."

I nod. A spark of pity nearly ignites something in my chest

that gets quickly snuffed out. "You never fancied a woman of your own class?"

"Never trusted them. All their toil, they're tired of working. Looking for a day off, not a husband." He clears his throat, eyes widening slightly as I fold a pillowcase. "Not that the labor's the issue. Find it mighty attractive you stuck by your husband even when he treated you poorly."

I almost laugh, offering a wry smile instead. "I suppose someone might consider that a compliment."

He shakes his head. "All I'm saying is there's no shame in finding company under the same roof, you and me."

There's the offer, quiet but clear—finding company, paying for company. It's all the same while I live under this man's roof, earning my keep.

"There's shame enough already, Mr. Collier. Best we not add to it."

Something flickers in his eyes—irritation, maybe. "Suit yourself, Mrs. Sherman. I was only being neighborly."

"Of course," I murmur, watching him turn toward the porch.

"When you're done there, help Mrs. Baxter with supper."

Have I hurt his feelings? Wounded his ego? I hope so. I offer a lopsided grin. "Yes, sir."

That night, I carry a folded towel to my chamber, slow on the stairs from the weight in my hip and the ache in my arms. My door creaks open and I step inside.

The floorboards shift behind me.

I turn, heart pulling tight. Collier stands in the doorway, coat off, boots muddy from the porch, face blank.

"This isn't proper," I say, loud enough for the corridor to carry it. "You have no business here."

He props a shoulder to the frame. "Calm down. I only came to talk."

"There's nothing to talk about."

Steps echo from down the hall. Fred's voice. "Everything all right up there, Miss Alice?"

"I'm fine," I call. "Mr. Collier was just leaving."

Collier doesn't budge. "Go on back to bed, Fred," he says calmly. "No need to play chaperone."

Mrs. Baxter's voice joins from further down. "You can't go in a lady's room!"

"That's enough out of both of you," Collier snaps. His friendly mask crumbles. "Back to your bunks. This is a house matter."

A pause, then reluctant retreating footsteps.

He shuts the door behind him. The latch clicks.

I take a step back. "This is not your right. I belong to this house, not to you."

"Calm yourself." He crosses the room in three strides but does not touch me. His voice is heavy. "You belong nowhere. You said so yourself. It doesn't need to be that way." He leans in close, breath warm with whiskey and want. "I could give you a home. A warm bed. A bit of comfort. That's all this is."

"No." I make it sharp, complete.

His hand shoots out, catching my wrist. "You think you're too good?" he sneers. "A woman defiled by an outlaw?"

Something inside me cools. I lift my eyes to his, steady. "You don't know what you're saying."

He leans closer. "Don't I?"

I let a breath slip slowly through my teeth. "He didn't do anything I didn't want. And he's not the only one with blood on his hands."

He blinks, thrown.

"You think you can force me out of here, throw me to the street, and I'll just fade away?" My voice is soft, but the words bite. "You won't even see me coming. I've made widows of women who loved better men than you, Mr. Collier. You ought to mind your p's and q's."

For a moment, the only sound is the hiss of insects outside.

His fingers slacken just enough for me to pull free. But instead of retreating, he closes the distance, a shadow blotting the lamplight. "I didn't need to take you in, you know. Virgil explained your circumstance, and I took pity on you," he says, thick finger in my face. "You've nowhere else to go. Least you can be grateful."

"And I suppose you can think of ways for me to show my gratitude."

He scoffs, curling his lip in disgust, giving me a once-over like he can't believe how wicked I am. "Be downstairs at dawn." Then he's gone, the door swinging shut, latch clicking, his boots echoing down the hall.

CHAPTER 37

KODIAK

When Alice wrote those words, I don't think she realized how difficult returning to her would be. I lay low in the shadows, still in my jailbird denims. First thing is I need to get to looking different. Lord knows my size already sticks out like a bucktooth, but it never ceases to amaze me how far a gentleman's costume can get you.

I keep to myself till dark, resting in an alley till my wound quits bleeding. There's a gentleman's outfitter I passed on Market Street. Behind the glass, mannequins in suits and bowler hats, gloves on wooden stands, polished boots on a shelf. This joint should have just what I need.

Alleys nearby marine supply shops and blacksmiths are rich with scrap metal, bent nails and short, useless strands of wire. Those scraps find utility in the haberdasher's lock as it clicks open. Much more subtle than a brick through a picture window.

Inside reeks of perfumes and tonics, nearly chokes me. But it's a good sign. They'll have toiletries here. I scan the space in the dark; a copper pipe travels along a brick wall behind a long oak counter. Indoor plumbing. Seems I'll get cleaned up proper here.

The register till gapes like an open dresser drawer, nothing but moonlight gleaming inside. Looks like my pockets'll stay empty a while longer.

I move quiet through the rows, running a hand along the wool. French loom, most likely. My father had a tailor in the capitol that would order swatches from overseas. Fine weave, dark gray—something a banker might wear to church. From a hook, I lift a bowler hat and a pair of gloves, soft as milk. I take the jacket and matching trousers, then a clean shirt from the stack. Too small at the shoulders, but most are without a bit of tailoring.

Alice would know just what to do. Have me cleaned up in no time flat.

Goddamn. The thought of her hits me square in the gut, knocks the wind out of me. I been alone most my life, never thought I'd feel this kind of loss. But since she's been gone, I'm all outta sorts. There's a wound in me no one can see, runs straight through like I ain't whole no more.

Ain't just the things she'd do—making my coffee, fixing supper. It's looking for her when the sky turns that bruised purple, when it smells like rain and I realize she ain't there. It's laying under the stars wanting to hear her go on about this one and that one, asking stupid questions just to make her laugh. The grief wants to choke me, but I shake it off. I'll get back to her soon enough. In the meantime, need to clean myself up some.

In the rear room, I find the basin beneath that copper pipe.

The handle groans, then gives a thread of water, cold enough to sting. I strip off the striped denim, stiff with dust and dried blood, and let it fall in a heap. The wound along my side's crusted over, ugly but holding. I wash the worst of the dirt away, the water turning pink before it clears.

A shaving kit waits on the shelf. Straight razor, a cake of soap that smells of cloves. I work a lather, careful round the scabbed edge of my jaw. The blade's sharp; each stroke takes years off me. I trim my hair with the scissors, clumsy but better than a prison barber's hack. When I finish, the man in the mirror looks almost respectable.

A bottle of cologne stands among the brushes. I dab it on, too much maybe, but the scent covers the road and the blood. The gloves slide over my hands like a disguise sealing shut.

I gather what I've used and set it back near enough to right. A glass case out front is loaded with watches and gold cufflinks. Once the lock talks, the panel slides open. I just take what I need. One watch to add some legitimacy to this act. Another to pawn in a pinch. It'll be a day or more before the shop owner knows what's missing. Let the law think I'm traveling in my old denims, that Galveston is already a speck over my shoulder.

I shove all my shit in a leather bag for the road and pull the door open a crack. Outside, the lamps along Market Street burn low, and the Gulf wind whispers between the buildings. I step into it, collar turned up, a gentleman by moonlight and nothing more.

The fog's rolling in off the bay, thick enough to hide a man if he moves quick. I stick to the shadows along Strand Street, boots scraping on the cobbles. Seems every window's got a poster—Train Robber Still at Large—and though the face sketched there looks half stranger, the name cross the top is mine.

The rail yards are out. They'll be watched. A man who robs trains can't run from them the same way. So I head for the docks. Lamps along the piers are smothered in yellow halos. The wharf creaks underfoot. Out in the dark, ropes groan as the tide pulls at them.

One ship's working late. Small cargo steamer, maybe a dozen men moving wearily, stacking barrels under the hiss of lanterns. Across the barrels I read the letters PASC.

Pascagoula, maybe. East, out of Texas.

I watch a minute, counting heads, listening. One man, the purser maybe, sits behind a crate with a ledger open. I straighten the bowler, smooth the coat, make myself tall and certain. A man with purpose draws less attention than a man skulking in the dark. When I step into the light, the nearest deckhand don't even pause.

The purser looks up, squinting. "Passenger business is daylight hours."

I meet his eyes. "Not passenger. Freight. Wallace & Sons. Textile shipment under McKinnon. I'm to ride with the crates, sample inspection when we reach Pascagoula. McKinnon swore it'd be cleared."

He frowns, ledger open, but don't find the name. I press before doubt sets in.

"Look here," I say, reaching into my vest and pulling the gold watch. The shine of it is enough to help him see things my way. "Invoice might've been misfiled in the rush, but you'll surely find it in your morning post. Freight's paid, that's certain." I hold the watch out to him. "Here. I'll let you hold it. Collateral."

The purser glances again at the watch, then at my gloves.

Men trust gold, always have. He takes it, turning it over in his hand. The lamplight glints on the glass face like a wink, and he closes it in his fist with a knowing look. I ain't getting that watch back.

"You'll ride quiet, then. No meals, no complaints."

"I'm nothing if not quiet," I say.

Dropping the watch into his pocket, he nods toward the gangway. "Find a bunk aft."

Seems we understand each other. I step aboard, boots thudding on damp planks. The ship smells of oil and iron. As we push from the wharf, the city blurs into fog, only the cathedral spire left to mark the place I've burned behind me.

Two nights of keeping my head down later, we come into Pascagoula through thick air, rich and green with pine and mud. The docks smell of fish and coal. A poorer sort of town, less polished and more forgiving than New Orleans and Galveston.

No one stops me when I walk ashore. The purser don't even look my way. He's got his watch, and I've got a name that don't belong to any poster in Mississippi. Fair trade.

The streets off the wharf are a cross between boardwalk and mud. A telegraph office buzzes two doors down. I pass a grocer hauling shutters open and a barefoot boy sweeping sawdust into the street.

My pocket is light, the pawn watch gone. But I'm clean, dressed, and standing in a place where nobody cares who I've been. No wagons idle, no horses hitched. From here, the road bends north and I start walking. Alice is a long way off, but I'm finally facing the right direction.

By the second day on foot surrounded by a lot of nothing, I'm half starved, half limping, and aching for a meal. Toward dusk, I come on a store at a crossroads. L. Poole Mercantile &

Sundries, the sign says, letters faded, shop wrapped in honeysuckle.

A cat sleeps in the window beside jars of penny candy. Smoke rises from the chimney out back. I straighten my coat, brush the dust from my cuffs, and step inside. The bell over the door gives a sharp little ring. Smells sweet inside, like peppermint and sugar.

An old woman stands behind the counter, white hair wound in a tight knot, apron faded to the color of flour. She looks up from her ledger and takes me in, eyes moving slow, measuring.

"Evenin', ma'am," I say, touching the brim of my hat. "Name's Wallace. Been on foot since Pascagoula. Horse left me short of town."

She looks me over again. "You don't strike me as a man used to walkin'."

"Never planned to," I say, smiling tired. "Luck turned sudden."

She nods like she's heard it a million times. "You'll eat first. Then talk about luck."

She has me wash up at the pump, then sets me at her kitchen table. Beans, cornbread, fried chicken. I try to mind my manners but the hunger wins out, and I eat something fierce till my hands stop shaking.

When I look up, she's watching me with a small, knowing smile. "You're headin' somewhere important?"

I set my fork down. Lying to her would feel like kicking a dog, so I give her half of the truth. "Yes, ma'am. North. There's a woman waitin' on me there. Alice. We were to be married, but life came between."

"You plan to set it right."

"I aim to."

She stands, crosses to a cupboard, and comes back with a folded paper. When she presses it into my hand, I feel the crisp edge of bills.

"Enough for a train ticket to Meridian," she says. "You'll make better time."

I start to shake my head, but she stops me with a click of her tongue. "Don't argue with an old woman. I got no use for money I can't spend, and the world needs a few more weddings."

I laugh. "You're kind, ma'am. Kinder than I deserve." I pocket the bills and stand. "I'll see her right. I promise you that."

She smiles. "I reckon you already did, just by walkin'."

Before I go, she hands me a warm biscuit rolled in a cloth.

"For the road," she says.

Outside, the air smells of wet pine and rain. I walk on, the road narrow and the money burning a hole against my chest. A proper man would buy a ticket, catch the next north-bound and be halfway to Meridian by nightfall. But a proper man's face don't hang in post offices and train depots.

I keep to the back roads till I find what I need—a horse trader's pen just outside town, men loading wagons with corn and salt. The trader's a fat fella with a cigarette on his lip.

"Fine animal," I say, leaning on the fence. I nod toward the smallest of the bunch, a black mare with a kind eye and a limp in one leg. "That one looks sound enough for the road."

"She's slow."

"So am I."

He squints at me, measuring coat and gloves against the dust on my boots. "Three dollars."

"Two," I say, spreading the bills out so he can see that's all there is. He stares, then spits into the dirt and takes them anyway.

"Bridle's extra," he says.

"I'll make do."

I lead her out by the rope and walk until the town falls behind and the road opens wide. The mare's gait is uneven but steady. I call her Birdie.

By afternoon, the pines thin to fields, and every mile I put between me and the Gulf feels like penance. That night, I camp under an oak, eat the last of Mrs. Poole's biscuit and think of her standing in that kitchen, flour on her apron, believing every word I said.

It's a clear night and the stars come out. Ain't never looked up the same since I met Alice. Wonder if she's somewhere looking up too, mapping out the constellations. Three stars low in the east, just clear of the horizon. The hunter chasing north like he always does.

She'd name Orion's belt, and I'd say something stupid like, *yeah, but where's his suspenders?* She'd laugh, that real one that starts in her chest and bubbles up bright. The thought of that sweet sound puts a smile on my face.

"I'm comin', Alice. Just a little slower than I'd like."

Sleep don't hold me long. The wind changes sometime near dawn. Carries a smell I don't trust. Woodsmoke, faint but wrong for this stretch of empty land. I sit up, listen. Nothing but the steady rasp of Birdie's breath and the whisper of leaves overhead.

When daylight comes, the fog's burned off and the world's clear again. Birdie limps worse. I walk beside her for a spell, my boots stirring dust that hangs low in the sun.

By midday, she's sweating hard, each step a labor. I stop by a creek to let her drink. She lowers her head, water shivering round her muzzle, but she don't take much. I reckon she knows what I don't want to say out loud.

"Don't quit on me yet, girl."

I let her rest a while, then climb back up.

The land starts to roll gentle northward, fields turning to pine hills. The air grows cooler, sweeter. I almost let myself believe we'll make Meridian by week's end. Then the sound comes—faint, like thunder.

But it ain't thunder.

Hoofbeats.

Dust rising on the eastern road, just a flurry at first. Then shapes. Riders.

Three of 'em, maybe four.

My gut goes cold. Birdie feels it too, her ears flicking back, muscles tensing under me. I press my hand to her neck. "One more run, girl. That's all I ask."

We lurch into motion. Wind bites at my face, coat tails snapping behind. The road north twists through woods. If we can reach the bridge by nightfall, maybe we stand a chance.

Behind us, the riders fan out, silhouettes dark against the glare. No lawman's shouts, no gunfire yet. Just pursuit. Cold and patient.

Thirty miles north, the road narrows to a ravine where roots crawl like rope ladders down the slope. The creek below flashes white through the brush. I risk a glance back, dust cloud swelling, riders closing the gap.

"Come on, girl," I whisper, nudging her forward. She stumbles once, catches herself, then pushes on.

By the time we hit the far bank, I can hear the jangle of tack behind us, the hollow clatter of shod hooves on rock.

Birdie's limp worsens. I feel the tremor roll through her muscles. I pull her up short in a thicket of sweetgum, slide off her before she can fall.

She's shaking as I press my forehead to her neck.

"You done good, Birdie. You done real good."

The riders' voices come faint through the trees—one calls orders, the others answer.

Birdie stands a moment longer, head low, then eases herself down with a sigh that breaks something clean inside me. I reach out, touch the warm velvet of her nose. "Rest easy, girl."

Then I run.

Not sure where, I just move. Branches claw at my coat, roots twist underfoot, shadows swallowing me with every step. My lungs burn, stitch flaring in my side.

Behind me, hooves crunch through the forest floor. I veer off the trail, tumble down a shallow embankment, and crawl beneath a thicket, the earth damp, pine needles sticking to my face.

Silence. Just the sound of me sucking in air and my heart beating in my ears.

They pass close—so close, I hear their horses panting. Then a pause. Something not right. One of the horses shifts, snorts.

"He's close."

Bootsteps. Too many.

I make a move, but before I'm upright, a hand grabs my ankle. I lash out, wild, catch a cheekbone or a jaw, but a second man slams me down. Knee in my back, arms twisted till I see stars.

"Easy now," says a third. "Ain't no use getting broke before Sherman sees him."

Sherman.

Son of a bitch.

I stop fighting. The cold numb settles in slow.

They haul me to my feet. One wipes his split lip with the back of a glove, grinning at me through blood. Another rifles through my coat, comes up empty.

"Thought you'd make it farther," he says. "For a train robber, you sure ain't got much sense."

They laugh.

"You're out here riskin' your neck for daddy Virgil?" I mock. "Wonder how else he puts that neck to use, you cocksuck—"

Before I can finish, a fist to my cheek shuts me up, blood surging in my mouth.

"That'll do," says the third man, voice flat. "Bring him in alive."

CHAPTER 38

ALICE

Virgil knew precisely what he was about, that small and calculating man. He could not simply cast me into the street. What would that have said of the illustrious Sherman name? No, he must appear benevolent, must send me "home" under the care of another. How thoughtful of him, to place me in the keeping of a stranger.

The cruelest part is more than once I have glanced across the yard and felt my heart rise at the sight of a tall, broad silhouette, foolish and wild, before I realize it's only Collier. Kodiak would never loom so uncertain, as though the weight of his own limbs perplexes him. There is nothing of a leader in Collier's posture, nothing of a man who knows his own mind. Collier slouches even when he stands still. Kodiak stood tall, walked like he owned the ground beneath his feet.

Collier has not spoken to me since that night. He passes me in the hall as one might a piece of furniture, yet his temper speaks in other ways: a heavier pail to carry, a longer list of linens to scrub. Still, I keep my head high and my work neat. He can pile on every burden he pleases; I would sooner die than give him the satisfaction of seeing me stumble.

It has been weeks now since I've seen my bear. I remind myself that the journey from Ohio to New Orleans took weeks, and his path now will be far rougher. Since his flight from the courthouse, every newspaper from here to the coast carries his name. The whole world knows of his escape. And yet, I cannot help but believe he is out there, making his way to me.

This afternoon, I dare the upper hall, meaning to climb to the observatory. The key hangs on its nail by the door, though the stairwell has gone unused since before Collier took the house. I thought perhaps, just for a moment, I might look again through the great brass telescope.

But before I reach the first step, Collier's voice stops me.

"Where do you think you're going?"

I turn, careful to keep my tone even. "The observatory, Mr. Collier. The lens must be cleaned, and it seems no one has been up to maintain it."

He leans against the wall, hands in his pockets, a lazy smile at the corner of his mouth. "That contraption's a waste of space. I'm to have it stripped and converted to rooms. Bedrooms earn their keep. Stargazing don't."

The blood drains from my face. "You cannot mean that. The Astral Society brings half the county each year. It is the inn's proudest tradition."

"Then it's time this house learned new ones."

"But it's one of the rare amenities that sets us apart."

"Mrs. Sherman, it's high time you remember there is no us. You are a servant. Nothing more."

"And you are a dolt," I say before I can stop myself.

His smile vanishes. For a heartbeat, the hall is quiet but for the clock ticking on the landing. Then he straightens, lazy posture gone, and takes a step toward me.

"What did you say?"

I lift my chin. "You heard me."

The slap comes quick. A backhand meant to teach a lesson. My head turns with it, but I keep my eyes on him.

He grips my arm hard enough to bruise. "You'll remember whose roof you're under."

I open my mouth to answer, but the next blow takes the air from me. Then another. The room spins and I hit the floor hard, my hip catching first, pain bursting white.

When I lift my head, he's already coming toward me, his face red, twisted with fury. I see the glint of his belt buckle, the tremor in his hands, and I understand what he means to do.

I scramble backward, skirts tangling at my knees, palms slipping on the boards. "Don't you dare," I hiss.

He kneels, catching my shoulder, pressing me down with the weight of his arm. "You can end this," he says, the words hot near my ear. "Say the word, and you'll live easy. Or—"

I twist hard, my bad hip screaming, and strike at him with whatever strength I've got left. He swears, loud and ugly, claps a hand over my mouth. Somewhere below, laughter drifts from the dining room. He freezes, head cocked.

The guests will hear. Won't they?

"No one's coming," he mutters. "They won't hear you. You could've come to me easy. You had the chance."

I kick again, clawing at his sleeve, and manage a muffled shout. He jerks back, eyes flicking toward the stairwell. The sound of a chair scraping below. Voices pausing.

Gideon shouts from downstairs. "Miss Alice? Is that you?"

"Help," I cry, but it's mostly lost against his hand.

Footsteps pound up the stairs.

He releases me, standing so fast he knocks a candlestick from the table. "Mind yourself," he says, voice steady now, almost polite.

"Miss Alice?" Gideon asks, appearing on the landing. He takes it all in—Collier red-faced and panting, me on the floor. "Are you all right?" he asks, extending his hand to help me up.

"Bless you, Gideon."

Collier straightens his cuffs as though nothing at all has passed between us. "You should take it easy while you're healing, Mrs. Sherman. Things can still get worse."

CHAPTER 39

KODIAK

Three canvas tents. A wagon. Cookfire smoking low. A man sits sharpening a blade beside a crate marked SHERMAN CO. The others nod to him like they all know the drill.

They shove me toward the central tent. Inside, it's neat. Sparse. A chair, a canvas cot, a lantern hung from the ridgepole. One man stands there already, hands behind his back. Neat mustache. Shirt without a wrinkle. Boots too clean for the trail.

Not Sherman, but one of his hounds.

He glances over his shoulder. "This him?"

"That's the one," says the man with the busted lip.

The man with the mustache turns to fully face me. Eyes pale and slow-moving, measuring me—not with anger, with interest.

I spit at his feet. "Ain't polite to stare, unless you're plannin' to ask me to dance."

He ignores my taunt, rolling his eyes and turning to the other one. "Virgil's coming," he says. "Wants to see for himself."

They sit me in the chair and tie my ankles to the legs. I don't bother struggling. Ain't no leverage in rope this tight. They leave me tied to that chair long after the fire's gone to embers. The night hums with crickets and the low mutter of men on watch, boots crunching soft over pine needles.

Sherman's a no-show. Maybe he's on the road. Maybe he's back at some polished desk, sipping bourbon and smiling.

I breathe deep, but it don't fill my lungs, like my ribs are too small, the rope too tight. I lean my head back and stare at the seam where the tent poles cross.

Lord, don't let Alice think I ain't tried. Don't let her think I wouldn't travel from Galveston to her doorstep on foot if I had to, just to get back to her.

Maybe this is my fate. This is what the stars had in mind to teach me a lesson. I've taken more than my share in this life. Robbed men blind. Told myself I was a decent man so long as I didn't kill nobody who wasn't asking for it.

But sitting here now? I don't feel like a decent man, and I fear Alice'll think I took her favor and ran off with it. She might even doubt if I ever loved her at all. Lord, what kinda lesson is that? What kind of universe blesses a man like Virgil? Puts me in his net to have the satisfaction of taking me down after all the Shermans have done. Shawnee blood's just as red as mine. A man like him will take what he wants from a tribe in broad daylight, then sit in the front pew on Sunday without anyone questioning him. But a man like me, who steals from men like him...got to slither on our bellies in the dark lest we end up some fool's pair of ugly boots.

Either way, the son of a bitch ain't here yet.

And that means I still got time.

I work at the rope with my fingers till they bleed, till one loop feels loose. Outside the tent, voices drift in and out like smoke. I test the chair legs, rock gently side to side. One creaks, just a hair. Dry pine. Maybe split somewhere near the base. I lean into it, careful not to tip, just enough to feel the give.

Then I freeze.

Bootsteps, crushing the earth right outside the tent.

A shadow breaks the light, one of the men peering in.

I go still. Head slumped like I'm half-dead.

He watches a moment, then moves on.

When his steps fade, I press hard into that weak leg. It groans again. Then cracks. Not loud, but noise enough I quit breathing.

No one comes.

I twist the chair, angle it sideways, and slam my weight into the seam where the seat meets the leg. Once. Twice.

Snap.

I'm free of one side.

The rope fights me, but I've got leverage now. I wedge the broken chair leg under the binding, twist hard till the cord slices deeper into my wrist. My fingers are slick with blood when it finally gives.

It's pitch-black outside the tent. I crouch by the flap, listening.

Three men. One near another tent—maybe an armory. One pacing the wagons. One just outside my tent, dozing upright, chin tucked to his chest. Rifle strapped to the bastard.

I wait.

Count ten breaths.

When the wind stirs again, I move.

Slipping out from under the flap into the moonless night, I keep to the tent's shadow. My hand wraps the broken chair leg slick with blood. Not much of a weapon, but it'll do up close.

I get behind him. One hand covers his mouth, the other jams the wood hard against his throat. He struggles, but sloppy —half sleep, half stupid. I hold till his weight slumps into mine, front of his shirt painted dark. Then I ease him down gentle.

Now I've got his rifle.

I drag him out of view behind the tent, cover him with the edge of a tarp. His canteen's full, his belt's got a knife and three cartridges, his satchel has some coin and the box of matches the bastards stole off me. I take all of it.

The man pacing the wagons is next. He walks a loop— confident. No idea someone's missing. I wait for him to pass the tents again. When his shadow slips out of sight, I duck behind the wagon, rifle ready.

A lantern hangs from a hook near the rear, with two small tins of lamp oil resting beside it on a crate. I tip one over the wagon's sideboards, the other across the firepit's half-dead logs.

My lamb's match flares soft between my fingers. I touch it to the wagon and walk away without a backward glance.

A beat.

Flame finds oil, loosing a hungry *whoompf*. Fire races up the soaked wood, leaping tent to tent like the whole camp had been built to burn.

"What the hell?" someone shouts. A gun cracks wild into the night.

"Fire! Get the barrels!"

Too late. The crates pop as the heat reaches whatever they

had stashed. Black powder? Ammunition? Don't matter now. Flames bloom like hellfire, lighting up the pines.

I'm gone, headed for the horses.

Four of them, still tied. They shuffle, nervous at the scent of smoke, the flash of fire. I choose the black one—stocky, already saddled—and let the others loose.

She huffs once as I mount.

Someone's yelling names, kicking tents, cursing in half-sleep.

I'm already galloping, the black mare's hooves digging deep into the night while the world burns down behind us.

CHAPTER 40

ALICE

Weeks pass, and autumn comes in full. The mornings are cold now. Breath fogs in the washroom, and the water bites when I rinse the linens. Smoke from the chimney settles low across the yard, caught in the damp. I work till my hands go numb, then warm them over the stove and start again. Busy hands keep the mind from breaking.

In the early morning, I stand in the kitchen before a cutting board, dicing carrots. The water bubbling and the cadence of the knife hitting the block—Mrs. Baxter's humming as she moves about the kitchen with practiced ease—is soothing in its own way.

Then heavy footsteps announce the dolt's arrival.

"Fred needs a hand unloading the carriage."

Mrs. Baxter squeezes her eyes shut over the sink, her back to him, shaking her head ever so slightly.

"I'll be right over to help, sir," I say.

"Don't dawdle," he grunts. His boots scrape against the hall floor, growing faint.

"Why he expects you to do a man's labor when you're—"

"It's fine, Mrs. Baxter," I interrupt. "I've spent enough time fretting over the way Mr. Collier uses my chores as punishment for rejecting his courtship. I'll manage."

"It was most improper for him to enter your sleeping quarters after dark."

"I know." I hum softly, chopping the last of the carrot. Wiping my hands on my apron, I think about the way Collier's hand had locked on my arm, how his fury had filled the narrow corridor, and how Gideon's voice had saved me from whatever he meant to do. The butcher's blade gleams across the board, glistening from the root's moisture. There's a drawer full of knives just like it, collected over the years. I wipe this one clean and wrap it in a dish towel, stuffing it into my apron.

"He knows not to cross me now," I say, more confident than I feel. "That's why these silly tasks keep being added to my plate. He's no other way to hurt me."

"I wouldn't count on that, Miss Alice. Don't take your eyes off him for a second. I've never trusted the bastard."

I chuckle at the sound of a curse on her elder lips. "I'll be fine."

Though I'm not sure. Nights have grown colder, and I find myself wondering if I'll ever feel Kodiak's warmth again. I wonder if the chill has reached him too, wherever he's gone. I picture him on some long road, coat buttoned to the throat, eyes on the horizon. I tell myself he's coming, that he's just delayed. But the silence has gone on too long. The papers have stopped printing his name.

Perhaps he's realized that having me at his side only ever

made his burden heavier. The thought roots deep, and I press my hand to my chest as if I could pluck it out, but it stays. In any case, I cannot afford to wait for him to come to my rescue while I'm darkened by the shadow of Mr. Collier's threats.

At night, once the house has gone still, I take the key from its nail and climb the spiral stair to the observatory. The air up there is colder, cleaner. The roof groans in the wind, and the boards smell of dust and old varnish. I find the room empty. The brass telescope is hidden in a shed until Collier can find a suitable buyer, he said. He's stripped the room bare—no charts on the walls, no lenses, no brass fittings—but the sky is still there, just as I left it.

Outside, wind sweeps through the trees, scattering leaves. Collier's laughter rises from the parlor below, rough, too loud. The hunters are back from the fields, men with red faces and full pockets. He'll be showing off again, boasting of improvements to the inn, the fine company he keeps. When the guests retire, he'd better not come calling for me.

I open the shutters just enough to see the fields below. The town lights blink miles off, just like the stars. Somewhere out there my Kodiak might be walking, head bowed against the wind. The thought should bring comfort, but it only hollows me out further.

I strike a match and light a single candle. Its glow spills across the empty floor, pale and gold. I kneel by the window, watching my breath drift in the cold air.

It comes to me then, like the slow settling of ash after a fire. All my life I kept the ledger neat, every kindness in one column, every sin in another. I thought if the sum stayed in my favor, the world would leave me standing. I thought suffering had a reason, that virtue was a shield you could raise against whatever storm came howling.

But here I am, hidden in an empty room, the telescope left to rust, my prayers falling like stones into a pond dry from drought. I've sinned, yes. I won't lie to myself about that. I lay with my Kodiak. I lied. I murdered. Those things will never wash clean. I know it. God knows it. Yet even so, I was caged here before, even after all my small obediences, my careful keeping of rules. And after all my sins, I've wound up here, in the same place, under Collier's roof—a servant in my own home.

It isn't that I've lost my faith. I know God and the stars are out there, burning steady. It's only that I see it differently now. Faith isn't a tally you keep, or a promise that pain won't find you. It's just what you hold to when you've nothing else.

I bow my head and press my palms together, and I imagine delivering my thoughts out across the dark to where Kodiak walks—if he walks—through ice and pine.

"If you're still breathing," I whisper, "find your way back."

After silent hours pass, I blow out the candle. Smoke curls up and fades. The sky beyond the window stays patient, the stars bright and cold, and I stay there a long while, neither praying nor despairing, just breathing, until the chill of the boards seeps through my skirts and the first light of dawn brushes the fields below.

Footsteps crunch up the stairs. They're heavy, oafish. I brace myself for what's to come.

His figure hovers at the top of the stairs. "It's odd for a woman to lurk in an empty room all night," he says, voice sluggish with drink.

"I'm not lurking, sir. I'm praying."

"Hmm," he hums, almost with approval. "I need you to lend a hand in the stable."

I blink. For a moment, I think I've dreamed the voice.

Collier's breath smokes in the cold. He's already in his riding coat, gloves half pulled on, the smell of whiskey clinging to him even at this hour.

"The stable?" I repeat. My voice sounds small in the hollow room.

"Is there a problem?" he says, tilting his head with a faint smile that never reaches his eyes. "One of the guests' bays is down. You've a steadier hand than Gideon, and I'd hate to see the animal suffer."

The way he says it makes my stomach twist. He could have called Gideon, could have gone himself. He wants me out there—in the dark, in the cold, where no one will hear.

"Of course, sir," I say at last. I smooth my skirt, hiding the tremor in my fingers. "Let me fetch my shawl."

"Don't dawdle," he says, turning toward the stairs. His boots echo down the hall.

In my room, I take my shawl, wrapping it over my shoulders. Before I go, I pause, remembering the kitchen knife I'd tucked away at the bottom of my sewing basket. I have prayed and waited and endured, and nothing in heaven has moved to spare me. This time, if he means to harm me again, I will not leave my safety to chance.

Outside, the wind rises, scattering the last of the leaves across the yard.

I lift my skirts and start down the steps, the sound of my heartbeat louder than the creak of the boards. The yard is slick with frost. The lantern I carry throws a thin circle of light before me, trembling with every cold gust. The air tastes of woodsmoke. From the stables emanates a soft glow against the dark.

I pause at the door. The night is so calm I can hear the slow drip of water from the eaves, the wind combing through the pines beyond the field. Hinges squeal as I push the door open. The smell of hay and dung rushes out to meet me. A row of stalls glow, the soft light catching on the curve of a bridle, a pile of feed sacks, a pitchfork leaning against the wall.

I check each stall until I find Collier standing alone inside one. He's not tending to any horse. Just waiting. His coat hangs open, his shirt half-unbuttoned.

"You said a horse needed my hand," I say, keeping my voice steady.

"There is," he answers. "Only it ain't a horse."

He takes a step closer, boots scraping on the packed dirt. His eyes glint like wet stones. "You make a habit of sneakin' up there at night, do you? Prayin'?"

"Sometimes," I say.

He grins, crooked and mean. "Funny thing, a wicked woman prayin' to God."

I take one step back toward the open stall door. The knife's weight in my apron pocket steadies me. "You've been drinking again."

"Only enough to speak plain." He wipes his mouth with the back of his hand. "You ought to be grateful, you know. Could be worse things than bein' mine."

He comes closer and I take another step back, my free hand brushing the edge of a bridle hook. "You're not making any sense, Mr. Collier."

He laughs softly. "Ain't I? You think Virgil would lift a finger for you now? He's washed his hands of you. I'm offering you a life, Alice."

The words sting, but I keep my eyes on him. "Step back, sir."

"Why do I offend you so?" he says, closing the last of the distance. His breath reeks of whiskey and bile. "Why won't you see reason, woman?"

He reaches for me. Reflex moves faster than thought. I twist away, the knife already in my hand. His fingers catch my shawl, jerking me off balance, and we crash against the stall door. It bangs open with a sharp crack. The lantern rolls across the dirt, its flame guttering and flaring.

"Quit fighting. I don't want to put hands on you again," he warns, though his hand grabs for my wrist. I drive the knife forward. He grunts, the sound guttural and shocked.

"You brought a knife?" he rasps, voice wet. "What'd you bring a knife for, you wicked woman?"

We struggle—his weight nearly flattening me, one arm pinned—but the knife finds him again, lower this time. The breath goes out of him like a sigh.

He stumbles back, eyes wide with disbelief, one hand pressed to his middle. For a moment, he just stands there, mouth working soundlessly. Then he folds to his knees.

I back away, the knife slick in my hand.

Collier lies on his side now, breathing shallow, eyes already fixed on nothing.

"I told you to leave me be," I whisper.

The lantern's flame steadies in its glass. The horses shift uneasily, but none make a sound.

The cold settles quick. His breath frosts once, twice, then stops. I watch until I am certain. Leave the knife where it fell. The frost will do the rest—keep him through the night, stiff and unmoving, till the morning light finds him.

Outside, the wind has quieted. The yard lies pale under a wash of dawn. I wash my hands at the pump with frigid water until the blood rinses off my fingers. From the house comes no noise, no alarm. The early morning holds its breath, and I start back toward the kitchen door.

The inn resumes its patterns, hands ticking round a clock. Once the sun slants through the kitchen window, I know someone will be running up at any moment. The teapot's just begun to whistle when the back door bursts open.

"Miss Alice!" Gideon's voice cracks like a whip. "You best come quick!"

I pour a cup of tea as Mrs. Baxter turns from the stove, startled.

"What is it, boy?"

He stammers, breath puffing white. "It's Mr. Collier. Out in the stable."

Her hand flies to her chest. "Lord have mercy."

My lips purse as I blow gently at the steam.

"Come," she says. "We mustn't let this get away from us."

I don't ask questions. I set my teacup down with a soft tap against its saucer and follow them outside. We cross the yard together, frost snapping underfoot. The stable door yawns open, the lantern inside burned low.

Collier lies where I left him, still and pale in the straw.

Lucas and Fred arrive soon after, drawn by Gideon's panicked cries. They stop short in the doorway, faces going slack.

"Christ," Lucas mutters. "You think he froze solid?"

Mrs. Baxter covers her mouth, whispering a prayer.

"He didn't freeze," I say.

I kneel beside the man who nearly ruined me, the man who will never raise a hand again. My voice is steady. "He came at me. Now he won't come at me again."

"Oh, dear," Mrs. Baxter says.

Lucas stiffens. "What are you saying?"

"I seen him come at her before," Gideon chimes in.

"You killed him?" Lucas finally sputters.

"Lucas, please," Mrs. Baxter says, holding up a calming hand.

He ignores her. "We ought to send word to town. Get the sheriff."

"No." Gideon steps in front of me before I can open my mouth. His face is bright with heat from the run, chest rising hard. "Miss Alice'll hang for it," he says, meeting Lucas head-on. "After all that's happened, do you think they'll hear you out? Or me? They won't ask questions. They'll drag her off before sunrise."

Lucas's voice thins. "She took a man's life. That's the law."

"She done what she had to!" Gideon snaps. His voice shakes but refuses to bend. "You think she aimed to be a girl that makes men do wrong? Ain't her fault."

The boy's courage is raw and ridiculous and true. For a long, breathless second, no one moves. Mrs. Baxter steps closer and lays a hand on Gideon's shoulder, as if to steady them both.

"Best we not be askin' the sheriff just yet," she says. "We know how folk will take it. We'll do the decent thing here among us."

Fred shuffles, uneasy. "What if Virgil gets here and—"

"He's due," I say. "He'll be here any day. We'll tell him what must be told. For now"—I breathe deep—"we move him, somewhere cold, until we decide."

Lucas's panicked expression slowly calms, the lines at his temple tightening as though he's aged a year in an instant. "If you're certain, if you all stand by her, then I won't tell. But this is a weight on all of us. If it should come back—"

"It won't," Gideon says, his small voice like flint.

Fred retrieves a canvas tarp from the shed and we roll Collier onto it before we lift. The canvas scrapes, rough in our hands. Fred takes him under the shoulders, Lucas the feet. Gideon and I shoulder the middle, while Mrs. Baxter carries the lantern. The body is cold, heavier than any of us guessed. We walk carefully, breath steaming white, the yard a field of small silvers of glass under the thin morning.

"Easy now," Mrs. Baxter whispers.

We've just cleared the garden path when Fred stops short. The canvas slips from his grip. "Sweet Jesus," he mutters, awed.

"What?" Lucas snaps, glancing up. "Holy shit."

Across the yard, through the fog and weak morning sun, is the specter of a man. For a heartbeat, none of us move. The air itself seems to hold still.

"Christ almighty," Mrs. Baxter breathes. "Collier's ghost."

It's as if he's moving through the mist like he never died at all.

Gideon's hands fly from the canvas, his face white as milk.

Lucas staggers back a step, crossing himself.

The breath snags in my chest. My mind won't make sense of it. I know where Collier lies—wrapped at my feet, heavy and cold—and yet that shape keeps coming, tall and broad and steady in the pale light.

The fog parts around him, sunlight glancing off the dark of his hair. And then I see him—straight-backed, unhurried, grace in every motion.

"Kodiak," I breathe.

The others stare, caught between awe and disbelief.

He stops a few paces off, boots dark with mud, breath steaming in the chill. His gaze sweeps from the canvas to my face, quiet understanding dawning there.

"Wasn't expectin' a welcome party," he says, grinning at me. He glances down at the corpse wrapped in a tarp. "Or a funeral."

CHAPTER 41

KODIAK

After Alice explains I'm not a danger—at least to her and hers—I help 'em drag that Collier bastard to the root cellar. Never met the man, but if Alice helped him give up the ghost, reckon he earned it.

Hell, all I wanted was to lift her, spin her, kiss her deep. That's how I saw it playing out the whole way from Galveston. But finding her there with a dead man on the ground sure took the shine off the moment.

I hole up in the main house while the others go about running the inn. Come nightfall, Alice finds me there. She's limping some. Stops in the doorway like she ain't sure she's welcome.

"Why you hangin' back, sweetheart?"

"I can hardly believe it's really you," she says, quiet-like. "I keep thinking you'll vanish."

I grin. "Been called a ghost already today. Seems I'm gettin' a reputation."

She laughs a little—worn thin but real. I reach out slow, letting her choose. She don't move. Just watches me with those wide eyes I've seen in dreams every night since Galveston.

"I kept thinking you might be gone for good," she says. "That you'd realized life would be easier without me."

I shake my head. "Ain't nothin' about this world easier without you."

Her face softens, shoulders drooping like she's been holding up the world alone. She leans into my hand like a kitten purring against a leg, and I draw her close, one arm at her waist, the other sliding up her back. She smells of woodsmoke and cold night air.

We stand quite a while, fire crackling behind us, her breath warm on my throat.

"I feared I'd never feel safe again," she says, barely a whisper.

I bend to kiss her. Her fingers knot in my shirt as though she'll lose me again if she loosens her grip. And God—her taste—it's like finally laying down the ache I've carried through every empty mile without her.

When she pulls back, her body eases away.

"Virgil is coming," she murmurs. "Any day now."

"Good. Been lookin' forward to seein' him."

"Kodiak, I don't know what to do."

"Don't fret none. I'll see it handled."

"With guns?"

"That strikes me as a sensible plan."

"You cannot keep solving every problem with bullets. Aren't you weary of all the running?"

"It's the only life I've ever known."

"I understand. But we could have something better."

She steps into the firelight, shadows shifting across her

face. "You said you wanted cattle. Hogs. Chickens. We can do that here. Live off the land. Run the inn."

Being a hotel man don't sound like a dream. I'd sooner chew nails. But she's right about one thing—me wanting to live clean, quiet, and with her, whatever comes next. I've dreamt of Alice heavy with my child more times than I care to admit. Trouble is, it ain't a life I can promise.

"We can't. Not while there's a price on my head."

"I cannot run again," she says, voice firmer now.

Then her fingers go to the buttons at her hip, undo 'em. The fabric parts, and there it is—the scar. Pink, ropey, like a railroad track etched into her flesh.

"It aches when the weather turns. I can walk, work, but it's not easy. If we had to run, really run, I'd only slow you down."

For a long spell, I just stare. That wound damn near took her from me.

"I remember that day," I say. Wind off the Gulf, her skirts soaked in blood, me screaming for a doctor like a madman.

"It's ugly," she murmurs. "I walk like a lame mule."

"You're the finest thing I've ever laid eyes on. I'd do it all over. Swing from a rope if it meant keepin' you alive."

Her hands come to my face, trembling. "Don't die for me, Kodiak. Live. *Stay*, and live."

I sink to my knees before her, pressing my lips to the scar. The skin's warm, raised. I kiss it again, slower this time, mouth moving along the jagged ridges. My hands find her hips. She leans back against the wall, breath catching.

"Let me see you," I murmur.

With shaky hands, she tugs the skirt open the rest of the way. It drops past her hips in a soft whisper of cloth. Ain't nothing underneath—just her, bare and trembling in the firelight.

One hand finds the wall behind her. The other grips my shoulder.

I start with a kiss to her inner thigh—slow, reverent. Her skin's hot under my mouth. I drag my tongue along her, feel her jolt. When I part her and kiss the place she's burning for me, she lets out a gasp.

She tastes like sin and redemption both. I take my time, tongue drawing soft circles, then deeper strokes. She moans, nails clawing at my shoulder.

"Kodiak."

I hum against her, sucking gentle on her pretty little button, feeling her whole body start to quake. She's close already, hips grinding. When she comes, she don't cry out. She whimpers, legs shaking, head thumping against the wall.

I hold her through it, mouth gentling, letting her ride the wave.

After, I rest my head against her thigh, breathing hard.

She laughs, breathless. Hands cup my face, pulling me up. She kisses me deep, like she don't care what I taste like.

"Come with me," she whispers.

I nod, chest tight. "Lead on."

I follow, one step behind, watching the sway of her hips, the soft dip of her spine where her blouse hangs loose. Her skirts are pooled downstairs, so all she's got on is that blouse. The hem barely covers the round curve of her backside. She hasn't even touched me yet, and I'm already half crazed with want. But it's more than that. It's need. It's months of hunger, loneliness.

My voice comes quiet. "You're the prettiest thing I've ever laid eyes on."

She pauses at the top of the stairs, turns her head just enough for me to see her smile—soft, tired.

The bedroom door creaks open. She steps through and halts at the edge of the bed—the same bed that held the man she was bound to by name only, and later, the scoundrel we dragged down to the root cellar.

I catch up to her, slide my arms 'round her waist from behind, and kiss her shoulder. The scent of her clings to my mouth.

"This all right?" I ask, voice hushed against her ear. "This room?"

She nods. "It doesn't belong to them anymore. It's ours now."

I press in closer, resting my cheek to her hair. My hands splay across her stomach, thumbs brushing slow.

"You tell me what you need, lamb," I murmur. "How you want it."

She takes my hands and guides them up—over her ribs, her breasts, her throat arching just a little. Her body knows mine. Missed mine.

"Slow," she says. "I want to feel every part of you."

She leans into me, like she's certain I'll catch her.

"You want me to lead?" I whisper, my mouth brushing the shell of her ear. "Want me to take care of you proper?"

Her breath shivers out. "Yes," she whispers. "Take care of me."

I turn her gentle and stop her hands when she reaches for the buttons of her blouse.

"Let me."

She lowers her arms, lets me do the honors.

I take my time, each button a small undoing. I kiss her as I go—her collarbone, the hollow at the base of her throat, the soft curve of her breast. She trembles under my mouth, breath catching like she's near forgotten what this feels like.

When I slide the blouse from her shoulders, she stands there bare, the dim lamplight dancing across her skin. Her nipples are drawn tight from the chill, gooseflesh crawling up her arms. I cup her chest, my thumbs rolling gentle over those pretty peaks. She gasps, bending into me, and I lower to her— tongue flicking soft at first, then firmer, sucking her into my mouth while her fingers curl into my shoulders.

"You feel that?" I whisper, moving to the other. "That's me takin' my time with what's mine."

She's breathing harder now. Her fingers tremble where they grip me.

I let go, slide my hands down her waist. "Bed," I whisper. "Go on, lie back for me. Nice and easy."

She does, careful of her hip. Helping her down, I guide her until she's settled—flushed, bare, eyes wide and waiting.

I step back and start to strip. Hook my thumbs in the suspenders, let them fall slow, one at a time. "You miss me?" I ask, the corner of my mouth curling.

"I dreamt of this," she says.

I shrug off my shirt, one shoulder then the other. My belt's already loose, trousers hanging low. Her eyes drop, lingering on the trail of hair, the heavy shape of me straining beneath the fabric. *Christ*—how it aches for her. I grip my rigidness through the cloth just to hear her breath hitch—watch that slight needy roll of her hips.

"Tell me what you want."

"I want to see," she says, voice like silk. Thighs parted, her arousal glistens in the lamplight.

I toe off my boots, fingers working the buttons of my fly one by one. When I push the trousers down and step free, her gaze don't leave me, not for a second. Wrapping a hand around the base of myself, I stroke slow, thumb passing over the crown. A slick bead of desire wells there, and her lips part as I smear it in a slow circle until the swollen head glistens wetly.

"This what's kept you up at night?" I murmur. "Dreamin' on how it'd feel to be stretched full of me?"

Her thighs part a fraction. She don't answer, but she don't need to.

"Spread for me, darlin' and let me take what's mine."

She parts her thighs for me, her little wince not lost on me. I place a hand on her knee, gentle-like.

"That hurtin' you?"

"No," she says, voice steady but breathing fast. "Just tight."

"I'll go easy," I murmur, leaning in to kiss her stomach, the line of her hip. "You just keep tellin' me if somethin' don't feel right. You hear?"

She nods.

"I need to hear it."

"Yes," she says. "I promise."

I wrap a hand beneath her thigh, lifting it to cradle her just right, taking care to mind that ache in her hip. With the other, I guide my length down and slide the tip through her slickness, dragging slow over that tender little bundle of nerves. She is dripping—wetness slicking my length the instant I touch her, a hot, silky flood that tells me how long she has ached for this. I slide upward, pressing the flushed crown against that sensitive bud, rubbing back and forth, circling, teasing until it swells harder beneath the pressure. Again and again I torment it—slow drags, light taps, firm circles—until her hips jerk helplessly upward, chasing more.

"Easy, now," I whisper. "You ain't in charge here. I am. I decide what you get and how hard you get it."

I press forward slow, my teeth gritting tight at the feel of her stretching around the thick of me. Her warmth grips me like her body remembers every inch. She gasps, back arching like I lit a match to her spine.

"You're mine," I rasp. "Ain't no one else ever gonna have you like this." I draw back slow as cold sap then sink in again—deeper this time, harder, claiming more of her with every roll of my hips. "My woman. My home."

Her back arches, mouth parting as tries to tilt her hips up into mine.

"Ah, ah," I chide, gripping her good hip tight. "I warned you once. You don't get to chase it. You take what I give. Understand?"

She swallows. "Yes."

"Say it proper."

"Yes, sir."

I smile. "There's my good girl."

Then, I move. Slow, dragging strokes—out until the crown barely brushes her entrance, in until I'm seated deep, brushing that hidden place that makes her quiver. I watch her unravel, eyes fluttering. My thumb seeks out her swollen pearl and traces lazy circles—light at first, then firmer, rubbing until it pulses under my touch.

"You like that?" I murmur. "Like me teasin' you here while I fill you slow? Feels like heaven, don't it, little lamb?"

"Yes, sir," she breathes, legs trembling against me. Her breath turns uneven. She makes a sound—half moan, half plea—and I know she's close. Her fingernails dig into my shoulders like she's hanging on for dear life.

Her head falls back, exposing the pale column of her throat. I can't resist—I slide my hand around it, fingers curling possessively as my thumb leaves her bud. I squeeze just enough to feel the frantic flutter of her pulse, just enough to remind her who I am.

"Your heartbeat's hammering against my palm. You trust me not to hurt you, little lamb?"

"Yes, sir," she whispers, the words strained and soft under my grip.

I rock deeper inside her, slow and deliberate. "But you know I could, don't you?"

She answers with a broken cry, arching sharply beneath me. Her diamond-hard nipples drag across my chest with every desperate heave of her breath.

"You're right there, ain't you? Right on the goddamn edge?" I rasp against her ear, holding her pinned. "Come for me," I growl, thrusting deep and grinding hard against her core.

She shatters—Christ, does she shatter—clenching around me in waves that drag me deeper, her body pulling at mine like it's starving for every inch.

I give her no reprieve. I drive into her harder, relentless, chasing the fire she's lit inside me. Her thighs clamp tight around my waist and the feel of her unraveling beneath me splits me wide open.

"Fuck," I choke out, burying myself to the hilt one final time. I come with a ragged curse, spilling deep and hard, everything I have pouring into her. My body locks rigid, jaw clenched against the damp curve of her neck as the world flares white-hot and still.

Her fingers tangle in my hair, her lips brushing soft kisses along my throat while we both breathe ragged like we just outran the law.

When the spinning finally slows, I stay buried inside her, chest heaving against hers. I trail a lazy hand down her thigh, stroking the sensitive spot behind her knee. Her skin is slick with sweat, glowing in the firelight, and she's never looked more beautiful—bare, breathless, utterly spent, and still full of me. The room hangs heavy with the raw scent of us.

I press my forehead to hers. "I could live right here between these thighs, little lamb...fillin' you up till it takes."

She trembles at that, fingers curling against my back with a gentle laugh. "Do you expect us to run with a baby strapped to my chest?"

I don't answer straight off. Just breathe her in, cheek restin' against her temple, hand idlin' at her waist.

"I ain't never expected nothin' but trouble," I say finally. "And I damn sure never thought I'd be so lucky to have a woman like you. But that don't stop me from wantin'. From seein' it clear in my head: you in a warm cabin, belly full, hair comin' loose from the heat. Me out mendin' fence or tendin' to the stock. Maybe a boy trailin' me, maybe a girl sittin' on your lap listenin' to stories."

She's quiet a long while, then she pulls back, the pads of her fingers brushing sweat from my temple. "Then why do you keep riding toward death?" she asks. "Why keep chasing a fight, Kodiak, when you just described peace?"

Because it's all I've ever known. Because every time I've hoped, I've regretted it.

But I don't say all that.

Instead, I kiss her forehead.

Her hand slides to my cheek, thumb stroking lazy. "If we're going to run, I need to know it will not be forever. I need to believe there's an end to it. A cabin. A fence. A child."

"Wakin' up with your legs 'round me and the sound of chickens out the window. Hell yeah, that's what I want. I just don't know how to get us there."

She leans in, presses her lips to mine. "We'll find a way," she says. "But not if you go off getting yourself killed chasing vengeance."

I blow out a breath. "I'm still gonna kill Virgil," I mutter into her hair. I ease my weight off her, careful not to jar her hip, and cradle her close as I lie us down side by side. My hand finds the back of her head, fingers sifting through damp hair. She presses her face into my neck like she needs to hide there a minute.

"You can't kill everyone, Kodiak."

"I know. Let's not worry about that right now," I say, pulling her closer. "You feel so good wrapped around me. Been thinkin' about this since Galveston."

She hums low, content but worn through, like her bones melted out of her.

"Ain't lettin' you go again," I whisper into her hair. "You know that, right?"

"You'd better not."

I drag my fingers along her spine, feeling the sweat start to cool on both our skin. We lie there a long while, tangled up in each other, just breathing. Letting the fire crackle down and the night stretch quiet.

"Sleep," I whisper. "I'll keep watch."

CHAPTER 42

The notice we hung at the gate sways in the wind, the ink bleeding where the rain had touched it:

INFLUENZA OUTBREAK — CLOSED TO TRAVELERS TEMPORARILY

It would keep the curious away. Illness always did.

I peek through the upstairs window. Two riders turn into the lane. Virgil rides in front, posture straight as ever, his coat immaculate despite the muddy road. Behind him comes a thinner man, a satchel balanced on his knee.

My pulse quickens. Why had I assumed he'd come alone?

Oh no. This won't do at all.

When his knock finally comes, it echoes through the empty rooms like a bell tolling. I draw a steadying breath and open the door just wide enough to meet them in the threshold.

"Virgil," I say. "You shouldn't have come. There's sickness in the house."

He removes his hat, polite as if he hadn't abandoned me

here with a strange man, as if he hadn't beaten me bloody the day we left the courthouse.

"Always some ailment about, Alice. I won't be long. Mr. Collier and I have unfinished business."

My hand tightens on the door's edge. "He isn't receiving visitors. The fever has quite undone him."

The younger man shifts behind him, uneasy. "Perhaps we might return another day."

Virgil silences him with a glance. "Nonsense. A few signatures, that's all. You've no objection to me stepping inside, do you?"

I hesitate just long enough to make the lie believable, then step aside.

"Very well," I say quietly. "But please, don't linger."

He steps aside with a small gesture. "This is Mr. Brown, a notary from the county. He'll see to the papers once we're settled."

The younger man bows, awkward but earnest. "Ma'am."

"Lovely to meet you, Mr. Brown," I reply, inclining my head.

They cross the threshold with the careful air of men entering a tomb.

I've left the lamps low and the curtains drawn. It makes the hall feel smaller, closer. The scent of carbolic and smoke clings to the walls, proof enough of "disinfection."

"Apologies for the state of things," I say, leading them toward the front parlor. "We've been doing what we can to cleanse the air."

Brown presses a handkerchief to his face as though the contagion might leap from the wallpaper. Virgil, by contrast, seems invigorated by his own fearlessness, his boots striking the floorboards in bold defiance. His eyes wander over the room—the closed door to the kitchen, the fire burning low, the ledger waiting on the side table. "Mr. Collier's up to bed, then? I should like his signature before the ink dries on my patience."

"He's resting," I tell him. "The fever took him quite hard."

Virgil seems to weigh how much truth I might be worth. "I imagine you've been playing nurse," he says. "Always did have the constitution for it. But I'll need to see him. I may be a respected man, but the bank won't simply take my word."

The tremor seizes my hands before I can still them. "He's scarcely fit for company."

"Then I'll be brief."

Brown shifts again, clearly wishing himself elsewhere. "Mr. Sherman, if he's truly ill—"

Virgil turns on him with a touch of ice in his tone. "You're here to witness, not to diagnose. Sit yourself there and prepare the papers."

The notary obeys, fumbling for his pen.

Virgil faces me. "Show me to him."

Upstairs, Kodiak waits behind a locked door, Collier's hat and coat laid ready on the chair beside him. The smell of lye is stronger up there. Even through the floorboards it bites the back of my throat.

I smooth my skirt and force myself calm. "If you insist. But you mustn't linger."

Virgil offers his arm with mock gallantry. "After you, my dear."

I take a single steady breath and lead him up the stairs. The house creaks around us, old wood complaining as if it meant to warn him. *Stop! Turn back!* Every step sounds louder than it should, as though the walls themselves wish to betray me.

At the landing I pause, hand on the banister. The air is close, heavy with soap and smoke.

Virgil's boots creak behind me. "Still smells like lye," he says. "You always did like things scrubbed raw."

I ignore him, turning toward the east corridor. The door to the sickroom waits at the end, light leaking through the keyhole.

"Best keep your distance when I open it," I say, loud enough for my voice to carry. "He coughs when the air shifts."

Virgil makes a sound, amusement perhaps. Let's see how amused he is inside. I reach the door, hesitating. My blood pumps so hard I can feel my heartbeat against the doorknob.

Inside, silence. Then, the faintest movement, the creak of a chair, the whisper of cloth.

Kodiak is ready.

I knock lightly. "Mr. Collier," I call, as the door squeals open. "Virgil's come about the deed."

A rough cough answers, convincing. "Not now, Alice." His voice is thick, unrecognizable.

Virgil's expression shifts, a flicker of discomfort. "I need his mark. Nothing else will do."

"Then keep back," I say and push the door open.

The curtains are drawn, only the fire lends shape to the room. Kodiak lies half-turned from us, face lost in shadow.

Virgil steps inside, the smell of carbolic and damp wool strong enough to sting the nostrils. "Collier, you look worse than I expected," he says, tone half teasing.

Kodiak shifts but does not rise. "You'd look the same, Sherman, a fever to your bones."

Virgil chuckles, uneasy. "We just need your mark, friend. Then you can go back to dying at leisure." He steps closer.

I move to intercept him, setting a hand on his arm. "Please. The doctor says exertion worsens the fever."

He looks down at my hand, then back to the bed. "I'll be careful," he hisses.

Kodiak turns slightly, enough for the firelight to catch the line of his jaw.

"Paper," he says. "Bring it here."

Virgil hesitates. For the first time, I see doubt in him—something calculating, something wary.

Downstairs, a board creaks, the notary shifting perhaps.

Virgil hands me the papers. "Very well. Have him sign."

I cross to the table, dipping the pen. Behind me, Kodiak coughs again, the sound raw enough to make Virgil flinch.

"Hold still," I whisper, and pass the pen into Kodiak's waiting hand.

He scrawls the name in a single deliberate stroke, the ink soaking into the page like blood.

When I turn back, Virgil is studying the shape beneath the blanket, his mouth drawn tight, lingering by the foot of the bed. The fire pops and a thin coil of smoke slides toward the ceiling.

"He's drifting. The fever takes him under for hours."

Virgil smiles without warmth. "I should like a closer look." He takes another step.

My breath catches. I can see the muscles in Kodiak's forearm tense beneath the blanket, his hand closing over the pistol always holstered beside him.

"Please," I say quickly. "He's contagious."

Virgil hesitates, amusement flickering again. "You truly think I fright so easily?" He reaches for the edge of the quilt.

Before he can draw it back, Kodiak speaks, voice deeper now, clear.

"Leave it be, Sherman."

The words freeze him. Recognition hits like the crack of a whip. His gaze darts to me, then back to the bed. "That's not—"

Kodiak throws the blanket aside and sits up, firelight in his eyes, pistol leveled between Virgil's. For an instant, Virgil doesn't breathe. Then he laughs, short and sharp.

"I'll grant you ingenuity, Alice. I'd thought you'd taken this creature to your bed, but I never dreamed you'd domesticate him." Virgil's smile does not falter. He rests one hand on his hip, fingers curled near his own piece, a passive motion that betrays the true threat of violence, that blood could be drawn at the twitch of a finger.

"You don't want to gamble which of us is faster with a pistol, Sherman." Kodiak's voice is soft, measured, but there is iron under it.

For a heartbeat, Virgil lets his hand lie there, as if he were caressing the thought of it. "So this was your plan? To pretend to be Collier and send me on my merry way? You nearly passed for Collier, I'll give you that. What have you done with him?"

"Take a wild guess," Kodiak snarks, but I've been hooked by Virgil's words. Just then, it comes to me all at once.

Collier. That's it.

Virgil's smile remains, but his eyes lose their edge—too still now, too calculating, all his focus on the pistol. "I'll ask again. Where is Collier?"

I step between them. "He's...passed on."

"He's fuckin' dead, Virgil. Alice, get out of the way."

Virgil sighs as if I've disappointed him. "You let this animal kill an innocent man?"

"I killed him."

"Alice," Kodiak warns, "get out of the goddamn way."

"It was self-defense," I explain.

"Alice, move. Now!"

His shout makes me jump, and I stumble back. I turn to face him. "We are not doing this, Kodiak. Both of you, put your guns away at once. We will discuss this like civilized adults."

Virgil scoffs. "Civilized? With a murderer and a fugitive? He killed ten men in Galveston. More if you count the innocent men on that ship."

"I don't expect this yellow-bellied dog to know a goddamn thing about honor." Kodiak's arm swings blunt against my chest, sweeping me backward and out of the line of fire, his other hand snug on his gun.

"Kodiak!" I warn.

He ignores me. "Go ahead, draw iron. I dare you."

Virgil studies him. "You've got gall, Randolph. If you fire your weapon, the man downstairs will ride into town and have the sheriff up here by nightfall for the both of you."

"You need the law to settle your scores, boy?"

"Enough," I say. I turn to Virgil. "I know you well enough to know your true concern is not with Kodiak. This is about business and the Sherman name. It always has been. So what if we could give you the satisfaction of claiming the bounty on Kodiak."

"What?" Kodiak shouts.

"Calm down and let me finish!" I shout. "You want to be done with this?" I ask them both. "Then we end it. For good." I address Virgil. "We both know the only reason you want to see Kodiak executed is to impress the railroad men at L&N so you can make permanent their arrangement with Sherman Hotels."

"You assume much. What is your point?"

"My point is, there's a body downstairs. Same build. Same height. No people to miss him. Take him in. Say you found Kodiak holed up in the cellar. You took him down with your own hands. You collect the bounty. The law crosses his name off the books and you play the hero."

"Oh, come on, Alice. Virgil couldn't take me in a fight," Kodiak complains.

I face him. "Do you care more about your reputation than our future together?"

Virgil chuckles to himself, shaking his head, but his attention stays fixed on Kodiak. "You'd let the world believe you'd perished? For a woman?"

"Yes, I'd die for that woman," Kodiak says, unflinching. "Alice, what are you saying?"

"I'm saying you can stop running. Live for me. Here. Put down roots."

His eyes flutter slightly and he exhales—one sharp, soft breath.

"So let me get this straight," he says, half to himself. "You want to fake my death with Collier's body. Hand him over to this bastard"—he nods at Virgil, who merely raises an eyebrow —"and let him walk into town a hero with a bag of bones for a bounty check, while I pretend to rot in a shallow grave and go dig potatoes behind this inn for the rest of my life."

"It doesn't have to be here," I say gently. "Just not running. Not killing. Not hiding."

Kodiak shakes his head, gun pointed at Virgil. "This is madness."

For the first time, Virgil relaxes, hand slipping off his gun. He crosses his arms. "It is madness—but it'll pass. Disfigure the face, strip the clothes, leave something to identify him by. The law will see what it wants to see."

"Kodiak, put the gun down," I say.

He shakes his head. "You might trust this bastard, but I'd sooner wrestle a rattlesnake than take his word."

Virgil snorts—half disgust, half boredom. He lifts his hands in mock surrender, then slowly unbuckles his belt and sets the holstered weapon on the bed. "Unlike my brother, I do not let emotions cloud my judgment. I'm nothing if not pragmatic. And it seems our dear Alice has offered quite the novel solution."

"She ain't *our* anything," Kodiak growls.

"Kodiak, please. Put down the gun."

He exhales slow, eyes scanning Virgil for hidden steel. Then, at last, he holsters the pistol.

Virgil smooths his sleeves. "This debacle has cost more than I care to admit—chiefly, my time. Then, of course, there is the chore of reuniting our New Orleans guests with their missing trinkets and soothing the gossip that followed. I've no interest in petty revenge games with you and Princess Stargazer. My concerns lie in investment, expansion of our metropolitan hospitality divi—"

"Get on with it, Virgil," Kodiak snaps.

"It's in everyone's interest to end this in a way that serves us all. From the beginning, we only meant to resolve an inconvenience for our partners. Now, if Kodiak Randolph is to die, well, then his crimes die with him."

Kodiak's gaze drifts to the fire's low glow, the damp coat slumped across the chair, the pistol at his hip. The deed on the table. Fragments of a life come apart. He rakes a hand through his hair. "You'd carry this lie into town?"

Virgil's jaw sets. "Not if you plan to make a fool of me. If I stake my name on your death, Randolph, you best stay dead." Virgil turns to me, voice edged with skepticism. "And why in

God's name should I trust the word of an outlaw? Be damned foolish of me to do such—"

"I'm a man of my word," Kodiak cuts in. His voice is quiet, but it lands like a gunshot. He looks to me, then back at Virgil. "And why should I trust this dandy won't go whisperin' to the sheriff anyway?"

Virgil lets the silence stretch, the faintest smile tugging at the corner of his mouth.

"Well, since we're all speaking plain," I add, "there is the matter of the property."

Virgil narrows his eyes. "What about it?"

"Collier's money would have bought the deed, but he's gone now. I assume you'd prefer to complete the sale. We get peace. You get the bounty, the sale of the inn, and to walk into town every inch the hero. Seems like quite a rich bargain for you. Why would you spoil it by crossing us?"

I glance at Kodiak, his jaw tight, shoulders coiled, but he doesn't move.

Virgil nods, satisfied. "Of course I'd honor my end of the bargain, assuming you deliver on all of your promises and stay well out of sight and memory."

I nod in agreement. "I'll see that we do, and I'd be happy to spare you the displeasure of our company ever again."

Virgil steps toward the door, then pauses with his hand on the frame. "Very well then. I'll collect the body come first light tomorrow." His gaze flicks to me. "But try not to make it too neat. No one trusts a clean story."

Then he's gone, boots echoing down the stairs.

CHAPTER 43

KODIAK

The door shuts with a click that settles too hard in my
chest. Footsteps fade. Then nothing. Just the fire
and her.

Alice don't speak. She watches, waits—like she knows
what comes next could break either of us. She's by the hearth,
one hand gripping the mantle like she's fixing herself there.
She breaks the quiet first.

"You could still run. If...if you'd rather keep the life you
have, then you're free to. I won't try to stop you."

That pulls a string that snaps in me, hurting as it breaks.
"You think I'd run from you after all this?"

"I want you to have a choice."

"I do. I choose you. Always will. Just..." I start, trailing off.
"Give me a minute."

Since I was a boy I was running, stealing just to survive.
Associating with the likes of thieves and killers. It's all I know,
except for that small piece of me. That piece I use when

convenient. The piece that remembers being proper. Feels like a costume. Like a mask I slip on to fool some dumb bastard into letting me past the gate.

"So, what am I...an innkeeper now?" I ain't mean to say it like the thought is a fate worse than death, but that's damn sure how it sounds.

Alice don't flinch at the question. Don't smile either. "You're whatever you decide to be," she says. "That's the point."

"Slickest train robber in the country fluffin' pillows and flippin' mattresses."

She lets out a soft laugh. "I'd never put a brute like you in charge of linens. Or managing guests. I'm sure the first dissatisfied lodger would find himself under the inn." Her palms graze up, resting on the thick meat of my arms. "Though I would enjoy watching you unload a wagon or two." She offers a smile I can't return, the weight of this notion heavier than all hell.

The fire pops.

"You know I ain't never stayed put," I say. "Not anywhere."

She nods. "I know."

"Most I ever stayed in one place was a jail cell."

"Would this be a prison to you?"

I imagine the way the sunlight hits her face in the morning before she wakes up. How after months of sleeping on dirt or stone, these sheets feel like swimming in butter. It's nice. Maybe *too* nice. "No. It's just that if a fella gets too comfortable he goes soft, and my luck's never held long."

"I've been thinking," she says. "About the stars."

"You're always thinkin' on stars."

"Hush," she says, but ain't no bite in it. "I mean, on why the stars might have put us together. I think this is it, bear. I think...maybe it was to free each other. You helped me out of my cage, and now I help you stop running. You can finally rest. Let the hunters think they won, but live a life."

I run a hand down my face. How is this not the easiest decision I ever made? I love Alice. I know I do, there ain't a doubt in my mind. But...Archibald Kodiak Randolph—dead. Can't wrap my head around it.

"You think we can trust Virgil?"

She nods. "Virgil isn't sentimental. He never believed I was kidnapped. Still he went along with this because all he cares about is protecting his reputation."

I watch the coals in the hearth sink in on themselves. "Don't feel real," I say. "Thinkin' of myself buried in the ground while I'm still breathin'. Folks believin' I'm rottin' somewhere just so I can walk free."

Alice kneels beside me. Her hand finds my knee. "You've been buried your whole life. Under the burden of being orphaned. Under wanted posters and aliases. This is the first time you get to come up for air."

I breathe deep, lungs stretched against my ribs. "You really think I can be someone else?"

Her voice don't falter. "I think you already are someone else. You've just only ever showed him to me."

Silence stretches long between us. I listen to the wind outside, the boards in the wall shifting in the cold. My old life's out there somewhere, waiting to catch up. But here—in this room, with this woman—it's warm.

I nod. "All right. Guess I'm...Dead Man goddamn Collier. What's his name?"

She jerks back, and her face puzzles. "I don't rightly know."

I bark a laugh at how stupid this whole thing is. "Well he's probably got somethin' in here with his name on it."

She goes rifling through the desk drawers, the firelight catching her hair like copper. Papers, bills, a cracked pipe, a few coins. Then she stops. Fingers pinch something small between them—a card, frayed at the edges.

She steps closer, the card in her hand, eyes bright. "Merrick."

"Huh," I say. I take the card from her, study the faded print. Merrick Collier. Plain as any man's name, but it hums somehow, like a thing already mine.

"Merrick," I repeat. "Guess I can live with that." I glance at her, half a grin twitching. "Suppose you wouldn't mind bein' Mrs. Collier, then?"

Her lip curls before she can catch it.

"Damn. That's how you respond to a man's marriage proposal?"

Alice's eyes widen a touch, then she huffs out a laugh, kneeling on the floor before me. "It's not you, bear. It's him. Collier. He courted me brutally. The idea of belonging to that man—" She shudders. "It made my skin crawl."

I lean forward. "You wouldn't be his. You'd be mine," I say.

That stops her. Her gaze softens, all the fight slipping out of her shoulders. Like she's seeing the promise beneath the words. "Yours," she repeats, almost whispering.

"Mine," I say again.

She rubs her hands on my thighs, and the tingle of her touch paired with seeing her on her knees looking up at me makes my root twitch.

"So it seems you've made your decision," she says. "Virgil gets the reward and plays the hero, but you get a life, you get *me*."

"You're the sweetest part of this deal," I say with a smile.

"Collier was a wealthy man. Suppose he probably has his account ledgers around here somewhere."

I nod. Ain't bad news, but it does remind me of something important. I sit back, scrub a hand over my jaw. "I ain't been completely honest with you, Alice."

Her hands still where they rest on my legs. "What do you mean?"

"Well, when your husband and that dandy brother of his ambushed me, I was comin' off a job. One of the jobs that pissed a lot of them railroad men off. Now, they think they got it all. Between what they found on me then, and the haul they recovered off that ship in Galveston, I reckon they thought they got everything I hadn't spent. But they ain't. Not by a long shot."

She stares, wary now. "What are you saying?"

"I'm sayin' that was the biggest job I ever pulled—L&N line outta Kentucky carryin' payroll for half the state. I hit that train clean and split the take before the smoke even cleared. Stashed it where no one'd ever find. Gonna take some travel to get it, but it's there. Enough to start a life on."

"Merrick and Alice Collier," she says, testing the sound. "Has a ring to it."

Outside, the wind scrapes at the shutters. Inside, the fire keeps on burning, and for the first time in a long damn while, I start thinking maybe my best days ain't behind me.

CHAPTER 44

ALICE

Summer has arrived, and I busy myself with the work of wiping lenses and twisting calibration dials into precise positions. I focus on the task in order to push the thoughts away, deep into the pit of me, but it seems every time I pause, the cold reality of my empty nursery bubbles back up.

The observatory is full of notebooks tracking the moon and stars, and our bedroom is rife with notes of my womanly cycle. Kodiak even purchased one of those glass thermometers; the doctor having said my temperature would show patterns in my cycle. Tracking the moon phases, my daily temperature, waiting fifteen minutes with a glass rod under my tongue is less than appealing before forming our romantic union, and so far it has been no help at all.

Bless Kodiak and his tender hazel eyes when he tells me, "you're all I need." But I'm no fool. He's been talking about making me "round with his young," almost since the day we met. I know what he says now is nothing more than kindness.

That's the worst of it; knowing deep down that something in him is missing and he can't express it while sparing my feelings.

Footsteps creak up the observatory stairs, and from the weight and cadence, I already know it's him before his tall, broad silhouette darkens the landing, his hair tousled from the pillow or the wind. The moonlight catches the dark scruff along his sharp jawline.

"Thought I'd find you up here fussin' with that thing," he says. "It's late, sugarplum. Why don't you come to bed."

"The Astral Society will be here in two days. The eyepiece alignment on the new telescope was off."

He shoves his hands into his pockets and ambles over. I keep my attention on the telescope as he nears. The sting behind my eyes, the tightening in my chest—I know if I look at him now, I won't be able to stay in control.

He stops beside me, close enough I can feel the heat of him even through my sleeve. He smells of smoke and soap. "You're frettin' again."

I bite down on my lip, fighting the quiver there. "It isn't fair," I whisper. "It isn't fair that my body won't do the one thing it was made for."

He steps closer, rough palm cupping my cheek. "You were made for more'n that, Alice."

For a long while we just stand there, the silence between us stretching. "When Joseph and I never conceived," I say quietly, "I always assumed it was him. But now..." My voice catches. "Now I think maybe it was me all along."

He says nothing. The silent confirmation makes it worse somehow.

"I keep telling myself it shouldn't matter," I continue. "But it does. Some part of me refuses to stop wanting—" My eyes burn, so I turn toward the open slit of the dome where the clouds have just begun to thin. A single star blinks through, then another, before the tears blur the sight of them.

"Didn't I tell you a man that's always wantin' never has enough? A man content with what he's got's already rich. You gotta stop worryin' about gettin' what you want, lamb. You know as well as I do, life don't give a damn about fair. What's meant to be will be, and we just gotta make the best of it."

I turn on him, temper flaring. "Spare me your philosophy. You just stomp in here with your calm voice and think you can fix everything."

"Usually works," he says, grin tugging.

That grin does it. My frustration bubbles over. "Get out," I say, pointing toward the stairs.

He doesn't move an inch. "Now why would I do that when you're just gettin' good and feisty?"

"Because I asked you to."

He steps closer. "No, you didn't ask. You told. And that tone's gonna earn you a consequence, Mrs. Collier."

My pulse jumps. "Don't you dare."

"Oh, I dare," he says, and before I can take a step back, he's caught me around the waist and turned me against his hip.

"Bear!" I squeal, half laughing, half scandalized.

He sits on the low bench and pulls me across his lap. "Go on then, say you'll mind your mouth."

"No," I say, knowing full well what it will earn me. He catches the back of my skirts in his fist, pulling them up where they gather around my waist. He yanks down my drawers before I can even catch my breath.

His hand comes down sharp, a fiery sting that startles the breath out of me and scatters the sorrow right out of my chest.

"Kodiak," I gasp, the name breaking loose before I can stop it. He strikes again, and I jolt with the impact.

"Quit your squirmin', woman. Your rear's gettin' what it deserves for that smart mouth. Now apologize."

He swats again, harder, his broad palm searing across me, too big to miss a single inch. My knees weaken and heat floods my cheeks, my core, warmth spilling where I'm most tender.

"I'm sorry, sir."

"I bet you are. This hand'll teach you manners," he says, another swing coming down with a vengeance. I squeeze my eyes shut, seeing white. His palm soothes, fingertips grazing my center.

"You're gettin' all slick and soft, ain't you?"

I wriggle, my face flaming as I try to deny it, but my body's betraying me, melting under his touch. "I can't help it," I whisper, barely audible.

"Is that right?" he says, teasing, his fingers slide lower, teasing that secret warmth. I gasp, my whole body tensing. He glides down, pressing at my entrance.

"That smart mouth of yours," he whispers. "I know this is what you're really after, ain't it?"

I can't hold back my moan. I push back into him, but he draws his hand away. "Ah ah," he says. "Tell me what you want."

My breath catches. "I want you inside me."

"Beg for it," he growls, his voice laced with that dangerous edge that makes my pulse spike. His fingers pause, teasing just outside, denying me the fullness I crave. "You don't get a damn thing till you say it right."

"Please, sir," I whimper. "I need you inside me." The words nearly catch in my throat, but they spill out, my pride crumbling under the weight of his dominance. He hums low with satisfaction, a sound that strikes like a match, igniting as he gives me what I begged for.

"That's better." His fingers, thick and unrelenting, stretch me with precision, teasing that aching heat inside me until I'm trembling, my thighs slick with need. "You been wantin' it deep, ain't you?" He works me open, making sure I feel every inch of the ache. My body jerks, instinctive, desperate to take more, to be filled. He curls his fingers just right and I cry out, a raw, choked sound I can't control. I'm his to unravel, and he knows it.

"You ready for me? Ready for me to fill you proper?"

"Yes, sir."

"Up," he says, pulling his fingers free. He pats my rear end and nudges me up onto my feet. My skirts fall into place, drawers tangled around my legs.

My heart slams against my ribs, each beat a frantic drum as his command cuts through the air. "Strip."

My fingers fumble, clumsy as they tug at the laces of my bodice. I can feel his eyes on me, patient and hungry, as the garment loosens and slips from my shoulders. It falls to the floor with a soft thud. The warm air grazes at my exposed skin, raising goosebumps and tightening my nipples to aching peaks.

Kodiak leans back slightly, arms folded, watching me like a man admiring his favorite view. There's a slow, satisfied curve to his mouth, equal parts amusement and dominion. My skirts follow, crumpling in a heap, and my drawers snag around my ankles, leaving me bare.

"That's it," he breathes, approving. "Look at you, mindin' so sweet. Knew you could behave when you wanted somethin' bad enough."

He crouches slightly, takes hold of me and lifts me like I

weigh nothing. His arms band around me, thick with muscle and the warmth of him. His chest is broad, heart beating against me in a steady rhythm. I wrap my arms around him, carried by him until the observatory table's hard edge digs into my flesh. My legs dangle, useless, my body open and vulnerable, and a shiver racks me—not cold, but a raw, electric need that pulses low in my belly. I'm exhilarated, caught in a storm of his quiet power.

His mouth casts heat against my collarbone, and my pulse spikes, a frantic rhythm. "You're perfect," he growls, his voice a rumble that vibrates through me. He steps forward, his firm body filling the space between my parted legs, the scent of leather and sweat rolling off him, laced with his raw musk. It wraps around me, thick and familiar, like heat rising off sun-warmed earth. I could drown in that scent. It always does something to me, sinks deep, dredging out every ache I have for him.

His fingers, deliberate and slow, work the buttons of his trousers, each soft clink of metal against cloth striking my senses. I watch his hands—those capable, calloused hands—quick enough to draw a pistol, steady enough to calm a wild mare, and tender enough to touch me gentle like I'm the most precious thing on God's green earth. Now, they part fabric like pulling back the veil on something sacred, revealing the hard, undeniable proof of his desire.

His hand moves, guiding the thick length of him. The faint dew of his desire paints my inner thigh, an intimate mark that sends fire through me, a rush of warmth pooling at my core.

"You'll take all of me," he vows, the blunt velvet crown of him notched at my entrance. "And when I spill deep inside you, your cries'll carry my name to those stars."

His voice is a promise and a prayer together, and for a

heartbeat, I forget the ache, the sorrow, the months of trying. All that's left is the wanting.

I close my eyes and breathe, feeling the weight of him before he even enters me. I send the thought upward, past the rafters, past the glass, past the reach of air, up where heaven begins. Let this be the time. Let something take hold so I may carry a piece of him.

The stars blur above, and I almost imagine they're listening. I picture a spark tumbling down from the sky, a seed of fire small enough to take root within me.

If the heavens ever wished me kindness, let it be now.

CHAPTER 45

KODIAK

Nine Months Later

She's standing by the window in the late afternoon light, backlit and soft, hands pressed into the small of her back like she's trying to ease the pull of carrying what we made.

I pause in the doorway.

Sunlight's spilling through the glass, painting her in gold. Swell of life plain under her chemise, clinging to every curve. And those breasts—Lord, those breasts—near ready to spill over the neckline, heavy and swollen with the promise of life.

It's sweet, but then my hands go cold, numb. My chest tightens. Lately, it's like the Devil's hiding 'round every corner. Ain't normal. I should be overjoyed—and I am—but then I think on my ma, on how I came into this world killing, and I can't help but wonder if maybe fate's been sitting back, waiting patient for me to get soft, to love something enough for it to hurt.

She don't see me at first. I take a step in, boots scuffing the floor just enough to catch her ear. She turns. Her lips part like she forgot whatever it was she meant to say and holds the round swell under her dress.

I walk up close. "You feelin' all right?"

Her cheeks flush. "I'm fine. I'm starting to wonder how long she plans to keep us waiting."

I never paid no mind to those old wives tales about high bellies or low ones. Whether it's a boy or a girl, I don't care either way, long as at the end of this I got a wife and a child both.

"You know how long you take gettin' ready. Our little girl wouldn't be no different."

I lean down, press my forehead to hers, and for a moment I forget the fear and the ghosts and the stories I been telling myself about fate. There's just her, warm and alive, smelling like rosemary soap. God, she's perfect like this.

"I been watchin' you," I say. "You glowin'. Every time you move, I can't think straight. I swear I ain't had a peaceful thought since that bump started showin'."

She breathes in slow, chest lifting high, and it draws my eye to what I been hungering for.

"Mercy," I mutter. "Your breasts..."

I reach for the ties of her robe, waiting for her to stop me. She don't. She just watches, breathing shallow.

I part the fabric, let it fall open. There's the chemise underneath—thin cotton, stretched tight across her chest. Her nipples press through the fabric, dark and soft and aching to be touched. I bring my hands to her waist, trail my thumbs up her sides, feeling the newness of her curves. She ain't just changed —she's bloomed.

"You looked in the mirror lately?" I whisper, leaning close. "Seen what you've become?"

"A house," she says flatly, defeated.

"Don't you dare. You're a vision," I say. "Made to be worshipped."

She sways toward me. I slip one hand higher, cupping the underside of her breast through the chemise. "Lord above," I murmur, brushing my thumbs across her nipples through the thin cloth. They pebble tight, sensitive as ever.

That makes something primal twist low in my gut, my rigid length straining against my trousers. I drop my head, press a kiss just above the neckline, then another lower, tongue darting out to taste her through the fabric, and she makes a broken little sound in the back of her throat.

I pull the chemise down, letting it slip off one shoulder, then the other. Her breasts spill free, perfect and heavy. "Look at you," I breathe. "Goddamn, sweetheart."

Her hands find my hair as I lean in, kissing the underside of one breast, then the other, leaving soft, open-mouthed kisses. I suckle gentle at first, and her head tilts back, mouth falling open, a soft cry spilling out.

Every time I draw her in deeper, her fingers tighten. Her knees start to tremble, and I wrap one arm around her waist to keep her steady. The gold light catches on her skin, her breasts full and flushed, nipples wet from my mouth.

"Mm," I hum low against her, feeling her tight flesh rigid on my tongue. "You're achin' here, ain't you?"

"Yes," she whispers, voice raw.

"Bet it's been throbbin' all day, beggin' for my mouth."

She cries out, high and breathy, her hips shifting like she needs something more. I keep her right there—floating in it.

"Bet I could make you come just from this. Just from suckin' your pretty tits and whisperin' how perfect you are."

She lets out a broken sob, her head falling forward, hair spilling over her shoulder. I shift my hold, supporting her ripe middle with one hand while the other keeps its rhythm— rubbing, circling, pressing—until her body starts to quiver again, legs a little unsteady, but I've got her. "Come on now, sweetheart," I murmur, straightening up slow. "Let me get you comfortable."

One arm under her belly, the other cradling her back as I guide her upstairs to the bed. She sinks down onto the edge with a soft sigh.

"Lift your arms for me."

She does, breath hitching as I take my time, pulling her chemise up over the curve of her, over her breasts, over her head. I drop it to the floor. She's flushed and breathless, bare as the day she was born, and so damn beautiful it near levels me. I ease her back against the pillows, arranging them just so, supporting that precious swell of her.

"Christ almighty, you're a goddess."

She snorts—a quick, embarrassed little puff of disbelief.

My gaze sharpens. "Now what in God's name was that?"

Her cheeks go red. "You're just being nice."

I cup her chin, lifting her face to meet mine. "Don't you dare discount what you are."

She tries to look away, but I tilt her chin back. "You're gonna take the compliment like a good girl. Understood?"

Her eyes soften, and she nods. "Yes, sir."

"That's better. Now spread your legs and let me worship you proper."

She does, breath catching as I settle on my knees between her thighs. Her bump rounds soft and high, and just beneath it —rosy and glistening.

"You're beautiful like this," I rasp, thumb parting her gently.

She whimpers, eyes fluttering shut. I dip down, mouth pressing to her inner thigh, then the crease beside it, working my way up slow. I lick her open, tongue wide and slow, dragging from her entrance up to her bundle of nerves.

She gasps, sharp and sweet.

"God, Kodiak."

I groan into her, sucking her soft, then harder. She bucks beneath me, hands fisted in the sheets. I slide one hand beneath her, holding her still while I feast on her, letting her ride the rhythm. Every sound she makes just spurs me on. She's squirming, whispering my name. And all the while, I talk to her, full of hunger.

"God, I could spend all damn day here," I murmur, vibrating against her skin. "Lickin' every part of you." *Lick*, long and teasing, tracing the length of her. "Watchin' you lose your damn mind from my mouth." *Suck*, pulling her bud between my lips, gentle at first, then harder, feeling her pulse against me.

I pull back just enough to speak, my breath hot against her slick skin. "Goddamn, you taste so good," I growl, my voice muffled against her. I flick my tongue, light and teasing, then press harder, flattening it against her, letting her grind against the pressure.

"Kodiak," she chokes out, her voice trembling.

I can tell she's teetering on the edge. I don't let up, keeping my pace relentless, dragging out the pleasure until she's gasping, her body tensing. When she finally breaks, it's like a dam bursting—her cry is sharp, raw, her body convulsing as she comes undone on my tongue. I don't stop, lapping at her gently, guiding her through the aftershocks. Only when her breathing slows, her body sinking into the sheets, do I ease up, pressing soft kisses to her inner thighs, her hips, her stomach.

I crawl up her body, hovering over her, my lips finding hers in a slow, deep kiss. She moans into my mouth, tasting herself, her hands weak but clinging to my shoulders. "You're a wicked man," she whispers, a shaky laugh in her voice.

"Damn right I am." I grin, brushing a strand of hair from her face. "And we're just getting started."

Her hands tighten in the sheets, knuckles white, and I grin against her, diving back into our kiss, letting my tongue dance with hers. I pull back from the kiss, her taste lingering on my lips, and catch the way her eyes flicker with a mix of exhaustion and want.

"Ruin me," she breathes, catching her breath, chest rising and falling. The way she's looking at me—hungry, despite the way I just wrecked her—makes my blood run hotter. I smirk as I slide my hand down, letting my trousers down, gripping myself.

"Oh, I'll ruin you, sweet." I drag the tip against her damp and her hips shift.

She nods, a desperate little sound spilling from her lips, her eyes half-lidded and hazy with want. "Don't be gentle."

I chuckle. "Brace yourself, little lamb. I'll be as rough as you please."

I press just the tip inside, stretching her slow, and she gasps, her body tensing at the size of me. I groan, easing out some, then back in, just an inch, teasing her with shallow thrusts. Her moans turn crazed, her legs wrapping around my hips, trying to pull me deeper, but I keep it slow, torturing us both. She flinches—small, sharp—and the swell of her goes tight as a drum.

"You all right?"

"Hard, Kodiak," she whispers, guiding my hips.

"Easy," I murmur, nipping at her jaw, my voice strained as I fight the urge to bury myself in her. I slide in a little further, then pull back, watching her face—her parted lips, her pink cheeks, the way her eyes flutter shut. "Gonna make you feel every damn bit of me first."

Her hands claw at my back, nails digging as she tries to pull me deeper. But I'm in control, and she's gonna feel every second of this. She whimpers, her hips tilting up, chasing, and I can't help the growl that rumbles in my chest as I sink in to the hilt, feeling her clench around me.

"Bear," she breathes, her voice breaking.

I think she's just losing herself in the moment until her hands clutch at me, hard, and a low groan tears from her throat that don't sound like pleasure at all.

"Bear," she gasps. "Something's—"

I freeze, pulling out quick and drawing back enough to see her face. Her brow's tight, sweat starting at her temple, the color draining fast.

"Oh no," she huffs, then holds her breath as if bracing herself.

"What's wrong?"

She's breathing quick now, both hands flying to her middle. "I think it's starting," she says through a shaky breath. "She's coming."

The words hit me like a gunshot. Everything inside me stills.

"Shit. You tellin' me it's time? Now?"

She don't answer, she just screams in pain.

"Christ almighty. Holy hell." My mind sputters, switching tracks. I draw in a breath. "All right. You just stay put, I'll get the midwife."

Then I'm moving—one heartbeat I'm staring at her, the next I'm yanking up my trousers, jumping into my boots and running out the door, bare-chested, half-dressed, the cold spring air slamming my lungs awake as I tear across the lawn to the inn.

"Fred!" I bellow, boots hitting the floorboards like gunfire. "We need to get the damn midwife!"

Fred bursts out of the side room, coat half on, looking more startled than I've ever seen him. "Now?"

"Now!" I roar. "Alice—she's startin'!"

I'm already out the front door before he can answer, sprinting into the yard, mud splashing my legs. The sky's bruised purple, April storm rolling in from the hills, thunder low and mean. Fred brings the carriage 'round, and when we hit the midwife's door, I'm banging my fist against it like the house is on fire.

"Mrs. Clay!"

The door creaks open, and I'm staring at a man I ain't expecting. Native, by the look of him. Tall, weather-lined, salt-and-pepper hair pulled back neat, dark eyes sharp even in the low light. I'd come looking for our little Appalachian midwife. I take a step back, look at the name on the house.

He gives me a long, measured look. "You're here for Lula?"

"Mrs. Clay?"

He nods again and pulls the door wider, voice raising toward the back of the house. "Lula! There's someone at the door for you!"

Mrs. Clay saunters out like she's got all the time in the world, short and compact but sturdy on her feet, with arms that look like they could carry a baby in one hand and a cast iron skillet in the other. Shawl already in hand, she swings it over her shoulders. The thick wool smells of camphor and starch. She gives me a once-over, head to boots, like I'm some half-dressed fool hollering nonsense on her porch.

The man who answered the door stays back, watching, still and unreadable.

"It's Alice," I tell her through the screen door. My voice cracks. "It's time."

Mrs. Clay gives a slow nod and waves me inside like she's inviting me to supper.

"Settle yourself now, Mr. Collier. You're white as snow on a tombstone. Come in before the cold takes you under."

"Please," I rasp, stepping in to get out of the cold. "She's hurtin' bad."

"All right," she says, already turning for the hall. "I'll go on and get my things." No panic. No rush. Like she's seen a thousand men look just like me.

"Who's knockin' like the world's endin'?" Another man stomps into the front room—gray-bearded, flannel half-buttoned, boots still caked in fresh mud. He looks me over, top to toe. "Show up bangin' like that, I figured somebody'd been shot."

Before I can answer, the man who opened the door speaks up. "His wife is birthing a child."

The wild-looking one blinks at that. Some of the edge slips from his face. His gaze drags over me again, this time softer. "Well, hell. Congrats."

My jaw tightens. "I ain't celebratin' nothin' yet. Mrs. Clay, please..."

She reappears just then, pulling on her coat, satchel already in hand.

"You look like you've been runnin' through fire," the wild one mutters. Then, "First?"

I nod once. Can't speak around the knot in my throat.

"Big thing," he says.

The first man steps in, calm as ever, hands up like he's trying to reassure me. "Lula's delivered near every baby in this valley. If there's anyone who knows what to do, it's her."

The other one nods, arms folded now. "Ain't no one better."

"Can we go?" I ask, sharper than I mean to. "Please."

They don't flinch. Mrs. Clay lifts her shawl and heads for the door without another word. I'm right behind her. I scoop her up onto the wagon myself, climb up, and snap the reins like my life depends on it. Every tick of the clock stretching my nerves tighter.

I keep hearing my ma's name in my head, seeing the ghost I never knew. Not again. Not this time.

By the time we reach the house, I can hear Alice from the porch—those pained sounds she's making twisting my insides. I follow them up the stairs, my heart pounding so loud it drowns out everything else.

Mrs. Clay don't waste a second, shoves me toward the hall. "Out," she orders. "I'll call when she's through."

"I ain't leavin' her."

"You'll do her no good fainting at my feet," she snaps. "Go fetch water, boil it, and keep your hands busy if you can't keep your head."

I want to argue, but another scream rips through the door, and my knees damn near buckle. So I run—anything to keep from losing my mind.

At the stove, I fill the kettle, my hands shaking so bad I spill half of it, the water scalding my hands. Steam hisses, metal clatters, and I whisper to myself.

"She's strong. She's stronger'n anyone I ever knew. She'll be fine. She's gotta be fine."

Evening falls and she's crying out, but now I can hear Mrs. Clay's voice, calm and firm, coaching her through the birthing pains. It guts me hearing my woman suffering, fighting hard, and me stuck down here useless as boots in a flood.

Finally, sometime past midnight, there's a lull.

No crying. No shouting. Just silence.

And that's worse than anything.

I'm halfway up the stairs when I hear it—a low moan, then her voice, wrecked and breathless, saying, "I can't...I can't..."

My whole soul flinches.

But Mrs. Clay, cool as ever, replies, "You can, Alice. You are. Baby's almost here. You just breathe through it."

I sit on the step. Head in my hands. Sweat dripping down my back. I don't even realize I'm crying till my shirt's damp at the collar.

The screen door creaks.

I turn, thinking maybe Fred again, but it ain't.

It's Gideon.

He's barefoot, dressed in his nightshirt, hair mussed like he rolled outta bed in a hurry. He don't say nothing at first—just stands there. "How's Miss Alice?"

I blink at him. For a second, I can't even talk. That lump in my throat swells damn near choking me. "She's still goin' up there."

He nods once and climbs the steps quiet as a whisper. Sits down next to me, shoulder to mine.

We don't speak.

Not for a long while.

Just sit there together listening to her fight.

Then, real soft, he says, "She's gonna be fine."

I glance over. He's looking straight ahead, jaw set like a man twice his age.

He adds, "She always is."

I scrub my hands down my face and nod. "Yeah," I say. "Yeah, she is."

The night stretches long, cruel and slow.

The storm rolls off just before dawn, leaving everything slick and silver outside. I've been sitting on these damn steps so long my back aches and my legs have gone numb, but I don't move. Can't.

Gideon's head slumped against my shoulder sometime after three. He's breathing slow, passed out cold. I didn't have the heart to wake him.

Upstairs, Alice's cries deepen with grit and fury and pain.

Mrs. Clay's voice cuts through, gentle and reassuring: "That's it, Alice. You bear down. Don't you hold back now, girl. You've got her almost here."

I press my fist hard to my mouth.

Lord, you don't take her from me.

Then—I hear it.

A cry, high and wet. Tiny lungs testing the world for the first time.

I realize I ain't breathed in what feels like a full minute.

Gideon stirs beside me. Lifts his head, blinking. "That the baby?" he asks.

I nod once, but my throat's too tight for words.

There's scuffing upstairs, hushed voices. Then soft footsteps on the stairs.

Mrs. Clay appears, framed in the pale light of dawn. She's smiling. Just barely. "She's here," she says. "Your wife's all right. Baby too."

I make a sound—could be relief, could be a sob, maybe a mix of both.

"Come meet your daughter, Mr. Collier." She steps aside.

So I stand.

And I go.

Up the stairs I ran down what feels like a lifetime ago.

The door creaks as I push it open. Light of dawn filters through the lace curtain, pale and gold. And there she is.

Alice.

Propped against the pillows, hair damp and clinging to her temple, eyes heavy. She's got a bundle in her arms, wrapped up tight in a yellow blanket Mrs. Baxter knit as a gift. The little thing is tucked in so careful, just the tiniest pink face peeking out, lips pursed, nose scrunched like she's already pissed off with the world.

Alice lifts her eyes to me. "She's perfect," she whispers.

Something breaks clean open in my chest. I cross the room. I can't speak. Just look.

Alice shifts the bundle, easing the baby toward me. "Kodiak...meet your daughter."

"Lord above," I whisper, like anything louder might break her. "She's so small."

My hands hover in the air like I don't dare touch her, but Alice nods gentle. I sit on the edge of the bed, and Alice lays her in my arms.

She's warm. Lighter than I expected. Delicate, like her momma.

Her tiny fingers flex once, then curl back in like she's ready for her first fight. She's mine all right.

I swallow hard, trying to keep it together. The baby—our baby—lets out a sigh, like she's bored of the fuss.

"What do we call her?" I ask.

Alice smiles. "Stella."

"Stella," I echo. "Like the stars."

Alice nods, eyes welling with tears. "Because she came from the sky. Like we asked."

I press my lips to the downy crown of our daughter's head, and something inside me settles. All that fear, all that running...it goes still.

She's here.

She's real.

Our spark of love and strength.

I'd lay down all I am to keep her safe...until the stars quit shining.

CHAPTER 46

ALICE

Late Summer

The sun's just slipped behind the hills, and the sky's caught in that soft stretch of twilight where everything glows rose and lavender. Inside, the world is peaceful.

Stella lies between us on a soft blanket, reaching for her little feet in the air. We're upstairs in the observatory, all three of us curled up in a pile of pillows and blankets under the dome. The telescope's pushed aside tonight, the stars free to shine down on us to admire their handiwork.

One of the windows is cracked open, letting in the song of crickets, the soft evening breeze rustling through the trees.

Kodiak rests back against the curve of the window seat. My legs are draped over his lap, and his hand rests on my shin, thumb brushing circles there like he doesn't even know he's doing it.

"Tell her the story," I whisper, and that soft, crooked smile finds its way across his lips.

"You wanna hear a tale?" he asks Stella, who kicks in reply. He lifts his head up toward the sky above us, stars pricking through the deepening dusk.

He begins, voice deep and warm:

"Once upon a time, there was a bear who lived up in the stars. He was big and ornery and didn't much care for people. He liked the mountains and whiskey and playin' cards. Despite what some folks might have you believe, he ain't never paid for the company of a woman."

He winks, and I give him a chiding nudge. "Kodiak."

"Oh, come on. She don't know what I'm talkin' about."

"Finish the story."

"The bear was always runnin'. From the law, from the past. Maybe even from himself."

I watch Stella's eyes go wide, little chest rising and falling with each breath.

"Then one day, the bear met a fine little lamb. Pretty as can be. And gentle too. But she wasn't all soft like folks expected. She was clever. And brave. She helped that bear trick the hunters into thinkin' they'd caught him. But really, the lamb and the bear just disappeared into the trees."

His hand moves gently over Stella's belly.

"And in those woods, they made a life. A good life. And after a while, they had themselves a little one. Half bear, half lamb. Fierce and gentle. Strong and kind. And they didn't need much. They had a warm fire and soft quilts and stars overhead."

He leans down and presses a kiss to Stella's forehead.

"And even though they loved lookin' up at the sky, they

weren't waitin' for anything to save 'em. They knew they were already safe. Here on earth. Together."

Kodiak turns to me. "Ain't that right, Momma?"

I nod, voice caught in my throat.

Outside, the stars burn bright.

And for the first time in a long, long while, I don't wish for anything at all.

I already have it.

THE END

THANK YOU

Thank you for picking up this book. If you enjoyed it, please consider leaving a review. Your feedback is invaluable and helps other readers discover my work.

About the Author

Halle Oak is an attorney living in Florida with her husband and two pugs. Fascinated by the nineteenth century and the American frontier, she is particularly drawn to the era's lawlessness and rough justice. Halle loves crafting stories featuring characters who are deeply flawed yet fiercely compelling. When she's not writing, she spends her time imagining the enduring kinds of love that could thrive amid the challenges of the past.

Her debut novel, *The Bear and the Lamb*—a dark historical Western romance expanding on an earlier short story—is scheduled for release in January 2026 as the first book in the *Fated Outlaws* series.

Sign-up for updates:
www.halleoak.com

CONTENT WARNINGS

This novel contains mature themes and may be distressing for some readers. Content warnings include:

- Alcohol use / intoxication
- Attempted sexual assault / sexual threat
- Choking / breath restriction (sexual context)
- Crime / criminal activity (outlaws)
- Death of a spouse
- Domestic violence (including past physical abuse)
- Explicit sexual content
- Graphic violence, injury, and blood
- Gun violence
- Hospitalization / medical scenes
- Illness / infectious disease references
- Imprisonment / restraint and legal proceedings
- Kidnapping / abduction and captivity
- Maternal mortality (including death during childbirth)
- Murder

- Non-violent animal death
- Pregnancy and "breeding" / reproductive coercion themes
- Religious themes
- Robbery / theft (including train robbery / holdup / heists)
- Spanking (kink and non-kink)
- Suicide
- Threats of execution / hanging
- Threats of violence

It is important to approach this work with caution if you find these topics particularly distressing. Remember to practice self-care and seek support if needed.

While every effort is made to capture all potential triggers, the above list may be updated after publication. For the most up to date trigger warnings, please visit:

halleoak.com/contentwarnings

ACKNOWLEDGMENTS

Dusting off an old short story and expanding it into this novel felt special from the very beginning. First and foremost, thank *you* for reading. If you're holding this book in 2026, there's a good chance you've never heard the name Halle Oak before. I've been completely blown away by the support *The Bear and the Lamb* has received and by the genuine excitement shared with me by new readers. There are only so many reading days in a year, and I'm deeply grateful that you've chosen to spend some of yours on this book.

This work would not have been possible without the unwavering support of my handsome husband. Thank you for handling all the things I ignored so I could become a one-woman publishing house and marketing firm. Thank you for not asking follow-up questions when, in response to your "What is this several-hundred-dollar charge on our bank statement?" I simply replied, "Something for my book." You support me in all my wild pursuits, and I love you for it.

I'd also like to thank my early readers and editing team. Were it not for the unhinged comments from my alpha readers, would I even have found the motivation to write every day? Special thanks to Allie Oleander, Poppy Fitzgerald, Des Devivo, Layna James, J.B. Laree, Kelly L. Clarke, and Madison Diaz for their help with every stage of alpha and beta reads, editing, and proofreading. Thank you to Elizabeth A. White for being with me on this writing journey from the very start. And, of course, to Moody Bitches LLC—thank you for supporting all my various identities. Thank you, Benjamin Twigg, for being you. Thank you, Tember Sapphire, for being genuinely pumped about my marketing efforts. Varsha Chitnis, D.W. Brooks, Regina Sage, and Lauren Lopes—I feel incredibly lucky to have found a group of authors who truly lift one another up.

Thank you to Theresa Chiechi who designed this gorgeous cover. I can't wait to see this beautiful series all together one day. I'm grateful for your creativity and professionalism. You're a pretty cool human to boot.

To all the artists who have brought aspects of this world to life, thank you.

Thanks to everyone who followed the various iterations of my work, to my street team, and to my PR support.

To my law school friends who didn't laugh when I started publishing books—thank you.

To my friends who *did* laugh when I started publishing books—thank you as well, because your doubt only made me more confident that I was fully committed to this path.

And finally, to my sister, who will not read this book because it's "pornographic": I hope the algorithm starts feeding you exclusively dark romance content so you can clutch your pearls forevermore. Love you.